The Rose
Vol 2

QUILL AND BIRCH

PD Alleva

This is a work of fiction. Names, characters, places and incidents are either the product of the author's imagination or are used fictitiously, and any resemblance to actual persons living or dead, business establishments, events, or locales, is entirely coincidental.

The Rose, Vol 2

COPYRIGHT © 2021 by PD Alleva

Quill and Birch Publishing, LLC
Treasure Coast, Florida
Quillandbirch.com

ISBN: 978-1-7351686-8-5 (Paperback)
ISBN: 978-1-7351686-9-2 (Hardcover)

Dedication

For everyone and anyone who enjoys a damn good
sequel.

"Introduce a little anarchy. Upset the established order, and everything becomes chaos. I'm an agent of chaos..."
~ The Joker (The Dark Knight)

"The hammer of the gods will drive our ships to new land
To fight the horde and sing, and cry
Valhalla, I am coming." ~ Led Zeppelin (The Immigrant Song)

Part I

The Phantom Opened His Eyes

1

ROBYN Winter watched the confiscated starship from his private chambers and saw how Phil powered on the ship; Robyn's telepathic ability on high alert. He wasn't just seeing Phil on the ship; he was standing in the ship watching Phil, a phantom hidden in the void, between two spaces, the physical and the mental. The antigravity vessel headed to China hummed out of the cave, followed by the cruiser holding Cam and his crew on their way to New Mexico. And then the pause...

Transmission being received, Robyn thought, when the door to his chambers hummed open. Robyn watched the room's reflection in the window. The pristine room gleamed with light reflected off the metal walls; a conference table, large and round, sat in the middle.

Silas walked into the room, one of the human nine who informed Lao about China's new visitors. Robyn knew it was Silas, even though Silas' face never reflected in the window. He could sense his vibration, his ether, and his energy. Clean except for the fear vibration beneath the folds in Silas' confidence. Robyn felt Silas pause, felt his breath constrict. He too knew what was happening on Phil's ship; Sanos was providing Phil with his location, and Phil undoubtedly will take the bait just as Robyn had informed Silas before Phil and Cam arrived after their battle in the underground compound. The record was shifting moment by moment, reflecting this new time and space, but the shimmer continued to gleam across the record, changing the landscape reflecting what was to come. Time, Robyn thought, once a set anomaly, has been changed by the corrupt.

Robyn saw his eyes in the window, those white gleaming eyes staring back as he followed through his reflection to the starship. Robyn locked in on Phil's thoughts, Phil's vibration filled with rage.

"You know what this means, Robyn," said Silas. He took a seat at the conference table, the chair scraped across cement when he sat close. "You said so yourself." He paused and Robyn could feel Silas' eyes on him.

"I know," Robyn said.

"Are you sure about this? I don't mean to question you, but… is there another way we can survive without…"

Robyn understood the truth was often difficult to accept, even for Silas. Robyn understood this more than anyone. Accepting fate when every atom in your body fought to stop it. Acceptance being a virtue so few could master. There was no need to answer Silas. Like many under Robyn's command, he, too, was grappling with the inevitable.

Instead, Robyn kept his focus on the starship, on Phil.

Some are meant for so much more, thought Robyn. But we are all nothing more than stardust, wrestling with the inner working of the universe. Most never understand true purpose until after the purpose is revealed. Phil is no exception. We have to face our fears to find who we are.

Robyn reached his hand to the window, whispered, "And Here We Go," and watched as Phil's starship raced out of the cave. Robyn closed his eyes, his head bowed.

Silas said, "Will you give the order?" Robyn heard Silas clear his throat. "We should act now, knowing what is coming. The survival of the human race depends on us. But the process will take a bit of time, its best to begin sooner rather than later."

Robyn could feel Phil's essence dissipating from the cave, the starship no longer in sight. But the essence remained.

"To be able to do what is right, for the survival of our species, Robyn, give the order…"

"All my life has come to this moment, Silas. I've crossed oceans of time, traveled across the universe, and dove into alternate dimensions for this moment. Of course I will give the order." Robyn looked at his open right hand, studying the bones, flesh, and palm lines.

Clenched his hand into a fist and squeezed, tightening his grip. This skin, he thought. This body… never had I thought it would see this end. Robyn watched as the flesh and bone in his hand and arm turned to steel, Robyn manipulating the chemistry in his body. He did the same to his left hand and arm.

Silas said, "I know I keep questioning your prediction, master Robyn, and I don't mean to. It's just that I…"

"It's just that you're scared. I understand Silas, believe me I do." Robyn's voice just above a whisper.

"Do all these people really need to perish?"

Robyn turned to see Silas; he was on the verge of tears.

"It is the only way."

"Like pawns," said Silas. "We're all pawns in the game of time. While those we are saving know nothing of our sacrifice. I don't know if my heart can take it, there's got to be a better way."

"You know as well as I Silas, this is the only way."

Silas paused before nodding, his eyes downtrodden, staring at his hand resting on the table. "This also means that he will return. The one who has been searching for you? The one known as Sephtis."

"Yes," said Robyn with a hush. "Once the Dracs are aware of my presence, they will send for him." He felt Silas, felt how his body tensed.

"What is to become of you, master Robyn? Have

you been shown your fate in the record?" Silas' voice was low and gruff; Robyn could sense how the situation was difficult for Silas to accept.

"I have… yes." And he said no more.

"What will happen to us? How will we know how to continue?"

"That is why there is Phil."

"Does he know?" asked Silas. He raised his eyes to Robyn. "Does Phil know what he is about to become?"

Robyn clenched his jaw, feeling how the bone had turned to steel. He looked at Silas and his heart sank. Robyn had endured the pains of the human heart for millenniums, nonetheless, it still stung to see a friend and confidant in pain, having to choose one life over another. Having to choose the greater good at the sacrifice of the ones you love.

"At one point in history, all the earth and all who lived within its embrace were made of magic. We shall return to it soon."

Silas touched his quivering jaw, then ran his hand through his hair; an attempt, Robyn thought, to stifle his tears. "But does he know, Robyn? What waits for him?"

"He does not," said Robyn. "But he's about to find out."

2

SANDY felt Moth's hot breath before she felt the puncture from his fangs in her neck. Maybe it was that click, or maybe it was this newfound curiosity, or maybe, just maybe, Sandy had become tired of being treated like a feeble child, that brought out the rage that sent Moth flying back against the wall. His neck snapped back, the back of his head smacked the metal wall and he dropped to his knees, clenched his fists and jumped to his feet, trampling across the floor with a roar in the back of his throat. "Insolent witch," he growled, his eyes wide with rage, but Sandy never flinched, nor did she cower.

She felt a snarl tear across her lips, her nose crinkled with rage; she clenched her fists, her eyes wide, waiting for Moth's attack.

"Dare to bite me!" Sandy hollered, seething and clenching her jaw. She could see the rose in front of her, what would be just beyond the reach of her fingertips. The air between her and the rose thickened like a protective shield.

Moth stomped forward, ready to attack, and

Sandy braced herself. His tongue lapped across his mouth where Sandy could see her blood on his lips. And he stopped cold, confused.

"Come on!" Sandy, she felt different, and different still, her eyes wide with rage. Not a moment to think, only to react.

Moth reached his hand to his lips, wiped blood over his fingers. His eyes inquisitive, studying Sandy's blood when he raised his eyes to Sandy, his snarl plastered across his lips. A moment later, his snarl turned to a grin.

"You don't even know, do you? What they did to you?" Moth moved his head back and forth as Sandy relaxed her arms, sensing the threat was over. "This is most unexpected."

"Of course I know what happened. They took my child. Tore him from my womb."

Moth did nothing more than laugh, a slight chuckle beneath his breath, followed by a grin. "Just as I thought, you know nothing. And you'll find nothing from me in return."

He said nothing more. One moment he was in front of Sandy, the next, walking down the pristine hall towards the darkness as Sandy felt her lips tremble. Fear had now subsided and in its place, pure adrenaline rushed through her veins. She noticed her hands were shaking.

Where did that come from?

Sandy looked at the wall where Moth had

crashed into, crushed by his weight and the force of Sandy's thrust.

Strength, thought Sandy. She felt powerful, clenching her shaking hands into fists. She searched down the hall for Moth, but he was gone, devoured by the darkness. Sandy knew change was coming, felt her organs changing, her stomach twisted with a stabbing pain, anger boiling into her throat. She looked at her fists, consciously peeling the fingers from her palms, and noticed how her fingernails had turned sharp and long, like talons.

3

CR115 is an abandoned district just south of the Colorado Mountains. Phil had arrived in Colorado within seconds from the cave in Atlanta, the entrance to CR115, a hundred yards away from where his ship hovered. Phil sat back, holding the starship above the earth, waiting, thinking, planning, playing the tape through, and the multitude of ways his battle with Sanos could go.

Sanos, he thought, what had become of him? How did he change into the monster Phil saw in the pit? Different from the image projected on Phil's screen from the transmission signal Sanos had sent. Which Sanos waited for him now? The monster or the monster?

Phil gazed over the desolate landscape, buildings crushed and crumbled, scorched earth where once there had been life, now, nothing but death greeted him. His people were dying, had been dying since before he was born, in a war waged beneath the shadows of time.

Time, Phil thought, hearing Robyn's instruction:

The person who holds time in their palm is the one who writes history.

Phil clenched, then unclenched his fists. His new armor, his new suit, came with upgrades, as Silas had so eloquently described. More than a few, Silas had said. And more than enough to help you through your mission.

Thinking of a battle strategy, Phil opened a small compartment on his left shoulder, retrieved two red pills and popped them inside his mouth. Silas had said they would dissolve after a few minutes.

See through the present to what will and can be, Robyn, a forever voice in Phil's head.

Phil scanned the screen, the taste of the pills bitter and chalky in his throat. His eyes stopped on a blinking red light, bottom corner, his eyes locked on it, then moved the signal center screen with his eyes. The blinking light now small inside the mapped CR115 landscape displayed across his screen; a beacon to Sanos.

4

I CRAVE new blood, thought Sanos. The human, Phil, and his ship hovered a hundred yards away from CR115, a beacon on Sanos' screen.

Why does he wait?

Sanos squeezed his keyboard. His insides hurt; pain a side effect from the pills he'd taken from Dr. Blum's lab, the pills that served as a catalyst for new blood. Every bone and muscle in his body ached as if bruised and battered, his innards too; they felt raw and hollow. Keyboard snapped within his tight grasp and Sanos tossed the pieces across the room, watching as they clanked and skittered to a stop. CR115 was a vast open area beneath Colorado, once used as a monitoring station for US government officials to monitor citizens' online movement. Now, rows of desks, chairs, and ancient computers held the purpose of collecting dust like some inanimate graveyard. A wide staircase led to the second floor, ascending to a foyer that led to an entrance to the offices on the second floor. Dark too, although Sanos was able to draw a weak electrical current to combat total darkness, allowing a dim light to stretch its soft glow and provide power to the computer where he watched Phil.

He'd chosen wisely for the upcoming battle, wanting no eyes to watch, no ears to hear, and no mouths to talk about his actions; a necessity to ward off any possible misinterpretation so often common among Drac socialites. Wanted no one to know his plan.

Sanos required the human who lived inside of Drac lore, Phil the phantom in their myths. Sanos was sure of it for what other human could accomplish the mayhem Phil had brought to the Dracs in the underground compound, stealth and elusive, and defeating Saiph? And Sanos had to deliver his prize to Moth, to gain trust with COR. Only then could he gain access to Dr. Blum's formula, the chemistry in the pills, and replicate them. But first, did he have the strength to best Phil?

(Of course you do. You are Sanos, the greatest Drac of all. You must capture the human; he is our key to new blood)

That voice again, the one from the pills, had followed him from the underground complex. Now a consciousness Sanos was familiar with. Hurt welled into his throat, his hands shaking, windpipe swollen and arid, Sanos ground his teeth, his jaw quivering.

(Take him alive. Deliver him to Moth and you will have the formula. Moth won't be able to resist your gift to him. You will have all. Best to be clear in mind, Sanos. Best to be the monster Phil expects.)

Sanos closed his eyes.

(Yes, Sanos. Breathe. Clear your mind; supreme focus is what we require. Yes, breathe, Sanos. Breathe.)

When Sanos opened his eyes, he watched as the starship hummed towards CR115.

(You will be hailed a hero, Sanos. You will have all.)

5

MOTH stomped through the hallway, listening to the sounds of a screaming baby. His eyes on the door leading to those cries. The door opened on his command, and Moth trampled into the room to find Mintaka, Alnitak and Alnilam, hovering over the baby and the bassinet. Alnitak and Alnilam on the far side from Moth, Mintaka closer, she turned to greet him.

Master Moth, said Mintaka telepathically. *How may we be of service?*

He'd tear Mintaka limb from limb if he wasn't aware the greys would retaliate, a circumstance that would compromise the larger plan. He already had to answer for Mono's death, and the grey representative was on his way to Drac City at this very moment. Moth suppressed his taste for blood in the face of the witches. The baby's cries were relentless.

"Can you shut up the abomination?" said Moth. "Its presence irritates me. I must speak with you, Mintaka, about a great and dire discovery."

Mintaka answered telepathically and with a bow, *As you wish.*

Mintaka turned to the witches, who, a moment after, bowed and gathered the baby, then glided to the back of the room and through a second door. Adam's cries softened when the door closed.

"I must have lost my mind to agree to that thing being born."

Mintaka said, "Adam will serve his purpose. For us and for the greater good."

Moth thought he caught a smile cross Mintaka's lips, a knowing conniving smile, if there ever was one. But no such smile graced Mintaka's mouth; she stood tall and patient. Perhaps it was the soul that smiled beneath the skin?

"How may I serve you?" said Mintaka in that echoing grey voice.

Moth gazed into Mintaka, assessing, scrutinizing, attempting to see inside her mind, to discover any secrets Mintaka may be hiding. He found nothing but a dark void and for a brief moment he struggled to move his eyes from Mintaka, struggling to break his concentration when his head snapped back, incapable of accessing Mintaka's thoughts. He turned to the bay windows, those large and tall windows that looked over Drac City. The crystal silver city beaming with skyscrapers. He could hear wind chimes beneath the fold. Hands clamped behind his back, he moved to the window, closer to Mintaka.

"Something troubles you," Mintaka continued. "Come, let me set your mind free. Tell me what it is."

Moth kept his gaze on Drac City when he said, "I have to meet with your grey representative about Mono," he hissed. "And COR to provide an update."

"As expected. Our victory was a success; you should have a most successful and honorable council."

A slight laugh escaped Moth's throat. He eyed Mintaka out of the corner of his eye, drew in a deep breath before returning his gaze to his beloved city.

A moment later, he addressed his concern. "Are you sure Mono was accurate in her assessment of the human Sandy?" He turned to Mintaka, looking down on her from his tall stature.

"Without doubt. Mono was selected for this purpose. She has always been the most efficient in identifying the indigo trait. I am confident in Mono's assessment."

"And she is human, correct? Sandy, that is."

"I took part in the procedure," said Mintaka. "Sandy is undoubtedly human."

Moth pursed his lips, curled his nose, clenching his teeth with a snarl, his eyes wide; he could see them reflected in Mintaka's black eyeballs. He could see his own anger. "Then tell me, Mintaka, *why* does she taste like Drac blood?"

6

SANDY returned to the room where she first awakened in Drac City. She couldn't stop the trembling. Her hands shook beneath the faucet as she splashed water across her face. Her skin was rough, like sandpaper. The water beaded off her skin, not the moist flesh she was used to seeing, and not dripping off her chin. The water moved and coalesced across her cheekbones. Sandy studied her skin; she could see a brownish auburn color beneath the flesh, just a hint, but it was there.

Shit!

Sandy stifled her tears in a whining breath. She regarded her fingers, noticing how the tips had grown sharp, although upon further examination, it wasn't her fingernail that had grown sharp but a new fingernail had grown beneath her human nail with the new nail protruding beneath. Her fingertips were swollen; Sandy squeezed her fingertip, and a gush of pus and blood streamed across the nail. Sandy squeezed harder, sliding her fingers across her held finger and her nail, her human nail, tore off. More blood on her finger, more pus. She did the same to all her fingers, her new nails sharp at the tip and growing longer. Sandy curled her fingers, hands shaking as she gazed at her reflection. Her new blonde hair glowed in the mirror; she tugged a wet clump of hair.

Thick and strong, more like rope than hair. But she saw nothing else, only blonde, and as she moved closer to the mirror, wanting to examine the thick clump as close as possible, the hair pulled loose from her scalp with ease.

Sandy muffled a whimper in the back of her throat. Her breathing turned heavy.

What did they do?

She ran her hand through her hair and when she looked at her palm, it was covered with hair.

Can't be. No. Please.

Caught her pupils in the mirror, now green with a glint of gold. Her upper lip twitched, trembling as if her lip had a mind of its own, wanting to reveal what was beneath. Slow and steady Sandy reached her fingertip to her lip, pulled it back. The gums were dark but her teeth were white and she could see beneath the gums a thick, dark protrusion. She pinched a tooth between her fingers, pulled down, and the tooth caught her gum. Sandy winced, craning her neck to the right, then regarded the mirror, opening her jaw wide, pulling on the tooth as blood pooled into her mouth, across her lips. Sandy tore the tooth from her gums and blood filled her mouth. She dropped it in the sink, within a wad of blood and phlegm. She opened her mouth wide and dipped her mouth closer to the mirror. A new tooth had sprouted beneath Sandy's human tooth. The tip was sharp, razor sharp, and punctured Sandy's thumb. Her finger grazed a second tooth, also loose. They were all loose. And that pain in her gut, she now knew, was hunger.

7

PHIL stepped into the vast open area that is CR115. Another abandoned post, thought Phil. Another relic of a world now gone. To Phil, walking in places like CR115 was like a twentieth century archeologist discovering the pyramids, a world from long before his time.

He saw death where once life had thrived. Felt cowardice in the hearts of the people who once walked these halls, and deception hovered above the landscape like a stain from a vile time that would take millenniums to dissipate. He could sense it, smell it, in the room, that dark energy consuming the earth, descending upon its inhabitants with an iron fist, constricting the atoms surrounding him, thickening the air he breathed.

Use the rose to scatter the atoms, Robyn's instruction. What was once heavy, closely packed atoms can then breathe like vapor from your core and shine the way through the darkness.

Phil closed his eyes, breathed deeply, manipulating his ethereal sphere, the atoms around him sparkling gold and white.

Now expand the sphere with layers of light energy.

Phil remembered how Robyn told him he could capture solar systems within his vibrational frequency by mastering his expansion of the rose. Be pure at heart; you are more than crude matter. You are stardust and within the stars you are free.

Phil opened his eyes to see how light now illuminated CR115, sparkling white and gold.

"Useful trick," said Sanos. He was on the second platform, standing close to the wall in the foyer outside the second floor entrance. He looked over the newly lit room. "But I prefer the darkness."

"Most monsters do." Phil turned towards Sanos, staring, waiting.

Sanos clucked his tongue, stepped slowly towards the staircase, dragging his nail across the wood banister, splintering a string of wood, his head bowed in thought.

"Do you believe the light will save you?" Sanos ceased walking and glared at Phil. "As if the light is some mystical being expected to bring peace to a dying breed."

"I choose to live in the light. I fight for love and for what is right. You fight for destruction and chaos. For self-preservation with the purpose of making others suffer."

Sanos cocked his head to the right, a laugh in his throat. "So true, and yet, dear phantom, it is still fighting. And fighting will always bring death." He laughed out loud. "Perhaps we are both on the wrong side; we both give purpose to violence. Don't deny your nature." Sanos' head moving back and forth. "You love the battle. The fight. The carnage. After all, you are only human even if you are the phantom."

"Phantom?"

"Of course, do you really believe that only humans have their devils and monsters? To us, you are the monster. A ghost set on destroying our way of life. Whirling into our plans with destruction and murder and then gone, vanished without a trace. A *phantom* in our lore."

"Glad I can make an impression."

Sanos jumped from the second floor and landed on his feet fifty yards from Phil. And Phil stepped forward, turning so that he was eye to eye with Sanos.

"This is our planet, Sanos. You're just an uninvited guest. An alien parasite infecting our world."

"And you the exterminator. Dear phantom, what makes you think this planet belongs to you?"

"You're the father of lies, Sanos. Enough with the chitchat." Phil stretched his arms in front of him. He pressed the handles in his palms, extending the blades down his arms as a helmet formed around his head, smooth and silver. Sanos staring inquisitively at Phil's new armor. "Let's dance, vampire."

Sanos shook his head. "See, I was right." His eyes beamed with rage, his voice a sinister hush. "You *are* a monster."

8

CAM was lying on a bed in a tiny room on the cruiser, alone, thinking over the events he'd witnessed. He could hear the children, Cameron and Annison, playing. Odd as it was, the fact he was flying across America on a vessel he never knew could exist seemed perfectly rational. The war behind him, the war he'd fought for so long, a pawn in an elite game of chess, with the winner claiming the planet he so loved, with children, one he was sure was a genetically altered vampire or monster or whatever the young Cameron would become, the girl, Annison, who came with some strange antenna on the back of her skull, and a giant, Perseus, who had to remain hunched over to fit inside the vessel; all seemed completely rational, rational in his new reality. But there was more. He couldn't help the sensation boiling in his gut that told him…

All these people and yet I feel alone. Detached from them. From all of them. From myself.

Grimes was flying. He had jumped at the chance to fly the cruiser like a child who'd been given a surprise toy.

And what a difference a day can make.

Aliens do exist. Vampires too. For shit's sake, we are not alone in the universe, not by far. But how long have they been here, toying with us? Infecting our planet. Turning us against each other?

The vessel jumped up, then back down in a quick thrust, then settled back to its smooth ride.

Get it together, Grimes. Quit playing around.

And his thoughts kept returning to Robyn Winter. He could see Robyn as clear as his hand in front of his face. Those eyes? Why are his eyes like that? But it wasn't just his eyes; Cam saw Robyn's mouth move, his words too soft for Cam to discern.

Robyn.

Cam couldn't shake the notion that he somehow knew Robyn Winter; there was a familiarity and comfort Cam experienced in Winter's presence.

Safe, Cam thought, like an old blanket that provides comfort on multiple levels.

The vessel turned on a dime, and Cam had to brace himself to not roll over.

"Friggin' Grimes!" Cam hollered, jumping off the bed, his hand on the wall to brace himself, when he heard the speaker on the wall crackle to life.

Grimes' voice shouted through the speaker, "Cam, get up here. Now!"

The vessel jolted to the left, and Cam shifted his hands to keep himself from falling. A second later, he pressed his hand to the panel next to the door.

"We've got company," said Grimes through the

speaker as the door opened.

Cam rushed out of the room down the hall. Doors on his left and right, the hall opened to a large room where Cameron and Annison sat strapped in their seats. The giant sat on the floor.

"What is it?" asked Cameron. He looked pale, sick even.

"I'm sure it's nothing. Stay here and stay strapped in." He looked them over. Fixed his eyes on the giant. "Keep them strapped in." The giant answered with a quick nod before Cam rushed through the room to the cockpit. Grimes flying the vessel.

Cameron saw the screen before he heard Grimes speak.

The image was clear, a UFO behind them, a replica of the starship Phil had flown from the compound. Its movement on the screen was erratic. One second it was behind them, the next hundreds of yards ahead and on their right.

"Sit down!" Grimes hollered.

"What is it?" Cam said as he strapped into the seat beside Grimes.

"I think it's been following us. It showed up not long after we left Atlanta."

"Hostile?"

"Now, how am I supposed to know that?"

"Alright, alright. Let's not get our panties in a bunch." Cam craned his neck, searching the sky for a sign where the UFO had gone. "Where'd it go?"

A pause. The UFO was in front of them. They were barreling directly towards it.

Grimes screamed, "Shit," and dipped the vessel down, banking a hard right. "I'd say definitely hostile."

The vessel banked left and Cam saw the UFO outside his window further on the left. "How the hell do they move so fast?"

"I don't know? But it's messing with me, and I don't like it."

"Following us, trying to find out where we're going?"

Grimes propelled forward, the vessel lurching into a fast break straight away.

Cam braced himself, his hands on the wall to his right, his left hand squeezing his armrest as the vessel turned left, then settled straight away.

"Well, maybe we should get out and tell them we come in peace."

Grimes shot Cam a wild stare. "This is not the time for humor."

"Oh, Corporal, it's always a time for humor."

Grimes banked hard left and Cam's stomach twisted.

"Well, at least they're not engaging." Cam breathed deeply, thinking.

And then he heard the shot before he saw a green beam race past their cruiser.

"Shit!"

"You were saying, Lieutenant?"

9

SANOS caught Phil's fist. Phil pulled and tugged, but struggled to free his hand from Sanos' grip as Sanos laughed, when Phil used Sanos' strength as leverage to propel himself up. His boot thrashed against Sanos' chin as Phil flipped over onto his feet and Sanos stumbled back with a grunt, crashing into a desk that crumbled under his weight.

Sanos' mouth filled with blood. He shattered a fang, he was sure of it. Phil standing, ready for Sanos to launch another attack; his helmet's shield around the eyes gleamed a glowing white. Sanos rubbed his chin, grimacing. He spit a wad of blood to the floor. And yet his phantom stood unmoving, waiting, unfazed. The phantom's moves were smooth, cold, calculated. And yet he was still a simple human, or perhaps there was more to Phil than Sanos had thought.

Sanos rubbed his jaw, his breathing heavy; he felt weak without the pills, without new blood. His body labored when he pushed himself up, and the phantom waited for his next move. He looked up and over the room, still filled with light from the phantom's rose. His eyes settled on the phantom.

There is more to him than expected. Who is this phantom? Who is he indeed?

(He is the key. Dismantle him. Take him, Sanos… *take him.*)

Sanos tightened his fists and rushed at the phantom when Phil met his pace, lifting off the ground. Two kicks to Sanos' torso and head, and Sanos felt himself fall back, slammed against the ground with a heavy thud. Sanos jumped up quickly as Phil engaged, crossing blade against blade. Phil swiped Sanos' legs from beneath him. Another fall. His body ached, his skull beating with a heavy, painful thud.

"C'mon, Sanos," muttered Phil. "I thought you'd put up more of a fight. You're not gonna make this too easy, are you?"

Sanos gathered himself to his feet. He felt blood cascade across his forehead. He wiped it clear from his eyes. Phil raised his arm; blood stained his blade, Sanos' blood.

"I'll take you piece by piece if I have to."

Sanos glared at the phantom, thinking, my strategy is wrong with this one. There's too much light. Sanos stepped forward, slapped his hands together, bathing CR115 in darkness. Phil's light was now gone and Sanos rushed at Phil, slammed into him, and watched as Phil was tossed back into the wall, to the staircase that led to the second floor. He landed with a thud, his face pinched in a painful wince. Sanos standing tall, growling, clenching his fists.

"Two can play the rose game, dear phantom."

Phil catapulted towards Sanos, rushing at him with his blades. Blade against blade they fought, Phil's movement lightning fast and packing a thrust so powerful Sanos found it difficult to counter. Sanos backed up from Phil's relentless fury, and Phil crouched down, sliced his blades across Sanos' thigh. One cut, two, three, and followed with an uppercut to Sanos' jaw. Phil kept coming as Sanos reeled back. Phil raced towards him; his foot barreled towards Sanos, but Sanos caught his foot in the crook of his left arm, swiped his right blade across Phil's helmet, the metal crushed and cracked from the force of his blow. Phil's head snapped to his left, but Phil followed with his free leg, a kick to Sanos' already bloodied head. Sanos lost his hold on the leg. Phil's legs like a windmill, leg over leg delivered two kicks to Sanos that dropped him to the ground on his back, sliding away from where Phil was. And Phil stood, eyes on Sanos as his damaged helmet detracted.

Sanos wiped blood from his lips, glaring at his phantom. He shook his head with a growl in the back of his throat, then pushed himself to his feet.His eyes narrow as he looked at his phantom. "There's my phantom," said Sanos. He could feel his blood seeping down his leg. "What else have you got up that sleeve of yours?"

Phil was bobbing on his feet. "You'll find I'm full

of surprises." And he rushed at Sanos, but Sanos was quick. He slapped his hands together, turning the air between him and Phil into tightly packed atoms with the weight of concrete that wrapped around Phil with an iron grip. Sanos thrust his arms to the left and Phil went crashing into the wall. His back arched, his neck thrashed back.

"Come on!" Sanos hollered as Phil dropped to his knees. Phil's jaw clenched, his teeth grinding, staring at Sanos. "Dear Phantom," Sanos chuckled beneath his breath. "Time for round two."

10

CAM jumped up from his seat.

"Where the hell are you going?" Grimes banked left. The UFO appeared in front of them. "Shit." Turned on a dime to the right as Cam braced himself.

"Probably a good idea to shoot back, don't you think?"

Grimes eyed him. "About time, Lieutenant."

Cam raced down the hall. According to Silas, one of Robyn Winter's lackeys, the cruiser was equipped with a battle pod beneath the vessel. He stumbled but caught himself as the ship continued its winding, jutting, cutting movement. He opened the hatch in the floor and climbed into the seat in the pod, a clear sphere, controls across the thin desk surrounding the seat. Outside the vessel attached to the pod was the gun, a weapon unlike any Cam had ever seen. He strapped in quickly, took hold of the trigger and handles, set his feet on the pedals beneath him, and looked down. The pedals told their purpose; the right pedal swiveled left and right, the left pedal up and down.

He saw another green blast coming straight for

him as the vessel swerved hard left. He saw a metal halo beside the pod's controls with the word HEADSEAT engraved on it. Cam fit the halo over his head; he could now hear Grimes in the cockpit when he saw the UFO barreling towards him.

Shit.

Cam squeezed his trigger, and two bolts of green lasers shot from his weapon. But the UFO disappeared, the green blasts racing through open air.

"Holy shit, we got green shit too."

"What?" Grimes hollered. "Where the hell are you?"

"Gunroom, Corporal. Keep eyes on them, the flying's erratic. We need to catch them spot on."

A second later Grimes screamed, "Three o'clock."

Cam swerved, shooting beams of green across the sky. One of them grazed the UFO before the starship disappeared. "Ha, ha," Cam uttered. "A little chin music for ya."

"Below us. Below. Directly below."

Cam slammed the pedal and the gunner pod turned fast; the UFO was there. Cam shot another four times, but the UFO vanished before his lasers had a moment to reach its target. He saw a flash in the corner of his eye, turned on a dime, another four shots. The UFO gone.

"Fuck," Cam screamed. Then, beneath his breath, "How the hell do they do that?"

11

PHIL'S adrenaline-fueled blood raced through his veins, his head becoming weary. The pills' effects had begun and soon, Phil knew, those effects would arrive in full force. Vital signs were dwindling, and he felt his veins constrict, restricting access to his precious lifeblood. He could hear his heart ache, pounding in his chest with a heavy hammering thud like a blind man unnerved by an unknown cause.

But he must continue to fight, Phil told himself. After all, he couldn't just troll into Drac City and expect a warm welcome while they handed over Sandy effortlessly. No, he needed to get in to the city, move around unnoticed. What better way to accomplish his task than for them to think he was already dead? He thought it ironic how Sanos referred to him as the phantom, for it was a phantom they would receive.

And Sanos was his ticket inside. Sanos waited, arms stretched, and Phil still crouched against the wall. Sanos was using the rose now, manipulating the surrounding atoms to his advantage. Phil would need to counter his strike, but Phil's mastery of the rose was still out of his reach. He needed to reach down, let the magic flow from his veins. Had to. There was no other choice. Sanos must believe he won, through whatever means he needs to secure victory, and that meant believing his victory was difficult. Yes, Phil was taking a chance with his strategy, but what strategy did not play under the thumb of chance and risk?

See through the moment to the future. Make that future your present and it will become as you see it. Robyn's voice an echo in his mind. And Phil could see himself arriving in Atlanta with Sandy in tow as he manipulated the atoms in his sphere. Tiny bulbs of light ignited inside those atoms, charging, circulating into a loud sonic boom that raced towards Sanos and thrust him across the room. Phil ran behind his light as Sanos crashed against the wall with a groan. Phil, on top of him, lashed out with his blades, but Sanos was quick. He caught Phil's blade with his, and his boot barreled into Phil's torso. Pain swelled in Phil's gut and raced to the back of his skull. Phil hunched over, the pain in his abdomen excruciating and unnerving. Sanos on top of him, Phil had no time to think. Blade against blade, they fought, Sanos on the prowl, Phil on the retreat backing up as they fought. Sanos expanded his ether; the desk beside them turned to sand, then the sand to daggers aimed at Phil's head, speared towards him on command from Sanos. Phil welcomed them into his ether, turning those sharp spears into bursts of light. His blades met Sanos' as he manipulated those atoms into thickly packed ice that wrapped around Sanos' feet to his shoulders, encasing him in a block of ice.

Without conscious thought, it came from beneath. Instinctively, Phil thought.

Sanos struggled within its icy grasp as he looked at Phil. Phil's mouth agape. I did that? he thought, looking at the ice encasement, bottom to top. A smile graced his lips when he locked eyes with Sanos, and Phil shrugged. Sanos dissipated the ice with a force that exploded into Phil. He felt himself reeling back, slamming into the ground and sliding, but Phil jumped up quickly, steadied himself on his feet, a fighting stance, on guard. Sanos watched, shook his head, and snarled. And Phil smiled.

"Arrogant human," grumbled Sanos.

"What's wrong, Sanos, having some trouble?"

"If it wasn't for COR, I would have killed you already. But now I know, phantom, your death is required."

"Death," repeated Phil. "What an extraordinary adventure." He tapped his middle fingers into his palm, and his jet pack propelled him towards Sanos, fists first. Sanos' eyes wide unbelieving what his eyes revealed, a flying phantom barreling towards him too fast for Sanos to react when those fists slammed into Sanos, reeling him back as he crashed into desks, chairs, and computers, all crushed under his weight, as Phil stood tall, erect. Sanos looked at the surrounding chaos, his eyes found Phil.

"What do you say, Sanos?" Phil's lips curled into a grin. "Ready for round three?"

12

"WHERE the hell did it go?"

Cam hovered inside the pod, listening to the crackling from the headset, waiting, his breathing shallow. The pod hummed when it moved into position. Cam's feet now had a mind all their own. The cruiser propelled forward.

"Maybe it's gone?" said Grimes through the headset. "Got what it wanted and went back to... wherever the hell it came from."

Cam listened.

"Like a scavenger, gathering information to bring back to the flock."

"I don't think so," uttered Cam, barely audible, his gaze fixed on a spot some hundred yards away. He cocked his head, staring, noticing how the air around that spot swirled, and Cam felt his chest constrict as the UFO propelled out of the void. "There it is, seven o'clock." Cam shot four times, two shots hit on impact. The UFO faltered, spiraling, turning down. Three more shots as the UFO banked right and vanished. Cam swerved his pod around; the UFO was there whistling four shots at the cruiser. Gone again and Cam heard the explosion before black smoke billowed from the cruiser.

Grimes' voice loud in Cam's ear. "We're hit. We're hit!"

The cruiser banked down and to the left. Smoke plumed from the cruiser with relentless fury. "We're going down, Lieutenant." Grimes again, Cam could hear his grunting as the ship leveled in the air.

That same comingling circle in the air, Cam's eyes on it. He started shooting immediately, and the UFO spiraled out of thin air. Cam's shots direct hits, four in a row, ripping explosions across the UFO. The UFO burned on its way down to crash into the earth. Cam watched as an explosion erupted from the UFO and a burst of fire leapt into the sky.

Cam hollered, "UFO going down, Corporal." He watched as the UFO slammed through the desert, fire jutting from its bowels, then heard the screeching, humming, burning of his vessel.

"We're going down. Brace yourself."

Black smoke wrapped around his pod like a dark nightmare. He could see nothing beyond the pod. This is when Cam remembered he was at the bottom of the vessel. He'll be crushed on impact. Quickly, he unlatched himself.

13

SANOS gripped Phil by the throat and slammed him into the ground. Phil's foot kicked the back of his head, but his grip around Phil's throat held. Sanos shook his head, warding off the pain from Phil's kick. Phil wriggled in his grasp across the floor. Grunting, Sanos dragged Phil to his feet, gripped his head in both hands, and tossed Phil into desks and chairs. Sanos expanded his ether, barreling thickly packed atoms towards him, turning the desks and chairs into metal ropes that wrapped around Phil and squeezed. But Phil used his blades, cutting those metal ropes into quarters, which turned to sand at his feet. Sanos rushed at him, his pace inhumanly fast, slamming into Phil. Sanos continued his advance; he was on top of Phil, now pressed between himself and the wall, Sanos' hands on Phil's throat, squeezing. Phil dug his fingernails into Sanos' hands. Phil's blades' claws jutted from his fingers and tore through Sanos' hands as a loud grunt escaped Sanos' throat.

Phil pulled Sanos' hands from his throat, the pain excruciating for Sanos as he dropped to his knees.

Phil hovered over him, staring, apparently enjoying the pain he was causing when Phil's boot crushed into his face, dropping Sanos back, where his head rattled against the floor. Phil used his jet pack to lift off the ground as if he were on a spring, floating behind Sanos, back down to the floor. Sanos held his trembling curled claws, blood jutting from the wounds.

He had him. Had the phantom in his talons, squeezing the life from his lungs. How does he do it? How does he know with such miraculous instinct what to do? As if he can see his next move before it happens. And yet, he is only human, bound by human thought, a slave to human programming. How have the laws impeded upon his people not touched him? When he was in Sanos' grip, his eyes revealed no cause for concern, nor fear, as if he had Sanos right where he wanted him. Phil, this human, represented a flaw in Drac thinking and belief, Sanos was sure of it. His people were never debriefed about humans with Phil's skill, nor his wit, or....

Sanos gathered himself to his feet, clutching his shaking, bleeding hands against his abdomen. The phantom waited, watching, poised and ready.

Evolution!

The thought stuck. Sanos saw it clearly, the Draconian's reasoning for destroying the human race. Should they be allowed to evolve with the phantom's abilities, they would reign supreme. Phil bent his head, watching the heavy breathing Sanos.

Why does he not advance?

Every inch of his body throbbed with immense pain. His head bled into his eyes, his fang broken, his leg sliced three times and was still bleeding. And his claws, his hands, punctured by phantom claws. And still the phantom remained unscathed, other than a host of bruises. If it was fate for him to die at the hand of the phantom, then so be it. Sanos stood tall, arching his back as Phil began that bobbing motion, readying himself for the coming threat.

(You must take him, Sanos. He is the key to our future.)

Sanos shook his head, an attempt to ward off the voice. He snarled and spit blood to the floor, his eyes never leaving Phil, cradling his torn talons.

"Ready to give up, Sanos? Tell me where Sandy is, and I'll let you leave here alive."

"I'd rather die." And he rushed at Phil, who flew quickly over him, now behind him, his arms wrapped around Sanos' neck, wrapped around his throat. Sanos thrust the back of his head against Phil's face, breaking Phil's nose and releasing his arms from Sanos' throat. Sanos spun round with a punch that carried the strength of an atom bomb. Phil reeled back, and Sanos was on him with his blades, caught by Phil's blade. Crossing blade against blade, Sanos saw how the blood jutted from Phil's nose across his lips. His eyes welled with tears as he stretched his leg up high, his body swerving, and Sanos found himself in the crook of

Phil's knee, his throat gagged, felt his head and neck twist and his skull rapped against the floor when Sanos manipulated the surrounding atoms, sending shards of broken desk and metal that slammed into Phil.

Sanos jumped up, grabbed Phil's body, and tossed him into the wall. Phil's eyes rolled to the back of his skull as Sanos slammed his forehead into Phil's eyes. Phil reeled back and fell to his knees. Sanos stomped over to him, took hold of a talon full of bloodied hair, and yanked back. A painful wince and grunt erupted across Phil's lips. Phil's neck exposed, Sanos snapped his teeth around his neck, drank down a gulp of blood, and yanked his head back. Just a bite, a little taste of phantom blood. The blood was exquisite on his tongue. His hands squeezed Phil's head and slammed his skull through the wall. Phil's feet shuddered up his legs before falling limp, his body half in and half out of the wall.

And Sanos raged with a victorious roar that filled the vast void. And then the pain came full force, like a tidal wave slammed into his veins. All he felt was pain as he looked at his phantom and those limp, unmoving legs. He craned his neck to see Phil inside the wall. Phil's eyes were closed, his neck lined with puncture marks where Sanos had bitten him, the skin beneath his eyes moist, where tears had fallen now turning black and blue above a crushed, bloodied nose. No breathing. No chest rising and the blood had ceased jutting from his wounds. Sanos furrowed his brow, inquisitive as he reached his hand to Phil's neck.

No pulse.

His phantom was dead.

14

THE cruiser crashed into the desert sand mere seconds after the giant had lifted Cam from the pod, enveloping him in that giant embrace as the cruiser barreled into the earth. Cam never felt the impact; the giant had taken the brunt of the crash. Even when they tumbled, tossed, and slammed across the cruiser, Cam felt nothing more than shuffling, safe in the giant's embrace.

Cam could hear the cruiser screech to a stop, and with one last explosion, the cruiser dipped to the left, and all movement ceased. A second later, sprinklers erupted throughout the ship. An alarm raged through the halls. Cam looked around the ship; his eyes squinted by falling water. The giant's grip was tight.

"I think you can let me go now," said Cam, watching Perseus whose mouth gaped open, looking over the ship as if he needed to confirm all was safe before loosening his grip. Cam stood up with a wobble, needing to steady himself on his feet, when he saw blood across the giant's skull. "You're bleeding." Cam gestured to the giant's head, and he wiped blood from his skull, grimaced and snarled at the sight of his blood. He put his hand over the wound and gathered himself to his knees.

Cam hollered, "Everyone all right?" while offering his hand to Perseus. Annison and Cameron hollered back they were fine. Perseus cocked his head; his expression revealed the fact that Cam's offer wouldn't do anything more than hurt Cam, as if the giant's heavy weight would cause significant pain. Instead, Perseus lifted to his feet, hunched beneath the roof when the sprinkler ceased.

"Fire Out!" said a mechanical voice from the cruiser's speaker system.

Cam eyed Perseus. "Thank you," he said. "I was about to meet my maker out there." He cocked his eyebrows. "Thank you for saving my life."

Perseus pointed at him, then through the window to the battered UFO outside their ship, a hundred yards away, and he bowed.

"Well, either way big man, thank you."

Perseus winced, touching the wound on his forehead.

"Keep your hand on it. The bleeding will stop." Cam looked over the cruiser, then went to the back, where Annison and Cameron were still seated. Annison gave a thumbs up.

"You got 'em," said Cameron. "Good shooting."

"Lucky shot is more like it. Perseus is hurt, take him outside and try to assess any damage…"

The speaker crackled to life, Grimes on the other end. "Cam. Need you up here."

Annison and Cameron unbuckled.

Cam pushed the speaker button to talk. "On my way," he said, then to his two preteens, "Get him off. I'll be out in a minute."

Cam went to the cockpit as Annison and Cameron walked behind him to help Perseus.

"That was one hell of a crash, Corporal. Never knew you could crash so well," Cam said as he entered the cockpit. Grimes was in his seat. Pinned to his seat was more like it. A metal rod had impaled him. Blood dripped from the metal point that had gone through not only Grimes' shoulder but the seat too. "Well, that's not good."

"No, it's not good at all," said Grimes. "And I don't think I'll be flying anything for a while."

Grimes was soaking wet along with the cruiser's controls. Cam heard the last few electrical sparks burn out with a fizz and pop.

"What do we do now, lieutenant?"

Cam cocked his head, assessing. "Simple, we take that rod out of you."

"How?" Grimes shot back.

"Well..." Cam gripped the rod and pulled, assessing how stuck the rod was. Grimes hollered in pain.

"Don't do that."

"What do you want me to do, Corporal, leave

you here impaled to a seat?" He gave up on the rod.

"I don't know," said Grimes.

Cam thought it over. "Stay here," he said and walked from the cockpit.

"Not like I can go anywhere," Grimes hollered.

Cam called for Perseus, his wound being tended to by Cameron and Annison. "I need him," said Cam.

Perseus looked at Cameron before gathering himself to his feet and following Cam back into the cruiser. "Need your help again, big man. Follow me." Cam went into the cockpit; the narrow hall stopped Perseus from moving forward. He looked over the hall and doorway to the cockpit, snarled and gripped the entrance lip, crushing the wall back and tearing it off.

"What the hell is that?" Grimes asked as he attempted to look over his shoulder.

"This is the best and quickest way," said Cam.

Grimes' eyes widened. He started shaking his head. "No way, lieutenant."

"It's the only way." He went behind Grimes, wrapped his arms around him. "Just don't move."

"Holy shit." Grimes' body jumped as Cam held him firm and Perseus yanked the rod with one quick thrust. Grimes hollered something awful and Perseus tossed the rod across the room.

"Like pulling off a bandaid."

"Definitely not like pulling off a bandaid," grunted Grimes, hunched over, gripping his wound.

"Now, Corporal, let's get you fixed up."

15

SANDY was sitting in the bathroom corner, shaking, alone. Clumps of hair in her palms. Hair scattered across the floor, and draped over the sink where a host of teeth and nails rested in a pool of blood and spit. Blood smeared across her lips and more blood dripped from her fingers as her stomach raged with a hunger she fought to suppress. And then there were the voices, like echoes raging across the room, competing for a permanent space in Sandy's mind.

"You are Drac."

"How is it possible?"

"You're human, Sandy. Don't forget your human nature."

"You must feed. Dracs don't last long without feeding."

Were these her thoughts, or had she gone mad? She attempted to wrap her head around what in blazes was happening and how it happened? It could have come from the greys. The greys who took Adam. Adam, her boy, her son, was gone, but still she could feel him, sense him, see him in her mind's eye. And then Mono, that evil witch, the cause of Sandy's suffering. Her change.

What did they do? Desecrated everything I hold dear. But she was sure Adam was still alive; Moth had to be lying. He'd said it was her fault, Telas' fault.

My fault for fighting back. I can't believe that, he…

She could hear crying, a baby's cry. Everywhere in the room, although faint like a whispered calling for help.

"Adam?" She clambered to her feet, listening. The cry again, wailing, as if calling to her. Sandy walked out of the bathroom; she was alone, her head moving left and right, her hands shaking by her side.

Where is it coming from?

Sandy went to the door, put her palm on the reader next to it, and walked out of the room on a mission, listening, following the cries.

*****

Moth sat in front of a large screen, watching Sandy. One of his subordinates, Kaal, sitting next to him. Moth was shaking his head.

"Putrid abomination."

Kaal said, "What do you wish for me to do?"

Nothing from Moth; he couldn't take his eyes off Sandy.

"She'll find him without a doubt. It's only a matter of time. If the connection is the same, she will undoubtedly find him."

"That... human... is never allowed to know her baby is alive." Moth stood up. "Deter her, Kaal. Send her towards the archives study. I'll meet her there."

Kaal looked over his shoulder at Moth. "What about the baby? COR requires him; we can't dismantle the child without their accord."

"I'm completely aware of what COR desires, Kaal. This Sandy poses a new conundrum."

"Just kill her then. Be done with it and it won't be a problem."

Moth gripped Kaal's shoulder. "In time. But first I need her."

"For what?" Kaal said. "I think you just want to play with a new toy."

Moth chuckled under his breath. "Not at all, Kaal. There is something rotten in Drac City. I must weed it out. Too many players at hand to believe any of them. The truth exists between the lines and there's something I'm missing. The truth hides in what has not been told. What I do know is that baby needs to leave Drac City before she does find him."

"You know as well as I she will always find him. If this human has become Drac, she will always find him no matter how far he is."

"See through the present, Kaal. In the future, I would have killed Sandy. This is simply a distraction from the inevitable to gain intel on whomever our traitor is. If Mintaka is correct, the grey's may be moving towards insurrection."

"What did Mintaka tell you?"

Moth paused. "Mintaka is limited in her knowledge. Her species of grey are subordinate to Mono and I believe she is not aware of Mono's grey lineage and desires. There're missing pieces to her story more than likely not shared with her by grey superiors."

"But what did she say?"

Moth scoffed. "She said it was simple; the only way Sandy could become Drac is if she was Drac already."

Kaal burst into laughter. "That's impossible. Do you know what that would mean? If Drac's were to hear such blasphemy, we'll have insurrection within our own."

Moth said, "Than let's make sure they do not know."

"But the archives are lies. You said so yourself."

"Even lies hold some truth, Kaal. It's simply a matter of how they are perceived. Either way, I'll tear her heart out before she's able to cause any more concern." He walked to the door that slid open on his command. "Notify me when COR has gathered, Kaal. And when the grey representative arrives." And with that, he walked into the hall, ready to meet with his guest once again.

16

CAM had cleaned and bandaged Grimes' wound. Perseus carried him to the bed Cam had been using. Grimes complained about the wet bed, and Cam had laughed it off. All the while, he kept his eyes on the UFO.

Nothing had emerged from within the starship's hull. For all Cam knew, whoever was flying had perished in the crash. Cam himself wasn't sure how they all survived when the cruiser went down, but all the same, he planned on making a trip to the UFO once he'd gotten things settled on the cruiser. He needed to get word to someone to let them know what happened, Robyn Winter being the first on his mind. They were marooned in the Mojave, somewhere not too far from New Mexico, but the cruiser's mechanics were damaged in the crash, and the sprinkler system had finished it off. There was no signal getting out today.

"All this way just to die in a desert. How ironic is that?" His voice carried a whining cry. He kicked the control desk, ran his hands through his hair, thinking, Ok, we got food, we have weapons–Cam had seen the arsenal in the back of the cruiser and pantries filled with the kind of food Cam was sure was used by astronauts during their voyage to Mars and the Moon. The same food they used when first terraforming the red planet. And he could build a fire for warmth. He hoped his contact in New Mexico, the one provided to him by Silas, would be concerned when they had not arrived, prompting him to send out a search and rescue.

Possible and likely... but we can't depend on it.

But what's the alternative?

Cam scrunched his eyes to ward off the sudden bright glare that glinted through the cockpit from somewhere out in the desert. The light wavering, almost dancing, with the shape of a small rounded box moving across the cruiser's control panel. Cam watched it, followed it to its source hundreds of yards away. He shot up from his seat, craned his neck, looking at the sun, then back down to where the reflection had come from.

Maybe they weren't that far off from civilization after all. Cam was sure of it; they were not alone in the desert.

17

EVERY time Sandy thought she found the source of the cries, she hit a dead end. They were coming from all directions; the baby could be anywhere; she couldn't wrap her head around it.

Another wailing cry dissipated into the void. Sandy turned on her heels; quickly she followed the desperate call, trampling through hall after hall. Everything looked the same, like a maze she couldn't figure out. The only differences were the hieroglyphic symbols engraved on the walls at the start of each new hall. She stopped cold when she rounded another corner, a statue at the end of the hall; behind it were two large double doors.

The statue was tall, towering nine feet above Sandy. Made from what Sandy surmised was marble, depicting a female vampire dressed in a robe with two childish figures at her feet, huddled close to her legs and looking up as she looked straight ahead, as if devouring Sandy with her eyes. Her arms stretched in front of her, palms up. A phoenix hovered above the female vampire, attached to the nape of her neck.

Sandy wasn't sure if the female was a Drac; although the skin carried scales, there remained an odd resemblance to a dove, the nose being the most prominent, or beak, as Sandy thought. And the face, the face was likened to a human. In each palm was a feather, as if offering a gift to whoever approached, or to the children at her feet, both with the same features as the vampire.

Sandy assessed the statue, up and down, left to right. She saw symbols on the base, but not hieroglyphics like the ones marking each hallway. No, this was a language similar to Chinese. Sandy read them from right to left. "And you shall be free," read Sandy while mouthing the words. She followed the base to the vampire's eyes, completing what was written, softly speaking, "With this gift of passion." Sandy couldn't take her eyes off the vampire with its beak and feathers as an icy shiver crossed her skin, noticing the still quiet that clung to the moment with a subtle depth revealing the end of mystery. She crossed her arms. Her scaly skin bubbled with gooseflesh, the nape of her neck cringed, and the thought that dropped like an anvil in her mind exploded with resolution.

The statue vaguely familiar; Sandy knew she'd seen it before.

A baby's soft cry, tender, loving. Sandy could hear the cry in her mind's eye when those thick double doors opened softly, welcoming Sandy. She peered into the room, taking in what Sandy believed was a museum. It went on forever. The doors locked into place, opened wide. Above the door a word, more alphabetical symbols. Sandy read them.

"Archives."

I understand them? I can read their language? Without a thought or struggle.

"As if I've always known." She looked at her hands; the Drac skin had spread to her elbows. Looked at the statue and gnashed her fangs, jaw tight, head shaking. "To hell with you," she snapped. "You have your children... I want mine."

She raised her fist, screamed, "DO YOU UNDERSTAND ME!" And the statue continued its gaze into the unknown.

That soft cry again. Sandy stepped back, despising the statue for not hearing her plea. She turned to the room, walked to it. But she knew then, she knew Adam was not in there. Some insipid game was at play, and she was sure Moth was behind it all.

18

SANOS gathered his phantom, his prize, his ticket to new blood, and brought Phil to his starship. The ship, once he stepped inside, beamed with life, lights turned on and a slight hum gathered beneath the folds. The hull open, on the right the cockpit, on his left, staterooms. He went left with his phantom over his shoulder. He felt pressure, not just from the dead phantom's weight, but from pain, suffering. His breath labored through a wheeze in his chest, his hands shaking, bleeding from his leg that stung something awful. He thought himself weak, and not because of his battle with Phil, because of the pills. The side effect was itself an abomination, depleting his will and strength. Should he had been at optimal functioning, he would have dispatched the phantom quickly, he was sure of it. Nonetheless, he would need to gather his strength; he would need to heal before addressing COR.

And he needed to feed. The thought of his last feast rifled through his mind as he dropped Phil on a raised slab with a grunt. Phil's blood had tasted sweet, delectable, but dead blood was cold and tasteless and turned Drac blood with a shiver. Those who drank from the blood of the dead always turned mindless and ravenous, as if the cold blood turned the heart hollow and the mind vile. He would need to wait until his arrival in Drac City to satisfy his hunger. A ripe young human child was the first on his list. A soldier's thirst took many humans to satisfy. The thought of his youth sprang into his mind, running through the fields and tearing humans apart. Some, like Sanos, liked to play with their food, taunting their minds into fear and suspending the moment before filling the gullet. Fear always tastes better. It does something to humans, heats the blood, and adds a tinge of bitterness Drac's find exquisite. Such fond memories, fond memories indeed.

Sanos' hand twitched. He raised it to his eyes. Bleeding. Phil's claws had penetrated his hand, two puncture holes through his palm, and a third had nipped his finger. Two gaping holes. He stared through them, turned his hand around, a hole through his palm, another by his thumb, and his phantom lay dead through the hole. Sanos strapped the body to the slab. No need to have the dead slumping across the room on his way to Drac City. He fastened the belts tight, all the while watching his phantom.

Phantoms are dead already. Will you rise again, dear Phantom?

Sanos dipped his nose to Phil's lips, closed his eyes with a slow inhale. The blood was cold, the sweetness in the phantom's blood erased by the hand of death. And the body was already rotting, discolored; a greyish tint had formed across the phantom's skin. He sensed no movement within the body, no blood coursing through veins, no electrical activity in the brain, no beating heart. Sanos snarled, his growl in the back of his throat. He lifted his head, looked at his hand.

"At your worse you were a worthy opponent. But like all myths, you too have been revealed as a fallacy. You were only human, dear phantom, and humans are inferior." He gripped Phil's jaw, moved his head right then left, the bones crackling, cartilage stretched and popped. He clutched the jaw between his fingers, his lips curled in a snarl; fingertips sank into Phil's skin.

"See you in the next life, dear Phantom. Perhaps then victory will be yours."

19

DEATH, thought Phil. It's not so bad.

All he could see was darkness, a vast void of darkness. Eight hours; Silas had said the pill's effect will subside in eight hours. Plenty of time for Sanos to bring his prize into Drac City. Phil stepped across the darkness, his footsteps echoing into the void like a pounding between his ears. Lights now overhead, Phil snapped to it, looking high above to a stream of stars rushing across the sky. Shooting stars, blazed white and gold within a blanket of suns and planets, raced overhead as if competing towards a final destination. Each constellation disappearing into darkness, leaving Phil, once again, bathed in a dark blanket.

Now a struggle, a thick swelling rose in his chest, his heart ached, pain erupted in his veins, excruciating, billowing to every part of his body. Phil clutched his chest, dropped to one knee. His heart like a stone, difficult to breathe. He gasped for air, one hand on some invisible ground, the other across his heart. The heart that swelled with a painful gasp, cold like ice. Felt heat across his skin, his face burning, flushed, his heart in his throat, gagging. And then a release as if floodgates had opened, allowing blood to race through his veins, and Phil knew then his heart had taken a beat. Silas said the heart will continue to beat, albeit infrequently. The pain lingered like an echo too strong to dissipate. Phil gasped for breath, his inhale raging, drawing air into his lungs.

A light in the corner of his eye, Phil moved his head towards it. White and blinding, over his shoulder. He could see now an outline from a staircase, leading to the light high above. A line of human beings, wide eyed, on those stairs, like moths to a flame, unblinking, jaws hung open as one by one they stepped off the stairs and into the light. It mesmerized Phil, his eyes wide, hypnotized. All suffering ended in the light. But the people appeared worn, disheveled, their movements labored, zombie like. Phil turned to his left, his attention drawn to a sparkle in the dark void. The sparkle brought colors like the northern lights. A sea of light, thick unwavering reds, orange, yellow, green, blue, indigo, and violet, the colors warm, and Phil could feel his skin ripple with warmth. He thought the colors continued for eternity. The light over his shoulder strengthened as if the white light above the stairs competed with the rainbow. His jaw dropped, felt his body release as if he'd carried a heavy load torn quickly from his shoulders. He stepped towards the white light.

"It's a trap." The voice had come from the

darkness.

Phil heard footsteps tap across the invisible floor.

Phil's eyes narrow, staring into the darkness.

"One meant to cause strife and usher anxious attachment back to our planet. And with it, confusion and unrest with the purpose to strangle a lucid stream of consciousness."

Phil turned to the waiting line; one by one they stepped into the light and disappeared.

"They're confiscating our energy. Keeping it from entering the stratosphere and attaining knowledge necessary to bring to the next life." Phil would have sworn the voice had swallowed before continuing, as if a lump had formed in the throat. "Only few of us have leapt into the correct light." Phil saw a finger stretch from the darkness, pointing towards the northern lights. "That is the true light. When combined, the colors reflect the white light that has been spoken of. That is the light that brings us home."

Phil heard thick footsteps behind him; he turned to the sound as the voice stepped into the light.

"Robyn?"

Robyn Winter stepped closer to Phil.

"How can it be?"

"You're between life and death, but we can exist on multiple planes." He looked over his shoulder at the white light, his neck stretched, and Phil watched the souls in uniformed solidarity stepping into the light. "It's a shame," said Robyn as he turned to Phil. "With all the killing, all the wars and destruction, the recycled mass of consciousness has no recourse to claim a new earthly host." He craned his head, staring into Phil as his white eyes gleamed. Phil's mouth agape, looking from Robyn to the white light. "Soul energy," said Robyn. "And with no host to return to, they will walk eternally in that void. Confused. Angry. Tortured. And ravenous. Very few will return. And when a new host is born, the souls will claw and tear at each other to claim the new host. But with that return also comes the confusion, the anger and ravenous nature, essentially evolving the human heart into a malevolent beast, easily controlled by fear, easily influenced by hatred."

"Hell on earth," said Phil.

"For lack of a better phrase, yes. But that is nothing compared to what will become of the universe. As more and more become trapped in the false light dimension..." He was shaking his head. "The result will be catastrophic. A sonic boom more powerful than a supernova, more ravenous than a black hole, will envelope the universe. Picture all in the universe suddenly change over. Where once there was beauty, in an instant will become withered and decayed. Where once there was love..." he snapped. "Suffering will be the norm. Our entire universe will be made over in a Draconian image. It's not enough for them to take over one planet at a time. It's not enough for them to destroy one species after another." Phil could sense Robyn's dismay. "They want it all. They want to be God."

"How can it be stopped?" asked Phil. "How much time do we have?"

Robyn swung his left arm across his body like a maestro, revealing to his audience a new revelation. Revealed within the darkness was a never-ending line of human bodies. "With everyone who enters, the energy reaches closer to critical mass. This is what is not known in the physical realm. This is spiritual warfare within a quantum dimension. Even the most skilled and cunning warriors will become trapped in its mangled ball of confused and torturous energy. In order to reverse the polarity, in order to release those trapped souls will take something more. Something pure. A light like a child, energy like comfort, familiar and knowingly safe. Shining brighter than any star in existence with an energetic boom capable of building a bridge between the trapped dimension and the light so that they can return to the source." Robyn pointed to the northern lights over Phil's shoulder. "Allowing those souls to fly free and seek new hosts across the universe."

Phil bent his head, turned to the northern lights. "What is in there?" he asked.

"They wait for you," said Robyn. "Across the universe, for all to be revealed."

The northern lights, Phil was sure, called him to it, mesmerizing, hypnotic. He felt his arms tingling, trembling. "But what is it, master Robyn? Where does it lead?"

"To truth."

Phil turned to Robyn. "Truth? What is truth?"

Robyn Winter smiled. "Easy to find out, isn't it? Step in," said Robyn. "It waits for you."

Phil stepped towards the northern lights, away from Robyn.

"The universe is a consistently evolving pattern of recycled energy with competing vibrational frequencies seeking dominance in each pattern. The patterns seek balance. Whether fear or love dominates that balance is no matter as long as there is balance. It is our duty to be the balance that holds freedom in its grasp by accepting our dark nature"

Phil walked to the northern lights, Robyn's voice over his shoulder.

"In the beginning, when the light first beheld the darkness, the vast void of dark energy, it swallowed fear and anguish."

Phil moved closer. Lights swirled around him.

"And when the darkness gazed upon the light it experienced wonder… and a feast of delight."

Phil raised his arms; light everywhere, framing his mortal coil.

"Such is the nature of the universe."

Light through him. Everywhere there was light, a thick sea of light, high above, and so below.

"And the conflict in all of us."

Phil felt the push before the pull, as if some cosmic hand pulled him forward into a vortex, a wormhole spiraling bright with an electrical current and brilliant, beautiful light. And still he could hear Robyn's voice, as if his influence was carried on the heels of the cosmos.

"Do we evolve peacefully or fold into ourselves, implode into oblivion, and give in to destruction? If this is the fate we choose, then how will we rise again? What darkness will follow us across the universe?"

20

THE Archives room was like a museum. Cold and
clean, filled with ancient scrolls, and books so thick
Sandy thought they must weigh hundreds of pounds.
Some texts rested on podiums inside glass cases and
were open to a random page, others were on a vast
number of shelves. She stepped to a podium and the
book open in its case. On the page a pastel picture
depicting a serpent, a cobra, in the grass followed by a
vampire in his infancy holding a feather, the same
feather in the palms of the statue. Next a grown
vampire, standing, hunched over, primitive, its head
thick and square with cobra flaps reaching wide from
the ears. And the last figure a Drac as Sandy knew
them now. The evolution of Drac. And surrounding
each image was a pod of light, each with different
colors. Sandy craned her neck, staring. Something
about the image was off, as if there was another layer
Sandy could not see.

"The colors represent the evolution of vibration
within our species." Moth behind her, Sandy turned to
him. "And the levels of consciousness that bring about

the evolution of the spirit…" His nose curled in a snarl and he closed his eyes, as if allowing a sinister thought to pass. His eyes opened slowly to meet Sandy's gaze. "The colors dance across the page to represent the constant shifting of energy."

Sandy regarded the book. "Looks stagnant to me. Perhaps you're not as evolved as you believe?"

Moth stepped forward and Sandy stood tall, erecting her shoulders and clenching her raised jaw, devouring him with her eyes, and he grinned. "Your eyes are still human. That is why you cannot see it."

Sandy turned away, clutched her fists beneath her folded arms.

"Give it time," said Moth. "Once your eyes turn, I'm sure your vision will as well. I wonder what other abilities will accompany your change?" Moth paused, as if gauging Sandy's change. "Have your movements turned fluid?"

Sandy's brow furrowed. "What?"

"Movement? We come from the serpent; it is why our movement is smooth and quick, like water flowing in all directions, back and forth, side to side. We are fast on our feet, slight movements the human eye has difficulty to catch. And then we pounce on our prey, catch it in our clutches, between our jaws." His eyes burrowed into Sandy's soul. "Striking fear into the hearts of our prey before feeding on their blood."

The simple mention of blood twisted a knot in Sandy's stomach. The thought of drinking blood held both a nauseous reverberation and salvation. Moth took her hand; how he had gotten so close so quickly she hadn't seen. Sandy ripped her hand from within his grasp.

"I only mean to see firsthand what is true."

No response. Sandy closed her eyes. Moth's presence was irritating, but Sandy knew he would not reveal where Adam was. This was a game, and Sandy needed to learn the rules before she could make a move. Her lips trembled, and she fought to ward off the anger swelling in her heart.

"Come with me," said Moth, when Sandy opened her eyes. He hadn't moved except to clamp his hands behind his back. "Allow me to show you our great city, as few have seen it. Through my eyes."

He smiled before walking further into the room, his movements swift, gliding across the floor towards the wall that opened as if the wall expected Moth's arrival. A gust of wind rushed through the opening. Sandy could see the city from where she stood; Drac City stretched on for miles, glinting silver skyscrapers spotted with electricity in a sea of darkness. Moth walked onto the platform beyond the wall. She could see how the edge stopped, with no railing or wall surrounding it.

Moth looked back at Sandy. "Come," he said, then laughed. "No need to worry, my lady. I've given up wanting to eat you."

"That's not comforting."

"Cannibalism has never been a Drac delicacy. Come," he said. "See our great city." Moth glided to the edge, smooth and fast, reminded her of...

Phil, in the camp when he rescued Sandy. She remembered how Phil had torn through soldiers as if he could disappear and reappear, much like Moth did now. Sandy searched the outside; the wind blowing in through the open door was warm across her skin, humid.

She had no recourse, so Sandy went outside. Beneath the breeze, wind chimes rattled, clunked, and tinkled. Moth stood at the edge. Sandy went close to the edge, looked down, and immediately snapped her head back when she felt herself plummeting. There was no ground below. The skyscraper disappeared into a vast sea of clouds.

Moth laughed. "I see you still have some human left in you. We have no fear of heights." He craned his head, contemplating. "No fear at all to be truthful."

"No," said Sandy. "Monsters only fear the light."

"My lady, leave no doubt. You, too, are a monster. We always become what we fear most."

She thought of Phil again, saw him sitting, focused on the light from the rose.

"Who is this Phil? A friend from another life?"

He caught her thought, and Sandy cursed herself for leaving herself open. What else was Moth burrowing into? What other corners in her mind had he slithered his way to?

Sandy looked down into the void below. "He is no one," she whispered. She could feel Moth stiffen. Shrewd was the word on the tip of Sandy's tongue for Moth's calculated mind.

"What is below the clouds?" she asked, a quick change of subject.

Moth looked down at the clouds. "We call it the gallows. Filled with tenements," he said. "The unsavory. Laboratories. Laborers." He turned to Sandy. "The dead. Humans who have served their purpose. We honor those humans who have brought nourishment with a funeral pyre."

Sandy refused to flinch; she was sure Moth was attempting to stifle her thoughts with cruelty. She raised her chin. The city reached as far as she could see, set back in three tiers likened to a stadium. The building where Sandy stood overlooked the whole of the city, towering high above as a symbol of Drac excellence, the beginning of the city; everything began with the tower. From where she was standing, she looked over the top of Drac City, all three tiers dwarfed by the tower. Directly below, the building dipped into the clouds with a platform that jutted out from the building beyond what Sandy surmised was some under earth moat, but instead of water there were clouds. The platform was below the three tiers. A bonfire raged in the center of Drac City, three hundred meters from the tower. Then the three levels rose above the platform, one behind the other, each taller by far than the previous and all made from silver, reflecting a smooth, tranquil pattern. Crosswalks and platforms surrounded each tier as trains moved across buildings heading north and south, east and west. Satellites floated across the buildings, beaming with light energy.

"How do you have power down here? How is that possible?"

"The earth," said Moth. "There's unlimited power on this planet and we are close to its core, where stored energy could fuel a billion cities for eternity. Your human counterparts unfortunately refused the work of the one you may have learned of as Tesla. Probably one of the greatest credits to your race. Although, even he was limited in his very nature."

"Limited by what?"

"By the fact that he was still human." Moth's voice filled with rage. "Although he was a credit to your race. As in every devolved species, there are glimpses towards evolutionary minds."

Sandy regarded Moth, his eyes staring into his city. "Who are the others?"

Moth scoffed, shook his head. "There have been a handful. You have probably heard of them as mystics or loons." He laughed beneath his breath. "Humans have always been cruel to those who are more than they."

"You didn't answer my question."

Moth turned to her. A smug smile curled in the corners of his mouth. "Few. Very few." He paused.

"Your most valued specimen would be the vile Robyn Winter." He turned to his city, eyes closed. "He has caused more strife in the universe than any human in history."

Sandy slammed a door in her mind. Robyn Winter. Phil's Robyn Winter?

Moth stepped closer to the edge, the tips of his boots across the threshold.

"Thankfully, the insipid creature is dead." He turned to Sandy. "Unable to cause any more trouble." He turned from Sandy's eyes as a strong breeze rifled across them from the city. Wind chimes rattled with the wind.

Sandy cradled her arms, the skin rough beneath her hands as a shiver crossed across her flesh. "Why wind chimes?" she asked.

Moth turned to her. "Beautiful, aren't they?" He pointed to his city. "Flutes too, although you may not hear them. Their vibration is usually silent to human ears. They exist as a calming mechanism. Music and fire have provided my people with peace for millenniums. It's a common thread, something shared by all who live with us."

Sandy was quiet while looking over Drac City. It buzzed with a vibration Sandy could sense in her veins.

"Perhaps once your transformation is complete, you will hear the flutes too."

Sandy shook her head. "I heard them when I first arrived," she said, then looked at Moth. "Before you attacked me!"

"Well," said Moth. "I am a vampire now, aren't I. And that was before I knew what was happening to you."

"How is it happening?" Sandy said.

Moth caught her stare with his own. "Truthfully, I do not know."

Sandy shook her head. "Liar."

"Not so. I have no idea how you are turning, but the how is not our issue, is it, Sandy? What is true is you are Drac. You're turning by the minute." He stepped closer. "Tell me, Sandy, how much of your human nature will remain after you've completely turned?" Stepped closer still, Sandy raised her chin to see him towering over her as her eyes narrowed. "How much will you remember of your human existence? How much will you despise them, then? I wonder, Sandy. Wonder how long will it take before you are completely Drac."

Sandy felt her stomach twist, felt her blood turn cold. Moth reached his hand to her cheek. "You're growing pale," he said. "Tell me, do you feel pain in her veins, in your blood? Your gut? As if everything in your body is straining to break free."

"Yes," Sandy breathed in a hushed hiss of a voice. Staring into Moth's eyes, she saw the eyes of a snake.

Moth walked away, toward the museum, Sandy watching him. He turned to her before entering.

"Return to your stateroom," said Moth. "I'll have proper attire brought to you."

"For what?"

"Well, my lady, since your reflection is that of Drac, perhaps it is best to acquaint you with some of our traditions."

"Traditions?"

"Yes, my lady. Our culture. Tonight..." he said, "We welcome you to Drac City, my personal guest, our new mistress of the night."

Sandy looked skeptically at Moth.

"Someone, my lady, needs to show you how to feed."

Sandy shuddered. A grin curled across Moth's lips, and then he was gone, gliding across the museum as Sandy's veins swelled, her pounding heart calmed, and she could breathe freely once again, thankful he had gone. She wasn't sure how long she could keep that door in her mind closed.

Robyn Winter. Phil's Robyn Winter. The very person who sent Phil to snatch her from the clutches of tyranny. But if he's dead, then how did he send Phil?

Wind across her skin, wind chimes beneath the fold. Sandy gazed across the expanse of Drac City. The platform where she stood jutted away from the building, Sandy turned, arching her neck, looking high above, observing how the top was shaped in an obelisk. Above the obelisk, perhaps on the rooftop, she surmised, a wide electrical current cascaded across the sky, flowing purple and blue. The building stretched as high as she could see with those colors raging with electricity around it.

And she wondered then, how long would she need to play this game with Moth?

21

THE sun had gone, leaving stars to illuminate the night. Night had fallen on the desert and a cold tinge arrived with the wind.

Cam had ordered Perseus to stay on the ship, and he brought Grimes outside to sit by the fire with Cameron and Annison. Grimes may be hurt, but he could still pull a trigger with his left hand, and if anyone thought it best to cast a raid on the broken cruiser, they'd think better of it once Perseus greeted them. All staged to bring out whoever was watching them. Cam hid away from the cruiser. He'd found an infrared pair of goggles, scanning the desert with them while he hid behind a sand mound, the cruiser in clear view from his vantage point, along with the decimated UFO. His new weapon, a rifle resembling his classic AR15, sat next to him.

The fire raged high. Cameron and Annison laughing, Grimes was laughing too, although he winced with every gut busting cackle. Their laughter raged across the desert; Cam was sure that whoever was out there, hiding in the desert, could hear them. He wondered if it was human or alien.

Hopefully human, I don't think I can take another alien species at the moment.

Most people went to the safety camps during the war, but some remained home to defend their lands. Outliers! The military referred to them as outliers, doomsday preppers who scoffed at the military's declaration for safety camps. They believed they were safer in their homes. How right they were. Cam scanned the desert where he'd first seen that glimmering reflection of light. Saw nothing that would trigger his internal radar, nothing but desert.

"Come on, buddy," Cam whispered. "Come out, come out wherever you are."

His attention caught by a moving object in the clouds a few hundred yards across the desert. The clouds moved as if a shield for whatever ship moved within it. Cam removed the infrared goggles and looked with his own eyes. The cloud glowed a sickly green and crimson, moving slowly away from their camp.

"And where are you going?" Cam looked through his goggles, bringing the image up close, zooming his view closer to the cloud. He could see the outline of the UFO hidden within. "Gives a new definition to the term cloud cover." He scanned across the desert to the shipwrecked starship, then removed his goggles. There was no cloud cover for the downed ship during their battle. Cam bowed, thinking.

Why hide under cover? Our ship…

He looked at the cruiser.

Not a human ship is why. Which means…

He looked through the goggles to the cloud hiding UFO.

Surprise attack.

"Shit," said Cam. "They're heading to the nearest town."

Cam remembered how Robyn Winter's people reported the aliens were revealing themselves.

Yeah, thought Cam. Revealing themselves in a surprise attack.

He shuffled to his feet. We're sitting ducks out here. It's time to check if that UFO is operational. Obviously, anyone on board is dead or they would've climbed out. Cam looked through the goggles, the wrecked UFO revealed in his view.

He stepped closer, scanning the desert, turning, twisting, seeing the night sky. Seeing the figure that was standing behind him.

Cam felt the pain in his skull before he hit the ground with a thud. Pain scorched to the back of his brain and neck. His eyes bleary, vision blurred when the figure stepped over him, arms raised, holding a staff.

And then darkness.

22

SANOS awakened to a bleeping signal. The crypt he
was resting in casually opened, vapor rushed into the
open room from the crypt. Healing oxygen to aid Sanos
in his return to strength and health. The crypt was a
horizontal pod made from silver and gold. He had been
in a deep sleep, a much needed rest after the last few
days. Now the bleeping signal reached into the
subconscious, and took hold of Sanos. His mouth
gaped open, then closed, his head lolled from side to
side, drifting between sleeping and waking
consciousness. Eyes opened slowly with a flutter. Sanos
sat up; his back popped and cracked. Looked around
the room, all was quiet.

His first thought went to his phantom, the
second to his hands. He stretched his fingers, looking
them over. The holes had healed, leaving a circular
discoloration where Phil's claws had bitten him.
Touched his leg where Phil had cut him; also healed.
And he felt strong, his insides at optimal functioning,
strong and yet… starving. Ravenous. He could eat an
entire human family in this moment. New blood would

have to wait, can wait, and must wait. Sanos shook his head, stretched his eyelids and snarled as he twisted in the pod, his feet on the floor, standing. He felt normal, as if the effect of new blood had finally waned. His head clear, brain functioning with high acuity.

New blood drives Dracs into a frenzy, thought Sanos. Who among us wants to feel superior? The answer is all.

Sanos went to the door. Talking to the ship, he said, "How far to destination?"

The bleeping ceased, the ship's mechanical voice answered, "Ten minutes to arrival."

"Dock in the tenements," he ordered.

A second later, "Tenement landing confirmed."

"Good," whispered Sanos when the door slid open. Sanos went to Phil. Part of him wanted to make sure the phantom had not moved, as if the dead could move. And part of him wanted to gaze upon his prize. His ticket back to COR, and through COR, new blood.

Phil remained as Sanos left him. Unmoving. Undisturbed. Dead. Sanos breathed hoarsely, rubbed his head, and went to the cockpit. They were below ground now; the ship weaving between dendrites that raged with electricity. Drac City in the distance.

"My home," said Sanos. "My city. My people." And he grinned a conniving victorious grin. "*My...* people."

(Yes, Sanos, give them new blood and they will bow to your leadership.)

23

CAM was being dragged across the desert. His eyes drifted open, the figure dragging him bathed in darkness, a shadow in the firelight. He could hear Annison, Cameron, and Grimes talking around the fire. His hands and ankles tightly bound, a gag in his throat. The figure stopped cold, dropped Cam's feet, and crouched down. Whoever this person was, he was holding Cam's rifle, the butt of the gun between the crook of its arm.

Cam could see they were just inside the darkness. The glow from the fire dissipated fifty yards from where Cam and this unknown figure now waited. Cam was sure whoever had bound and gagged him was assessing a plan of action. Cam grunted through his gag, hollering as loud as possible when the figure turned, his face framed in the moonlight, silhouetted by the fire. His skin hard to see, covered in shadow, but Cam could see that the creature's face was not human. Looked more like those vampires, lizard like, but the head was small and Cam could only see part of its face; the creature wore a cloak with the hood covering the head and ears. Its yellow eyes gleamed at Cam before returning its gaze to the fire. Cam began screaming, but the gag was too much, muffling his pleas. He started pulling his restraints, tearing at his wrists. Started squirming backward when the vampire, or whatever it was, gripped his ankles and pulled Cam closer with ease, standing, now dragging Cam towards the fire. Cam hollering through his gag, trying to free his hands when this being tossed Cam towards the fire. His back cracked into sand, his head jutted back and twisted, pain rushed through him and he could hear Grimes and Cameron call his name and a hushed scream from Annison. And the thing who tossed him said with a groveled and echoing voice, "Human scum, arms up, let me see your hands."

Cam craned his neck to see Cameron, Grimes, and Annison were doing as they were told. The captor went to Annison first, patted her legs and stomach, made a gesture to Annison's head's protrusions, then did the same to Cameron, squeezing the boy's jaw to turn to it, Cameron whining in its tight grip, forcing his mouth open. Cam eyed Grimes, who gestured to him with a quick head nod. Cam's brow furrowed when Perseus gripped the gun from the captor's hand and lifted the captor off the ground in a whining fit, kicking its legs and protesting. Perseus tossed the being into the cruiser, keeping the gun for himself. The being tried to scurry beneath the cruiser, Grimes shot three times at the sand by the being's feet.

"Stay right there," Grimes ordered, holding the gun with his left hand as Cam grunted beneath his gag. "Cameron," said Grimes. "Untie Cam."

Cameron rushed to Cam's feet, cut the rope around his ankles. "I knew you were in trouble. I could feel it," Cameron said, cutting the rope tying Cam's wrists. "We were ready, right, Cam? We did good?"

Cam tore the gag from his mouth. "You did outstanding," he said, rising to his feet. The thing sitting fearfully beside the cruiser was a tiny little creature not more than five feet tall. Reminded Cam of a rat more than a vampire, although the skin was scaly, and lizardlike, its nose a sharp point like a small beak. Dark purple lips and those yellow eyes. It appeared to be more concerned with Perseus standing over him than Grimes' gun.

Cam stood close to Grimes.

"What do we do now?" asked Grimes.

"Simple. We question him. See what he knows and why the hell he's combing the desert."

"Nothing," said the thing, and he laughed. "From me you'll get nothing."

"Really, little man? I think Perseus here will have you thinking twice about that."

Perseus grunted and stepped closer to the thing, who scrambled backward.

"Ok, okay," it hollered. "Just keep the giant away please."

Cam and Grimes looked at each other. "That

was easy," they both said.

"Thought you'd see it our way," said Cam, then to Perseus. "I'll take that, thank you." Perseus handed Cam the rifle. "Now, Perseus would you be kind enough to escort our new guest on board for some much needed questioning."

Perseus stepped towards the thing and all Cam could see were his wide, yellow eyes filled with fear.

24

KAAL said to Moth, his head shaking, "I don't agree with it. If our people discover where she came from, it'll put us in a horrible position. Stop playing, Moth, kill the witch please."

Moth smiled, and said, "Kaal, I've never seen you so afraid before."

"You're playing with fire, Moth. She's not significant to our needs, only the child is. She needs to go. We can't have insurrection among our own people. It'll be anarchy in Drac City and you know it." His hands were trembling, his jaw stiff. "You can't program a species to believe something, then give it what it wants but still go against the grain. Moth," Kaal was shaking his head. "Don't do this, please."

"Oh, tire me something awful, Kaal. Enough with the doomsday prophesy. I haven't time to indulge in such a fantasy. She may be turning Drac but she is… like a newborn. Her thoughts are easy to find. I need more time to understand all she knows and the how and why behind the transformation. Someone's not playing by the rules. We need to squash it out, stomp on it or them, and make them pay. Our future depends on it. You know what happens when the plan is a success. You know what we will be given."

Kaal was shaking his head again. "I don't trust them either. This could be just another play in their cosmic game of control." He breathed deeply, his lips curled in a snarl. "The Draconians have always kept us under their thumb. They enjoy slaves and power, not setting people free."

"Not people, Kaal, us... us and COR."

Kaal was silent. Moth, looking down on his beloved, said, "Come with me then?"

"What?"

"Yes, that way you can see for yourself. Two are always better to reach into the mind of another. Plus, should any of our fellow Drac wish to press the issue, you can be there to assure them my explanation is satisfactory."

"And what if she tells them?"

Moth widened his eyes, cocked his head. "Not that it can't happen, but I'm sure our guest will wish to keep her secret safe. Considering she'll be surrounded by Dracs, she'll think twice before telling them she is human."

Kaal's attention drifted to his desk, where a signal bleeped with a blinking white light.

"COR is ready," said Kaal, going to his computer and turning off the signal.

Moth watched him. "Will you come or not?"

"I don't know. What about the baby?"

"I've already dispatched the baby. He will live on Atlantis until it is safe and Sandy is no more."

"And what if she doesn't die? She'll scour the earth looking for him."

Moth laughed. "There are plenty more places to hide a child than planet Earth, Kaal. So many barren systems in the universe. You know them as well as I."

Kaal shook his head, disappointed. "You better get to COR; they're waiting for you."

"Answer my question first, Kaal."

Kaal looked at Moth, grinding his jaw. "Yes, I'll come. But only to keep things safe. You know I don't enjoy social gatherings."

"Indeed," said Moth. "But it is always good to know what people are thinking. After all, Kaal, when this is over they will belong to us."

Kaal gazed through his window to Drac City.

"You think about them too often, Kaal. It makes you weak, pollutes your thoughts."

"All I see is tyranny, and suffering."

"Perhaps you should spend some time with the greys. Let them wipe out the attachment eating you alive."

"I don't think so," said Kaal. "Then I'd be like you."

Moth sighed. "So be it then. Live with your suffering. It's what you love the most, anyway. Leave it to me, Kaal. I'll take us through this…"

Kaal's head bent.

"... as I always do. Some of us, Kaal, are tasked with cleaning up the mess caused by weakness. A task I have become supremely confident in doing. Saving our people is all I have ever done."

Kaal turned to Moth, his eyes narrow, snarling, "But whose going to save them from you?"

25

SANDY sat by the window, thinking while gazing over Drac City. Her hand twitched, and within the light reflected in her window, she could see herself. Moth was accurate on one point; she was changing by the minute. She could hear her blood moving through her veins, and her heartbeat pounding between her ears. And in the distance, she could hear Adam's cries. She knew he was alive, somewhere, although she'd experienced a drifting, as if the cries had become soft or reached to her from far away as if he were across the universe.

Confusion, thoughts competing for a space in her mind, one human, the other vampire, telling her,

You must feed.

Blood is required.

Suffering. The human race needs your help.

We need you.

You are nothing. You have no place in the world.

Everything has changed. Change with it.

The voices were relentless; she could hear them

in all four corners of the room, in her mind, raking her consciousness, as she sat, head in her hand, wide eyed and trembling. And then there was the hunger; it drove her thoughts and actions. She wanted to feed, and the thought of feeding carried a sliver of freedom and relief. She didn't recognize the monster staring at her in the window's reflection. Couldn't recognize herself. She'd lost all her hair, now a smooth scaly skull, and she could feel the back of her neck, the bones swelling, boiling acid in the back of her throat, turning her stomach nauseous with a craving for blood. Her visual acuity had strengthened. She could see her pupils were still the same human shape, color different, but the shape was the same.

What will you see when the eyes turn to Drac?

Her thoughts went to her conversation with Moth. Move like a snake, he'd said. Slight movements too fast for the human eye to see.

She looked around the room, found a row of small crystal globes sitting on a shelf. Sandy moved to it, grabbed a crystal globe in her palm.

"Move like a snake," she said, tossing the globe up and then catching it. *How does Phil move like that?*

And who really is Robyn Winter? Does he have the answers to my questions? They had gone to great lengths to find me. Have they stopped looking? Are they aware of the change?

Caught her reflection in the window. *Did they do this to me?*

She tossed the globe across the room, the crystals smashing to bits to the floor as Sandy bared her fangs, hissing.

"Leave me here," she snarled, screaming. "Destitute. A vampire. A human vampire with a human vampire child." She twisted her neck, grinding her fangs, and her neck bones swelled, pain rifled through the back of her head.

You must be ready. Ready to fight for your child.

Sandy grabbed another globe. This one red like crimson blood.

"Yes," she said, tossing the globe high over head. "I will be ready." The globe reached its pinnacle and plummeted towards the ground as Sandy's torso dipped forward, her head close to the floor as her right leg sprang behind her, and the sole of her foot connected with the globe that spiraled against the wall, shattering into pieces.

Sandy looked at the broken shards of crystal, snarling as she said, "Ready for all of them."

26

CAM sat in front of the thing that had captured him. Perseus hunched over beside him, Grimes on his left and Cameron and Annison watching from the back of the hull.

Cam gestured to Cameron. "Outside," he said. "Keep your ears and eyes open." He turned to the thing. "Could be anything out there." He waited, hearing no movement, and turned again. "Go!" he ordered.

"C'mon, Anni, I think this is when the kids need to go to their rooms," said Cameron.

"Adult stuff," said Annison. "Always boring and so so serious."

They laughed as they walked outside. Cam turned his attention to more pressing matters. The thing stared him down as if he were a hot lunch. Cam bent his head, staring at the thing's head. He had only one ear.

Grimes said, "C'mon Cam, ask the first question."

Cam lolled his tongue inside his cheek. "I've got

so many questions at the moment, but I'll start with the most obvious. Who the hell are you?"

The thing turned away. Cam rolled his eyes. "Perseus. Our guest here has trouble talking. Could you squeeze the answers out of him?"

Perseus moved with a growl towards the thing, and its eyes grew wide.

"Hadock," the thing said, squirming in his seat. "My name is Hadock."

"Hadock," Cam repeated. He looked at Grimes. "These alien names are something special, aren't they?" Turned to Hadock. "And why were you trying to kill us, Hadock?"

Hadock squirmed in his chair. "I wasn't," he said. "I wanted the ship."

Cam shook his head. "Why? For what? Couldn't you tell the ship's inoperable? You must have seen us crash, or know at least that we did crash and wouldn't we have taken off if we could?"

Hadock said nothing, turned away from Cam's stare.

"Do we really need to keep this up or does every question need to involve a threat from Perseus?"

Perseus growled.

"Keep that thing away from me."

"If you answer my questions there won't be a problem."

"As if I'd believe anything a human would say." Hadock shook his head. "Vile species you all are."

"And yet, here you are, on our planet, hanging with us vile humans."

Hadock grinned. "What makes you think this planet belongs to you? It's only a matter of time until you recognize the truth. But by then, you won't care. Vile creatures turn to mindless subordinates. It is inevitable. And then…" He looked up as if addressing the stars. "The earth will be as it should, under Draconian rule."

"The vampires?"

Hadock grinned. "Foolish humans. Vampires are only the beginning of what's coming for you." He looked at Grimes. "For all of you."

"Cam, let me put a bullet in this fucker's head right now and be done with it."

Cam said, "Relax, Corporal. No one touches good little Hadock here… as long as he continues to answer our questions."

"This is a waste of time," said Grimes. "All he's going to do is tell you lies."

Cam pursed his lips. "Maybe, but there's always some truth in every lie. So, Hadock, what about the ship?"

Hadock rolled his eyes, and Perseus stepped forward.

"It's not inoperable," he said. "Stupid humans just don't know how it works." He looked around the ship. "This is a vessel from greys, is it not?"

"What do you mean?"

"The greys," Hadock repeated. "Seems the same technology the grey's use."

Cam was shaking his head. "Aren't they in the UFO?" Cam stretched his neck, looking at the starship outside the window. "Like that one there?"

"There are many ships in the universe, but this is a land cruiser, not suitable for space travel."

"Okay, genius," said Cam, crossing his arms. "So how do we turn it on?"

"Use the auxiliary power. Every ship like this has one. If you were more evolved you could simply just think it and the vessel will heed your command."

Cam's eyes narrowed, skeptical. Hadock rolled his eyes, shaking his head and gritting his teeth. A second later, he closed his eyes.

The ship said, "Auxiliary power on." And the ship burst to life with light and power.

"You've got to be kidding me," said Grimes.

Cam clucked his tongue, looking over the ship. Shook his head, looked at Hadock. "Useful trick."

"Why the hell didn't they tell us?" Grimes said. "That would have been useful information."

"Humans have no comprehension of telepathy. You wouldn't have understood it. Vile species you all are."

Cam stared at Hadock. "You keep saying that. I'm wondering why? What have humans ever done to you?"

"Any species like yours deserves to be

subjugated. You'd kill your own mother if it meant power. We deem all such species as vile creatures. Worse than Draconian; at least they don't eat their own."

"Yeah," Cam blurted. "I haven't come across any cannibals in my time."

Hadock said, "Give it time, and you will."

Cam paused, glaring at Hadock, said to Grimes, "Get on the horn. See if you can contact our people in New Mexico. They have to be looking for us by now."

Grimes paused.

"Corporal?"

"I'm on it," he said, although he remained standing. Cam turned to him, looked like Grimes could tear Hadock apart if Cam would let him.

"Corporal?" Cam hollered and Grimes snapped his focus, looked at Cam. "You wanna get out of here, don't you? Get on the horn. We'll leave shortly."

"What are you gonna do?" asked Grimes.

"Well," said Cam, standing. "I think Perseus and I will take Hadock on a little walk to the UFO. See if there's anything on there we can salvage."

Perseus lifted Hadock off his seat, stood him up.

"Don't touch me," cried Hadock.

"Plus," said Cam. "I've got a few more questions for our distinguished guest. A lot of questions."

27

MOTH walked through the conference door. Seven COR members were gathered around the conference table, holographic images from around the globe. They all stood when Moth entered, all with a bow to their leader.

"Gentlemen," said Moth. "Your presence is appreciated." Moth provided the respectable bow to his subordinates. "Please, sit, we have much to discuss."

All sat as instructed. Moth stood at the head of the table. "First," he began, "Let us hear updates from your posts. Have all necessary actions been taken at this time?" He turned to his right, addressing the China ambassador, Belial, directly.

Belial addressed COR, his head held high, a grin across his lips. "Of course. Our human allies have taken all necessary steps. All have been gathered in safety camps as we wait for the appropriate chemistry to begin the final phase. The grey army has eradicated all outliers." He laughed before continuing. "The citizens will wait in camps on government orders." He looked at Moth. "You will have no concern with our Chinese counterparts; their people follow in line with what is told."

Moth eyeballed his members as, one by one, they all agreed with Belial, providing similar updates on their respective territories. Belial then addressed Moth directly. "But holding all in camps will only last so long. We must begin the final phase and reconditioning with Dr. Blum's chemistry. We must reestablish societal norms among the humans. Their ambiguous training needs to continue. The dark veil must return for a time. All must be seen as normal and without question."

Grievous, the South American ambassador was next to speak. "What lie will provide the necessary accord with the humans to take the formula and when will the formula be ready? Have we addressed this issue with our human allies?"

All eyes on Moth now. "The grey's representative is on his way. The formula was provided by Mono prior to her death. He shall be here soon. The humans will inform their citizens germ warfare has contaminated the air prior to allowing the reestablishment of society. They will require all who wish to leave the camps to take the pills and, with it, a continued daily necessity to reduce exposure. We are a generation away from achieving the final phase. The pills will transfer to the unborn; we will erect a generation of human slaves. All in Draconian honor."

"Good," said Grievous. "The frequency grows

weaker every year; we have only this time to act."

Chatter among COR, speaking to or addressing each other individually.

"Time is on our side."

"The Arcturians will return and be handed their decimation."

"The universe will finally be under Draconian rule."

"Bathed in darkness."

"Wrought with fear and slavery." Laughter combined with scoffs and sarcasm erupted.

"And us with power in our hands. Finally able to take our rightful place by the Draconian side."

"Unquestioned loyalty from our own will maintain our status."

"As it always does."

"The star systems we will own... outstanding."

"How much time before the frequency is no more?" asked Grievous, and all fell silent, looking at Moth for an answer.

"Plenty of time, gentlemen. Plenty of time to implement the final phase with ample time to handle any possible insurrection. This is our time, my fellow Drac." He tapped his fingernails on the table. "Our time to rule."

"But how long do we have, master Moth?"

Moth paused before answering as a quiet hush fell across the room. "Thirty-six years," said Moth.

Heads nodding approval.

"Plenty of time indeed."

"More than enough to be sure all goes as planned."

"We are close. So, so close."

"I can feel it. It's beautiful."

Members of COR provided appreciative nods to Moth. He bowed in return before re addressing. "Now, gentlemen, are there any concerns or issues to discuss?" He noticed the Middle East ambassador, Romala, with rage in his vampire eyes. He was the first to speak.

"What has become of Zeta? I've been informed of his demise, and his number one, Saiph? Is this accurate and if so, what caused his death?"

"I too received this information," said Kalal, the European ambassador as he leaned close to the table, his hands folded, addressing COR. "I have also been informed that all Drac assigned to VG211 have perished." His eyes scanned his fellow Drac, settling on Moth. "Is this because of the human rebellion? Or is it a grey insurrection? Considering only greys have survived, we must consider the possibility the greys are compromised."

Chatter erupted across the conference table.

"That would be most unfortunate."

"If the greys are compromised, what does that mean to the larger plan?"

"Have we alerted the humans to Dr. Blum's death?"

Moth shook his head, waving off COR.

"Gentlemen," he said. "Gentlemen, please hear me." He waited for COR to settle their fears, waited for silence, all eyes on him. Moth raised his hand. "Ah, thank you." He breathed deeply before continuing, started pacing behind COR members, around the table, hands clamped behind his back. "It is true that Zeta is no more, but we have no indication of the how behind it. Was it human rebellion or grey insurrection? We do not know. As you said before, no Drac survived the events that took place on VG211. And yes, you are accurate in knowing only greys survived."

"What story have the greys provided to account for his death?" Romala, sitting back in his chair, eyeballing Moth.

Moth ceased pacing, raised his chin. "They informed me Zeta met his death by the hand of Drac."

A pause among COR, disbelief, followed by high-pitched commotion, COR members addressing each other.

"Impossible."

"If true, our own Drac have turned against us."

"Not from within our own. This can't be true."

"They grow weary of our leadership. Our own people, we must gain control."

Then, Kalal asked, "Where is the child, Moth? We must secure him. He's the only way the indigo resurrection will fail."

Moth said, "The baby will be brought to a secure location."

"Where?"

"With whom?"

Moth responded, "A secret, undisclosed location. He is being cared for by grey and Drac."

Romala snarled at Moth. "Why are we not allowed to know? Moth, this is insubordination, even from the highest member of COR. You must tell us the child's location."

"The less who know the more secure the child is. Gentlemen, you'll have to put your trust in my leadership. There are circumstances that may not make sense now, but in time, all will be revealed. Besides, other, more dire circumstances have arisen."

"As in?" Kalal, grinding his teeth.

Moth's smile grew from ear to ear. "Gentlemen, I am following a lead that I am certain will bring an end to the human rebellion. As you are all aware, we have been shown our victory; it quickens close to us now, but you have to trust me. You must move past your own beliefs and allow me to continue what has taken thousands of years to manifest. Once the human rebellion is decimated, our victory becomes inevitable. And then, we will be free. All of COR will rule over our people without influence. We will live like gods with Drac bowing to our will."

Heads nodding, grunting approval.

Moth waited as COR took to the idea, his declaration.

Romala addressed the empty seat where Zeta

would have sat. "What do we do about our vacancy? What Drac among us deserves the riches Zeta would have received? You know the ritual, Moth, Zeta's replacement falls on your shoulders. Who do you recommend to take his place?"

And then, at that very moment, as if on cue, the conference room door slid open and standing in the door was Sanos, a large and long bulky bag being dragged by his left hand.

Moth said, "Sanos?" when Sanos stepped into the room and tossed the bulky bag onto the conference table.

And Sanos said, "Members of COR," as he stepped close to the table. Some COR members sprang from their seats; some sat staring inquisitively, mouths agape, all eyes looking from the bag to Sanos, then back to the bulk on the table. "May I present a gift to the council, the human who has caused havoc and dismay among Drac. I present to you *the phantom.*"

28

"I FIND it disturbing," said Hadock. "That you have taken up cause with a vampire… and his tender little human. So sweet actually."

They were on their way to the UFO, Cam aiming his rifle at Hadock's back, Perseus beside Hadock.

"What's it to you?" said Cam.

"His thirst runs deep, only a matter of time before he takes his little morsel's throat between his fangs. Tell me something; do you think she will scream? I don't think so. Not at all. As a matter of cause I believe she will rather enjoy herself. Considering the way she stares at him, and her thoughts…" Hadock raised his chin, his head nodding, sniffing. "She leaves herself open. I'd watch out for those two, if you know what I mean?"

"The only one you need to be concerned about is yourself."

"Hmm, seems so." Hadock stopped, looking over the sky.

Cam followed his gaze; saw nothing but stars and the glowing moon rising above the horizon. He pushed his rifle into Hadock's back. "Move," he said. But Hadock remained still. Cam pushed him forward. "I said move."

"Okay, okay," Hadock said, walking again. "Don't have to be so forceful. You've got the giant here to help you, human. If it weren't for him, I'd be feasting on your skin right now." And he laughed, a wheezing little chuckle.

"Yeah, that's been tried already."

"Oh, so you felt the jaws of death around your throat, have you? What happened? Did Perseus here rescue you then, too? Human, I might say, you all don't stand a chance."

"For your information, it was a human. Cut that vampire's head clean off."

"Human? What human could do such a thing?"

"That's for me to know, Hadock. My question is, what the hell are you? Obviously not a vampire, or maybe you're just a lackey. Some vampire slave. And how many other aliens are on our planet? Seems like an alien exodus has come to Earth."

Hadock said, "The only species allowed on Earth are those invited by Drac and human alike. If it weren't that way, Earth would have already been a hub for all creatures in the universe."

"Great, an invitation only party. Let me ask you something because all I've seen so far are sick and depraved aliens. Are there any rational aliens out there in the cosmos or is everyone an ass like yourself?"

They arrived at the UFO. Hadock stopped in his tracks. Perseus on Hadock's left, Cam moved to the right, still aiming his rifle. Hadock ignored him, kept looking at the sky.

"Waiting for someone?" asked Cam.

"Oh, one never knows what's flying through the air tonight. So much activity going on." He turned his gaze to Cam. "They must be close to final phase."

"What the hell is final phase?"

Perseus growled.

Hadock regarded Perseus. "You feel it to don't you, Perseus? The end of the humans is imminent."

And he smiled, glaring at Cam.

"And when you're turned a slave, General, I'll keep you as my personal pet. Eat you up piece by piece. I'll even have you cut your own skin and feed it to me as I lick your blood off your fingers. Can't wait for that moment."

"Well, you'll be waiting a long time, Hadock. I'm a lieutenant, not a general. See, if you knew anything about anything, you would have known that too. Seems your powers of observation aren't as acute as you thought they were."

Hadock's expression burrowed inward as if he'd had a revelation. "But the corporal took orders from you?"

"We're beyond the chain of command, considering current circumstances."

"But that..." He locked eyes with Cam, said,

"Lieutenant Cameron Fisk?"

"How do you know my name?"

"Can't be," he said. "Then that means…" And his wide eyes raged with fury before his wings erected wide across his back, soaring at Cam.

****

Grimes attempted for the umpteenth time another frequency. He couldn't make contact; something he couldn't comprehend wasn't connecting. All he received was static, and he cursed under his breath.

"What is it?" asked Cameron.

Grimes turned to see Cameron and Annison in the cockpit doorway. "Cameron," he said. "I thought Cam told you to stay outside?"

Annison answered. "We heard you having trouble." She craned her head to look beyond Grimes at the control panel. Looked at Grimes and said, "Communication issues?"

"Yeah," said Grimes in a huff. Turned to the controls. "This thing is simple to fly, but everything else is a different language. I can't figure it out."

Annison walked towards him. "Let me try."

"You? What do you know about communication with alien ships?"

"Probably more than you," she said. "It's not as hard as you think." She turned to Cameron. "Get it, 'think'?"

"I get it," Cameron huffed. "Very funny."

"I have no clue what you're referring to nor do I have time for kid stuff."

"Can I try?" asked Annison.

Grimes offered the microphone and laughed. "Sure, why not. I've got nothing to lose."

Annison regarded the microphone, then put her hand up. "Keep it," she said, and closed her eyes. "The ship best responds through telepathy." Grimes' eyes narrowed. "Although I haven't perfected the practice…" Grimes could see her eyeballs roll upward beneath the eyelids. "I can communicate in other ways. Frequency vibration is one of my specialties. All us newbies have it."

Grimes shook his head, looked at Cameron who shrugged.

"Your guess is as good as mine," said Cameron.

"Oh, hmm," said Annison.

"What?" responded Grimes. "What is it?"

"Seems someone put up a firewall for outside communication." Her eyes clamped even further shut, her eyes twitching and Grimes noticed those protrusions on the back of her head moved, jutting out from her skull, erect.

"Who would do that?" said Grimes. "And why?"

Annison dipped her head left, then right. "Seems it was that guy?"

"Which guy? Hadock?"

Annison nodded. "Hm. That he did. When he accessed the ship, he ceased communication to outside sources."

"He can do that?"

"Yes, he can."

"Okay then. Gets stranger and stranger as the minutes tick by."

Annison smiled, a slight laugh in the back of her throat. "Tricky little guy, he is. And not a very nice person either." A pause, and then, "Oh, got it." Grimes could see how her eyes scanned left and right in rapid successions behind her closed eyelids.

The microphone crackled to life.

"What? Hello," he said into the microphone.

Annison said, "It's useless though."

Grimes looked at her, head shaking. "Why?"

Annison opened her eyes. "I don't know. Can't be sure exactly but there's no one there to hold the line."

"What do you mean?"

"Where we're supposed to be going. Doesn't seem like anyone is there. I could be wrong, but I don't think so. Usually these things are simple to discern. They monitor communications constantly. But now, I can feel it, there's no vibration on the other end, only open space."

Grimes said, "Well, that's not good," when he heard Cam hollering outside.

****

Hadock flew towards Cam and right into the giant's hand that gripped his throat and squeezed. His hands still bound, screeching, thrusting to release Perseus' grip, kept attempting to break his wrists free.

"He must die," Hadock was screaming, trying to rush at Cam, his wings batting the giant's head with successive thumps.

Cam lowered his rifle, thinking Perseus had Hadock when Hadock's hands broke free and his wings jabbed at Perseus, fluttering across his skull as Hadock continued to screech and gawk. Perseus gripped Hadock's skull with both hands, his massive paws squeezed and then Perseus plunged his fist into Hadock's skull and Hadock fell back with a thud to the sand. Green bile, what Cam thought was blood, dripped from Hadock's skull as Perseus roared at his fallen foe. Grimes racing over, gun drawn as Hadock's wings continued to flap.

"What the hell happened?" Grimes, looking from Hadock to Cam. Cam with a dazed stare. "Cam?" Grimes shouted and Cam shook his head, shaking off his thoughts.

Hadock wretched something awful, his head bleeding ferociously, started speaking in a foreign language, rapid speech, garbling on his own blood, his body retching and shuddering. His voice high pitched with rage, squawking, piercing their ears with a painful stab. Grimes gripped his ears but Hadock's gawk thinned, dwindling to shallow gasps as he tried to breathe, to breathe deep, gargling his own blood, his eyes fixed on Cam as his chest heaved.

"You," said Hadock, drawing in another deep breath. "Must... Die."

Cam stepped to Hadock, his rifle aimed at Hadock's head. "You first." And he pulled the trigger; a round beam raged from the rifle disintegrating Hadock's head, his body fell lifeless.

"What the hell was that all about?" asked Grimes when the UFO burst into life. Mechanical hums and blips; lights beamed from the ship's bottom before the UFO slid out of the sand, cut through the air humming into the night sky and disappeared in a flash. "Well, that's interesting." He turned to Cam, said, "You okay?"

Cam replied, "He knew my name."

Grimes raised his hands. "So what? It's written on your uniform."

Cam, wide eyed, looked down at his nametag. Put his hand over it, WALLABY embroidered across the patch. He looked at Grimes. "This isn't my real name."

29

MOTH asked Sanos to sit after he dismissed COR.
There was much to be discussed with his officer. The
body bag unzipped. The dead phantom's skin had
turned grey, darkening by the minute. His body
bruised and battered. COR had questions for Sanos,
namely what had transpired on VG211. Was the
phantom the cause of Zeta's death? Did you notice
insurrection from the greys? Did Dr. Blum achieve his
victory–a question that flew in the face of Moth's
declaration. He was not pleased. Sanos' presence was
irritating, and the cause of Moth's current indignation.

Perhaps, Moth thought, Sanos is the traitor.
After all, his surprise visit was unexpected. Moth had
believed Sanos was dead. Perhaps there is more to
Sanos' resurgence than he's letting on to. Mintaka had
reported Sanos and his Dracs had formed a coup in
VG211 against Zeta and the greys. The result was a loss
of Drac life, namely Zeta and Saiph. And here was
Sanos, who, according to Mintaka–and from what
Moth had learned through communication with
Mono's greys–was the catalyst behind the insurgency.

What had happened in VG211?

Somewhere in the middle was the truth.

And there were more pressing concerns Moth required clarification on. Namely, was Sanos aware of Sandy's transformation; an abnormality Moth wanted to hide from his fellow Drac? Sandy would falter under Moth's observation into her mind. The rebellion was coming to its last breath, and Moth wanted to be the vampire who delivered the planet on a silver platter to the Draconians, essentially securing his legacy and control over his people. An event he had been shown would manifest, and that right soon.

Sanos was fidgety, nervous. Moth craned his head, staring at his fellow Drac. Kept itching his arms, scratching, raking his skin. Moth regarded the phantom.

"This is the one," said Moth. "Doesn't look like much. Looks like a boy. A child. How could he be the phantom?" Moth's eyes burrowed into Sanos, whose eyes twitched, his lips curled in a snarl.

Sanos raised his hands, and Moth could see the discolored spots on his skin. "Phantom claws," said Sanos. "He may look like a boy, but he fights like a Drac." Sanos raised his chin to Moth. "This rebellion scum is unlike any other human. He is schooled in the art of the blades… and the rose."

Moth's eyes narrowed. "Impossible!"

Sanos shook his head. "Not impossible. True. This is the phantom we've been looking for. Look at his armor; the blades are there."

Moth lifted the phantom's arm, the armor thick, the blade down the arm stained with Drac blood. Moth turned to Sanos, placed the arm back. Sanos' breathing seemed shallow. Moth regarded the phantom, gripped the chin with his fingernails.

"Why do you question me? The evidence is right in front of you," said Sanos.

Moth ignored the question. "He's so young," said Moth. "Who provided his training? All indications are that no human is schooled in our ways. This phantom is also an enigma."

"Perhaps there are circumstances we do not yet know," said Sanos, his stare locked on Moth. "Or perhaps our leaders wish not to inform the rest of us that such..." he regarded the phantom, "monsters exist."

A small grin curled in the corners of Moth's lips. "Perhaps," he whispered. "But still the question stands, who provided training in our ways to this... infectious human."

"It matters not," said Sanos. "The phantom is now dead. He can't cause any more trouble."

Moth craned his head. "Please, Sanos. Where there's one, there's another. He came from somewhere and someone. The rebellion has always hid in the shadows. Where are the rest of them hiding?"

"I've done my part, master Moth. I give you the phantom, the rest is up to you."

Moth paused, thinking. "Why did you not return to your post after VG211 failed? Did you really scour the earth looking for this phantom? Or did he find you, Sanos?"

"He came for me."

"Why? What could you possibly have offered him for him to come and find you?"

"The human female," answered Sanos. "She is here, is she not?"

"She is, although not for long. I have slated her for reconditioning. She will leave by daybreak," he lied.

"Be careful with that one," said Sanos. "Any human who bested Telas and Mono must be a unique human."

"And who was it that bested Zeta, Saiph, and all Drac's under your command? You say it was this phantom, but how could that be so? One phantom to all those, Drac." Moth's head shaking. "Can one human really pull off such a task, Sanos?"

"He had help. Human soldiers were on his side. VG211 became a haven for insurrection."

"So you say."

Moth pursed his lips, breathed deeply, turning from Sanos, walking to the window. He knew Sanos was hiding truth; Moth had a burning inclination that Sanos had dealt Zeta his death. Of course, he would never admit to it, couldn't admit to it. Punishment for killing a member of COR was public death by fire. Sanos was covering for himself and Moth had to admit, he would have done the same.

Sanos said, "Have the greys provided the chemistry to reconstruct Dr. Blum's pills?"

Moth sensed desperation in Sanos' tone. "Mono provided the formula to her greys prior to her death. The grey representative is on his way... may have arrived already. We will have what we require once he is here."

"Why not just send the formula? What is the reason for the grey's visit?"

"Perhaps there is more to tell." He turned to Sanos. "Perhaps there is additional information from VG211 than we know of. The greys desire to be heard eye to eye." His jaw clenched staring at Sanos. "Is there something the greys may know that we do not? About what happened in that forsaken outpost? Anything else you wish to tell me prior to our meeting?"

Sanos' eyes narrowed. "Nothing more than what I've already provided, but I would recommend not trusting the greys, nor our human sympathizers. Something has spoiled in our plan and it rots with a foul stench even stronger than this decaying phantom." He pushed Phil away.

After a pause Moth said, "What is it you want, Sanos? You've brought in one of Drac's most wanted humans; this will inter a rather joyous celebration. COR is obviously taken with you. I wonder Sanos where will you go from here? What will satisfy your ambition?"

Sanos grinned ear to ear. "Everything," he said.

"I want it all. A seat in COR. Now that would befit a warrior such as myself."

"That would also give you access to truth, Sanos, and supposedly, you are the reason for Zeta's death. Giving you his seat would be cause for alarm among our people, even if you've provided the phantom to us. No, I don't think so. Not at this time at least."

"Not at this time," Sanos repeated, seething and snarling. "Then when?"

Moth smiled as he stepped towards Sanos. "I enjoy your ambitious nature, Sanos, leave no doubt about it, but our people require more from you. Let's be honest, Sanos, your history has charged you with insubordination, rebellion and an incapability to follow orders. Now we have a rumor that your antics have caused the death of more than a handful of Drac, including those who were under your command. The greys themselves may request your destruction as a result of losing Mono."

"I told you the human female dismantled Mono…"

"SILENCE!" Moth erupted. "Do not dare interrupt me."

Sanos turned stiff. If his eyes told the truth, he'd eat Moth's heart right now.

Sanos said, "I don't mean to my lord." Then a second later, "I bow to your leadership."

Moth started laughing. "Oh Sanos," he said, shaking his head, clucking his tongue. "Spare me your loyalty speech. It's beneath us both. It's quite obvious you could care less about the chain of command and yes, I believe it was you who murdered Zeta. Your rebellious antics prove that much."

Sanos turned from Moth's stare, his jaw clenched tight.

Moth stepped closer to the table, gripped the back of a chair in both hands. "Being a member of COR has its benefits, of course, but COR is loyal to each other. Why would I elect a member whose allegiance is to himself and not COR."

Sanos snapped, "My allegiance has always been to Drac."

"I said COR," Moth hollered, shaking his head. "Not Drac."

Sanos' expression registered Moth's statement. "Understood," said Sanos. "What is it you wish for me to do?"

Moth cocked his head, turned away. "Something devious," he said. "Something to be hailed in the Drac archives. You've already handed us the phantom. Perhaps when the rebellion is no more... perished by your command and hand, will your fellow Drac welcome you as a leader. We must always maintain order among our people. They must have supreme confidence in our ability to lead without question. A Drac who has handed them their freedom on a silver platter would be welcomed as a member of COR." He turned to Sanos. "Do you agree?"

"Yes," responded Sanos. "Without question."

"Should you be responsible for the rebellion's decimation, you will earn my favor, Sanos. And then, perhaps, I will show you something that will change the way you think about the future." And he grinned a wide and sinister grin. "What do you think Sanos, do you have the ability to dismantle the rebellion? A task no Drac has been able to do for millenniums."

"Of course it can be done by my hand." Sanos observed Moth. "You have a lead, don't you? You know where they are hiding?"

"In time, we will have the location to their hidden front. But you must trust in my leadership. All that is happening now has transpired according to the Draconian plan. It is inevitable, we shall win our future."

"So it is written..."

"So it is done," Moth completed the adage as Sanos raised his chin. "Go Sanos, be ready for tonight's festivities. The phantom will be on display for all to see before he is buried in a funeral pyre." Moth raised his head. "A gift to the gods of our people..." Moth turned to Sanos. "COR."

Sanos cocked his head, inquisitive, allowing Moth's words to sink in as a grin graced his lips.

"Rise Sanos, we will usher in your star tonight and when we have our information on the rebellion base, you will lead our victory over the humans."

Sanos did rise. Rose from his seat and bowed to

Moth.

"Good," said Moth. "Good." He placed his hand on Sanos' head.

Sanos raised his eyes to Moth. "Thank you, my lord." And Moth gave a slight bow, noticed how Sanos' arms were raked with tiny streams of blood beaded across his arms.

"Go," said Moth, and Sanos did just that. The door slid open. "Oh, Sanos," said Moth. "I forgot one question."

Sanos turned to Moth.

"You tasted Dr. Blum's formula, did you not? This new blood, tell me, what is it like?"

And Sanos responded, "Delightful," with a gleam in his eye and a smile across his lips. And then he was gone. The door slid closed, leaving Moth alone with the dead. He craned his head, staring. He was so young, so soft; Moth couldn't see this youthful presence destroying his people. Not alone, at least.

"Who trained you dear phantom?" said Moth. "Who indeed." He zipped the bag up over the phantom's head. He raised his chin, said, "Kaal," through a telepathic consciousness to the main access computer.

A moment later, Kaal answered. "Yes, my lord."

"Have the symbiotes prepare the dead human for celebration tonight. Seems this evening will be a host of intrigue."

Kaal shot back, "Yes, sir."

"Good Kaal. Good." And he placed his hand on the body bag before retreating towards the door that slid open on his command. At the moment Moth stepped through the door, he heard it, as if the heartbeat was in his throat. A thick wallop comprising pain that once completed opened a floodgate. And Moth craned his head, glaring at the phantom.

And he whispered, "Something wicked may be at play."

30

PHIL glided across what he assumed was a library, with its rows of thick books that reached into a never-ending row of books. The floor was made of marble, with pillars constructed of the same, reaching high above to a night sky. There were no walls; the room went on forever, disappearing into the void that was the Milky Way. Phil could see stars forming in the cosmos, the pillars of creation thumping and pumping with electricity. All around him in all directions was the universe, a fitting backdrop to the library where a mix of chaos ensued. Fires blazed inside black cauldrons scattered across the library. Books were being burned in those cauldrons. Pages revealing the minutes of people's lives like a flipbook that told a life tale. And every so often, a shimmer raged across the library, changing the landscape with a glimmer, revealing a new change. A change Phil couldn't see nor touch, but a change in the dimension, in the fold of energy, a flux in the wavelength, as if the charge had changed. Phil could feel it in his bones, the change. Something was different. Something was very, very different.

"Hello," he called, his voice echoed into the cosmos.

After Phil stepped into the northern lights, he arrived here, in this place, alone. None had greeted him, and for all he knew, the library was abandoned.

But who started the fires? And what is this place? A library at the end of the universe?

Phil went to one cauldron. Fire raged from within as Phil put his hands to the flame. "Cold," he whispered. Watched as the books burned in a funeral pyre, pages crumbled, flapping open, revealing pictures like stenciled images cut in stone disintegrating into a plume of smoke. The picture revealed a father with two children, sitting around a television, their jaws hung open, wide eyed while staring at the screen. But the picture burned before he could see what had captured their attention.

"Hellllooooooo!" he called, his voice echoed into the cosmos.

"It's useless."

Phil snapped to the voice. There, he could see, stood a woman of unremarkable beauty. Flowing white gown, dark hair with rolling curls and the bluest eyes. He recognized her immediately. "Mom?" Phil's eyes narrowed, craned his head, staring at the ghost of his mother. "How can it be?"

She stepped forward. "You took the pill, didn't you? Before your fight with Sanos."

Phil blinked rapidly, confused. "How do you

know?"

And his mother smiled. "Because it is written in your record."

Phil looked around. His revelation brought to the forefront of conscious thought. "This is the Akashic Record?" He scanned the library and the many cauldrons raging with fire. "What has happened here? Why are the records being burned?" He stared into the cauldron in front of him. "These books represent people's lives..." His head shaking, he turned to his mother. "Why are they being destroyed?"

She stepped closer. "It is because of the shimmer." She looked up, Phil watching her, studying, observing. "What was once written in stone has become no more. The records are shifting to reflect this change." She looked into the cauldron. "So much has been destroyed already." Her eyes lost in the fire. "Entire systems will never be born. Slaves will be made of those who had once been free." And she looked at Phil, her eyes fixed with an adoring stare. "The future of the universe is at stake. Will you have the strength to transcend?"

Phil's hands were shaking, his lips quivering, when he said with a crack in his throat, "I don't know."

"It's the anger within you that keeps you from the light. The anger initiated by fear. The fear you felt on the island."

"One day you were there, the next you were gone," he said, his voice soft, unnerved. "I know what they did to you… I… I couldn't think about it. Wouldn't think about it."

She bent her head, a small smile across her lips. "It's ok," she said. "I understand, sometimes the mind signals to the host to not go there, to not allow the thoughts to conceive the harshest of human indignity. But you fight with anger, my love. And that is no way to usher in a new human faculty. That is no way for a species to evolve. Only love should do that."

Phil looked over the library. His arms shivered cold. Thought about the scene, the fires raging, the emptiness, and the cold. A reflection of his heart and soul. He turned to his mother. "Are you saying this is all happening because of me? Am I the cause of this effect?"

She put her hands to the flame. "The fire rages cold," she said. "Just like you. Burrowing that rage inside an icy pocket until rage is all you will know."

"Can't be," he huffed. "I fight for our species to survive and to not be turned into slaves."

"If it is the fate of humanity to be subjugated, then that is what is written. Every species experiences slavery. They either discover the means to overcome or they drift into the void and are no more. Look around you, this is your Akashic Record, and it is filled with rage… you must be more than your fears, son. You must fight because you see the love in all… even if their love is corrupted. When those who see your change know you fight for them with love, they will do the same."

"That doesn't seem fair. Why does it have to be me?"

"Because you have made the choice to do so. Truly, it could have been anyone. All humans have the same power, all are given the same choice, and all are more than they are given to believe; you just accepted the choice. You have taken up arms all your life. When will the fighting be done? Does victory rage with anger... or manifest inside of love? The wheels of time turn continuously. You, like all, are a spoke on the wheel of time. It is the energy you leave that directs the wheel."

"I don't understand. I thought we were changing everything, giving humanity a chance to be free."

She laughed. "Against the will of others. Tell me, son, whose will is stronger? The one who uses fear and rage, or the one who uses love?"

"I have fought all these years to avenge your death..."

"No, son, that is not true. You fight to satisfy anger, to place your fear at rest. But has it found rest, or has it grown to be its own monster? Look around you, my son, see what anger has done to you." She gestured to the cauldron. "What it has done to the universe."

Phil raised his head from the burning books in the cauldron. He looked at his mother. "This... this hasn't happened yet, has it? You are speaking of events

The Rose ~ Vol 2 | PD Alleva

that have not taken place... I mean..." he looked into the fire. "Not to me, not in my time."

"Correct," she said and gestured across the library. "What you see here is a result of your future actions, should you not learn to accept what happened. To face fear within a manifestation of love. This happens after you die, Phil. Cold and bleak becomes the future. Humanity will perish into the void... nothing more than a blip in a timeless universe. Forgotten and never inclined to a future existence."

"But I love so much," his voice rose. "Robyn, Esta, Cathryn... the baby... all my love is for them. Are you saying that isn't good enough?"

"Show them more, my son. Show them what we *can* be and you will make the future, and all this..." she gestured to the library, "... will change."

He looked over the room.

"Time, my son, is constant, but it moves like waves in a furious sea, back and forth, an inevitable construct, like evolution and change... and energy. Energy is forever, always evolving, always transforming."

Her voice drifted into silence, and when Phil turned, his mother was gone. Again, he was alone. His heartbeat gagged in his throat, he closed his eyes, seething, swallowing hard with a heavy loud breath when he felt warmth on his skin, heard hollering and painful screams. And then laughter as tears cascaded across his skin. He didn't have to open his eyes to see

130

where he was. The smell was enough to elicit his memory; the rank decay of burning, cooking flesh turned his gut. He didn't have to open his eyes because he knew already.

He was back on the island.

31

"OKAY, so spill it. What's with the name change?" asked Grimes.

They were flying to their original destination when all Cam wanted to do was go back to Robyn Winter. Now in the cockpit with Grimes, Cam was flying the cruiser as Grimes sat beside him, nursing his shoulder. Perseus, Cameron and Annison in the back. Cam looked over his shoulder.

"They can't hear you if that's what you're concerned about."

Cam looked at Grimes.

"Although I'm not sure about Annison. Seems that girl has some special abilities."

Cam looked forward, said, "I used my mother's maiden name when I joined the force."

"Got that, but why?"

Cam shook his head. "Well, let's just say that the Fisk family has a very sorted past. I was afraid I wouldn't get in so I used another name."

"That bad?"

"You can say that."

"Okay, I get it, but how did Hadock know it?"

"I have no idea," said Cam.

Grimes shook his head. "Great, more mystery to figure out."

"You got that right." Cam looked over the monitor on the control panel, watching their destination–a blinking red dot on his screen–as the cruiser raced forward.

Grimes asked, "Where are we?"

"Just outside of New Mexico. We should be there soon." Cam paused, thinking about their destination and what waited in New Mexico. "And you're sure, right?" He looked at Grimes. "Sure about what Annison said?"

"Yeah, she said there was no one there."

"So why are we going?"

"The ship may work, but it's got issues and we're too far to go back to Robyn Winter. Not even sure we could make it there. I'm hoping we can find a new ship or spare parts or something to help repair the ship. Plus, let us remember why we're on this mission; Winter's people said the vampires can track Cameron through telepathy."

"If they're aware he even exists."

"Well, I haven't been schooled in exactly how vampire telepathy works, so I'll just have to take their word for it. Plus...," he shook his head.

"You're not really convinced she knows what she's talking about?"

"Well, let's just say I'm trying to be optimistic."

"A change in tune I see."

"Yeah, well, pessimism wasn't working out too well. They way I see it, where we're going is just a stopover, always was. Then to the final destination, as Winter said. We can hide there for a while; regroup before... well, who the hell knows. Friggin' alien war and all." He shook his head. "There's got to be some human beings who are on our side."

"All alone," said Cam, staring into the night sky.

"What?"

Cam shook his head. "What about our military brothers and sisters?"

"Who take orders from the very people who sold us out."

"But if they knew the truth, of course they would fight with us."

"And who's going to convince them? You and I have more than likely been declared enemies of the state. They'd shoot us on sight before you even opened your mouth."

"But they think we're dead. Might be worth a try."

"And tell them what? Our government, the people you take orders from, have conspired with aliens to turn us into slaves? Where's the proof?"

Cam thought about the grey female from the camp. "If we could make them see with their own eyes these aliens, they'd stand with us."

"Possible and likely, yes."

"How do they do it?" said Cam. "That lady in the camp, the short one, we always thought she was… different. How did she pull a veil over all our eyes?"

"Probably a question we should have asked Winter."

Cam watched the rolling night sky, with its blips of stars and a moon that seemed to be crashing down on the desert, so large and beaming with light. He remembered gazing on the mystery of the moon as a child, never knowing how our celestial neighbor was turned into a space station, with nuclear bombs aimed at the Earth.

And Cam whispered, "We are truly alone."

The ship said in that monotone mechanical voice, "Arriving at our destination."

Grimes looked at Cam. "Be ready, lieutenant. Ready for anything."

32

MOTH looked over his three soldiers, Drac warriors who stood proud and by his side for over a century. As the leader of COR, Moth was assigned three personal guards; guards who killed at his command. Guards who received special assignments, gathering intel as needed.

His Dracs stood at attention, their armor shining under the light, drenched black and purple. Dalious, Moth's right hand, stood center stage. On his right was Plagesous, the sinister Drac who enjoyed skinning his victims alive, a form of torture he'd become supremely confident in. On Dalious' left stood the massive Drac referred to as Calla. His size was enough to strike fear into those he fought. Standing close to seven feet tall, his thick frame could easily tear off a human's limbs with one quick thrust. It was once said that Calla tore off a human arm and drank from the spout of blood raging from the limb as if he were drinking from a cup as his victim screamed and wailed. Moth gathered his most trusted Drac warriors for a special purpose concerning the phantom, informing his warriors with the how and why behind the phantom's capture. They snarled when learning it was Sanos who had brought the phantom to Drac City.

"But I smell something rotten with our phantom," said Moth. "I want you all on guard during tonight's festivities. Dalious, you will stand over the phantom and usher his body, crypt and all, into Drac City. I want our people to know we have their best interest in mind, unquestioned loyalty being the reason. Once they see how our resolve towards creatures that murder our own are dealt with, their allegiance will grow even stronger."

Dalious said, "What expectation do you have for this phantom?"

Moth craned his head. "Could be nothing. Could just be a great funeral pyre and a night of Drac legend. But I want you all on guard in case we've been handed an evil seed. Plagesous, you will oversee the festivities from the south, Calla from the north."

Dalious said, "Do you wish for military personnel to oversee the festivities?"

"I do not," said Moth. "A military presence will do nothing more than stifle our Dracs. The less they see, the better. I wish not to engage them in speculation of an occupation, as has been the rumor spilling through our great city. Should something occur with this phantom, I want him taken alive."

Moth could sense the disdain in his warrior's ether.

"Do you understand this order?" He looked over at the three of them. "The human rebellion will be wiped off the map of existence, so it has been written. This is our time to rule. The events that have transpired over the last twenty-four hours lead us to this inevitability. We shall not falter due to blood lust, nor the carnage of our enemies to satisfy personal desires."

"And if he does not abide by your rules?" asked Dalious.

"All indications are that the phantom is dead, but until I see his body burn, I'll have no recourse but to lend a skeptical ear. But should there be something rotten in his death, should he rise like Lazarus, then we shall enjoy our day with a human god. And drink from his veins for an eternity."

His warriors all grinned; satisfied with the answer they received. Moth said, "Go, gentlemen. Tend to your duties."

33

SANOS gathered inside his military quarter. From his window, he could see ships docking in Drac City. He was waiting for the grey representative to arrive. The formula was with the greys. Sanos saw it fitting that the species continued on the side of Drac.

Now what riches did the Draconians promise the greys in this cosmic game of chess?

Sanos required the formula; the concoction would hail him a king among his people. It was dire for him to keep it for himself. In order to unleash holy hell on the humans, new blood was required. Turning his fellow Dracs into ravaging vampires would secure his victory over humans and Drac alike. And then he can rule, for anyone who desired new blood would have to bend to his will. He could taste the carnage on his tongue as much as he could taste the lingering effect of new blood.

His people were simple. They desired to live in peace, but peace was not a Drac delicacy to be feasted on for eternity. No, such living was an insult to Drac pride. We are monsters, Sanos thought. This peaceful change in Drac needs to be eradicated. The Draconians can have the Earth. I want Drakulon, my home, my planet of vampires.

Sanos stepped from the window, head bowed, thinking.

"Draconians," he scoffed. Treacherous vile creatures of the universe. They require Drac, not the other way around. Absentee gods in a galaxy filled with the meek.

But they have power. What other species has stretched its vile fist across the universe with such profound elation than the Draconians?

(They can make all happen. They can hand you the pride of Drac.)

And then we can rule.

(Earn the favor of the Draconians Sanos. Earn their favor and Drac's will bow to you.)

Simple minds ought not to be counted on to provide leadership. COR must be no more. For millenniums has COR ruled.

(No. For millenniums Moth has ruled.)

Moth, thought Sanos. He suspects deception within the phantom.

(Wants you to bow to him. To raise him on your shoulders and pledge undying allegiance.)

Sanos shook his head in a fit of rage, groaning beneath his breath.

(He stifles you, Sanos. We must eradicate him. Decimated. Destroyed.)

But he is the leader of COR. If I take his life, they will deem me a catastrophe. No Drac will ever bow to me.

(Lead him to his death then. In the spirit of war, he can lose his life by our hand.)

And none will be any wiser to our cause.

(And all Drac will hail Sanos as their new leader. Sanos, destroyer of phantoms, savior of Drac legend.)

And proprietor of new blood.

Sanos looked through his window where a grey ship was waiting to doc. Sanos felt his lips curl into a devious grin.

Time, he thought, quickens to meet my desire.

34

CAM saw smoke rising from the compound. A plume of grey lifted into the night sky. Fires were raging inside their destination. A battle must have taken place and recently too, considering the smoke and fires. But he could see neither ships nor soldiers. No vampires or Hadocks running amok. No greys unleashing telekinetic hell. Only a barren wasteland greeted them.

"Seems like a wild goose chase," said Grimes, the cruiser hovering a hundred yards away from the smoke plume. "Everything about this trip… it's like we're battling an invisible force or something."

Cam was watching the smoke rising when the cruiser sputtered. The ship dipped down, then back up.

Cam said, "Maybe the ship wants us to go in?"

Grimes looked around. "I wouldn't be surprised if this thing turned into an alien and ventured off the planet."

"And us with it."

"No doubt."

"I'll take it down, but not too close. Let's see what we're dealing with."

"Looks abandoned," said Grimes. "Whoever was here left in a hurry. Who's to say there's anyone even down there."

"Could be no one. Then again, there could be a survivor or two. Someone who's hurt and needs help. With the way things are, I'll take as many human beings as we can."

"Considering this place is in ashes, maybe we should go back to Robyn Winter."

The cruiser dipped as if in protest; Cam pulled the nose up, leveling the cruiser.

Cam said, "I don't think this ship likes us."

Grimes looked at Cam as he shifted the controls, and the cruiser jumped forward. "The feeling's mutual," said Grimes.

"I'm sure it is." Cam watched as the compound drew closer. He set the cruiser down a hundred yards from the opening, and it landed with a heavy thud. Grimes shot Cam a wicked stare.

"What? You fly this thing if you think you can do better." Cam shook his head, looked outside as the moon's glow bathed a slivery light across the rock formed entrance. His jaw dropped when he saw the bodies strewn in front of it.

Grimes said, "Well, that's not good. They look like they were vaporized. Most of them, anyway. Jesus, friggin' vampires did this? I thought they just drank blood?"

Cam whispered, "Not these vampires." He

rolled his tongue inside his cheek, thinking. Craned his head to look outside, into the sky.

Grimes did the same. "No flying Hadocks out there."

Cam stood from his seat. "No UFO's either." He pulled his 9MM from his holster, checked the clip, then punched it back in, and wedged the weapon in his back belt.

"What about the kids?" asked Grimes.

"They're coming too. All of us. I don't want to leave anyone behind."

"Can't wait," said Grimes. "Cam and his crew of misfits."

35

KAAL had alerted Moth that the grey representative had arrived.

A day of events, Moth thought. Truly, there is more to be revealed.

He wanted the formula. Finally, Dr. Blum had succeeded in his lifelong ambition; the chemistry had to be perfect, requiring no adverse effects to be noticed by the recipient, at least none to cause more than a second thought. Slight changes in cognition over time were required, and the ability for the effect to transfer from mother to child during pregnancy, essentially creating a generation of humans satisfied with less, a life of servitude with no ambition or drive to succeed. Never wanting more, never questioning what they were told. Mindless, simple creatures served with an exquisite taste.

Moth trekked through the corridors to meet with the grey representative, thinking, remembering the many ways in which they'd tried to dismantle the human race. More than a century of trial and error. Small victories over time, leading them to the here and now. Dr. Blum had arrived forty years ago to take on the task, a lifetime to humans, Moth knew. A lifetime of work resulting in the ultimate success; the humans would hand over the planet without a second thought, destroying the prime directive keeping the Draconians from ruling with an iron fist. Moth always wondered what the humans were like before the frequency imbued their minds with confusion, nervousness, and paranoia. He'd been told prior to his arrival that the planet had been drenched in riches, magic, and freedom, an evolution of the mind and spirit destroyed by the Draconians, helped by the elite, and fought against by so few, the tiresome and weary Robyn Winter being on top of the list.

The Draconians always said it the best, "Teach them they are nothing. Less than. Dependent. Make them look beyond themselves for safety and security, and they will die from within. Show their eyes what they cannot have and provide the dream that they can. And then laugh as they claw at each other to receive what they will never gain."

"Brilliant," Moth whispered, thinking of the Draconians. Scoff at the past, create division and destroy what was and you will change all that will ever be.

Except the humans always knew. Somewhere deep within the subconscious, the truth was locked inside their minds, stuffed inside a dark room of fear where not even the bravest of humans would venture.

And so began the steady decline of an evolved species. And millenniums of suffering, anguish, and war. But the Draconians failed on one level; the frequency was dissipating and soon, thirty-six years soon, the frequency would vanish; gone in a blink, and their plot revealed. The formula was now essential to the Draconian victory.

And the extinction of the indigo trait.

Moth grinned, thinking of the baby. The Akashic Record now beamed with delight in favor of Dracs. Inside the record it was revealed that the Drac indigo would be born on VG211 and his life would lead to the indigo's destruction; the final riff in the Draconian occupation would perish, allowing COR to rule over their people and return to their planet, rich with control and power.

"One step at a time," said Moth. "One step in time."

He curled his fingers into fists, tightening his bones as he stepped effortlessly into the conference room. Upon his entrance, the grey representative, Nero, stood and both the grey and Moth bowed.

36

THE stench of burning flesh turned their stomachs. Annison couldn't take it, vomiting where she stood as Cameron stood over her, his hand on her back. Perseus snarled, shaking his head, and Grimes covered his nose. Cam slumped to his knees.

Grimes said to Cam, "Maybe we should put the kids back in the car?"

But Grimes' words disappeared from Cam's consciousness. He couldn't take his eyes off the carnage. Their flesh was seared off, leaving nothing more than innards and organs, bones and traces of blood. There had to be hundreds of bodies across the ground, all leading into the cave and reaching as far as Cam's eyes could see.

Maybe thousands, thought Cam.

"Cam!" Grimes said in a hushed and stern tone. Gestured to Cameron and Annison. "They need to go back on the ship." Grimes turned to the carnage. "This isn't anything a child should see."

Annison shouted, "No. I'm not going anywhere," between a fit of coughs and choked back gags. "I need to see for myself what they're doing to us."

Cam looked over his shoulder when Cameron said, "It's okay. I got her." He looked at Cam, his head with a slight shake. "The smell... doesn't bother me," his voice carried a sliver of shame behind it.

Nothing was said in response. Cam dug his fingers into sand; let the grains slip through his fingers, clenching his fingers inside his fist, then stood up.

"What's the plan?" said Grimes. "We going in or not?"

Cam nodded, turned to Grimes. "Yes," he said, then walked over to Cameron, offering the boy his 9MM. "Take this," he said. "Do you know how to work it?"

"Yes," said Cameron, taking the gun. "Point and shoot..." his voice trailed off. He looked from the gun to Cam.

"Exactly," said Cam. "Safety's on." He regarded Perseus. "The giant here is your first defense." Turned back to Cameron and Annison, looked them both over. "Understood?"

"Yes," said Cameron, and Annison, looking rather pale and sickly, gave an understanding nod.

"Good. We go in single file. I'll lead us in, Grimes behind me, Perseus last. Got it?"

They both nodded.

"You see anything say something, but keep the voices low. Understood?"

Cam scanned his crew, receiving nods and agreements before turning to the cave, walking towards it and stopped next to Grimes. The moonlight dissipated inside the cave, where a black void waited to swallow them whole. He followed the bones and bodies from the cave to his feet.

Grimes said, "What do you think is in there? Other than more dead bodies."

"Hopefully nothing Corporal." Cam stepped towards the cave. "Hopefully nothing."

37

NERO slid a thumb drive across the table to Moth, who placed his hand over the drive.

"Your formula is on the drive," said Nero in that grey echoing voice.

Moth pinched the drive between his fingers, studying the device.

The future exists on this drive, Moth thought. The power of control is in my hands.

Moth regarded Nero, put the drive on the table.

Nero asked, "What information do you have about Mono's demise?"

"Only what I've been told. Mono was dispatched by the human who birthed the child."

"And who is this human?" asked Nero. "What matter of human has ever dispatched a grey?"

"She had help," said Moth. Nero raised his chin, regarding Moth, waiting for him to continue. "The human rebellion," he said. "It was carnage. What happened on VG211 will live in infamy within Drac legend. So many were sacrificed…" His eyes burrowed into Nero. "On all sides. Drac, grey, and human."

Moth had gone deep into his subconscious prior to this meeting, not wanting to give Nero even the slightest access into the depths of his mind. He was sure that Nero wouldn't miss an opportunity to read Moth's thoughts if the chance was presented. The greys were a tricky species.

Nero said, "And where is this human now?" He looked over the room and at the ceiling. "I sense no presence of human other than those existing in the gallows. We want her," he said, his eyes bulging black and Moth could hear pain writhing from those eyes. Nero opened and closed his fingers. "We have questions for her."

Moth knew he couldn't present Sandy to the greys. Nero and his people would never believe a human had turned to Drac. Moth's people would be blamed for Mono's death, causing insurrection. A war within a war. Of course, there were the witches, Mintaka, Alnitak, and Alnilam, who could provide Nero with this information. Although the witches are a different species of grey from Nero's, but still they were grey; thankfully they took orders from Moth. He'd done right dispatching the witches and Jayda with the baby, far from the telepathic stronghold of Drac and grey alike.

"Perished," said Moth. "She died upon arrival. A brain death. We assume whatever was done to her by Mono resulted in a lack of oxygen to the brain. She is no more."

Nero paused, his enormous eyes devouring Moth.

"Trying to see inside my mind, Nero will not be a benefit to you, this I assure you. I'm not that frightened naïve young Drac any longer."

"We only wish to know the truth."

Moth shook his head. "I have provided the truth. Do what you want with it, but do not attempt to see inside my head again." He moved his head back and forth. "I will not be so diplomatic if you do."

Nero bowed his understanding and turned to the window.

"Good," said Moth. "Now if that is all I'd like to be ready for tonight's festivities."

Nero turned slowly to Moth. "I have more to discuss. Much more indeed."

"Proceed," said Moth and he could have sworn that Nero smiled.

"Prior to Mono's... death, we received a download of information."

"Of what nature?" asked Moth.

"Of a disturbing nature," answered Nero. "A most dire disturbance."

Moth sat closer to the table, his hands folded over the thumb drive.

"It appears," said Nero. "The fabled Robyn Winter is alive."

"Impossible," Moth huffed. "Robyn Winter has been dead a long time. His atoms were scattered across the universe; you and all creatures in the universe are aware of this."

"It appears not. He is alive and leading the rebellion."

Moth's head shaking now, grinding his teeth. "How did you come across this information?"

"From Mono. As you know, we greys have telepathic abilities that cross space and time. We received communication through Mono of Robyn Winter's presence in the rebellion. Seems he is the one who dispatched the rebel fighters to VG211. Strange, the communication was…"

"How do you mean?"

Nero paused. "It was as if Mono had been blindsided by the revelation. We can only assume she did not wish for the information to be revealed. No further communication was received."

"Why would she not want this?"

"We are not entirely sure on that matter. And to us greys, this revelation is quite the cause for concern. On many, many levels."

"Do you suspect insurrection?"

"We assume nothing. Considering Mono has perished, we would say no."

Moth paused, thinking. Robyn Winter alive? There was no reflection in the record about such a circumstance. How can it be?

"There is more," said Nero, his head bent, eyes gleaming at Moth. "Also revealed within the communication was the rebellion's hidden base. Or bases as I should say."

"Where?" Moth growled.

"Underground," said Nero. "Right under all our noses. In plain sight. Ancient and abandoned for hundreds of years. Scattered across the planet inside pockets close to our own. This is the information that kept me from arriving here earlier."

Moth sensed there was more in Nero's story. "What orders have you given about this cause?"

Now Moth could see a smile, as if Nero's mind alighted with certainty.

"As a part of our duty to destroy the Outliers, we've uncovered multiple bases, now that we know what we are looking for."

"Go on?"

"We've eradicated all bases we've discovered."

Moth's eyes widened. "And Robyn Winter?"

Nero shook his head. "No trace, but we are confident he is alive. It is only a matter of time before we find where he is hiding."

Moth thought and thought. "It is possible he returns to those bases you've destroyed, have you..."

Nero cut him off. "We stationed cathagers at every base. Should anyone return to those bases, they will have a rather awful surprise."

"Good," said Moth. "We must find him. If this is true and Winter is alive, we must find him before the Draconians become aware. They will not be kind should they learn of our failure."

Nero bowed. "Agreed. We continue to search for him."

Moth thought about Sandy. Is it possible Sandy could lead them to Robyn Winter? Was Winter's location locked inside Sandy's mind, and that is how Mono discovered he was alive? So much more to Sandy than met the eye.

"What are your thoughts Moth?"

Moth leaned back in his chair, then sat up, the drive in his palm. Went to the window. He always thought better when he looked over his city.

"There is only one being who can eradicate Mr. Winter. The one known as Sephtis. I shall contact him, bring him here."

"Sephtis has allegiance only to himself."

Moth breathed, "The enemy of my enemy is my friend."

"He won't care to destroy the rebellion. His only focus will be on Winter and he'll dispatch anyone who gets in his way, grey and Drac included. You know the history between them, Moth. This may not be the manner in which we wish to proceed."

"Robyn Winter poses a dire threat to us both, Nero. We may require Sephtis to dispatch him. Considering he is alive, there's only one way that can be. None of us would be strong enough to take him down. It would take all our power and all our people to even try."

Nero thought on this before saying, "Would Sephtis consider the information confidential... and not inform the Draconians?"

"Indeed," said Moth. "Sephtis looks on all of us under a Draconian rule as sheep, but he despises Draconians above all. He will not say a word, not at least until after Winter is in his clutches. Then nothing will matter to the Draconians; they will accept what was because Robyn Winter will cause no more trouble. The how and why behind it will not matter."

"And if Sephtis fails?"

Moth turned to Nero. "Than we all do what is most necessary."

"That may leave all our people in ashes. Perhaps we should inform the Draconians. Let them deal with Winter."

"That, Nero, would cost me and you our lives. No, we will take care of this ourselves and call on the one known as Sephtis when the moment is right. Keep him out of the public mind and eye to cause no entanglements beforehand. Keep searching, Nero, as will I. Once Winter's location is determined..."

Nero raised his chin, meeting Moth's stare.

"Be ready for all out war."

38

KAAL retreated to his workstation. He was waiting for Moth to provide the formula so he could transfer the chemistry to their human counterparts. One step closer to final phase.

His concern was with the human female and Moth's refusal to destroy the human turning Drac. Sandy's change embodied the will of Drac legend, and should she be discovered his people would become disenfranchised with COR. Moth was skating on thin ice and Kaal knew it. Kaal didn't like loose ends, and certainly despised what Sandy represented. The possibility of what she could be twisted his gut. Sandy was an abnormality, nothing more. A concoction of grey genetic experimentation, outrageous and blasphemous.

I'll cut her throat myself should I see any sign she is…

"She is what?"

Kaal turned to see Sanos sitting on a ledge above the room.

"Sanos?" Sanos made Kaal's blood curl. He

never enjoyed his presence; his ether was foul. Sanos sat in darkness, but Kaal could see his gleaming eyes and how his hands gripped the lip he sat on. Of course he knew it was Sanos, for what manner of Drac would dare to enter Kaal's workstation without permission from Moth, plus that voice. It turned Kaal's stomach.

"Yes, Kaal, I am Sanos. But please continue. Whose throat do you wish to cut?"

Kaal turned from Sanos. "Get out of my study," he ordered. "Your presence is irritating, and you're not allowed unless Moth grants permission."

He heard Sanos jump from the ledge, and Kaal shuddered. He could feel Sanos approaching. Could hear his heavy breath as he stepped towards Kaal.

"Oh Kaal, I only wish to make friends with you. Better indeed if we do."

Kaal refused to look at Sanos. He kept his eyes on Drac City and his computer system.

"Why would I want to be your friend? You're a disgrace to Drac and COR."

Sanos laughed. "So precious Kaal. You, on the other hand, are a credit to all Drac, me included."

"Fine," Kaal muttered. "Now get out or I'll have you removed."

"Kaal, Kaal, Kaal. So pretentious and… afraid. I have no reason to hurt you, Kaal. There is no concern here. We are brothers. Bound by Drac blood."

Kaal snapped to Sanos. "I'm no brother to you, Sanos. You… only think of yourself."

"Ooh, now that hurt Kaal. Do you think you could use a bit of that kindness that has worked so well for you? Isn't it easier if we are friends?"

Kaal's head shaking. "You're disgusting."

"Nothing but words, Kaal." Sanos dipped his head to the right. "Is that any way to treat a future member of COR?"

Kaal felt the air rush from his lungs. His mouth hung open. Started shaking his head. "Not a chance. Moth would never allow you to take a seat with COR. Not you. Never."

"But it is true," said Sanos. "You can ask your... master, once he returns." Sanos turned his gaze to Drac City.

"I don't believe you."

Sanos shrugged. "It matters not what you think, Kaal. What you believe and what is true are not the same." He turned to meet Kaal's stare. "It would be better for you to accept this inevitability."

Kaal shook his head. "Why would Moth do that? There's no logic in such a decision."

"Please. I brought the phantom to his knees. And the rebellion will meet its end by my hand. There's only a matter of time before I take my seat with COR."

Kaal gnashed his teeth, his upper lip quivering. "What is it you want, Sanos? How can I quicken your leave from my personal space?"

Sanos turned back to Drac City. "Well, I have questions, Kaal, and I'm hoping you have some answers."

"Questions?" said Kaal. "What answers do you seek? And… keep in mind Sanos you are not a part of COR yet, so anything deemed classified will not make its way into that conniving head of yours."

Sanos regarded Kaal with a smug and grim grin. "It has to do with a discovery that was made on VG211." He shook his head. "That forsaken outpost caused more strife to Drac than was necessary."

"What discovery? Are you referring to Dr. Blum's work? That's privileged…"

Sanos growled and caught Kaal's throat in his hand. Kaal's eyes wide, feeling the choke of his throat in Sanos' palm. He lifted Kaal off the ground, meeting him eye-to-eye, snarling, as Kaal's feet thrashed, struggling to free himself from Sanos' grip.

"I grow tired of your attitude, Kaal. I came here to be kind but I see only fear will stifle your tongue."

Kaal gritted his teeth, said through gasping breath. "Release me. Master Moth will hang you from your innards if you don't."

Sanos tossed Kaal onto his chair, his back snapped, pain jutted up his spine to the back of his head. Kaal had no time to react. Sanos was standing over him, his hands gripped the armrests, snarling and growling.

"Be gone, I told you."

Sanos snatched Kaal's chin, his nails raking across his skin. Kaal could see scratch marks across

Sanos' arms.

"What Drac does this to himself?" said Kaal. His eyes narrowed. "You're a fiend. Master Moth will hear about this, I promise you."

Sanos gripped tighter, his nails cutting into Kaal's skin, as he dipped his head closer to Kaal with a growl beneath his throat. "You're pathetic and weak," said Sanos. "What makes you think I won't rip your heart out right here and now?"

Kaal's eyes widened. "You wouldn't? COR will banish you from Drac City. You'll be an outcast."

Sanos shook his head. "Even so, you'll be dead and my slave in the afterlife." He squeezed Kaal's jaw tighter, his nails drawing blood. "Destined to walk with blind eyes. And your master..." He looked to Drac City. "And his wretched species of slave you all fight to keep in your grasp... like grains of sand between my fingers."

Kaal ceased thrashing, his eyes wide.

"You will give me what I want, Kaal, or you will meet your death by my hand as will all who you hold so dear."

"No," said Kaal. "Please."

Sanos tossed Kaal's head back. "Pathetic," he snarled.

Kaal rubbed his chin, his jaw tight and hurting. He could still feel Sanos' fingernails as if they remained in his skin. "What is it you want?"

"It's simple, really," said Sanos, standing tall

over Kaal. "There are only two things I want from you."

39

TIGHT black leather. Those were the garment choices they provided Sandy, mostly at least. On the rack of clothes brought to her there was one red robe. Woven from a thick fabric, a thick stripe made of gold symbols–much like the hieroglyphics etched into the walls in Drac City–ran down both sides of the robe. Sandy chose this red garment; the hood would help to hide her human eyes.

She could feel power surge inside her veins, her heart pumping blood in all directions, but the power sensation would pass quickly as if the blood thinned before reaching its destination to bring the precious life to fruition. Her throat arid turned to heat inside her mouth, her teeth seething and wrought with pain.

Hunger!

And she was becoming restless, pacing across the floor, back and forth. Back and forth. She wanted to rush into Drac City. Wanted to tear apart any living creature that posed a threat to her motherly intuition.

But that would not bring Adam here.

She ceased pacing, standing, looking over the

circular vision of Drac City outside.

Move like a snake, she thought, looking over the room.

Sandy sprinted and jumped to the wall, ran across it, then landed on her feet. Repeating the same continuously, she had energy she could never understand in human form. She ran towards the back wall, jumped to it, her feet scampering up to the ceiling. She flipped over, landed on her feet, crouched down. Thick inhaling breath, her tongue pressed against the roof of her mouth, muscles and spine tense, and she started walking, slow steps one in front of the other. She could feel her breath rise to the back of her skull, energetic power rising to the top of her head. Sandy saw herself in the window; her tongue still pressed tense to the roof of her mouth, those bones behind her head swelled, and when she exhaled, her breath came out with a hiss across her lips. She had difficulty recognizing the cobra staring at her in the window.

It is me, she thought. A snake. A vampire. A cobra. A queen.

Sandy stretched her neck slowly to the left, taking in her reflection with apt focus. Moved her shoulders with a slow movement, her eyes wide, breathing still, inhaling the same, exhaling with a hiss.

And then, a vision. Adam's cries. She could hear his heart beat, feel his blood in his veins. Saw where he was, a place of pure effervescent beauty and wonder in a blanket of darkness. Those grey witches surrounding him seemed to look into Sandy's mind, knowing her presence was with them. With Adam.

And a vampire was with them. A thick and tall vampire, although Sandy sensed a softness beating in his heart.

Grey alien eyes, round and black, burrowing into Sandy's mind.

Mintaka!

Adam crying, being fed from a vein. Quiet now, young one. Quiet down. The pain you feel satisfied by blood.

Mintaka with the witches, Alnitak and Alnilam. All three staring into Sandy's mind.

When you are ready, their unison voices rang in Sandy's mind. We will be waiting.

Sandy felt the pull in her stomach, and the vision vanished in a flash like a spaceship had propelled at lightning speed, gone with the speed of thought.

And Sandy's heart with it.

40

"THIS happened," said Grimes, standing in the cave, looking over the multitude of bodies strung across the ground. "In a flash. Unexpected."

Cam ran his tongue inside his mouth; the stench was god-awful and grew stronger the further they ventured into the cave. He remembered the UFO he'd seen hiding in the clouds before Hadock had arrived. Silas had said how the rebellion's bases were hidden from the enemy.

They weren't expecting this at all. Secret hiding places were a secret no more.

They hadn't ventured more than a hundred yards into the cave. They had yet to step into the back of the cave. Cam remembered how Phil used his eyes to enter Winter's abode, looking at a similar wall torn to shreds where whatever alien had reaped carnage on this base had blown the rebel's security system off its hinges. There was quiet beyond this wall. Too quiet, Cam thought.

Grimes said, "It's possible they did the same to Winter."

"We don't know that. Maybe communication got to them during the battle."

"It's possible we're all alone now." Grimes' head shaking. "This is annihilation." He looked up from the bodies on the ground. "Where do we go from here?"

"Hang tough Corporal," said Cam. "We're still alive."

"For how long?" Grimes whined. "This is a schizophrenic nightmare."

Cam looked at Annison. "Annie, can you detect any communications? Any live feeds? Something we can use to..." he swallowed the lump in his throat. "Get word out on what's happened here."

Annison looked around the cave and Cam could see those two protrusions on the back of her head erect as if reaching for wavelengths that didn't exist. Her eyes found Cam, said, "There is nothing, no frequencies or wavelengths to catch. Whoever was here destroyed everything."

Grimes huffed, "Covert attacks. Of course, they would dismantle all possibility of communication. You're reaching Cam."

"Just assessing, Corporal."

Annison interjected. "The starships sent an electrical pulse prior to invasion. All communication was destroyed."

"That's great. Just great," said Grimes.

Cam ignored Grimes. "How do you know that?" he said to Annison.

"It leaves a stain in the air." She looked around the cave, in the spaces in between. "It's still here. I can feel it."

"Wonderful," said Grimes.

Cam turned to Grimes. "Corporal." Grimes lifted his eyes to Cam. "Get back on the cruiser and see if you and Annison can get communication out to Winter."

Grimes interjected. "We tried that already," Grimes huffed. "I told you, there's nothing getting through to their location."

"Then keep trying," ordered Cam. "Use Morse Code if you have to but do whatever is necessary. We've got to keep trying."

Grimes raised his rifle to his shoulder, head bent, eyes wide, thinking.

"And scan for a return." He looked at the dead bodies. "Whatever did this, we don't want coming back. See what you can do to fix the cruiser." Cam looked over the land cruisers, vessels, and vehicles in the cave, all destroyed. "It may be our only way out."

"What are you going to do?"

"Scan for survivors. Maybe someone survived… somehow. Plus, there may be weapons we can salvage. We'll need everything we can get our hands on."

"And then what?"

"One thing at a time, Corporal."

Grimes paused before ordering Annison to follow him. Cam watched as they walked away.

He's losing faith, Cam thought, looking around the cave, then to Cameron and Perseus. Keep up hope, he told himself. No one ever said war didn't come with loss.

He looked through the hole in the cave.

I hope we're still alive come morning.

41

PHIL could hear his own crying before he was aware there were frightened tears in his eyes.

He was four years old again, and his mother held him tight and close, huddled in a corner bathed in darkness. The only light came from the hallway. He could see it beaming from beneath the door.

"It'll be okay," said his mother. "It'll all be over soon." She smoothed her hand through Phil's hair. Her touch so gentle, caring, and soft.

But Phil couldn't stop his ears from listening. Hearing the screams, terror in the hall. Loud slapping slashes across skin and then screams again. Muffled hollering, voices in the dark, inflicting pain.

They were bred on the island. Bred as food. Bred for pleasure, but not their pleasure. Pleasure for the host, and pleasure for the guests who arrived on frequent occasions.

Phil shuddered in his mother's embrace when the panel on their door slid open with a crack. Wild yellow and green eyes gazed upon them from the hall. Phil tried to remember where he was, where he actually was, his body had to be in Drac City by now, but his mind, his soul, was entombed on this horrid island as if attempting to revisit a memory long lost in the recesses of his mind. The vampire in the window snickered with a grunt. Phil felt his mother tense when the lock on the door slid open with a metal scrape and bang. The door opened and in poured light.

Phil could see boots enter the room; saw the vampire pointing. "This one," the vampire's gruff voice ordered.

Phil's mother's voice, strong and steady, said, "Not him." She held Phil tight against her. "Take me," she said. "I won't fight. Leave him for another day, please."

The vampire hovered over them, a hiss in his throat, a low growl beneath the hiss, assessing Phil. Assessing his mother.

"I'm no longer fertile," she said. "I have no use any longer. Take me. Spare the child."

The vampire's head nodding, his eyes devouring Phil's mother. He turned and said, "Take the mother," then returned his stare to Phil. "Don't worry young one, we will have our time with you soon."

From behind the vampire came two beings, dressed in black gowns. They grabbed Phil's mother. Phil pleading not to take her, gripping her waist and refusing to let go.

Phil's mother said, "It's okay, my baby. It'll be all right." He could hear how her voice carried a tearful whine as the beings pulled her towards the door. Phil slid across the floor with a screech and wailing plea when the vampire's boot slammed into Phil's stomach, breaking his hold on his mother. He slammed into the wall, falling to the ground with a thud. Phil hunched over, clutching his stomach, pain in his abdomen turned his gut. He snapped his eyes open, his mother's arms forced behind her back and those beings holding her he could see were human.

Heard his mother say, "It'll be okay." Tears cascaded across her skin. "Live to fight another day."

She was being strong for him, Phil knew. In that moment, she was giving him hope.

The humans pulled her from the room and the vampire stood over him.

"Pathetic creature," said the vampire. He stepped to the door and turned back to Phil. "No need to worry. I'll take special care of your mother." And he laughed, a sinister cackle of a laugh. Laughing when he closed the door, slid the lock back into place, then slid the panel closed, leaving Phil alone.

Alone inside the darkness.

42

THERE were more dead bodies behind the wall. Cam led Perseus and Cameron through the cave to the rock formed bedrooms where bodies lay dead in their beds. Families had been resting, playing, before the slaughter.

Why didn't they run? thought Cam. Looks like they were still playing with no idea they were about to meet their death. If it was an ambush, they would have been alerted to what was happening outside. Cam looked back at the wall that was torn to shreds. The entrance from the outside in, upon closer examination, revealed a thought Cam never thought to assume.

The slaughter happened here first, in the cave.

He looked outside, through the door and the bodies strewn across the ground.

Then the UFO waited for them to run out. Came from inside?

"Find something?" asked Cameron.

The boy looked pale, sick, and drawn. "See the doors there?" Cam pointed to the wall that had been blown off its hinges. Cameron turned and looked, then turned back to Cam.

"Yes. That's how they got in."

Cam shook his head. "Look how the wall is forced out, away from the cave."

Cameron's eyes squinted, thinking. "So it happened from inside?"

"Exactly."

Perseus growled.

"Which means the ambush started here, inside the cave."

"How?"

"That is what we're going to find out." Cam moved past Perseus and Cameron. Standing in the room's center, he looked up. The cave reached a hundred yards high and a hundred yards around. Another opening in the cave, also torn off its hinges, opened into a dark room opposite the cave's opening to the outside. Cam went to the opening, Cameron and Perseus behind him. He could feel a breeze and raised his hand. The wind's direction showed it originated inside the opening. Darkness greeted him, but Cam could see a light glow within the cave, glowing blue. Faint was this light, but light enough. He turned to Cameron and Perseus.

"Keep your wits about you. You see something say something."

"Understood," said Cameron, and Perseus growled his accord.

They stepped into the darkness, Cam leading

them further into the cave, where the stench of scorched flesh stained his nostrils. His rifle aimed into the darkness, towards the blue light. The only sound came from their footsteps crunching into earth and rock. The blue light illuminated a large open area, much like the pit Cam remembered in the underground compound with the same opening into the earth.

"Maybe this is how they arrived. Through the underground cities." Cameron stood beside the opening, looking down.

Cam studied the opening, surveyed the room, noticing there were no blast marks in this area, the exception being the door to the common area. Saw a control panel close to the open pit and went to it, allowing his rifle to hang from his shoulder when he pressed a red button and the pit opening closed. Cam's eyes narrow, brow furrowed, thinking.

"What is it?" asked Cameron.

Cam was shaking his head, watching as the pit closed.

"Cam?"

Cam snapped his eyes to Cameron, the boy waiting for a response. "I don't like to assume but, there are no blast marks in here and the pit is perfectly operational unlike every other door or opening in this cave."

"Meaning?"

"Meaning, someone let them in."

Cameron shook his head. "Why would someone

do that?"

Cam whispered, as if he needed to swallow the truth before admitting it, "Because they were on their side. Someone they trusted… let them walk right in and…" His voice trailed off, staring at Perseus whose nose was crinkled, looking around the room.

"What is it Perseus? You smell something?" Cam moved away from the controls, looking around the room. Perseus was circling now, his head raised. Cam followed his gaze to the ceiling. Cam's first thought went to Hadock with his wings. But what jumped down from the ceiling wasn't any Hadock.

What jumped down on top of Perseus was human.

A human with red eyes.

43

MOTH went to gather his new vampire from her living quarters. He'd provided the thumb drive to his most trusted symbiote to deliver to Kaal to transfer the data to their human counterparts. Confident in Kaal's ability to do so, Moth turned his attention to Sandy.

What will she do when she sees her savior burn in a funeral pyre? The phantom's flesh will cook in the center of Drac City and be hailed as a monumental achievement.

Moth was hoping Sandy would leave herself open in that moment, long enough at least for him or Kaal to gain access to the whereabouts of Robyn Winter. He had yet to contact Sephtis, knowing Nero was accurate in his assessment about Sephtis and his loyalty to himself. It would be better if the Dracs could take down Winter. He could taste triumph on his tongue. The phantom and Robyn Winter dismantled on the same day and all because of Sandy. She is the catalyst that will transfer his Drac's to supreme victory and raise his species to a new light in the galaxy. Although, the phantom was nothing more than a Drac myth, but Robyn Winter? His destruction would be hailed across the universe.

Everything Moth had been working towards was coming to fruition, as if time were catching up to his ambition. He had the formula. The phantom was dead, and the greys were destroying any possibility of the human insurgence and rebellion. The outliers would serve him well between his teeth.

When he entered Sandy's living quarter, the room was empty, although he could smell the faintest trace of human. Outside he could hear the rumble of drums, flutes behind those drums. His Dracs had gathered in the center of Drac City, a celebration in vampire culture, burning the bodies of their food in honor of the great god Odin, purveyor of Drac life. And what a gathering they would have tonight, so many victories to celebrate, so many lives lost to honor, Zeta being one of them.

Moth looked around the room. He wasn't the type of Drac to be left waiting. Patience was not a virtue a Drac of Moth's stature could afford, his patience receding when he heard the slightest of footsteps behind him. Moth turned in a snap to grab the throat of whoever was behind him, but Sandy was fast; she caught his hand before it gripped her throat.

"Now that's no way to treat a lady, is it?" Sandy's eyes gleamed, her grip like iron, a hiss in the back of her throat.

Moth's eyes wide, staring at the Drac in front of

him. She released his arm, and Moth felt a tinge of pain in his wrist. "Changing by the minute?" He rubbed his wrist with his free hand. "Seems it's by the second." He touched Sandy's cheek, staring into her pupils. "And yet you are still human." Moth snarled, looking her over. "Of all the clothes brought to you…" his fingers pinched her garment. "And you choose this one." Moved his head back and forth with a tisk of his tongue.

Sandy grinned at him, pulled the hood over her head. "It's best to hide the eyes," she said.

Moth saw how her eyes changed beneath the hood, as if the slightest darkness brought out a red glow.

"Wouldn't want anyone to think I was… human."

Moth looked over Sandy. Her transformation was almost complete. Once the eyes change, she will be completely Drac.

"Yes, I thought about that myself. Kaal will accompany us. He is the only Drac privy to your… change. Stay close to the two of us; we don't need any Drac's learning of your human origin. Stay close and keep your eyes from making direct contact with all Dracs."

"And who is Kaal?" she asked, with a subtle hiss behind her voice.

"A friend," said Moth. "A trusted companion to COR and myself."

Sandy paused, nodding. "Is it time then?" She looked to the outside. "Sounds like the festivities have begun."

"Indeed," said Moth. "And I can't wait for you to see what we have in store for tonight."

Sandy met Moth's grin with her own when she said, "And neither can I."

44

THE red-eyed human jumped off Perseus as if he were sitting on a spring, lurching towards Cam with his thick six foot five frame, his dark armor a blur as he raced at Cam who fired his rifle but the human was fast and sidestepped the blast that raged into the far wall. He slapped the rifle from Cam's arms, gripped his shirt, and pulled him off the floor with inhuman strength. That rounded head like a bowling ball with soft gentle features that would have never struck fear into any victim's heart if it weren't for the red eyes staring at Cam with a sinister stare.

"What the hell are you?" Cam hollered before the human tossed him across the pit.

Cameron was beside Perseus. "Get up!" he hollered when the red-eyed human turned his attention to him, took two ferocious stepped towards Cameron and stopped cold as Cameron jumped to his feet, the gun in his hand trembling.

Cam rolled onto his front, shaking his head, and stood tall, pulling his knife from the sheath on his hip.

"Don't move," Cameron said as the human

looked over him as if studying who or what he was.

Cam jumped on the human's back, driving his knife into his spine, but the knife hit hard bone only an inch beneath the skin. The human's frame was solid strong and with a quick jerk tossed Cam off as Cameron unloaded six shots into the human's torso, reeling the human back. No blood in the human, but Cameron could now see the steel frame beneath the flesh. And the humanoid's eyes, those red irises, widened before lurching towards Cameron. More shots zipped from the 9MM but the humanoid dodged them, his movements smooth and fast and gripped Cameron by the throat, raising the boy to eye level. Cameron shot again, point blank, into the humanoid's chest as the air was squeezed from his throat. The humanoid looked at his chest, then back to Cameron, wriggling and grunting in his grasp. He used his free hand to pull Cameron's top lip up exposing the sharpened teeth when Cam slammed with all his power into the humanoid's back with little effect–it was like ramming into a steel wall-but Cam wrapped his arms around the torso pushing with all his strength trying to get the humanoid to the ground when the humanoid dropped Cameron, took hold of Cam's shirt and hauled him overhead.

Before he had a moment to send Cam to his death, Perseus drove his fist through the human's back.

45

THE darkness needs the light to exist; otherwise, the energy would have no concept of itself; or purpose.

The four-year-old Phil had clambered into the corner; huddled close to the wall, his arms wrapped around his knees, his head against the wall, listening to the screams, the hollers, the painful inception of a horrible death. Every so often, a shadow would pass by his door, sometimes hurried, sometimes slow. But it was those screams, the terror filled blood-curdling screams that gripped his attention refusing to let go.

These were the screams of his mother, being sliced and diced like a deer under a hunter's knife. Alive!

"They live on fear," his mother had told him. "That is why the host is kept alive. Fear is energy; a vibration that leaves a stain long after the initial fear has subsided. Fear is a powerful energy that, when left in the wrong hands, will lead to hate and suffering. It is okay to be afraid, Phil. It is okay to feel fear. But fear can also turn into the best of all things, courage, strength, and hope. Do not allow this perversion of immoral fear to stifle your wits. Rise above my son. Rise and shine through fear."

Phil clamped his eyes shut, feeling his mother's gentle stroke through his hair, a memory that brought comfort in the wake of screams and carnage. He could hear her voice humming a sweet melody. Phil longed to be in her embrace. He longed to be off the island.

"We are stardust," she whispered. "To the stars, we return. Shine like a star, my baby. Shine like the sun."

Phil felt tears across his skin, a gentle trembling across his lips. His mother humming, her stroke gentle. He heard the final wail in the hall followed by a choked back gurgling stutter as the humming dissipated, and the gentle stroke no more.

Phil could feel how his mother's presence had gone from their cell, like tossing off a warm blanket to reveal a bitter icy sting.

Rise again one day. Shine like the sun.

Phil opened his eyes to an empty room, his breath caught in his throat, quiet stained the air, a horrid, terror-filled quiet. A space in between time. The light beneath the door flickered with shadow; the lock scraped against the door and the door opened.

"In you go." The voice was human, one of the humans who'd taken his mother. She tossed a girl into the room by her hair, young but older than Phil. She dropped to the floor on her knees. "You two will have your turn in the morning," she said.

The girl's eyes met Phil's, the roundest brown eyes he'd ever seen.

"Enjoy your last night," said the woman. "Tomorrow you enter the netherworld, and it is there that you will spend eternity."

Phil watched as the woman walked to the hall. The girl motionless on the floor.

"Our little pets forever."

The door slammed shut; the lock set in place. All Phil could see were the girl's eyes, and they brought him comfort. Comfort he knew would be his last.

46

THE red-eyed humanoid turned on a dime with a forearm that slammed into Perseus' head. The giant was tossed across the room, his body slammed against the floor. Perseus shook his head, lifted himself up as the humanoid slammed his boot into the giant's ribs that lifted Perseus off the ground. His fist barreled against the giant's face, but Perseus jumped up with an uppercut that sent the humanoid reeling back.

And Perseus rose to his feet as the humanoid slid into a fighting stance. The two opponents glared at each other, a growl in Perseus' throat before the rumble; the two running at the other.

Perseus used the momentum, gripped the humanoid by the shoulder and throat, and slammed him into the wall that bent under the humanoid's weight. A knee to the giant's groin, and then the humanoid tossed Perseus into the wall with the same effect; the wall had bent in from the giant's weight. Perseus' arms unhinged the humanoid's grip from his shoulders and he slammed his head against the humanoids, whose head flopped back then snapped forward. But Perseus retaliated with a punch across the jaw that dropped the humanoid. The humanoid's head bobbed up and Perseus kicked him beneath the jaw; the powerful thrust from Perseus decapitated the humanoid's head that rolled across the floor. The body, arms and legs flailing with a mechanical confusion before dropping still.

The head across the floor, blinking as Perseus roared his victory.

"You're bleeding," said Cameron, standing close to Perseus, and the giant wiped at his forehead, a painful wince like that of a child across the giant's face.

"It's okay," said Cameron as he looked at the head still blinking, its eyes still red, wires and steel jutted out from the neck. "What is it?"

Perseus growled and groaned at the head as Cameron looked around the room, finding Cam on the ground, his eyes closed, his body not moving.

47

MOTH escorted sandy across a platform to a door; behind the door was the center of Drac City. She could feel the drum's vibration, the flute music gliding across her ears. A Drac stood in front of the door, his back to them.

"Kaal," said Moth. "It is an honor for you to join us."

Sandy noticed how Kaal tensed when hearing Moth's voice.

"Come," said Moth. "Meet our new vampire."

When Kaal turned, Sandy felt Moth tense. There were fingernail marks across Kaal's chin and above his mouth.

Kaal offered his hand to Sandy, looking her over, devouring her robe with his eyes. His jaw hung open as his eyes went to Moth, his hand floated to his side.

"You gave her the ceremonial robe?" said Kaal.

Moth's eyes narrowed. Sandy could see he was studying Kaal's chin.

"What is wrong with the dress?" asked Sandy, but received no response from either vampire. "Seems fit for a celebration."

Moth retorted, "Sandy has chosen her garments for tonight. Clever choice, don't you agree?"

Kaal looked at Sandy with a snarl of disappointment and disgust. "You're playing with fire Moth."

Moth gripped Kaal's chin. "And you don't play nice at all, I see." Then pushed Kaal's head away.

Sandy felt the tremble of shame in Kaal's ether. She looked at him with a sympathetic heart as anger boiled in her chest.

Kaal refused to look at Moth and Sandy as if he were shrinking beneath Moth's heavy gaze.

"Come," said Moth to Sandy. "Perhaps it is best if Kaal should return to his station." And then to Kaal. "Should he wish to treat his fellow Drac as such." Moth craned his head, snarling at Kaal. "Perhaps he has lost enticement towards his species."

Kaal looked from Sandy to Moth, sadness in his eyes. He bowed to Moth. "I bow to your grace. I do not mean to speak out of turn." He turned to Sandy, took her hand in his. "My lady, I welcome you to our home." And he kissed her hand.

Sandy watched Moth as Kaal's head was bowed. Rage revealed in his eyes. A stare that brought a slight grin to Sandy's lips. She could feel the tension, understanding that everything had a weak link. Her weak link bore the name of Kaal.

"Come Kaal," said Moth. "Open the door."

Kaal turned to the door, pressed his hand to the scanner beside it.

"Let us show our new vampire…"

The door slid open to the sound of thunderous applause. Drumbeats raged louder and louder, cheers from Drac's across the city.

"A night she will never forget."

And Sandy stepped into Drac City, a vampire among vampires.

48

CAM'S eyes fluttered open, felt pain in his neck radiating to the top of his skull. Cameron standing over him, slapping his hands in front of Cam's eyes.

"Wake up," Cameron called. Slap!

Cam stretched his eyelids, his breathing shallow, the cave becoming clear.

Slap!

"Wake up Cam."

Cam raised his hands. "I'm up. I'm up," he said, his head weary as he sat up. Hand on his head, eyes closed. His head hurt something awful. He remembered falling to the ground, the back of his head wretched against the floor. And then darkness.

"You okay?" asked Cameron, sitting on his legs next to Cam.

"Yeah," he nodded, stretching his eyelids. "What happened?"

Cameron looked over his shoulder to see Perseus nursing his blood-soaked head. "Perseus has many talents," he said, then turned to Cam. "Including destroying artificial intelligence."

Cam snapped up. "A.I.?" He looked around. The head was on the ground, the body by the wall. Cam could see the wires and steel hanging from the decapitated body parts. "No wonder that thing was so strong."

"Moved like a cat too," said Cameron, standing and offering Cam his hand.

"Tell me about it." Cam took the hand. Cameron lifted him with ease, as if Cam weighed nothing more than a feather. "You're getting strong."

"Side effects," said Cameron as he smiled at Cam.

"I guess so." A gleam ran through Cameron's eyes, to Cam's surprise.

"What?" huffed Cameron.

Cam put his hand on Cameron's shoulder. "Nothing," he said. "Head's still weary." He looked at Perseus. "You okay?"

Perseus snarled and growled, applying pressure to his facial wounds.

"Gotcha." He looked at the head on the floor. Looked perfectly human, aside from the wires hanging from the neck.

"I think it's dead," said Cameron. Cam turned to him and Cameron shrugged. "At least as dead as a robot can be."

Cam thought, if we were all human, this robot would have killed us all. And quickly too. He used his foot to push the head. A raging blue electrical current circled the head with a spark. He crouched down, studying the robot head.

Looks like something out of a movie.

Cam craned his head to see inside the severed neck. Steel rods and wires. And the eyes had gone dark. No more red glaring eyes. He picked up the head by the dark hair that felt like strewn silk.

Cameron said, "Should we get Corporal Grimes and Annie?"

Cam stared at Cameron, thinking about Annison's special abilities. Looked back at the head, said, "Yes, we definitely should." Cam put the head on the ground and rose to his feet. "Maybe she can hot wire this thing. Find out what it knows."

49

HER name was Esta, and she had a gentle nature, like Phil's mother. She seemed wise and caring, compassionate to the young four-year-old Phil. They spent the night together in that cold cell, waiting for death to find them. Two children drawing strength from one another. Children born into bondage, born with the purpose of serving as food in a diabolical game of carnage.

They talked through the night. Talked about dreams and hope, and things they would do should some miracle come to claim their future and vanquish them from their perceived fate. Mother always said it was good to keep hope alive, no matter what circumstance surrounded them. No matter how dark the day had been. How much pain the day had brought.

For a few hours, they experienced what they'd never known was possible… normalcy, or at least what they thought felt like normal. This self-deception cut short when the lock slid open on the door. Phil jumped into Esta's embrace, trembling with a whining crack in his throat.

"There's the little one," said the human female as she traipsed into the cell.

Esta hollered, "Don't touch him," and Phil could hear how she slapped the woman's hand.

"Little witch," called the woman. "You should welcome death," she shouted, regarding them both. "The two of you, pathetic creatures you both are."

And she slapped Esta across her face with such brutal force, Esta's head smacked the wall beside her. Phil could see tears in Esta's eyes as the woman tore Phil from her arms.

"You, you little nothing, your time has come."

The woman's voice was dull and muted in Phil's ears; all he could see were Esta's tears, all he could hear were her cries. And he smiled, as if the young Phil knew bravery would bring her hope, even if that hope only lasted the length of his smile when a vampire squeezed the back of his neck.

"Leave him be," Esta cried as the vampire carried Phil into the hall.

"Not gonna give me any trouble, are you little one," said the vampire, but Phil's attention remained with Esta, watching as the door slammed shut, leaving Esta alone with that woman. Hearing the hard, pounding slaps and continuous berating, the woman was doling out to Esta.

Heard Esta's cries and wails, being beaten like no creature should ever receive. The vampire dropped

Phil to his feet, took hold of his hair, and snapped Phil's head back. Blinding light from the ceiling clamped his eyes shut.

Heard the Drac whisper, "Such young blood. Such skin and flesh."

Phil felt the wind from the Drac's quickly snapped jaw before he felt the tear in his neck. Pain surged in his veins, his neck tense as the vampire swallowed his blood. Phil's body limp in the vampire's arms.

Don't give in to fear, he heard his mother's voice. They feed on fear.

The vampire snapped his head back and Phil opened his eyes, and all he could see was light. Soft white light bathed his eyes as a single drop of blood, his blood, dripped from the vampire's lips to his own. The vampire's hands trembling, he licked the crimson drop off his lips. Tears in Phil's eyes, but he refused to wail. His feet rattled with a mind of their own.

"So sweet," said the vampire. "One last drink before you die. One last kiss before you meet the blade."

The vampire placed Phil on his feet when the door opened to his cell. The woman slammed the door shut behind her and rested against the door. "So rich that one is. I could tear her heart out and cut her throat with my fingernails." The woman looked at her hands, her nails long and sharp. "Claw her eyes out," she said, and the vampire laughed. The woman's eyes met Phil's gaze, as Esta's cries reached a fevered pitch. Phil looked at the door and the woman followed his gaze. "No need for concern, young one. I'll be sure to look after her."

The vampire gripped Phil's hair, pushed him further down the hall to the steel door that stood like a gateway to hell and damnation, pain and torture.

"Enter, child," said the vampire, Phil's blood still on his chin. "They wait for you."

And in that moment, beneath Esta's continuous cries and wails, Phil could hear the scraping sharpening of knives behind that door. The vampire slid the lock away with a metal scrape. The door grinded with a metallic boom and the door creaked open, slowly revealing a butcher block stained dark brown–dried blood from ages of torture–in the room's center. Behind the block stood a husky human male, wearing a black apron, his hair short and dark, wearing goggles that made his eyes seem large and overly round, his eyes fixed on the knife he was sharpening. Behind him, fire raged within a large furnace. The room was cold, icy cold, as if that fire provided little in its purpose to produce warmth. Phil scanned the room. There were bones scattered across the floor leading to a pile of bones and carnage to Phil's left, his mother's severed head a fresh trophy among the collection of skulls and bones. Her eyes were open wide, black to the core, revealing a terrified stare forever plastered across her visage. Phil couldn't take his eyes off those eyes as he craned his head to the left for his eyes to meet his mother's directly.

"This is the one…" the butcher muttered. His knife sharpening turned furious. "Who's given us so much trouble?" He swiped the knife across the sharpening rod with one final loud stroke. "Let's proceed."

The human female gripped Phil's arm. "Let's go little one." She dragged him to the butcher block. "Time's wasting." She picked him up and slammed him on the cold, thick wood. His skull rattled on the butcher block. She tied his feet and ankles as Phil gazed at the yellow light overhead.

Shine like the sun, my baby. Shine like the sun.

The ropes were tight; his hands and feet felt numb. There were tears in his eyes, running across his temples to his ears. Felt his lips quiver, staring into the light.

Smelled the hot, putrid breath from the butcher's mouth as he said, "Will you not wail? Nor scream in this moment? Your eyes are tearful but your body is calm, perhaps just a little slice first, just a cut over that thick thigh of yours. Perhaps then you will scream." The word scream was choked back, garbled, as the butcher began coughing. The cough turned into a cackling laugh. Phil could hear the human woman and the vampire do the same, laughing at the little boy about to meet his doom.

Stay in the light, his mother's voice. Shine like

the sun.

Even when the butcher's knife sliced across Phil's leg did he not stir nor wail. His leg tensed from the pain but he relaxed his limb immediately after, as if instinct told him to do so, his focus supremely attentive on the light. He could feel the butcher's eyes on him, could sense the man's hands were trembling.

"What is with you?" asked the vampire.

"His eyes," replied the butcher. "I can't take him looking like that."

"Carry on," said the vampire, "There isn't enough time for pause."

"What's with his eyes?" asked the female. "You've seen many eyes wrought with terror before. Why should his be any different?"

The butcher said, "His eyes don't hold fear..." Phil heard the butcher swallow. "They hold peace. As if he is not afraid of death."

The vampire snapped, "Poke them out if you must, but continue and do so quickly."

Phil heard rattling now, as if the butcher had secured a new weapon.

"There you go," said the vampire. "Take his eyes out," his voice crackling, sinister.

Phil felt heat close to his skin before the sharp poker was revealed, the tip burning red with heat.

"Here you are, little one," said the butcher. "Such pretty, pretty eyes you have." He raised his arm. "I'll keep them in a box. Something to remember you by."

He snapped the poker towards Phil's eye, but his hand was stayed. Phil could hear commotion, hollering, and explosions raging through the hall. Could hear the woman's screams and the vampire's rage quickly dissipate. As did the butcher, as the poker dropped to the ground with a steel echo.

Phil's eyes never left the light, a fixed focus point where he sensed hope.

Never left the light until Robyn Winter gathered him into his arms and set him down in their cave. His wounds already healed.

50

DALIOUS entered the lair where the phantom was held. The rank and damp air existing beneath Drac City, in the gallows, turned his vampire gut. He loathed having to come down to this level; another reason to despise the phantom even more.

Upon his entrance, the symbiotes cowered away from the phantom, scurrying into dark corners. Dalious stood over the phantom, searching him over. The blood was cold and stale, the face ashen in blotches where the dark grime of decomposition had yet to touch.

"So young," said Dalious. "How could you be the phantom?" His eyes went to the crypt against the wall, seven feet high the crypt stood, crafted into the shape of a Drac but with the eyes cut out, holes to reveal the eyes of whoever they placed inside.

The symbiotes' eyes gleamed yellow in the darkness. Dalious addressed them. "Is he truly dead?" he asked.

No reply but he could see the symbiotes outline, its shoulders bobbing as if with heavy breath.

Dalious shook his head. "I mean no harm to you.

Speak freely," his voice gruff and frustrated.

The symbiotes, three of them, emerged from the shadows, their black slimy tentacles wrapped around their human hosts. The closest symbiote flicked its tentacle that was wrapped around the human's throat, playing with the vocal cords, forcing the human to speak. "This phantom lives in the netherworld. His body may be in front of our eyes, but his spirit has passed," the voice like a hushed whisper. The tentacles then squeezed the host's skull, emitting a breath wrangled with fear from the host's mouth that the symbiote drew into its tentacle mouth formed by the tightly wrapped wet appendage wrapped around the host's skull.

Dalious regarded the symbiote, looked down to the phantom, lips curled in a snarl as the symbiotes inched closer to him.

"Lord Moth requires many to be prepared tonight," said the same symbiote.

Dalious turned from the symbiote for the briefest of moments before regarding him as he stood tall. "Place this thing in the crypt and go. I'll usher this phantom into Drac City myself." He looked at the phantom. "Watch its pathetic life burn."

Dalious stepped away from the phantom as the symbiotes gathered the body, loading the phantom into the crypt, his feet on a block to provide the correct height, and locked him in. The eyeholes revealed nothing but closed, dead phantom eyes.

"They look so peaceful when they're dead," said Dalious as the symbiotes exited the room. Dalious stood glaring at the phantom before he turned around. Outside the window he could see nothing but smog stained green and brown. His nose curled from the stench.

"Putrid vile vermin. This is a waste of my time."

51

"CAN you do that... thing you do?" asked Cam to Annison.

He had placed the decapitated A.I. head on a desk beside a row of monitors. Grimes, Cameron, and Perseus looking on as Annison stepped closer to the head, her eyes scanning, head moving slowly right to left, and those protrusions erected as her eyes shone and the A.I.'s eyes lit up, red and wide.

Annison whispered, "There are many circuits with this thing. So many pathways to explore."

Cam's eyes narrowed, staring at Annison. "Can you tap into... it? Find what it knows. Maybe we can find a way out of here and know what happened."

Annison said, "His program is for destruction. His orders were to destroy any human who came to the cave." She craned her head to the left. "His superiors expected others to arrive. Human others." She looked at Cam, gestured to Perseus and Cameron. "Not them."

Cam looked at Cameron and Perseus, then turned to the head, and those red eyes constricted.

"He doesn't like you, Mr. Cam. Nor I or the

corporal. And he definitely doesn't like Perseus." Those red eyes drifted towards Cameron. "But for Cameron," she placed her hand on Cameron's shoulder. "Confusion."

"Why?" asked Cam.

"He has orders to not hurt or allow any vampire to be hurt."

Cam shook his head. "But Cameron doesn't look like... those vampires. He looks human, except for..." He looked at Cameron. "The teeth."

"It's okay," said Cameron. "It is true."

Cam smiled at Cameron. "How is he able to decipher that information?"

Annison stared deep into the robot's eyes. She turned to Cameron, stepped to him, staring into his eyes, then surveyed his skin, his lips, pulled the lips back, revealing a row of small although sharp teeth. Her eyes drifted to Cameron's hands. The nails were sharp at the tip, although short. Annison lifted her chin, staring into Cameron's eyes.

"What?" Cameron huffed.

No response. Tears formed in her eyes.

Cam craned his head to see Annison's expression. "What is it?" he asked, and Annison slowly turned to him.

"Specific features of a vampire are how he knows. It's in how it sees, it can switch from infrared to x-ray vision. When the robot scanned Cameron, it saw his bone structure, his teeth, and fingernails which caused the confusion."

Annison smiled at Cameron.

Cam looked at Grimes, who shrugged, his eyes narrow gesturing to Annison and Cameron.

"Okay," said Cam. "What else can you discover?"

Annison turned to the head, its eyes stared at her and Cam could have sworn he saw a sliver of fear in those eyes.

"What questions do you have?" asked Annison.

"Tons of questions."

"Hmm, let me see," she said and stepped closer to the head.

Cam watched her with apt focus as Annison's eyes widened in unison with the robot's as the power in the cave reached a new life, buzzing with light and the computers turned on. Her focus on the head was strict and unwavering. The head's eyes went dark, then beamed back to life, wide and with a soft, almost appreciative stare. The robot's mouth opened and closed.

Annison said, "You can ask him now."

"What?" blurted Cam. "Ask him?"

Annison looked at Cam. "I reprogrammed him. He will follow your orders, Mr. Cam, to the letter. He will cause us nor anyone any harm. And he'll answer all your questions." She looked back at the head and smiled at him. "Thank you," she said to the robot, and the robot blinked as if acknowledging her order.

Annison stepped back, her hand went to her head, Cam could see how her eyes fluttered beneath her eyelids.

"You okay, Annie?" asked Grimes, who shared a perplexed stare with Cam.

Annison nodded. "I'm tired. It's hard for me to tap into the ether. Drains the energy."

Her face was flushed. She appeared sick and worn.

She turned to Cameron, took his hand in hers. "Can you take me to the ship?" she asked. "I need to rest."

"Yeah," Cameron said, then looked at Cam. "Is it okay?"

"Of course. Maybe both of you should get some sleep." He turned to Perseus. "Get yourself bandaged up, my man. Look after them too?"

Perseus nodded his agreement.

Cameron led Annison away.

"Just one question, Annie," said Cam. Annison and Cameron turned to him. "How is it you're able to do…" He gestured to the head, looked up at the lights. "All this?"

Annison said, her voice weak, "I can pick up wavelengths and frequencies, like Wi-Fi picks up signals." Her eyes gestured to the sky. "They're everywhere around us. Always have been. I was told…" her eyes found Cam's stare, "it's evolution."

Cam's eyes narrowed. "By who?"

Annison shook her head, her eyes narrowed as if

Cam should already know. "By Robyn Winter of course."

52

MOTH stepped up onto a platform to provide a speech to his people. Sandy stood beside Kaal, the two of them behind Moth a few steps below where he stood. They were standing in the center of Drac City outside the main capitol building, the center of Drac City a large platform a hundred yards in both directions and over four hundred yards across. Moth's platform looked over a bonfire in the center of Drac City–packed with Drac's wearing similar red robes as Sandy. The three rings surrounding the center, the three levels of Drac City, one higher than the other, stood high above. Sandy could see how each level of the three rings also contained platforms where vampires stood waiting for Moth's speech and the night's festivities. The area rang with thunderous applause as Moth began his address. The center platform filled with Dracs packed tightly together. A few Dracs wore the black leather Sandy had chosen against wearing.

She could see young playful Dracs in the arms of their mothers looking on.

Moth began his speech, his words muted to

Sandy's ears. She couldn't take her eyes off the Drac child.

"My fellow Drac," Moth began. "I welcome you to tonight's festivities. Our celebration of life, from our newborns who have taken their first breath toward Drac lore, to the food that has provided us nourishment, and the fallen who have served the needs of all Drac, on this night... we honor all in our union."

The baby Drac caught Sandy's stare. Its head lifted from its mother's shoulder for a larger look at her.

"My people, we have lost many Drac soldiers in a recent raid by the human rebellion. Our trusted Zeta, a COR member, has perished under human vengeance. We will not take lightly his demise."

Moth paused as if he wished for Zeta's death to sink into the collective Drac consciousness.

"Something wrong, my lady?" asked Kaal when Moth continued his speech.

Sandy took her eyes off the baby. "Nothing at all," she told Kaal, then looked back at Moth. Her eyes floated to the child for one brief second, aware Kaal continued to stare, seeking her thoughts. She could sense his eyes were on her, and Sandy remembered to lock in her thoughts, bury them inside a dark room where neither Kaal nor Moth can penetrate. She was sure this was their mission tonight, for what purpose exactly she was unaware, but she could sense it.

Moth continued, "And tonight, we have a very

special celebration. Our phantom, the human who has caused such strife for Drac, has been captured." A collective hush fell over Drac City. "In the battle the phantom has perished, his death brought by the hand... of Drac." Thunderous applause, cheers, and calls for a bonfire death raged across the city. Moth waved for his people to calm as the thunder subsided. "You will all be able to rest your eyes on this phantom of Drac lore tonight. You will all watch him burn to our hearts' delight. And let it be known whoever seeks to destroy our ways, whoever stretches a dark hand across our great people, will meet with the same fate. We Dracs will not be slain. We will not give in to fear and they will not drive us from our homes with wretched resolve towards hatred. This is our planet my fellow Drac and we will not be driven from its heart under the threat of insurgence nor invasion." The thunder and rumble continued, rising high with drumbeats and applause. "We are Drac and together we will fight for our home, our planet, and drive off all who seek to remove us from our rightfully provided gift from our ancestors. The Draconians have sworn allegiance to us and will stop at nothing to defend our ways. All Hail the Draconian ways." He raised his hands, his chin. "Under the great leadership of ArAn Queens we shall be victorious."

Sandy noticed how Kaal squelched a laugh. She turned to him, and he wiped the smile from his lips.

Moth continued. "Under our leadership, we will

usher in a new era in the galaxy. An era under Drac rule." His voice rose when he said, "An era where the ways of Drac are taught across the ninth passage and will forever be in our favor. My fellow Drac, we have suffered through chaos and have risen from the ashes of subjugation to meet this moment in our victory. Forever will Drac ways be enshrined. Forever will we be gods."

Raging thunder gripped Drac City. The platform shook and rumbled beneath the gathering, feet stomping, cheers and hollers.

"Go my fellow Dracs. Be free tonight. Gather and celebrate the blood of Drac."

Drum's beating, dancing and celebration ensued as Moth bowed to his fellow Drac. Sandy looked over the city; raging applause and cheers of union could be seen on every platform. Vampires laughed and played, cheered, and danced. Her eyes found Moth, looking over his city, his right hand close to his navel, palm up, as he turned and took the two steps down from his podium.

"Indelible speech lord Moth," said Kaal as he gestured to the city. "They will feast tonight like no other." He bowed to Moth.

Moth staring at Sandy when he said, "As will we." A smile across his lips. "Come, Sandy, to the Palladium." He raised his hand, gesturing across the platform to the second level of the first ring of Drac City. Sandy could see Dracs coming in and out of the room, or whatever it was on that level. "From there we will have a grand view of our festive nature."

"What time have you declared the ceremony will begin?" asked Kaal.

"Midnight," answered Moth. "Until then, let us show our guest the best of Drac society."

53

ROBYN gently placed Phil on the ground and Phil, now his older self, turned to meet him eye to eye.

"It was you in the light," said Phil. "It's always been you."

Robyn shook his head. "No Phil. I am merely a catalyst for all things to come. It is my purpose. I provide influence to the cause, nothing more. And only to those who seek it. You sought the light, and in turn, I arrived. The fate of human evolution comes down to you and all the children of our beautiful planet."

Phil blinked, looking over the cave, his people working diligently, bringing food and water, supplies, and conversing.

"Where are we?" Phil asked. "Everything here seems different from what I remember."

"It is as it was when you first arrived. You have travelled through time. The pills Silas gave you allowed for this recognition."

"The pills," Phil repeated when he saw Silas, a young Silas, walk across the cave. He waved to Robyn and Robyn bowed. "They can see us? They know who we are?"

"He knows who I am, for you he will ask during our meeting."

"What will you tell him?"

"Nothing he hasn't heard already."

Phil bent his head, thinking. "Will I remember this?" He turned to Robyn. "When I wake up. When the pill's effect has waned, will I remember?"

Robyn paused before answering. "No, you will not. But you will take it with you, deep inside the subconscious, where only death will uncover what is known. With the right frame of mind," he craned his head to the right as if burrowing his eyes into Phil. "You will take it with you, that knowledge, that knowing, everywhere you go. In this life, however, it takes time for the conscience mind to catch up to the subconscious." He looked at the sky. "So many contradictory reverberations exist across our planet. The electronic blanket brings these contradictions; it is its purpose." Turned back to Phil. "Creates confusion, so the mind resets to what it knows. So few can handle time travel with consistency. It... does something to the mind. Some things, Phil, are better left for discovery."

Phil stared into Robyn's eyes. "Is that what happened to you, Robyn? Is that why you continue to fight? Because you know the outcome? What will and what can be?"

"I took an oath a long time ago. It was a choice, salvation through death or to continue in the ether, adding influence to the cause."

"Is that why you can't take life?"

"Yes, my purpose is only for influence."

Phil looked around the cave. His eyes landed on Robyn. "Why would you choose this desecration over salvation of your soul?" To this question, Robyn smiled as a bright red glow emitted from his eyes. "Oh," said Phil. "It is because of love. Because you wish to see us free."

"I wish to provide a choice for the future. An alternative. The reptilians must not have this planet. It will lead to total chaos, the death of a love vibration. The galaxy will become bathed in hatred, and for that cause have I taken an oath to dissuade. For the love of all in Eridanus."

"What is to become of us?" asked Phil with a quivering lip.

"Our fate is molded by choice. Are you able to love those who seek your destruction? Will you show mercy to those who did not show the same to you? Fate is forged through either love or fear. Which will you choose?"

Beside him, Phil felt a tingle on his skin. The air was spiraling, pulling into itself when a vortex punched into the atmosphere, creating a wormhole no larger than Phil himself inside the cave. He looked inside, seeing a tunnel to another space, another solar system, planets and stars shined bright in the distance.

Robyn said, "They wait for you."

Phil's mouth moved, but no words found their way across his lips. He looked back at Robyn, confused. "Who?"

Robyn Winter smiled, his eyes beaming white with electrical currents. "Those who made you. And all of us. I've already taught you our history, our true history, as is the education of all who live with us." He put his hand on Phil's shoulder. "Allow them to show you what we can be. Allow them to show you what beauty the future can possess. Unlock what ails you and become what you are meant to become."

Phil turned towards the vortex, put his hand to it as electrical sparks leapt towards his fingertips, catching his hand. Phil dragged his arm back, as those electrical sparks followed him.

"Go," said Robyn. "The pills' effects will soon subside. Time is of the essence."

Phil turned to Robyn, but briefly, with a slight bow, before turning to the vortex. He stepped in.

The wormhole sparked with electrical currents, pink and purple light spiraling across the universe. He was weightless within its embrace, traveling at the speed of light and without notice he stepped onto a marble floor inside a grand palace, the walls made from crystal prisms.

And the superior beings who waited for him, seated high above, a hundred feet above the prism walls on a tier above the wall, all gathered to their feet and bowed.

54

THE voice coming from the A.I. head was not what Cam expected. It was gentle, and Cam found it difficult to comprehend the robot had tried to take his life not an hour prior.

Cam sat with his rifle across his lap. Grimes beside him, his wrapped shoulder revealed blood circles seeping through his bandage.

Grimes raised his hand. "Ask the first question, lieutenant."

Cam nodded, staring at the head. "What happened here?" he asked. "It looks like they were blindsided. How was the cave found?"

"A communique was received from VG211. The greys deployed starships with sonar capabilities. Once the camps were discovered, a cathager was deployed to gain access from within. When the cathager was in place, the plan was set into motion. Initial EMPs were provided from overhead, destruction of communications was paramount to not allow any distress signals to be retrieved by additional undisclosed camps. And the cathager was set into motion, allowing underground reinforcements to enter without notice. Total obliteration was the order. None were allowed to survive. A cathager was to remain inside each compound with orders to eradicate any and all possible resurgence with one exception."

The A.I. paused as if waiting for another question.

"What's the exception?"

"Leave one alive for questioning by the greys. They were looking for someone specific."

"Who?" blurted Cam.

"Robyn Winter," said the head.

"Have they found him?"

"I have not received communication that he has been detained."

"Why is Robyn so important?"

"He poses a conundrum to the reptilians, the Draconians."

"How so?"

"Because he is dead, contradicting a report received in VG211 providing the contrary."

Cam eyed Grimes as the AI spoke.

Grimes said, "Is he a ghost or something?"

"No," said the AI. "He is something more."

"More?" said Cam. "Like what? An alien?"

"Transcendence," said the A.I. "Bound by cosmic law but free to walk in the realm of the in between, the sixth dimension. However, he is undoubtedly... human."

Cam and Grimes shared perplexed stares. Grimes said, "What is a cathager?"

The A.I. head answered, "Me, 1 am a cathager."

Cam was nodding, looked to Grimes. "That's how they got in. Everyone thought they were saving a human being…" he looked to the head. "Than you unleashed holy hell."

"That was my order, yes."

Grimes said, "They didn't notice something strange with your eyes? I mean, they're red. How did they not notice?"

The head closed its eyes, and when he opened them, his eyes were blue.

"Neat trick," said Grimes.

"How many more are there like you?" asked Cam.

"Our grey creators specifically designed us. Each of us unique in our mission. Cathagers have played a pivotal role in human history over the last two hundred years, preparing for the end of this age and the disintegration of the electronic blanket wrapped around Earth. All of us born with a single purpose, however directed that purpose might be. We are all the same in this regard. And to answer your question, there are one thousand of us on record."

Cam shook his head. "Why not just march all one thousand cathagers across the globe, destroy all of us, and take over? Why all the games?"

"Because it is the people of this planet, the

humans, who must make that choice. Should we dismantle all human life without consent from the home planet's offspring, we will have broken galactic law. The rest of Eridanus will not allow such a decimation of life and the Arcturians will reset what we've done. The only way to take the planet is to have it offered to us by the humans."

Cam and Grimes looked at each other, said together, "Galactic Law."

Cam asked, "What is Eridanus?"

"The proper name for the galaxy you know of as the milky way."

Cam shook his head. "Are there any aliens out there who are on our side?"

"Yes," said A.I. "Earth has been the focal point for many over millenniums, but the Draconians have kept it under their rule for over four thousand years. Many have attempted to enter in that time; however, the Draconians are masters of war. They have kept all invading star systems from entering your atmosphere and the electronic blanket keeps the humans subjugated, confused. It also does not allow for communications to be received from outside planets. The signals become lost or scrambled. There have been few who have made it through the Draconian armada, but all have failed in their endeavor. The Draconian hold is firm on this planet, its manipulation deeply embedded in the human psyche. Any deviation from that programming causes catastrophic stress on the human mind. That is why it is so difficult to release all humans at once. Most cannot confront the truth."

Grimes said, "But if this blanket is around the earth and the armada outside our planet, then how are all these aliens here right now?"

"They were invited."

Cam's eyes widened. "By who?"

"Your superiors. All alien species currently on the planet were allowed to enter the commons as guests to the human elite."

"Because they know already?" said Cam. He looked at Grimes. "Sold us out."

"Yes," said A.I. "They have bargained for power. They wish to be seen as gods to their human slaves. They wish to write their own history after the next coming cataclysm."

"And we're the bargain."

"Correct. Your planet is a young planet. Its riches in ore, metals, and gold can be mined for a million years. It offers those who control it with power across the ninth passage of Eridanus and therefore power over the galaxy."

Cam shook his head. His mind had gone blank with questions, having heard enough. He looked at Grimes. "What do we do now, Corporal?"

"I say we try to get back to Robyn Winter. Even if Cameron is who he is, there's nothing out here for us, plus we've got to warn him somehow. We need to get the ship operational."

Cam looked at A.I. "I do believe you're right, Corporal."

Grimes looked at A.I. "Are you able to help repair the cruiser?"

"I have detailed files on its construction."

"Perfect," said Grimes, sitting up.

"But if you reconnect me, I'll be able to help more efficiently."

"We wouldn't know how to do that," said Grimes.

"Understood," said A.I. "I can guide you through the process."

****

Cameron pulled a blanket across Annison. Her skin had gone red and blotchy, flushed and pale. And the look in her eyes was one of fear, unsettled fear. She couldn't take her eyes off of him.

"What is it?" asked Cameron. "Why do you look at me like that?"

She took his hand in hers. "I'm just scared of what I've seen." She turned from him. "All the death that exists here. It overwhelms me. Shakes me to my core."

He put his hand on her forehead, retracting quickly. His fingers trembling, his vampire fingers.

"Don't deny who you are, Cameron. Self-deception leads to suffering."

He looked down before locking eyes with her. "It's not who I am," he said. "This was… done to me against my will."

"But it is who you've become." She reached her hand to his cheek. "Either good or bad will be up to you."

Cameron paused before nodding. He craned his head, staring. "Rest now," he said. "Gather your strength."

Annison pursed her lips. "You should do the same. You grow paler by the minute."

He couldn't deny the pain in his stomach or how his blood was on fire. "In time," he said. "I'll rest soon. You first." He smiled while cocking his brow. "Go ahead. Perseus and I will watch over you."

Annison forced a smile, then rolled over, her eyes closed. Cameron pulled the blanket over her shoulder before walking out of the ship into the night sky and the burning essence of carnage. He looked at Perseus, standing on guard as he growled and gestured to the ship.

"She's sleeping," said Cameron, looking back at the ship. He turned to Perseus. "Keep a watch over her. Perseus," he said and stepped closer. Perseus met his eyes. "No matter what, I want you to always keep her safe." He was nodding. "Understood?" He could see how Perseus constricted, his eyes narrow, as if expecting what Cameron would say next. "Even if it's from me."

He turned back to the ship, wondering what had happened to Annison. Why she looked at him the way she did? What had she seen to cause her to carry fear in her eyes?

55

THE Palladium, as Moth called it, was a sophisticated high society social gathering place. The layout was much like a human club. Semicircle couches were placed around tables scattered throughout. Dracs sat and talked, cups of blood in their hands as human waiters and waitresses attended the tables. Each servant had a tube in their right arm and a serving tray with small empty goblets in the left hand.

When Sandy entered behind Moth, a round of applause erupted through the Palladium, which Moth graciously accepted with a bow before leading Sandy and Kaal to a table where three vampires sat waiting for them. Moth introduced Sandy as a Drac from the orient and offered Sandy a seat beside Kaal before excusing himself. The three Dracs, one female and two males, sat opposite Sandy and Kaal, each sipping on a crystal goblet filled with blood. Moth introduced them as Caila, Xeno, and Hensy. It was Xeno, a large and gruff vampire who spoke first.

"Do all the elite in the orient continue to wear ancient relics?" His remark brought laughter from his cohorts.

Kaal responded, "You'll have to forgive Xeno. He is unaware that some of us continue to cherish the old ways."

Sandy forced a smile, as if she understood what they were referring to. She looked for Moth through the crowded Palladium. Found him across the room talking with another Drac.

Xeno said with a laugh in his throat. "Next, they'll be consorting with the underlings. Those wretched fiends of myths long gone. As do you Kaal."

Sandy felt Kaal tense.

Xeno continued. "No wonder you give audience to this sentimental fool. What does Moth think of your pursuits?"

"I'd be careful with that foul tongue of yours, Xeno," said Kaal. "You might have it removed to prevent future catastrophe."

Xeno chuckled beneath his breath. He eyed Sandy, snarled, and turned away when one of the human waitresses approached. A fresh young blonde, no older than sixteen.

"May I offer convenience?" she said.

"Convenience?" scoffed Hensy. "Young lady, I'd rather drink from the fountain than be fed through a tube." He faked moving off the chair, and the girl jumped back.

"Not in here," said Kaal. "Go into the fields if you wish to be a raving loon."

"Always so serious Kaal," said Hensy. "Lighten up, I only mean to make the blood more tasteful… for our guest, of course."

Sandy received a telepathic message from Kaal. *Fear makes the blood taste better.* He ordered two goblets from the girl. She placed the glasses on the table, placed the tube inside the cup, and used a pump secured beneath her cloak to fill each goblet. Kaal took the first goblet and offered it to Sandy.

The scent was sweet and mouthwatering, effervescent. Her lips trembled; her body shuddered, looking at the blood.

"Go ahead," said Caila. "Before it turns cold."

Sandy paused, staring at the goblet.

"Don't tell us you're one of those who feed on synthetics?" said Hensy, shaking his head and clucking his tongue. "Such a pity."

Caila said, "Look at the dress, typical of low society. We should show her the fields. Perhaps this will enlighten our guest to our ways here in Drac City." She sat up. "Or does this go against your very nature?"

"What do you mean?" asked Sandy.

To this, Caila narrowed her eyes, confused. "Do you not know what garment you wear? Have you not been shown the deception behind that very robe?" She craned her head, glaring at Sandy. "That myth was disproven years ago. It's a pity you wear it now. Only fools still believe."

Perhaps, thought Sandy, Kaal had grown weary

of their banter, or perhaps he thought they would ask questions about Sandy he didn't want answered. Kaal rose to his feet. "Moth will hear of your disrespect." He turned to Sandy. "Come, my lady, let me show you a less obtrusive view of our city."

The vampires laughed. "Oh, come on Kaal. We're just having fun with our guest."

Kaal ignored them, offering Sandy his hand.

Sandy placed her goblet on the table before accepting Kaal's hand. Her eyes on the blood before she stood and Kaal guided her towards the front entrance, the one leading to the platform overseeing the center of Drac City.

"I apologize for their biting tongues," said Kaal. "We are usually more sophisticated than they prove." He led her outside through the many Dracs coming in and out of the Palladium. The bonfire raged beneath them in the center of Drac City, where a gathering of vampires danced and played flutes and drums around the bonfire. All wearing red.

"What is the difference?" asked Sandy. "Why do some wear red and others black?"

Kaal sighed before saying, "It is a caste system we live by. The Dracs who wear red do so because they consider themselves pure at heart. They wait for the phoenix to guide them back home."

"Phoenix?"

"Yes, the phoenix is the first Drac born of the feather, the gift of passion. They believe the phoenix will rise again to deliver them from the system."

Sandy thought of the statue, thought of her own people. "Not that far from ourselves," she said, and turned to Kaal. "Humans I mean."

"Mythos, lore and lies," retorted Kaal. "It's a fool's thought. No matter what evidence you show them to the contrary, they continue with their ways." He looked at Sandy. "The old ways must die if we are to transcend as a species. Master Moth has devoted his life to our survival. Now that is a Drac who should be hailed, not some gathering lie to the masses."

Sandy watched the vampires, felt her veins constrict, her blood on fire.

"They were right about one thing though, you need to feed," said Kaal. "Will you not take from the vein?"

She casually shook her head, and Kaal closed his eyes, disappointed.

"I'll retrieve some synthetic for you. After all, we can't allow you to dry up and perish."

Not yet anyway.

She caught his thought, eyeing Kaal, who seemed to cower beneath her gaze. He swallowed hard before saying with a bow, "I shall return."

She watched him return to the Palladium, disappearing into the throng of vampires. Sandy turned her gaze to the bonfire. To the baby Drac still staring, eyes locked on Sandy.

56

"I MUST admit," said A.I., "the two of you are more useful than I first calculated."

Grimes connected the last wire from the head to the neck when the A.I.'s arms moved as if the robot was flexing a new body. Grimes paused before twisting the head into place. He stepped back, more on guard than to give the robot its freedom to flex. Cam stood watching the robot, those red eyes looking over its arms and hands.

"Good work," said A.I.

Cam stepped to him, looking him over. "Remarkable how human you actually look, except the eyes, of course."

A.I. stepped back, closed his eyes and opened them, sparkling ocean blue. "Does this more accurately fit your perception of human eyes?"

Cam clucked his tongue and winked. "Perfect, actually." He turned to Grimes. "Corporal?"

Grimes paused before answering, staring at A.I.. He looked at Cam. "Yeah, that'll do. Looks like we got our own robot to add to our band of misfits."

"I prefer cybernetic organism."

"Yeah, that works for us," said Cam, continuing to take in his new toy.

"Cat," said Grimes. Cam turned to him and Grimes shrugged. "Well, we can't be referring to him as A.I. or robot. He's a cathager, or whatever he said before. I figure Cat for short."

"Makes sense," said Cam as he turned to his robot. "What do you think?"

"I'll respond to whatever word you choose for my reference."

Cam rolled his tongue inside his mouth. "Cat it is." He turned to Grimes. "Moves like a cat too, so it'll do."

"Let's get him to the cruiser. Hopefully, he can figure out what's wrong with it," said Grimes.

"Agreed." Cam gestured to the outside. "You ready?"

"Yes," said Cat.

"Follow along then. I've got a few more questions as we walk."

"Just a few," said Grimes. "More like a thousand."

"First question is, are you still receiving communication from the greys who sent you here? If not, are you able to tap into a computer mainframe or anything on their end?"

"Yes," said Cat, "I still have access to emergency response and I'm receiving real time intel as provided by our grey creators."

"Perfect," said Cam. "Let us know when new information is received."

"Confirmed," said Cat. "And the other question?"

They continued to walk, the air thinning the further they stepped to the outside. "Well, we encountered some... creature in the desert. Looked like a short vampire, but he had wings."

"Question, Mr. Cam?"

Cam shook his head. "Just Cam is fine. My question is, what is he?"

Cat craned his head as if thinking. He halted, looking around when a beam of light emitted from his eyeball to the wall. "Is this the creature you are speaking of?" On the wall was a replica of Hadock.

"Yes," said Cam. "That... that is definitely him. Called himself Hadock."

"Scavengers."

"Come again," said Grimes.

"Reptilian underlings," said Cat. "From the planet Floston in the twelfth sector of Eridanus. Not a very evolved species, but they do show promise. They're treated as pets for the Draconians, their purveyors. We refer to their species as the Chordata. I believe the human word would be rat. After our human counterparts signed the treaty, the Chordata were tasked to surveil the outliers because of their flying capabilities."

"Outliers?" asked Cam.

"Human's not in the internment camps. There were a significant number of humans who remained in their home during the war. They were selected for termination prior to the treaty being signed, an order that received outstanding success. The Chordata were ordered to provide intel on humans that may have survived. COR wishes for no human to not be in internment."

"Why don't you just ask him what you want to know?" said Grimes, eliciting a stern look from Cam. Grimes shrugged. "I'm waiting myself."

"What is it you wish to know?"

Cam looked at Cat, whose photo beam dissipated before he turned to Cam. "This Hadock Chordata creature." Cam shook his head. "Whatever he is. He knew my name. Not the name of on my uniform, my real name." Cat scanned Cam's nametag. "My real last name is Fisk. Cameron Fisk. Do you have any intel on why he knew my name?"

Cam could see how Cat's eyes were scanning his facial features, his body, his clothes as Cat's eyes glittered and glowed. Cat completed his scan.

"I do not," he said. "There are no files with that name. But that does not mean there is no file. It may be that I was not provided with it for the sake of my mission. There's none in the mainframe computer either."

"Maybe Hadock knew something the greys

don't?" said Grimes.

"Or the file has not yet been created, not in this time period."

Cam's eyes narrowed. "What do you mean?"

"The Chordata species is in its infancy, but they are masters at scavenging and their flight capabilities make them unique in their purpose."

"I'm not getting it," said Cam.

Cat continued, "They were brought through the time portal for their purpose here on earth in this time."

Grimes stepped closer. "Time portal?"

"Correct," said Cat. "From what my files show, the time portal is how the Draconians have manipulated the planet. But there is no other mention of the time portal in my files other than in this regard, as if someone purposefully deleted the information."

"Naturally," said Cam. He turned to Grimes. "A shimmer in the record."

Grimes' eyes narrowed. "What?"

"In the cave, Robyn Winter's cave." He turned back to Cat. "They said there was a shimmer in the record. Maybe that's why this is happening. Someone's messing with time. Using it to their advantage."

"That would make sense," said Grimes. He stepped closer. "So Cam here is set to take on the future? No wonder Hadock tried to kill you."

"Time is unfolding before us," said Cat. "But the future is delicate, like a butterfly. A change in one place causes catastrophe in another. Many species have already perished as a result."

Cam paused, thinking before he said, "Draconians?"

"What about them?" asked Cat.

"Maybe we should get to the cruiser, lieutenant," said Grimes. "At this point I can say with utmost certainty that time is of the essence."

Cat turned from Grimes to Cam. "I can provide all information on them as we explore your cruiser concerns."

Cam nodded. "Sounds like a plan." He gestured outside. "After you."

57

SANDY watched as the red-robed Dracs danced in circles around the bonfire, a useful distraction to squelch her tenacious timidity. Her hands shook, her blood pumped furiously as if confused with what direction to lead. Her head was weary; she needed to feed. She sensed how her telepathic ability was dwindling. Where had the ferocity gone? she wondered. When she was in her room, she had strength and tenacity. Now her stomach hurt something awful, as if her innards had been gutted and emptied.

Where is Kaal? Where is Moth?

She searched through the Palladium, noticing how eyes were on her. Drac eyes staring, getting a closer glimpse at the Drac in the red robe sharing space with the elites. She could sense their anger; it writhed with a vibration she felt in her shuddering bones.

Disgraceful!

Another Drac fool.

Why is she here?

A guest of our beloved Moth.

Tolerate the insolent witch? I think not.

Her head was weary, vision spiraling across Drac City, when Kaal grabbed her elbow.

"Are you okay, my lady?" He was holding a goblet filled to the brim with red liquid.

Sandy stretched her arm from his grasp. "I am fine," she said.

Kaal offered the cup. "It is quite apparent you need to feed," he said. "Our senses turn deranged when we don't. Like a starving human turns ravenous. Primal instincts kick in, survival of the fittest you could say. Here," he forced the cup towards her hand. "This is synthetic. No human was hurt in the making of this blood." He looked into the cup, a ghastly grimace across his lips. "Putrid if you ask me, but it'll do the trick."

Sandy paused, looking at the cup. She licked her lips, her eyes widened as her beating heart raged inside her chest.

"Quickly," Kaal said. "Seems we have an audience to appease." His eyes darted left and right, gesturing to the many eyes Sandy could feel were watching. "We wouldn't want to give them pause and discover your true nature."

Sandy reached for the cup, looked at Kaal and the smug smile across his lips. She tipped the cup to her lips when the most awful bitter taste curled her lips. "That's putrid," she said, at first. The effect waned quickly as she felt her veins open, blood flooding to her heart. She drank again, gulping the synthetic fluid.

"Good," said Kaal. "You'll be feeling better momentarily."

She felt warmth across her skin; her weary head gave way to focus. She sensed how her organs calmed, where before they were beating furiously now they felt strong with optimal functioning.

"Feeling better already," she said.

Kaal smiled and raised his chin. "Should try the vein. Now that is an extraordinary experience."

Sandy's eyes narrowed as Kaal turned from her gaze. "Or not," he said, leaning against the bannister.

"Where has Moth gone?" she asked. "Or does he normally leave his guests unattended?"

"He has many duties to tend to my lady." He turned to Sandy. "Much more important circumstances than a... human." He turned from her stare. "A member of COR of Moth's stature has many responsibilities you would find unnatural."

"Like decimating an entire species from their home?"

"Watch your tongue," snapped Kaal. His eyes looking over his vampires. "They can hear you, and I assure you they are all watching and listening. We don't have to be so accommodating to your needs either." He gestured to the goblet. "As far as I'm concerned, Moth should send you out on your own. Let's see how long your friends last when your veins cry out for their blood."

Sandy's eyes narrowed.

"Good to see the two of you getting along," said Moth, standing in the Palladium's entrance. He saw the goblet. "Oh," he craned his head to look at Sandy. "Feeling better I see."

Kaal answered, "It's synthetic. Turns my veins aflame."

Moth gestured to Sandy. "You'll have to forgive Kaal, his manners are not very diplomatic."

"Neither are his thoughts," said Sandy.

"Vicious fiend, stay out of my head," Kaal snapped as he rushed by Sandy into the Palladium.

"Temperamental," said Sandy.

"Forgive him," said Moth. "He's never been good at diplomacy. In his defense, however, you are a unique conundrum to accept."

Moth's eyes gazed into Sandy. He stepped forward, took hold of the rail. Sandy staring, attempting to seek his thoughts, but she found nothing but darkness, as if her psyche slammed into a black wall. The drumbeats ceased, the flute music faded, and the dancing Dracs subsided.

"Perfect," said Moth. He turned to Sandy. "The festivities will begin soon."

And Sandy thought, This won't be easy.

58

SANOS used the passcode provided by Kaal to access
the computer mainframe. One of his two requests, the
passcode will allow him to find the formula without
Kaal thinking anything of it. Let Kaal come to any
conclusions he wished. Didn't matter, not to Sanos in
the least. Not for what he had planned for his
superiors. It was time for Dracs to rise above COR's
leadership.

His requests were simple, and Kaal too weak to
give pause. The password and access to COR's
weaponry arsenal were his requests. His battle with
Zeta opened Sanos' eyes to many discoveries, one
being the sound frequency defense Zeta had used
against him. His ears continued to ring from the power
the frequency unleashed upon his equilibrium. Sanos'
rank in the Drac Military allowed him access to the
most state-of-the-art weaponry, but the fact that COR
had developed a weapon specifically manufactured to
dismantle Dracs–and hence squelch any possible Drac
insurgence or rebellion–and was provided only and
specifically for use by COR members led Sanos to one

conclusion: he wanted the weapon for himself.

Level the playing field, observe the enemy, know their minds, and then unleash holy hell. Everyone wanted something; there is only the simple fact of tracking it down and using it against those who required it. Moth should be no exception to this rule. Sanos just needed to find it. Humans were simple in this regard, but a member of COR? The members of COR wanted nothing more than power, control, and recognition by their Draconian ancestors. And Moth's resolve was unequalled in Drac history. It was Moth who brought his vampires from their home planet, promising riches and security, and an escape from persecution and poverty–the result of Draconian rule over Dracs. And it was Moth who established COR among the Dracs, the Commission of Raa, and what a joke that was, established under strict security and secrecy long before the Dracs had ever arrived. From what Sanos had garnered across his military career, COR had been created by the greys when Ra ruled over the earth, although Ra's reign had come to an abrupt end by the very greys he'd conspired with to take over the planet. The greys kept the name to maintain secrecy over the coup they started.

The greys governed through COR.

The Dracs did the same.

And all new COR members were sent into isolation for a year. Now what could they possibly need to isolate for a year for? thought Sanos, gnashing his fangs, his jaw tight as he gazed over the computer monitor. He'd been searching through folders, reading files on COR members. There have always been nine members of COR, and when one member perished, another was chosen to take their place. Over time, there have been eighteen members of COR, including the nine who currently held their seats. And always Moth was front and center, moving the pieces across the board to garner his ultimate power; Moth being the only COR member who maintained his seat since the inception. And, an interesting fact to Sanos, a pattern emerged. All deceased COR members had perished mysteriously. No other records were provided. No investigation had been started. Hand picked members replaced the vacancies. Hand picked by Moth, Sanos thought.

End the human rebellion and I will hand you a seat at the COR table. Moth's promise kept slithering into Sanos' thoughts.

So you can have all the power? I think not, lord Moth!

Outside in Drac City, the drumbeats wavered, the flute music dissipated. Sanos looked through the window.

The festivities will begin soon.

Sanos shook off his anger with a headshake and a growl. Slapped his head.

(Keep your wits Sanos. All in time.)

He stood up and smashed the computer's hard

drive. There would be no formula communique to the humans. None, and whatever suspicions Moth may have as to who had taken the formula will be for naught; Sanos would make sure Moth's reign would end. The formula was on a thumb drive secured in Sanos' pocket.

Whoever wanted it would have to bow to him.

This was his time.

It was the time for Sanos.

59

SUPERIOR beings stood high above Phil. Guards similar to ancient Egyptian pharaohs stood at attention, dressed in gold and carrying heavy spears. The horde circled around the room on the first floor, their stance beneath their superiors. Directly center and above him, three queens wore royal headdresses, their faces revealed with a reflection bestowed to evolved raptors. They snarled while standing, bowing to Phil, looking down at him.

On Phil's right, the three kings of Sirius, AnAn, EnLil, and Ea, clad in royal armor covered over with dark cloaks, snarled their wolf like features. King AnAn raised a golden goblet, and, while staring at Phil, bowed. And on Phil's left, three bird-like creatures all in white robes, scattered feathers across their heads and skin, their noses, beaks, likened to swans, smiled their approval. Phil eyed all three groups and bowed his allegiance, his gratitude towards them.

The guards stomped their spears before the guards directly in front of Phil parted ways. A door behind them opened slowly. Inside the door stood a female, nine feet tall, with wolf features, dressed in royal violet robes stitched with red symbols. Nin-Hur-Sag, princess and daughter of King AnAn, sister to Ea and EnLil, approached the waiting Phil.

She spoke in a language Phil had yet to learn, her voice garbled as if she were speaking underwater. Nonetheless, as the words graced his ears and burrowed into his mind, he understood what she said. "The nest must be sacred. The armada cannot fly. The nest must be sacred. The armada cannot fly."

His eyes narrowed, head cocked to the right. She must have registered the confusion across Phil's face, because Phil could see how her features changed to sympathy.

"The bird flies the coop through which all will be revealed. The bird flies the coop through which all will be revealed. Proceed as such," she said, reiterating the same, "Proceed as such."

Phil, not knowing what to do, nodded. "Okay," he said. Surprising himself, he added, "Message has been received."

Nin's lips curled into a smile. Her eyes, dark and round, looked at Phil with that same sympathy and a glint of pride. Phil looked around the room, noticing his own reaction to the scene; it was familiar, and in the presence of the superiors comfort clung to him like he'd come home. Nin stepped closer, her head leaning left than right, staring, devouring him with her eyes.

"You have grown into a great warrior… but to

be a great leader, you must learn to let go. In the moment of adversity, greatness holds no stance, it is seeing beyond the self that separates outstanding leaders from the fold."

The guards stomped their spears. Nin gestured to Phil's right as the door there opened and the guards parted ways. Beyond the door was a garden, an immaculate garden with trees and foliage Phil had never seen, filled with rainbow colors. The garden was welcoming, calling Phil to it. It seemed to go on forever, into the void of the cosmos surrounding the garden, high above as if the garden existed within the universe. Phil turned to Nin.

"Come," she said, her eyes staring at Phil. "I will guide you." She gestured for him to step towards the garden with her. Phil followed, the garden growing in his vision with every step.

He passed the guards, craning his head to take in all of their visage. So tall and towering over him they all were. He locked eyes with King AnAn before he stepped into the garden. Phil could have sworn he saw a single tear fall from the king's eye. He passed the overhang, turned his stare to the garden and Nin, standing with her back to Phil. The air turned cool although warm when he entered with an electricity he could not only feel but see as electric sparks raged across the garden, inside trees and foliage, in the surrounding air, and in the water. A slight wind rustled foliage with a slight hand. Water from a spring that weaved through the garden like a snake flowed with reckless abandon. In the center of the garden, a single tree of immaculate beauty exhaled precious clean oxygen and Phil could see the roots beneath, strong and unwavering, reach down into a translucent cosmos as if those roots took their hold in the universe. It was from this tree that Nin removed a small piece of bark. Phil turned around. The door to the Kingdom had closed and in its place vines and trees scattered for miles as if no door had ever been there.

He turned back to Nin, standing close to him, the bark in her hand. "What is this place?" asked Phil.

The wind captured her robe, waving the cloak behind Nin as dark clouds erupted overhead with thunder and pumps of lightning. "Genesys," she said when she stepped closer.

Phil, looking all around, felt his chest constrict. Hot pain stabbed his heart with a fierce pounding. He turned his head down, hand on his chest, letting the moment pass. Nin looked at him with sympathetic eyes. Phil looked at the bark, looked at Nin as the pain subsided. Looked around him, there was a sensation of familiarity; there was peace here. He could sense it in his bones, the sense of freedom. Desperation then filled his heart. Longing and fear gripped his throat.

I don't want to go, he thought. But I know I have to.

Phil pursed his lips, said, "Will we win?" he asked, his brow furrowed as he felt his heart sink.

Nin's focus was apt. Phil could sense how her stare burrowed into his mind, his heart. She said, "Sometimes, there is only so much one life can do." She bent her head as if to capture Phil's eyes, to remain still, to focus on her words, her lips and thoughts. "The fighting must stop. The carnage. The deception." A small smile graced her lips. "How it ends is up to you. We are stardust, my love. We are forever. Always do we return. The person who holds a mastery of time holds the future. And the person who..."

"Masters the rose master's time," Phil concluded. He'd heard the statement before, from Robyn Winter.

Phil looked from the bark to Nin's eyes. Looked back to where the door had been, then back to Nin. "With the door closed, how do we get back?"

She smiled at Phil as if she were entertaining the notion to not satisfy him with a response. "The pills you took have brought you here," she said, her eyes referencing the garden. She offered Phil the bark. "This will aid you in your return."

Phil stared at the bark in Nin's hands. Her fingers were wolf like; the bark between those paws.

"Once you go through, you will be shown a door. This door lives inside the portal, the dimension in between dimensions where the fold of space and time exists. This is the door only those pure in mind and heart can enter. Only human, as it has been for thousands of years. When you arrive, you will know which door to go through. It will bring you home."

Phil, looking around, looking at the bark, staring at Nin, his eyes blinking. "Have I been here before?" he asked as questions started arriving like missing pieces in a puzzle long gone, now found.

"Yes," she said. "Although you were very young."

Phil tried to remember, tried to think, but his thoughts kept arriving at a wall he couldn't penetrate.

"In the old days, before the blanket, individual travel to your planet had taken no time. It was simply a step through a door in between breaths." She touched Phil's forehead. "Travel through the mind exists between breaths. Mastery of breath when the pineal gland is unaltered has always been possible. Before the blanket. Before the systemic depletion of the human mind began. But the door has a spell on it, only earthly humans can enter."

Phil, mouth agape, looked Nin in the eyes.

"There are places in the universe that hold a magical energy. It is in these places where such travel is possible."

Phil shook his head. "My dear Nin, may I ask, how is it possible such energy exists?"

She bent her head, her eyes seeing through him. "Internal combustion, like a star that folds into itself, imploding to create a magical portal, puncturing a hole in the universe."

Thunder cracked across the sky, slicing bolts of

electric lightning raged inside the clouds as the wind thickened with a fierce, striking force. Phil looked at the bark.

"Are you ready?" Nin called over the wind.

Phil looked at her, his lips parted, trembling; he nodded reluctantly, and she placed the bark between his lips. The bark turned soft in his mouth and he swallowed quickly.

Nin put her hands on his shoulders. "Remember," she said. "Once you've gone through, find the door and walk through. Then you will be home."

Phil's eyes narrowed. He could see his reflection, frightened, confused. "Go through wha…"

He hunched over, the pain in his abdomen like a knife twisted in his flesh jutted pain to the back of his skull as he dropped to one knee. The air waved and fluttered around him, smeared across his eyes as his head shook, his body shuddered. He saw devils and vampires in the garden, waiting to devour his flesh.

He could feel himself tumbling, falling into the void. His body fell back, and he saw himself, as if he were outside his body, fall into the grass as a puff of dirt rose above him. His body wriggling and scampering, twisting with pain. And those devils and vampires inched closer to the body. Thunder. Lightning. Hurricane winds lifted Nin's robe into the air. Phil looked at her, and her eyes were staring directly at him.

"Give it no concern," she said. "It's nothing more than an ego death."

Phil looked at his body. Heard his voice, felt the screams in his throat, heard them as they pierced his ears.

"Happens to us all."

Phil covered his ears to stifle the terror of his bodily screams.

"It is meant to lose attachment."

Phil felt the pull as if his body called to him, pleaded with him to help.

"So the spirit can enter the ether unadulterated."

Devils and vampires scampered towards the body. Phil's physical form reached out to him, the pain showing across his face excruciating and terror filled.

"And give rise to a new spirit, unfazed by the past, with a mind and heart connection that can bring about the future, in bliss and harmony."

Phil's physical form uttered a single word, "Please," it called to him. Spirit Phil sensed acid boiling into the back of his throat. Wind blew through his spirit, reorganizing atoms that fluttered towards the physical form.

And Nin said, "Oh, that was a bad idea."

Phil's eyes wide as the vampires and demons came over him, slashing at him, wielding deep gashes across his skin, raking his chest, gnawing on his throat; Phil defenseless. He tried to fight, but his limbs had garnered the weight of a thousand fearful thoughts.

Heard Nin whisper in his ear, "Some of us have so much trouble letting go."

60

"YOU can see in the dark?" asked Grimes to Cat as Grimes looked at Cam standing on a sand mound behind them, staring at the moon. They were outside the cruiser. Cat had removed a cover from the ship, a metal plate he had leaned against the vessel. He was crouched down, staring into the mechanics behind the metal plate. Although the moon provided decent light, the light dimmed inside the inner working of the cruiser.

"Yes," said Cat. "My visual acuity remains the same whether light or dark."

"Typical," answered Grimes. His shoulder hurt and he could feel fresh blood seep into his bandage.

Cat's focus on the cruiser was paramount, his head moving left and right, searching. "Seems like the capacitor has been fried." He turned to Grimes. "Were you having trouble hovering?"

"Yes," said Grimes. "Damn thing would dip without cause. Can you fix it?"

Cat turned back to the cruiser, stood up, surveying the cruiser. He turned to Grimes. "Most cruisers have replacement parts loaded in the storage compartment. Without the necessary replacements, I won't be able to provide the appropriate repairs. Also, your communications system is inoperable; this will make it impossible for communications to be received. And, slightly more important and dire is the simple fact that the cruiser's main boarding system is damaged. It will need to be replaced. Unfortunately, such a large component is often not kept on board."

Grimes noticed how Cam turned around, his eyes on Grimes. Cam said, "Do what you have to, Cat. I think it's high time we get out of the desert." He turned back to the moon.

"Affirmative," said Cat when his eyes found Grimes looking at his shoulder. "Is the regeneration chamber on board not working?"

"Come again?" said Grimes.

"The regeneration chamber," said Cat. "There is always one on board. If you lie inside of it, your shoulder will be repaired. Quickly too."

Grimes swallowed, staring at Cat. "One thing at a time. Let's focus on the ship first."

"As you wish," said Cat with a slight bow, then walked around the cruiser. Grimes turned to Cam, walked towards him, his eyes on the moon hovering high above. "Ya know, this might not be that bad," said Grimes.

Cam shrugged as he sighed. "Still going with the optimistic approach?"

"Yeah, well, what else do we have?" Cam nodded while dipping his hand into sand. "We get the cruiser fixed and head back to Winter. He's got to know other places to go. Places where Cameron can hide. I believe we need to decompress, get our heads together and regroup."

Cam let sand drip through his fingers. He stood up, shouldering his rifle while staring at the moon.

"You okay soldier?"

Cam shook his head. "Can't say that I am."

"It's a lot to take in," said Grimes.

"Tell me about it."

"Doesn't mean we stop fighting. Doesn't mean we give in."

Cam nodded. "I know," he muttered, then turned to Grimes. "But is there any hope left?"

"Of course," Grimes huffed. "All we have is hope."

Cam's eyes roamed left and right. "Where? You heard Cat, Robyn Winter's rebellion has been decimated. He may not even be alive when we get to him. Every human being is locked behind walls we can't touch and our very own military brothers and sisters are secretly taking orders from an alien species hell bent on turning us into slaves and we're running around the desert on some foolhardy mission." He gestured to the desert. "We're... all alone."

"We have each other," Grimes shot back. "We may be a band of misfits, but remember, wars have been won by misfits and militia groups. What else do we have other than fighting." He gestured to the ship. "For them, if not for ourselves. Maybe we can spark the flame that ends this bullshit." He stepped closer to Cam. "Listen, I don't know where this will lead…" He shrugged, shaking his head. "We could be walking into certain death for all we know. But we just have to take it one step at a time. Like the battle in Wakefield." Cam turned to him. "You remember the call, don't you? Ten thousand troops and only a hundred walked out alive. It was hope that won them the battle, that soldier mentality to always keep moving forward. What if they gave up and gave in?"

"Need I remind you we lost the war, Corporal?"

Grimes was shaking his head. "No, we didn't. Don't you see, we were never meant to win? But it's the human will that keeps fighting. That's what they're afraid of, that's why they want to turn us into mindless slaves. They're afraid of the human will. Our capacity to overcome and our undying conviction to be free. This is… all we have left. And if we die fighting, then that is our destiny and I'll accept my fate, knowing I did all I could to give us all a chance to be free. We need to get word out to our military brothers and sisters. We need to show them the truth about what's going on and we need to put an end to this alien insurrection. Now I don't know about you lieutenant, but there's no way in hell I'm giving in."

Cam smiled at Grimes. "Can't argue with that

now, can I?"

"Do you remember the call? It came over every intercom during Wakefield. It brought hope to the rest of us."

"Stand Free. Stand Tall. The dawn breaks with blood to reveal our victory."

"Yes," said Grimes. "The dawn breaks with blood to reveal our victory."

"Let not the darkness conceal our honor."

"And go forth to be free." He stepped to Cam. "Don't lose faith. I know we're against insurmountable odds, but we will find a way." He tapped Cam on the shoulder. Cam nodding. "We will find a way."

61

"FIRST," said Moth. "The honoring of our nourishment will taint the skies red with blood." He looked up, a grim smile across his lips. "Carried to the surface to provide to the earth." He turned to Sandy. "The grand circle of life."

"I'm sure the people you're about to set on fire don't see it that way."

The smile wiped clear from his lips. "I'm sure they know nothing other than what they're told, as all humans do."

A single drumbeat rang through Drac City. All in attendance gathered around the city's center. The red-robed Dracs took their seats as a door opened on the far end and through it a mechanical float buzzed into Drac City. At the helm, sitting high on the float, was a Drac dressed in red.

"Ah, Clitis leads today's charge," said Moth.

Sandy asked, "Who is Clitis?"

Moth's voice was subtle when he said, "One of our very best healers. He is schooled in the old ways."

"I thought those dressed in red don't believe in

human feeding?"

"Clitis sees things our way," said Moth, a glare in his eyes. "He understands the need for appropriate nutrition. Synthetic blood dulls our true nature. He wishes for all Dracs to be free. Feeding is a part of that freedom, for it is only when we feed that we feel truly free."

Sandy searched across the float. Seven humans kneeled below Clitis, four women and three men, and she could see how their eyes revealed fear, staring into the bonfire where they would meet a blazing death. Their hands bound and how young they looked, how frightened and youthful. Surrounding Clitis and the humans were Drac soldiers, standing at attention.

"I wasn't expecting them to be so young," said Sandy, staring at the female center stage. Sandy turned to Moth. "If they serve a purpose, why destroy them at such a young age?"

Moth never looked at Sandy to answer. His voice was low, just above a whisper. "They have outgrown their use," he said. "Humans over a certain age have no purpose any longer. These seven humans have already provided us with all the offspring we can ask for. After too much breeding, we could be feeding on improper human nutrition. It is best to keep things neat and unaltered. The better the genes, the better the taste and nutrition."

Clitis rose to his feet. His hands extended in front of him, his eyes seeking Moth as he bowed and began to speak. "Lord Moth," he said, his voice echoing through Drac City. "We bow to your leadership. And we bestow on all Dracs to let our freedom ring across all of Eridanus."

Moth returned the bow before he called out into Drac City, "Flattery will get you nowhere Clitis, get on with it."

Laughter erupted in Drac City. Cheers and howls.

"I wish to see the night bathed in red," continued Moth, his words receiving thunderous applause.

"As you wish, my lord," said Clitis, bowing once again. He addressed his Dracs. "Fellow Dracs of the cloth, Dracs of labor, Dracs of art and philosophy. We honor what provides to us, we honor life and we honor death." Clitis raised his chin, looking over Drac City. "These humans have provided for us. It is through their blood and flesh that we have found peace. It is through our digestion that these humans have become a part of us. A part of Drac. And as with all Dracs, we commend their spirits to the heart of... FIRE!" Clitis tossed, from what Sandy could see, a handful of dark powder into the bonfire that set the flame ablaze with a boom and eruption as the flames licked at the air. The red-robed Dracs all turned from the flame as Dracs dressed in black clambered for a better look from the second level where Sandy was. As the flames softened, the female human front and center jumped and shuddered. Sandy could see how her body trembled, her lips, her hands shaking, her skin crawling with fear as Clitis forced her to her feet, a handful of blonde hair in his grip. Pain winced across the female's face. Clitis held her still. "In honor of COR, we salute this human for the offspring she has provided." He pulled a knife from his back, raising it high overhead. "In the name of Drac we honor thee."

He sliced the girl's throat, her head jerked forward as if attempting to swallow air into her lungs as blood poured from the throat and her eyes rolled up. Clitis pushed the body forward into the funeral pyre, the flames licking and dancing, devouring the flesh. One of the human males jumped up and tried to run away but was quickly caught by a Drac guard who forced him center stage. Clitis presented him, the human panting. Sandy could see his chest rising with quick successions. The knife slashed his throat and Clitis pushed him into the bonfire. Sandy felt herself cringe as she turned away. Her eyes downtrodden as she felt a sting in her heart.

The third human went into the bonfire. Sandy's hands trembling, fighting to conceal her reaction from prying eyes when she felt the touch on her shoulder and when she looked up, it was Kaal. His eyes caught with sympathy.

"Don't waver, my lady," he said. "They are watching you." His eyes gestured to the right as he forced Sandy's shoulder to turn, and Kaal stepped to her left, holding his arm around her, forcing her to watch.

Sandy's lips quivered as the fourth human was brought forward. The knife was drawn and Sandy searched the crowd for something, anything, to catch her attention, to bring a sliver of peace to this carnage. The child was watching her, and she settled on sharing his interest. The flames burst high when the fourth was tossed into the fire. Sandy kept her eyes on the youth. The fifth, then the sixth, followed by the seventh human, all burning, all being devoured by flames licking and lapping across their flesh.

Clitis stood over the flames, the blade in his hand, dripping with blood, watching the fire, the burning bodies. He raised his chin, his arms stretched, palms up. "Hail ArAn, the queens of Drac. We give honor to your purpose."

The collective "Hail ArAn," erupted across Drac City. Clitis provided a silent bow to Moth, then took his seat as the float moved around the bonfire.

"Now the celebration of the fallen," said Moth as he turned to Sandy. "Then, a special announcement for all Dracs to celebrate."

"Doesn't seem like all Dracs enjoyed the display you just put on," said Sandy as she gestured to the red robe Dracs. "Seems that some of you don't agree with your resolve."

Moth craned his head. "There's always those who refuse to adapt. But give it time and they will."

"And if not, they'll meet with your rage, won't they, lord Moth?"

"Indeed," Moth said, his eyes alighted with a smug smile as the second float entered Drac City.

Sandy shook her head. "I won't watch this any longer." She stepped back. Kaal and Moth's eyes on her. "I wish to go back to my room."

Moth scoffed. "After the last event," said Moth, wearing a devious grin that turned Sandy's gut.

Kaal interjected, "Lord Moth must remain in Drac City for the rest of the festivities. I as well. Come," he said, "I've been too hard on you. Perhaps it is too soon for you to witness such an event." He looked at Moth. "Would it be better if you were among the robes?" he asked.

Sandy looked at Moth, then at Kaal. Looked around the second floor and all the Dracs watching with bated breath for the next float to begin. Looked below, caught the eyes of the child. "That would be preferred," she said, clearing her throat.

"Come, I will escort you below."

Sandy caught the stare between the two Dracs. Moth's eyes narrowed, and for a simple second, before his grin captured his lips, Sandy was sure they had passed telepathic communication as Kaal took her hand. Sandy's stare remained with Moth.

Moth said, "I will find you once the ceremony is complete."

Sandy turned from Moth's stare, Kaal leading

her to the stairs.

"Do enjoy what you see," called Moth.

As she rounded the corner to the second set of stairs, Sandy glimpsed Moth. He turned around and was quickly enveloped by his Dracs, gone and out of sight, but she caught his thought.

Soon, he thought. Soon we will have all we need.

62

EVERY rip, every tear, every rake of talons were like phantom claws tearing away Phil's ether. They dipped into his flesh and bone like invisible claws. Each rake tore at him as his body jutted and squirmed to be free.

He saw vampires tearing at him, his vision fluttering like waves caught in a thunderous sea. His skin was wet as tears cascaded from his eyes. Phil could see his mother, Esta, Catherine, Robyn Winter and then another rake across his skin, his back, his legs. All the while, he could hear the Drac's voice proclaiming, "You lose this time, human. You lose this time."

The garden fluttered in his vision. He could sense vibrations in the garden, evil and tainted with fear.

Nin said, "Lose that mortal coil. Be done with it and give in."

A vampire raked his abdomen, and Phil curled in pain, screaming and whimpering.

"They are the relievers," said Nin. "They wear the face of your fear."

Phil snapped his eyes open, staring at Nin as

behind her, a horde of vampires rose around her.

"When will you give in? When will you let go?"

The stare in Nin's eyes unwavering although her face was solemn. And the vampires wretched and squealed around her, dropping to their feet, surrounding him as Phil, cradling his abdomen, clawed his way to his feet. He saw his mother, a ghost, her face, her eyes coming towards him. "Shine like the sun," she said as she passed through him. Phil felt her essence as she passed. The sensation was strange, painful yet comforting, and forced him to step back. Pain now in his heart, heavy breaths, hunched over huffing, straining for air to breathe free, suffocated and gagging.

"Let go," said Nin. "Surrender to the ether."

Phil scampered around, his right leg clawed with blood pouring from deep lacerations. He faced Nin as the vampires surrounded her and him, as if waiting for a command. Phil's mother stood behind Nin; he locked eyes with her and she smiled for him before closing her eyes.

"Let it take you," said his mother. "Let go."

Phil grunted beneath his breath, his head trembling as he stepped forward, staring at Nin staring at him.

"This isn't a battle you can win, dear Phil." Her eyes soft, caring. "Sometimes we must let go."

Live to fight another day. His mother's voice. *Shine bright like the sun.*

Thunder rolled overhead as Phil tasted blood

across his lips, and a vampire raked its claws across his back. Phil screamed and wailed, dropped to his knees.

"Let go," said Nin in a whisper.

Phil huffed, his hands shaking. He clenched his jaw and his teeth rattled. The vampires closed in around him, tongues clucking and their fangs rattling. He looked up, saw how the clouds parted ways, behind them the sun.

"Surrender."

Shine like the sun.

Warmth across his skin as Phil closed his eyes, forced his shaking, bloodied hand to his side and did the same with the other. He breathed deeply, allowing the vampires to tear him to pieces.

63

THE air was different with the red robes. It seemed cleaner, easier to breathe. Kaal hissed at the red robes who attempted to approach them as the celebration continued, honoring the fallen Dracs. Kaal led them through the red robes and gestured to a Drac standing guard.

"They'll bring seats," said Kaal. "Just one moment."

Sandy nodded. Looking over the city, she could see Moth standing on the second floor, his focus obvious and apparent; he was staring at her and Kaal. His devious grin tearing into Sandy's heart as he raised a goblet with a bow to Sandy. The vampires surrounding him all cackled and laughed, giddy to be in the presence of their leader, who walked freely among his people.

"Here we are," said Kaal as two Drac guards brought two royal thrones stitched with red velvet, placing both chairs in the center of the red robes. Sandy noticed how the Dracs watched her. Not just the red robes, but all Dracs, even those who hid their intrigue. "Please my lady," said Kaal, offering his hand, "Take a seat."

Sandy noticed how the air seemed to thicken around her as if every Drac watching had thoughts that rushed towards her with an ether and energy all their own, surrounding and suffocating the air from her lungs. The thoughts were not kind; the ether stabbed at her skin, clawed at her heart, and placed pressure on her mind. Sandy touched her forehead, hoping to ward off a dizzy spell as she felt her face flush and her feet felt heavy.

"You okay, my lady?" asked Kaal, continuing to offer his hand.

Sandy locked eyes with Kaal, if for no other reason than to have a focal point to keep her concentration on breathing slow and deep. In his eyes, she could see the bonfire crackling as the flames licked the air. Red, glowing flames consumed Kaal's eyes when a thought rattled inside her mind.

You're being attacked. Energetically. The purpose is to weaken your core, to open your mind with easy access. It's a common Drac trick.

Sandy bowed to Kaal. "Yes," she said, "Just taking it all in."

"Very well," said Kaal, gesturing to the seat.

It's better with the red robes. We mean you no harm.

Sandy eyed Moth and the Palladium, her stare continuing above the Palladium to the higher levels of Drac City, searching as she turned to take her seat. Kaal sat beside her.

"We can see better from here," he said.

Sandy had been so distracted she hadn't realized the second celebration had already begun. Clitis also led the ceremony.

Use the ether to your advantage. Wrap yourself in a veil of protection. They can't stab at you with their thoughts should you protect yourself.

Clitis' speech muted in Sandy's ears as she searched for the origin of the voice in her head. But all she could see was a sea of Dracs, all looking away from Sandy, all watching Clitis.

Sandy pictured the rose in her heart as she inhaled deeply, clearing her thoughts, calming her heart. And as she exhaled she pictured that protection billowing from her chest, expanding the ether, seeing the rose tall and erect at the edge of where her fingertips would be should she stretch out her arm, the roots firmly planted in the earth, unwavering with strength and calm.

Perfect, said the voice. Always protect yourself. Always.

Sandy's eyes searching, waiting for the click. That click in the stomach, an instinctive click of knowing. Knowing where the voice came from.

She caught Kaal's stare, and he offered her a smile, although Sandy saw through it; he was disappointed.

There's more happening in Drac City than meets the eye, thought Sandy. Never thought about a cerebral attack. No wonder I felt depleted and unnerved in the Palladium.

Now that her thoughts were clear, she could see truth.

They were all attacking, cutting through the ether. Devouring energy by overpowering mine.

Sandy breathed deeply when she found the Drac child resting in his mother's arms. And of course he was watching her.

The bonfire raged high, stoked by Clitis and the powder he tossed into the flames. Sandy watched as the flames licked and clawed high above and all of Drac City thumped and grunted all at once as Sandy gazed beyond the flames. Of course there would be no sky, she knew, but where did Drac City end and the earth's surface begin? All she could see was darkness. A sky with no stars. The flames seemed to circle, the smoke the same, spiraling and reaching towards the earth.

Keep your focus, said the voice. *That's how it happens. Distraction allows them in.*

Sandy snapped her focus back to Drac City as the second float moved from the bonfire. She turned to Kaal, sitting at the edge of his seat, his hands between his legs.

"Third show will begin soon," he said.

Sandy nodded, said, "Can't wait," as she clawed away at her thoughts, wondering,

What is it they want me to see?

64

SANOS watched the festivities from the third tier of Drac City alone. From this distance he could take in all of Drac City, watching with a keen eye and apt focus the energetic feel of the ether. There was a thick wallop of brutal energy surrounding the center of Drac City. Thoughts rose above the city like dissipating smoke from the bonfire. Hateful thoughts cut like knives.

Where are these thoughts directed to?

Something was rotten in Drac City. Something wicked Sanos was unaware of. He was sure Moth was at the center of it, playing the cards in his favor as he always has. Sanos searched the city, scoffed at the red robes.

Putrid vermin they are.

He turned his attention to the second tier. Of course, the Palladium was shoulder to shoulder as Dracs gathered in thick droves around the second tier. Moth in the center, a horde of Dracs surrounding him. Moth, as usual, was a beacon of unwavering thought. Always locked in, always locked out. He was a master at self-preservation, a simple fact that burned Sanos' blood. There had to be a way to get to him. No one is immune to coercion.

It's only a matter of time, thought Sanos. Sooner or later, everyone slips up.

Sanos was searching over Drac City. His vision passed a silhouette across the center platform, hiding in the dark. Sanos recognized the figure, one of Moth's three guards. His size was unremarkable.

Calla.

Sanos stroked his chin, staring. If Calla is here, then Dalius is not far. He scanned the crowd, searching for...

Plagesous! There you are.

Sanos found him on the third tier platform not far from where Sanos was himself. Alone and standing guard was Plagesous.

Strategically placed, thought Sanos. Now what could be their order? What is Moth expecting? Where is Dalius hiding?

Moth's three guards were loyal to a fault. They must go, thought Sanos, because there was no way they would join Sanos' coup. In fact, Sanos was sure they would cause insurrection, and challenge his leadership, and that simple fact was something Sanos could not afford.

Where there is one, there are three, and where there are two, there is definitely the one, thought Sanos. *Where is Dalious?*

65

CAT turned his arm, and the cruiser lit up with life, humming as it raised a few feet off the ground.

Cam watched the cruiser, nodding as he stroked his chin.

"See that," said Grimes, looking at Cam. "Hope does exist."

Cam looked at Grimes. "How long to reach Robyn Winter?" he asked.

"Judging by how long our travel was before the UFO attacked, I'd say no more than an hour."

"Perfect," said Cam. "Let's get going."

But Cat interrupted, asking, "A UFO?" His head craned, eyes staring red as if confused. "Attacked you?"

"Yeah, why? Over the Mojave," said Cam.

Cat stood unwavering as he pressed his finger to his temple and his eyes gleamed with electrical waves across his pupils.

"Cat?" said Grimes. "What's going on in that AI head of yours?"

"Connecting with source code," said Cat, his

pupils fluttering with information then suddenly returned to a solid red. "They're searching for you. And Robyn Winter."

Cam stepped up. "What?"

Cat said, "Communications received from the downed ship prior to the crash indicate a human at the helm. They've sent a search party to comb the desert."

"Are you saying there are aliens looking for us?" Grimes, his stare stoic, looking from Cat to Cam.

"Affirmative."

Cam turned to Grimes. "Hope," he scoffed when the squawk raged across the sky high above and his head snapped to the sound. Flying amid clouds were several Chordata circling their location. Cam looked at Cat. Cat looked up, then to Cam.

"They will not engage," said Cat. "Their orders are to gather intel on your location and report their findings."

Cam looked at Grimes. "Which means they'll be sending someone to find us."

"Which means we can't go directly to Robyn Winter," said Grimes.

Cam started walking towards the cruiser. "But we can do our best to make sure they don't find him."

Grimes cocked his eyebrows. "Hope," he said.

"Something like that. Get ready for some fancy flying," said Cam.

Grimes breathed, "Fancy shooting is more like it."

"Exactly," said Cam as he stopped and turned to Cat, looking at the Chordata. "Are you coming?"

Cat stood tall, turned to Cam. "Of course."

"Well, times wasting. Let's get the hell out of here. We've got a better chance in the air than we do down here."

****

Cameron sat beside the sleeping Annison. Perseus crouched on the floor, huddled against the wall as the lights in the cruiser came to life. Perseus looked up and growled.

Cameron looked around the cruiser. "Looks like we'll be leaving soon," he whispered when Annison stirred beside him. One word breathed across her lips before her eyes opened, "Aries." Her eyes opened and Cameron smiled, caressing her hair and cheek. "Cruiser's fixed," he told her.

Annison nodded, her skin wet with perspiration; she pursed her lips and swallowed.

"You were dreaming," said Cameron. "But you're all right now."

Her eyes carried a sympathetic stare.

"Are we going back home?" she asked.

Cameron nodded. "I believe we are."

"Good," she said as she closed her eyes. "I need to talk to Robyn."

66

THEY carried him through the darkness. Thousands of angels with fingertips so soft comfort had come instantaneously. Phil gazed through the dark void, watching shooting stars rage overhead as the hands placed him with caution to his feet. And when he turned to his angels- those once demons and vampires that tore into his flesh and heart-their wings erected, their lips drawn into soft comforting smiles, their eyes wide with wonder, strength, and beauty. One by one, the angels disappeared, turned into the darkness and were gone, their eyes like flashes of light in the void. Like those shooting stars, they drove across the universe. All but one.

Cloaked in darkness, Phil could see the angel's outline beaming with sparkles as gold dust glittered off the smooth angel wings. A wave in the void circled around Phil. He watched it, turning in unison, turning around and when he turned to where the angel had been standing, the angel was gone. Phil watched as the angel's eyes joined the void, like a child rushing to join friends on a warm spring day, joyous and carefree.

Phil could feel his skin tingling with a pure love vibration, a flutter of wonder, and a deep sensation, a knowing, effervescent freedom. He reached his hand into the void, into the wave that continued to spiral around him. It was as if he dipped his hand into magical waters where millions of stars rushed through his flesh and bone, sending vibrations directly to his heart. In his palm he could see galaxies and stars, the pillars of creation, planets and moons, trees and animals, flowers, budding vegetation, harmony.

All is right in the universe, he thought. He couldn't help but smile. Freedom was in his heart.

Light now on his right, a white glow cast across an invisible hallway. All he could see was the hallway's outline. Phil turned to it and one by one more lights turned on, thumping like dominoes, revealing doors on each side of the hall. Phil stepped into the hall, his eyes scanning, walking, finding a door with the same white light beaming through the edges from the other side. He touched the door, and the door opened, soft and welcoming. He craned his head, staring in, seeing two small round holes in a thicket of black. A smile crossed his lips as he understood where the door led.

And Phil stepped into the door, stepped into his body inside the crypt in Drac City. And slowly the phantom opened his eyes.

Part II

Then why don't you tell me

1

MY name is Diagon, said the voice in Sandy's head as Sandy gazed over Drac City, desperately attempting to be as inconspicuous as possible. Kaal beside her, but his attention was on Clitis as he paraded across the float like some foolhardy magician, dazzling the vampires with magic spells. His honoring of fallen Dracs, including Zeta, had concluded.

The air thickened around Sandy, heavy with tightly packed atoms she was sure she could transform into a concrete block. The use of the rose and its purposeful conceptualization was beginning to take form in Sandy's understanding. It was for protection, Sandy told herself, a metaphysical wall to protect Sandy from the onslaught of stabbing thoughts and ether eating fangs. But did she pack the atoms with her own thought, possibly out of fear, or was some Drac-perhaps this Diagon-attempting to cause confusion? Sandy was unsure. Clitis' antics muted in her ears. Sandy looked at Kaal when he burst into laughter. Apparently he was enjoying Clitis and his magic show. His laughter caught by a thick etherical wave and vanished, brushed away from Sandy's focused concentration and attempt to find Diagon. Sandy's heavy breath prominent between her ears as she continued to eyeball Drac City.

Her eyes roamed from one Drac to another, attempting to catch thoughts as they manifested. Felt her breath catch in her chest, heavy and constricting, billowing pressure into her skull to the point where Sandy was sure her skull was about to crack. Held breath, her tongue pressed to the top of her mouth, her spine tingled, seemed to breathe on its own. Slow motion, her shoulders moving like ocean waves back and forth as the breath exhaled across her lips with a hiss. Return to strength, and that confidence she experienced in her room clicked back into play as the tightly packed atoms surrounding Sandy eased into a flutter, free and like vapor from boiled water. Her thoughts returned clear and unfettered. Sandy saw vibrations in the fold, in the space between herself and Kaal, herself and Clitis and all of Drac City.

And then the click, as if the click captured pure confidence. The stare in Kaal's eyes as he turned to Sandy filled with amazement and yet fear. Sandy noticed how his hands were shaking, his lips trembled.

"My... lady?" he said, forcing a swallow down his gullet.

And Diagon said, *There you are. The vampire we've been waiting for.*

2

PHIL remained inside the crypt after he opened his eyes, assessing current circumstance. A vampire sat waiting in a dark room filled with putrid and rank decay that insulted his sense of smell. A window beyond the vampire, but all Phil could see were smoke clouds like fog on a winter morning. He was in Drac City, this he knew, for what other place could carry such a prominent and foul stench of vampire other than Drac City?

And the waiting vampire kept his thoughts wide open. Through this waiting vampire, Phil was able to map all of Drac City. The twists and turns, secret passages, military operations, docking bays, vampire living quarters, general structure and schematics like blueprints for Drac City, and... himself, the phantom that was about to be burned in a funeral pyre, but no mention of Sandy. Not even the slightest inkling about the human brought to the city, although two names continuously rifled through the vampire's mind, Sanos and Moth. Apparently, the vampire had more than a few choice words for Sanos, a revelation that Phil could exploit; insurrection from within was a more efficient method to dismantle a species than an outside force. Change comes most prominently from within, and, in turn, so do destruction and chaos.

As for the other, Moth had been on Phil's radar all his life. An elusive vampire sitting at the helm of COR, and it was with this vampire that Phil was sure he'd find Sandy for what other vampire would be in charge of a human prisoner other than the leader of COR? Burrowing into the vampire's mind, into his thoughts, Phil could see his memories, the vampire standing at attention with two Drac warriors, Moth speaking to them, providing orders, the scene moving inside Phil's mind with waves that drowned out Moth's voice. A few exceptions passed through, little tidbits or a word or gesture. Moth handed down orders to all three warriors, where they were to be stationed, where they would watch the funeral pyre, and orders to be on guard for the possibility the phantom would rise from the dead. Phil could see clearly where these stations were. He required Moth, which meant Phil would need to confront these warriors.

Phil returned to the vampire's memory, his focus on Moth, his eyes, as Phil attempted to go further into the Drac leader's mind, although to no avail; Moth was a seasoned vampire and schooled in the many ways of telepathy. The vampire was a walking testament to the rule and discipline required to suppress thoughts from entering the ether and into the larger cosmic current, where thoughts could be picked like fruit from a tree. Nonetheless, a seed could still hide in the ether, hidden in plain sight, a telepathic seed with a direct link to Phil. Even the most seasoned telepath could be tricked when the attack was unforeseen. The seed planted held no reason for discovery when the purpose was to sit and wait with no other cause other than to beam location to its originator.

The vampire, Dalious, turned to the ceiling and Phil could sense the thunder that caught Dalious' ears from up above in Drac City, laughter, dancing, and a gathering of vampires existed up above, all of them waiting to watch the phantom's demise.

Now is the time, thought Phil as he turned the crypt's atoms into sand and stepped away, walking towards Dalious, immediately building the crypt back to original form behind him.

The vampire, quiet, still staring at the ceiling, groaned and grunted. Phil ejected his blade claws, still stained with Sanos blood, from his armored fingers, an act that caused the vampire's head to snap around.

Phil drove his claws into the vampire's neck, throat, mouth, and head. Breath whistled from the vampire's punctured throat with a wet garble. The vampire's eyes turned stiff with shock as blood spouted from the wounds, streaming across the vampire and Phil's claws as Phil flexed his fingers, clawing further into the vampire's throat, then tore the windpipe, tendons, and bone when he thrust his claws from the vampire's body. The windpipe fell to the floor, his throat gutted. The vampire's head hung from a thread of tendons and spine as the body slumped forward, falling limp to the floor. Phil could feel the vampire's blood on his face and neck, wet and warm across his lips.

He looked over the room, raised his chin to the ceiling, and heard the thunder that raged from up above. A round door on the ceiling caught Phil's eye. He turned to his feet and observed the platform he was standing on had the same shape as the ceiling door.

The platform moves, he thought, looking up. Rises into Drac City. On full display for all to see. He turned to the crypt. *In celebration of their victory.*

Phil thought as he turned back to Dalious, If it's a phantom they want, I'd hate for them to be disappointed.

Phil retracted his claws, then gathered the dead vampire. He locked him in the crypt, bloodied, gutted, and dead. On display for all to see.

3

NOW Moth clutched his heart, felt a stabbing pain that raged and tensed his bones, curled his blood, and gritted his teeth. The attack an intrusion in his ether, but who had the tenacity and wherewithal capable of entering his etheric existence?

Moth was a master at manipulating ether and was supremely confident in his ability to ward off such an attack. Always locked in and always on guard, Moth operated on a trust no one philosophy, and it was in this simple philosophy that allowed Moth his position in COR. It kept him sharp. On point and provided the ability to never let his guard down, because the enemy was everywhere, even within his own. When you hold a position of power, everyone wants to knock you off the pedestal at some point. Being on guard became second nature, a must have, for who knew when betrayal would rear its ugly head. Better to be on guard than blindsided.

Nonetheless, he experienced his first attack in centuries. Someone, some vile cerebral enemy, had declared war against him with a personal attack, attempting to poison his thoughts and deplete the chemical composition of his internal system and his ether. Moth's head moved left and right, scanning Drac City, needing to find the source of this assault. The air in front of him thickened with a suffocating constriction of breath. He could sense the contraction; it barreled down on him, suppressing breath into a shallow constraint. The second wave was here, the second attack. Laughter from the platform; those damn red robes dancing and playing as Moth's jaw tensed, his eyesight keen and focused.

"Are you okay, lord Moth?"

The voice subtle and gentle. Moth regarded the young female vampire next to him. He bowed when he said, "Yes, my dear. All is well."

Of course, he had to play the moment perfectly. What would his people think if the leader of COR had been attacked and that the attack had gotten through? Weakness was not an attribute befitting a leader. The girl bowed in recognition before returning her gaze to the center platform. A bead of sweat formed on his forehead, his head weary. The attack was ongoing.

Block off your thoughts, he told himself, holding his hand to his heart and breathing deeply as he reconstructed his ethereal plane, forcing the attack from his ether. Whoever devised the assault was strong. They kept forcing the attack, refusing to give up. He craned his head, looking high above, searching when the attack ceased as if a tether had been cut, and the attack slipped into a void and vanished, and with it, the suppressed sensation ceased. His shoulders slacked, tension dissipated, and his thoughts flowed freely.

But he lost the ability to follow the train of attack, to catch the tether, latch on, and discover who his aggressor was. But they were here, in Drac City, with him now. Moth continued to scan Drac City, searching for hidden eyes in the darkness. An energetic flow like gravity pulls a close object towards its center. If someone were using the rose to get to him, there would be a residual effect, a solidification of atoms close to the assailant.

He found none.

Something wicked has arrived, he thought.

Whoever this vampire is, they hold a power unlike any I've ever seen.

4

"THEY'RE following us," said Cam, staring into the night sky. He was flying the cruiser. On his right and left outside the ship, he could see a row of Chordata. They flew in a V shape around the ship, their large wings flapping in the night sky.

"Finding out where we're going," said Grimes. "You didn't really think they were just going to leave us alone, did you?"

"More like *hoped* they would."

Grimes shook his head. "No faith," he said. "Where is Cat?"

"Looking through replacement parts and taking inventory, why?"

"We need up-to-date intel." He pushed the intercom on the panel board in front of him. "Cat," he said. "We need you in the cockpit."

"On my way," said Cat.

Cam rolled his tongue. "Got to be a way to outrun them," he said, turning to Grimes. "Can't this thing go any faster?"

Grimes shook his head. "Cat said the boarding

system is damaged."

"What does that mean?"

"Not sure. I'm not schooled in alien technology. But considering how fast we were flying before compared to now, I'd say manual controls have taken a hit." He looked at Cam. "Probably has something to do with our ability for faster speed."

"I don't like those things," said Cam, referencing the Chordata. "Not one bit." He banked the cruiser to the left, but the Chordata remained with the ship.

"I can understand why," whispered Grimes.

Cat said, "Here gentlemen."

Cam shouted, "Those things are still with us, and the cruiser won't go any faster."

Grimes said, "Is there a way to lose them, and have you received any information on their orders?" He looked at Cam. "Maybe they'll be told to leave us alone."

Cam shot Grimes a skeptical stare, then turned to Cat. "I thought we'd have enough muscle to outrun them, but I can't get the cruiser to fly any faster."

Cat stomped over to them, craned his head, looking at the Chordata. "They will follow wherever you go," he said. "They're sending your location in real time."

"Lovely," said Cam. "Any chance you can send them an order to leave us alone?"

"Negative," said Cat. "But why are you not using the halo? Manual controls and velocity are contingent on the boarding system's functionality. The halo is not a part of the same system. It's run through the capacitor I replaced earlier."

"What halo?" muttered Cam.

Cat pointed to a round piece of metal hanging beside his seat. "This halo."

"I was told not to touch it," said Grimes, garnering stares from Cam and Cat. "Silas," he said. "Told me we could end up in deep space."

"Have you not used one before?" asked Cat.

Cam shook his head. "Let's just pretend like we're novices to all things alien and humor us for a moment."

"The halo allows for interstellar travel on most ships and for planetary travel faster than light speed. The halo serves as a direct function of the ship when receiving communication from the wearer's thoughts."

"It reads our thoughts?" said Grimes, his nose curled, eyes narrow. "How does that help us in our current situation?"

"Thoughts travel faster than the speed of light. Wherever you wish to go, you will arrive within seconds."

Cam and Grimes let out a collective "What?"

"As long as there is a clear indication of the travel path, all you have to do is think through it and you'll arrive at your destination along the time line necessary to manifest the location through thought. Although a ship like this is not meant for interstellar travel. Those functionalities are only capable on starships specifically created for that exact purpose. However, the cruiser is capable of intra-planetary travel along all paths."

Cam looked at the Chordata when Grimes went to grip the halo.

"Don't touch it," said Cam. He looked at Grimes. "Who the hell knows where your mind will take us."

"I was thinking somewhere warm and sunny."

"Yeah and we'd wind up in Siberia." He shook his head. "I don't think so."

"Okay, but..."

"I am schooled in its function," said Cat. "If you wish to be away from the Chordata, it is best to use the halo."

Silence, Grimes shaking his head and outside the cruiser, Cam could see Chordata wings sailing in the wind. "Sit down," he told Cat, then looked at Grimes. "Get up Corporal. Get to the regeneration chamber."

Grimes unstrapped himself and switched seats with Cat.

"Where would you like to go?" asked Cat.

"Somewhere we can hide," said Cam. "Away from prying eyes so we can be absolutely certain we're in the clear with no one tailing us. Hide and wait. Maybe we can get in touch with Winter by then."

"If he's not dead already," said Grimes.

"You heard Cat. The man's already dead. I'm sure we'll find him."

Cat said, "There is no intel that says they have found him." He sat back and Cam could see how his eyes sparked with electrical currents.

"Is there any safe place in that computer brain of yours?" said Grimes.

"There's only one that meets our needs. Where we can obtain the equipment we require, and that is free from alien eyes," said Cat.

"And where would that be?" asked Cam.

"Miami."

Cam and Grimes let out another collective, "What?"

Cam continued, "Miami's been under water for years. There's nothing there other than decaying buildings. Nothing."

"Not true," said Cat. "The remaining skyscrapers serve a purpose in housing and manufacturing weaponry and vessels such as the one we're flying in now. Although my reports indicate the project was abandoned after the war, there are still replacement parts located there." He turned to Cam and his electrical fluttering eyes returned to red. "Our required replacement parts are included in the inventory."

"Miami?" said Cam.

"Correct lieutenant."

Cam looked at Grimes. "You said you wanted to go somewhere warm."

"There's nothing warm about Miami," he said.

Cam looked out to the Chordata, then took the halo off the hook and offered it to Cat. "Maybe one day you'll teach me how to work this thing." Cat returned his stare. "Until then, big boy, it's all you."

Cat took the halo. "Understood gentlemen." He fit the halo over his head, then turned to Grimes standing over him. "I advise for you to sit down and strap yourself in, Corporal."

"That fast?" Grimes said as Cat turned in his seat.

"Yes," said Cat. "I'll take us in from the southwest. We'll have a better indication on where to land from that angle." He gripped the controls. "We shall be there momentarily."

5

SANOS perched high above on the third tier, scratching his arms, tearing away at his flesh, watching Moth. His plan was simple; once the phantom is presented, he'd take out Plagesous, surprise attack being the best possible method to dismantle the loyal Drac. Moth's irrational fear of the phantom would become his demise. After Sanos removes Moth's trusted guards from the picture, there'd be no one to challenge him when he confronts Moth, and if those COR vampires refused to accept his rise over COR, they'd meet with the same fate. The Dracs belonged to Sanos now, their future in his hands.

And the humans will bend to my will, thought Sanos. King Sanos, ruler of Planet Earth.

Snarling, Sanos raked his talons over his forearm, clenched jaw, grinding his fangs, drawing blood down his arm. The itch was intense. He couldn't help itching and raking. His stomach twisted into knots. And he required blood. The scent of burning human bodies salivated his tongue. And where had the voice gone? The one from the pills? Dissipated into the void of the subconscious, thought Sanos. Waiting to be set free.

Wide eyes now as he snapped his head towards Plagesous, standing on guard on the tier three platform where light refused to reach. Sanos raked his nails across bloodied skin as his tongue lapped across his chin.

Now is the time, he thought. Phantom's coming up soon. The Clitis magic show was ending. Sanos leapt across the rooftop, barreling towards Plagesous.

He couldn't wait to try out his new weapon.

6

ONE thing Phil had on his mind when he tore the sides off his helmet, the parts Sanos had damaged during their battle, leaving the top of the helmet and the screen over his eyes, as he tossed the parts to the ground, was his dream. Arriving in blips, still images that stained his thoughts, his time beneath the fold of death, would arrive with a vengeance and disappear as quickly as they came.

He couldn't grab on to any single thought, image, or feeling as he searched through the sonar screen on his helmet. With this technology, he could see through walls. Silas had definitely done well with the upgrades. The man was a genius with technology; his latest advancements were indeed aiding Phil in his quest. He'd gotten out of the room with Dalious, made it through the hall while hiding from the eyes of the symbiotes. What a vile wretched species they were, taking control of the host while feeding on their very breath. Some say that being a victim of a symbiote was a living hell, as their tentacles would wrap around the brain, causing ongoing nightmares in a vast void of subconscious catastrophe. Although whether this was true or not was difficult to ascertain, as few had ever survived their wrath. Even if the symbiote was ripped from the victim, death would normally occur. Only a few have ever survived. He wished not to confront them if possible.

He went outside into the fog, searching, using the map he received from Dalious to coordinate his methods. Phil required Moth. Needed to follow him to Sandy and learn her location. Sounds of drills, talking, and laughter raged on the floor above him. The docking bay was on the next floor. Phil used his jetpack to propel to it, landed cautiously on his feet, crouched down, assessing. Vampires working on starships and cruisers, their attention on the work at hand as Phil assessed the ships; he would need transportation out of Drac City after he finds Sandy. On the far side from Phil was the entrance into hollow earth. He scanned the ships, so many ships, using the helmet's computer system to assess each one for any possible malfunction, finding three that would meet his needs.

Perfect, Phil thought, as he stood looking high above. According to the Dalious map, he was outside of the central platform, between the second and third tier. Nothing but fog existed above his head. Jetpack propelled him upward to the top of the third tier. Crouched down, scanning Drac City for Moth. Vampires everywhere twisted Phil's gut. He scanned across the central platform, craned his head when he found the Drac warrior standing guard within the shadows. Phil's eyes widened to take in the whole of the vampire.

Calla, he thought. Your size, like your reputation, precedes you. Now what could you be looking for? thought Phil. His sonar scanned the vampire for weaponry. He was holding a particle beam rifle in his armored arms, and his blades gleamed in the sonar. A bowie knife sheathed on his right leg, a handgun holstered on his left leg.

Particle rifle. Hate those things. Hiding behind a gun was as cowardice as stabbing someone in the back, although useful when the enemy carried the same. Should Phil need to confront the warrior vampire, he'd have a few surprises to contend with his particle beam. He scanned across the platform; two Dracs sat center stage among the red robe vampires. Phil scoffed as he shook his head, scanning to the second tier where black dressed vampires gathered; he followed the train to the center.

There you are.

Moth stood center stage, surrounded by Dracs, watching the center platform. He looked paranoid, uneasy, jaw tight, gritting his teeth, searching.

Searching for the cause of his ethereal attack.

He did not look pleased. There was rage in those vampire eyes.

I must have gotten to him, thought Phil. Even you can be gotten to Lord Moth, he scoffed, thinking of the attack he mounted through Dalious. No concern, he thought. I'm sure we will meet again. But not yet. Soon Moth, we will have our dance.

One thing about vampires that Phil knew was true, anytime you took out one another reared its ugly head to take its place. But how Moth had survived at the helm of COR for so long was baffling. He was indeed a powerful vampire. Phil scanned the rest of Drac City, second and third tier, when the second Drac warrior standing guard caught his attention.

A flash in the corner of his eye, Phil moved his head to see Sanos hovering above the third tier, above one of Moth's three personal guards, Plagesous. Phil ducked down; Sanos was in full range to see Phil's location, although his focus was on Plagesous. Apparently, Sanos was moving into position to launch an attack.

Now that is one ambitious vampire.

7

CAM gripped his seat's arms so tight he was certain that once the trip was over, they'd come apart in his hands. The vortex opened on Cat's command and the ship propelled at lightning speed. His stomach jumped into his throat. Outside the ship, spiraling light raged, his eyes circling, following the spiral and then...

Stop, as if the ship had never moved, never spiraled, never flew. There was no reverberation, no jump forward or back, just a simple and smooth transition to a new location. Hovering in a rainstorm, the ocean a black abyss beneath them, turning wave over wave crashing into the sparse Miami skyline. Blue and purple electrical waves cascaded across the sky.

"Are we here?" asked Grimes. He was sitting behind the cockpit where Hadock had sat earlier.

Thunder raged overhead as lightning thumped blue and white over the horizon.

Cam sat forward, staring. "I believe we are Corporal." He heard Grimes unlatch himself from the seat.

"Amazing," said Grimes, standing over Cam.

"That took what, like five seconds?"

"Something like that," answered Cam.

Grimes said, "You have thoughts in that head of yours, Cat? I thought you were made of computer parts and robot metal."

Cam looked at Cat, whose attention was focused on the electrical blue and purple current raging above the city. Cat turned to Grimes and Cam could see how his eyes raged with electricity, his head craned, staring at Grimes.

"You okay, Cat?" said Grimes with a slight stutter in his throat. "You look like you're confused."

Cat pushed his temple, and his eyes turned back to red. "There are a few things that are puzzling me at the moment," he said, garnering more intense stares from Cam and Grimes.

"What would they be, Cat?" asked Cam.

Cat looked at him, those red eyes beamed. "I rely on my creators coding to assess the outside world, however, I have reached conflicting information with my current programming in relation to the real time information I have discovered."

Cam narrowed his eyes, turned to Grimes. "Now, this should be interesting. Even the A.I. is confused. Join the club Cat. We're accepting applications."

Cat craned his head, staring at Cam. "What club?"

Cam shook his head. "Forget I said it. What's

troubling you?"

Cat paused for a moment, seemingly reluctant in his answer. "The first conflict pertains to… the two of you, or should I say, humans. My programming describes humanity as a powerful and evolved species. In fact, in a study conducted by the famed Cephalopod, Artemis, humans were discovered to house abilities for more evolved and powerful than any other species. However, current company does not seem to represent the findings of that study."

Cam and Grimes shared perplexed stares. "I think he just insulted us," said Cam.

"No," said Grimes. "He definitely insulted us."

"What brings you to that conclusion, Cat?"

"It seems I have misjudged the depths for which your knowledge reaches." He looked directly at Grimes. "Do you not know that your thoughts are electrical?" He tapped his forehead. "Like a computer."

Grimes raised his hands. "Sorry Cat, must have slipped my mind."

Cat made no subtle movement, nor did he register Grimes' gesture. "I have provided a new code in my programming to assist you with your limited knowledge. It is apparent that I know more about your species than you do. I can only compute that the two of you were raised in captivity and are not or were not a part of the human rebellion."

Grimes patted Cat's shoulder. "Now that's an optimal conclusion. Thank you Cat. We'll try to be more studious in our knowledge. Just pretend we know nothing and shout out anytime you feel it's necessary."

Cam looked from Grimes to Cat. "And the second?" asked Cam when Cat turned those red eyes on him. "What else are you confused about?"

Cat turned to the outside, pointing. "If the city is abandoned, as my intel shows, then who has taken occupancy?"

Cam sat forward, staring through the storm. On the rooftops were ships sitting idle. Inside the windows, the ones that weren't completely blacked out, he could see lights and tiny silhouettes moving about.

"And," Cat said as he looked up, pointing to the blue and purple electrical current raging within thick grey clouds. "Who scorched the sky?"

8

MOTH felt eyes on him. The same essence that had attacked before. He had checked in telepathically with Plagesous and Calla, receiving that all was right in Drac City. But Dalious had not provided the same. Moth's chest constricted. Something had gone wrong. Dalious always provided communication quickly. He searched over Drac City as the float and Clitis moved from the bonfire and a hush fell over Drac City as the platform opened and the crypt holding the phantom rose into the city.

Moth clenched his jaw. Dalious was not in attendance. Had he abandoned his post? Never, not Dalious, but what else could be the reason for his absence? Moth searched the crypt, his head craning, tilting to the right, seeing the closed eyes behind the two holes as Clitis climbed onto the platform. Moth, shaking his head, could see the skin over the eyes in the crypt as his own eyes widened.

That's no phantom.

"Dracs young and old," shouted Clitis, standing in front of the crypt.

That's Dalious.

"Behold," Clitis declared, "The phantom has perished."

Moth was about to scream to not open the crypt, however his voice caught in his throat as Clitis opened the crypt and Dalious' dead body slumped forward.

At first there was nothing, no sound, no screams, no fingers pointing, no chaos or mayhem, as if every Drac in Drac City held their collective breath. Moth's entire body tensed, his eyes wide, gritting his teeth as a red robe stood up, pointing at Dalious and Clitis with that stupid awestruck look on his face, staring at the dead Dalious by his feet.

"The phantom lives," hollered the red robe Drac.

"A Drac is dead," screamed another.

"The phantom is here in Drac City."

More hollers and screams raged across Drac City, all muted to Moth as he stomped down the stairs. He required Sandy; clearly the phantom had come for her. How he survived death was a question to be revealed later. Right now, he needed to grab Sandy before…

Drac City erupted into chaos. Red robes running across the platform in upheaval, swarming towards Moth. Fear had come to Drac City, chaos to his people, as he fought against the torrent of Dracs rushing at him. He pushed through the crowd, seeing Sandy and Kaal being barreled over. Their chairs dropped to the floor, hidden from his vision as Dracs raced around them.

Grab Kaal and the female he is with, said Moth to his warriors telepathically. *Grab them now.*

Frustration raged in Moth's eyes as he tossed one Drac after another, attempting to get to Sandy. But the platform was too wide, too long, with too many Dracs barreling towards him. Screams, terror filled, and pleas for help raged across the city, and as Moth forced his will over his people, another horde of vampires rushed at him.

"Master Moth," said one of the red robes. "What do we do? The phantom has come to Drac City."

"Get to your staterooms," he ordered, forcing his way through the thicket, searching for Sandy's location, finding her in a sea of frantic red robes. Kaal on the floor beside her. He watched as Sandy went to assist the unconscious Kaal, her attention taken by the vampire that gripped her wrist.

Moth's fingers clenched while staring at the vampire; Diagon was not who he expected.

9

SANOS thrust himself, feet first, into Plagesous, propelling the loyal vampire into the wall behind them as Sanos hung off the lip, dangled a second before dropping to his feet. Chaos ensued in Drac City. Vampires hollering, pleading, and scurrying to reclaim their homes raged across every tier.

"Hello, Plagesous," muttered Sanos. "Having some trouble?"

Plagesous held the back of his head as he looked up to Sanos, rage in his eyes as he snarled, "I'll tear you apart, Sanos." Plagesous pushed himself to his feet as Sanos craned his head. "It's you who have brought death to our city. Vampires like you bring dishonor to all Dracs." He clenched his fists and his blades jutted down his arms. "I'm going to enjoy this, Sanos. I think I'll tear off your arms first, then your heart. I hear you enjoy eating hearts, Sanos." His teeth grinding, his lips curled. "I'll feed you yours."

Sanos never took his eyes off Plagesous, his lips pursed tight as he reached behind him, clipped off the portable device he'd secured from Kaal. The same weapon Zeta had used on him in the pit. "Do you know what this is, Plagesous?"

"I don't care."

Sanos' eyes widened. "You should," he said as his forefingers and thumbs formed across the triangle. "It's one hell of a weapon."

Plagesous, eyes narrow as he stared at the tiny device and Sanos engaged the sound vibration, barreling the frequency towards Plagesous, who immediately grabbed his ears before dropping to his knees. His teeth clenched behind his parted lips, groaning and grunting as the wave ceased. Plagesous, breathing heavy, clutched his chest, gasping for air.

"See Plagesous, these are the kinds of weapons COR refuses to share." He sent another wave vibration that slammed into the weakened Plagesous. "I want you to know this, Plagesous. I want you to know before you die that your master Moth has kept secrets from you. I want you to know who will lead our people after Moth has gone."

Blood streamed from Plagesous' ears as he forced his head up, his face pinched in pain, his teeth seething, blood now across his lips pouring down from his nose. Sanos watched as the eyes boiled and burst from his skull as he screamed, clutching his bloodied eye sockets. His skin splitting, tearing across his arms, soaked in blood.

"Die Plagesous!" Sanos screamed as he slammed his left foot forward, tensing his hands over the triangle, forcing more power, more vibration onto his victim. "DIE!" he hollered, his face tense, his eyes wide with power and death.

Plagesous attempted to rise, but the vibration was too powerful. He dropped on his stomach into a pool of his own blood that jutted from his open wounds. His skull fractured, split in two oozing bile and brain fluid as his left foot shuddered against the ground. And Sanos continued, unrelenting. Plagesous' body, the flesh beneath his armor and clothes rising and falling as his body slackened and fell like a blanket drifting to its final destination.

Sanos ceased the vibration, staring at Plagesous as smoke slithered from the body with a putrid, foul stench. The bones disintegrating before his eyes from the vibration's pressure, pooling and mixing white and yellow in a pool of dark crimson. Sanos curled his nose. "Disgusting," he said, looking down to his triangle, then back to Plagesous as a thin smile graced his lips. "Well, that was fun."

Sanos latched his triangle on the back of his belt as he turned to the continuous chaos raging in his city. Eyes wide as he watched the turmoil scanning the platform, snickering when he saw Moth struggling through the crowd. Continuing to scan. Where was Calla? *No longer at his post. And Dalious?* He searched the bonfire and the wide-open crypt with the vampire lying dead in front of it.

No wonder my city is wrought in chaos, he

thought. The phantom has escaped.

And Sanos laughed beneath his breath. "Perfect," he said. "Absolutely perfect."

10

"COME with me," said the female vampire, gripping Sandy's wrist. "Lord Moth is heading this way. We must go now."

Sandy looked at the vampire. Her skin sparkled gold as if the sun directly reflected its brilliance. Her eyes gleamed with a crystal blue as her lips were parted. She was shorter than Sandy, about five feet four inches, small and fragile, as if she could be broken with ease. She wore black armor and Sandy noticed how the bones behind her head swelled and growled as she looked in Moth's direction.

"He'll tear out your heart," she said. She seemed like she was about to jump, her shoulders bobbing up and down as she locked eyes with Sandy. "We have to go," she ordered. "Now!"

She bounced with a hurried step, and never looked back to see if Sandy was following, which she was, weaving in between panic stricken Dracs to the bonfire when she followed the raging fire around to the platform where the crypt and dead vampire remained. She stepped onto the platform, then turned back to

Sandy.

"Come on," she hollered, her eyes looking beyond the bonfire. She offered her hand and Sandy took it, lifting her onto the platform. Sandy stood eye to eye with the vampire; her eyes carried panic, as if she were assessing Sandy, her eyes moving left and right in frequent successions.

And then a scream erupted inside Drac City, followed by a screeching squawk that brought fearful tension among the Dracs. This simple scream caused the vampire to tense, although that tensed system lasted mere seconds as she looked down at her feet and stomped on a thick, round knob on the platform.

Sudden movement, a jerk and a twist, and Sandy steadied her feet as the platform moved downward. The vampire now held Sandy's two hands, staring into her eyes.

"Use your power," she said as they descended. "All your strength, all your might, all your knowledge to keep the door closed." Another squawk and screech and her head snapped towards the bonfire. The platform close to finding common ground as Drac City rose high above Sandy's view as the platform came to a stop below Drac City.

The round door above them leading to Drac City began closing inward from both sides.

The vampire ordered, "Close it quickly. Keep it locked."

Sandy's eyes widened as she looked overhead,

the door closing.

"No fear," she screamed.

Moth was flying overhead with wings like ravens claws, death and rage in his eyes as he barreled towards the door, his mouth agape, snarling, those fangs like black daggers.

Sandy's entire body tensed, her heart stopped, breath constricted, held in her lungs as her eyes watched the door close and lock just before Moth reached the opening. The vampire watched the ceiling as a sonic boom raged from above it and Sandy's heart skipped a beat. The vampire gripped Sandy's face in both hands, forcing Sandy to look at her.

Her head shaking, she said, "No fear, focus on the door. Keep it closed. He's powerful, but together we can keep him out."

Another boom and Sandy's eyes went to the door.

"I can't," Sandy screamed. The air thickened around them with a powerful rage and essence created through hatred, anger. Sandy could feel Moth's presence in her veins, her skin crawled with loathsome flutters as her throat constricted.

"You have to," the vampire screamed, forcing Sandy's head back down.

BOOM!

The entire room rattled. The windows shook, and Sandy could hear screeches, grunts, and growls from above. Behind those guttural grunts, screams and hollers continued to rage in Drac City.

And the door opened.

Sandy could see rage in Moth's eyes as another screech belted from his throat and lungs. It was as if his jaws clenched around Sandy's throat and bit into her neck.

"He's trying to weaken you."

The door opened another inch and Sandy could see how Moth's hands, shaking and tense, were forcing the door open through an ethereal space. The vampire forced Sandy's eyes from his.

She said, in a gentle voice, "Now, Sandy." Her head craned to the left, her eyes burrowing into Sandy's soul. "Close the door."

Another screech from Moth as Sandy reached her hand over her head and brought it down in a quick thrust, tensing her fist. The door shut with a loud bang, the vampire's hand on Sandy's heart. Her head bowed.

"Keep it closed," she said, again in that same soft voice.

Another boom, followed by another, but Sandy's focus was on the door.

"Good," said the vampire, and she raised her head. "You've done it."

Sandy turned to the vampire, her eyes darting back and forth as she turned, walking to the side door. Sandy noticed the dead vampire. His head dangled from his spine, his throat gutted.

"They'll be looking for us," said the vampire,

opening the door. "We must leave now. Take you somewhere safe, away from the city." She turned to Sandy. "Are you ready?"

Sandy looked from the vampire to the ceiling, then back to the vampire, standing, waiting. Craned her head, seeing, feeling, hearing the vampire's heart thump furiously in her chest. A white glow in the center of that heart breached Sandy's mind with a sense of wonder; innocence likened to childhood, free and immortal.

Sandy asked, "Diagon?"

"Yes, I've been following you since you arrived." She stepped onto the platform. "We've been waiting for you."

11

MOTH stood on the platform. He was not pleased. Not only had the phantom escaped, and his people panicked, but Sandy and Diagon now presented a new conundrum. He cursed himself for not listening to Kaal; he should have killed Sandy when he had the chance.

Nonetheless, his inability to open the door stifled him. No Drac had ever defied his power before. And in front of Drac City, where he had to reveal his wings and fire above them with rage as he attempted to capture Diagon and Sandy. Centuries of planning, earning trust with his people and in one fail swoop, all he had worked for had become compromised. Moth looked around his city, looked for Calla and Plagesous, nowhere to be found. Neither answering telepathic communications.

He stepped around the fire, finding Kaal unconscious on the floor.

"Pathetic," he snarled, head shaking; he looked around the city when he received a communication

"Master Moth."

Moth recognized the voice immediately; Zon

was the lead member of the military faction housed in Drac City.

"Speak Zon." Moth walked from the platform towards Drac Tower.

"I've found Plagesous. He's dead."

Moth stopped cold, gritting his teeth. "In what manner did he meet his death?" Had to be the phantom, most likely it was the phantom, but one could never be sure, and he wanted to know exactly how capable this phantom was.

"I... I've never seen this before. It..."

"Get on with it Zon," Moth shouted.

"It's like his body has been boiled or something. There's blood everywhere and his bones... Master Moth it looks like they've been incinerated from within."

Now Moth knew exactly how that happened. It was obvious the phantom was not only aware of the sound vibration weaponry, but he had it and was using the Drac weapon.

"Master Moth?"

Moth shivered, clenching his jaw. "Clean it up," he ordered. "I want no Drac to know about his demise." He continued toward Drac Tower.

"As you wish."

"And Zon, we have more than a few current predicaments that need dire attention."

"I assumed so. What are your orders?"

"That wretched fiend Diagon is here. She's gone

into the gallows with a female Drac. I want them both found and brought to me immediately."

"As you wish."

"Kaal is unconscious in Drac Plaza. Have him brought to medical. And find Calla. He refuses to answer my inquiries. I want him brought to me to meet his consequence."

"As you wish, Master Moth. All orders confirmed."

"Then why are you still communicating?" Moth watched as ten soldiers gathered around him, two carried a stretcher, and continued to Kaal. Zon's silence irritated him. "Speak Zon, I haven't got time for games."

"What about the phantom? He's loose in Drac City, terrorizing our people."

"I'll communicate with Drac City for all to stay in their homes until we find the phantom. In the meantime, find Diagon and the Drac she is with. This is our top priority."

"Confirmed. And the phantom?"

Moth rolled his eyes as he entered Drac Tower, stomping through the atrium, the ceiling over fifty feet high, the white lavish walls covered in art, and the bronze statue of the phoenix stood prominently as if staring at Moth. He stopped in front of it, snarling at the statue with discontent. Seething, his breath hissing when he said, "Find Diagon and the phantom will come to us."

12

NOW Calla was on the hunt. He'd felt eyes on him when he was standing guard in Drac City. And his search revealed a conundrum that gathered light when Dalious fell dead from the crypt. He saw the phantom then, clawing across tier three, and gathered himself to seek the vile human out. And in his search he'd become aware that the phantom was following Master Moth using his telepathic capabilities with the ethereal manipulation, the rose, to attack Moth.

And that was something he refused to allow himself to be a part of. Common sense told Calla that the phantom had killed Dalious and, more than likely, had used his mind to gather intel on Drac City. Calla refused to allow himself to become a victim of the phantom's manipulation. He shut himself down from telepathic communication.

The phantom was following Moth. And Calla was following the phantom.

Soon, thought Calla, I will meet with him eye to eye.

13

THEY found a secure dock to land the cruiser. It had become apparent to Cam that when people are operating in a secret and by all supposed standards, abandoned base, there was little inquiry to the goings on in the area, assumption to the cause and secrecy being a comfortable conclusion to all happenings that may take place. As a result, they were able to dock unnoticed.

And Cam couldn't help the powerful sensation that kept funneling into his consciousness that he was required to be here. For whatever reason, he was unsure. And, for another reason he couldn't fathom, he felt like he'd been here before, as a familiar sensation kept arriving in his gut.

"What is it?" asked Grimes, standing over Cam and Cat in the cockpit.

Cam was staring through the cruiser. They docked in what had been a parking garage, now gutted to allow easy landing for any cruiser or starship. Numerous ships were stationed in the docking bay. All was quiet except for the raging storm outside, although the thunder, pelting rain, and ocean squalls softened once the cruiser entered the skyscraper.

"Earth to Cam," said Grimes. "You there?"

Cam sat forward, staring. "I have a strong feeling that I've been here before."

Grimes shrugged. "It's Miami. I used to take family vacations here all the time. Obviously, before the ocean tide destroyed everything all the way to central Florida. Remember that catastrophic event?" Cam turned to Grimes; he seemed a bit too excited. "Took years for the dead bodies to stop washing up on shore."

"Strategically planned and competently executed," said Cat.

Cam and Grimes shared skeptical stares.

"What?" said Cat. "You don't know about that either? The Florida destruction was a political game." Cam was sure that Cat could sense their unacknowledged truth. "A human order was given to the SST-3 submarine to torpedo rebellion base operations in Miami. The resulting attack created… what you see here. Since there were no survivors, there was no one to challenge the official story, as I'm more than sure a good amount of people heard the attack. Official and confidential documents revealed communication prior to the floods regarding the attack. These reports were suppressed and held back from the populace."

"Fuckin government's been corrupt for centuries," muttered Grimes.

Cat looked at Grimes. "Correct," he said. "It's a common game, suppress information that doesn't reflect the narrative. It's rather easy to call out a conspiracy theory, therefore segregating anyone questioning authority as a baseless fool or mentally ill."

"PsyOps," said Cam.

"Correct," said Cat.

"Make us think we are less than. Have us believe we are dependent and that survival requires big brother's help."

"Again, an accurate assessment. Human beings are all powerful; your enemies and leaders know this and will stop at nothing to make sure you never find out. Division has allowed you to be conquered; programming of a false narrative, including the God concept, religious superiority, and political division, has been your demise. When a species is taught to believe that any semblance of hope, order, survival, or peace in their lives in contingent on external sources, that species loses the ability to go within, always looking for an external solution to an internal challenge. Hence, the mind becomes confused and reaches for whatever can fill the void. But the power you possess still exists within the depths of your subconscious, creating a direct conflict between what you feel is instinct to what they have taught you to believe is true. Therefore, your species is susceptible to illness, addiction, and mental health ailments. You should be all-encompassing, and able to heal from within." He pointed to his temple, referencing the brain. "All healing has been given to you. All the answers exist within the subconscious realm of heart and mind, energy, emotion and the physical body. Should you have all celebrated your differences and looked within for evolution and prosperity, humanity would be far beyond most every species in the universe in terms of evolution; instead devolution has occurred." Cat's eyes gleamed, looking over at Cam and Grimes.

Cam turned to Grimes. "He's saying we're devolved brainwashed lunatics."

"That is not my calculation towards present company," said Cat.

"Sounded like it," said Grimes. He patted Cat on the shoulder. "Don't worry about it. I'm just glad you're on our side. Considering your contempt for our species, I wouldn't ever want to fight you."

"Thanks to Annison," said Cam.

Cat rose from his seat. "Affirmative," he said, "Now that human is a testament of an unadulterated mind. Her evolution is a credit to your race."

Cam rolled his tongue inside his cheek. "Grant it. Now that the history lesson is over, what's the plan Cat?"

"Simple," he said. "I've already scanned all necessary ships in the docking bay. Fortunately, there are three vessels here that have our necessary parts. Since I am the most unlikely to raise questions if discovered, I'm the best suited to gather what we need."

"So you want us to stay here?" said Cam. "Why not just take one of those ships?"

"Negative," said Cat. "Those ships have tracking devices. They'll find you rather quickly and discover your whereabouts and the Robyn Winter location. I have also received a communication that the Chordata tracked our trajectory. They are not aware of our exact location; however, time is of the essence. It will be best if we are not here when the search party arrives. If our goal is to remove all possibility of them finding Robyn Winter's location, if we depart prior to their knowledge of our whereabouts we will essentially achieve our goal."

"That was a mouthful," said Grimes. He patted Cat on the arm. "Okay, Cat, you're hired. Just don't leave us here."

"That would go against my current programming."

"That's a relief," said Grimes. He cocked his head and clucked his tongue. "Get to it then."

"I shall be back soon," said Cat as he trooped out of the cockpit.

Grimes took his seat, put his head back, and sighed. Cam couldn't take his eyes off the door leading into the building. He wanted to go in, to see what was happening in this undisclosed location. For better or worse, knowledge always wins the battle.

He suspected Robyn Winter would know.

14

CAMERON had gotten up to retrieve synthetic blood.
He was malnourished, he knew, could feel it in his
veins, his blood becoming dormant, struggling to bring
nourishment to his internal system.

He required blood; every instinct confirmed this
need. And the longer he remained by Annison's side,
the stronger his thirst became. But he would never hurt
his friend. He refused to allow the thought to manifest
inside his mind. Annison's innocence and gentle nature
were something to be cherished and applauded in a
world wrought with war. To Cameron, Annison
represented the best of humanity, the best potential
source of our evolution. The thought of corrupting her
veins with his desire to drink from her vein turned in
his mind with a guilt complex.

How could I ever even think about hurting her?

But he wanted to. Wanted to tear his teeth into
her neck and satisfy the hunger that drove his mind
wild. She looked so peaceful while sleeping. So
innocent. And she knew so much. She is very wise, he
thought. Knew so much more than he did, and it

wasn't because she was older, not by much, a few years if that. No, her knowledge came from what she'd been taught, and how she lived. And here he was, turned into a freak and, as a result, he had no recollection of any part of his past prior to waking up in the military camp where he found Cam.

He wished he could remember. Remember anything. His parents. His past. Did he have a brother or sister? Were they dead or alive, living somewhere in a safety camp? And his most dire question, are they looking for him or had they abandoned him, given up on trying to find him?

He popped the top off the synthetic blood and drank furiously. Blood raced down his chin as he gulped and finished the bottle. He leaned his forehead against the closet, breathing deeply. Could feel the blood rushing inside his veins. Could hear it like a thunderous tidal wave barreling towards its destination. His shaking hands ceased as he drew in another breath as his heart calmed to a normal rhythm.

Caaaaammmmmerrrrrooonnnnn!

He snapped his head up. The voice was in his head; he was sure. He looked around, craned his head to see Annison sound asleep and Perseus sitting quietly.

Caaaaammmmmmerrrrrooonnnnn!

Now the voice was everywhere. He stepped into the room with Annison and Perseus. Perseus grunted, staring at him.

"Did you hear that?" asked Cameron, staring over the cruiser.

Again the voice, this time outside the cruiser. Annison stirred in her slumber, moaned, and went silent. Cameron could see how she was sweating, her hair, saturated, clung to her skin. Her breath labored, her heart beating fast in her chest.

Caaaaammmmmerrrrrooonnnnn!

He snapped his head around, confident the voice came from outside the cruiser. He followed it, went to the door and stopped, scanning the dock. His attention caught by Cam and Grimes talking in the cockpit. Their backs were to him as he stepped into the docking bay.

Nothing, no one was there. On his left, he could see Cat working on another cruiser.

Caaaaammmmmerrrrrooonnnnn!

He snapped to his right, rounded the cruiser when the door came into full view. Perseus grunted behind him. He, too, was staring at the door.

"What?" said Cameron. "What do you think it is?"

The voice again, this time loud and sinister, like a heavy evil baritone. Cameron jumped, put his hand to his mouth.

Coooommme Caaaaammmmmerrrrrooonnnnn!

He tilted his head, staring, when he noticed his feet were moving. Moving towards the door.

15

PHIL traced Moth's whereabouts to the tower in the center of Drac City. According to Dalious, Dracs referred to it as Drac Tower. Moth was on the thirty-third floor. Phil had successfully planted a seed in Moth's ether, allowing him to locate Moth. At least until Moth became privy to the seed, which he undoubtedly would in time. Phil was certain that current circumstances deterred the vampire from initiating a temporal and ethereal scan. But once he did, Phil's ability to track his whereabouts and his ability to find Sandy would become exponentially more difficult.

He was confident in his ability to fight vampires, but battling every vampire in Drac City would take something or someone truly special, like Robyn Winter. He may not be allowed to take life, but he could definitely use all his power to disarm and dismantle his pursuers with general ease.

Robyn has abilities that fly in the face of all laws of physics, thought Phil, snaking around Drac Tower in the gallows, a phantom within the mist, the dark fog that gripped the gallows. All was quiet; all vampires had returned to their homes, turning Drac City into a ghost town. Phil found it ironic how he, known to Dracs as the phantom, was terrorizing vampire city. He'd been told stories about the Dracs from long ago, when they first arrived on the planet and would sneak up onto the surface, terrorizing small villages, eating and murdering as if some plague had gripped the village, draining all blood from their victims, hiding in the night and gone by day. Families would go to sleep in perfect health and upon waking would find a loved one dead in their sleep, completely drained. How awful it must have been for them, how horrific. And to think how humanity romanticized these creatures of death sickened him to his core.

They are vampires here with one purpose, to drive humanity into slavery and take over the planet. Romanticizing such a species was as foolish as it was consequential. Best advice, if a vampire ever confronts you, don't expect a romantic encounter; cut that fucker's head off and get out of Dodge. The only good vampire is a dead vampire; leave no question about it.

Phil stepped through the fog and looked up. The computer on his visor calculated his projection to the thirty-third floor. This side of Drac Tower had docking bays on every floor where smaller ships could drop off pedestrians for easier access into the tower when he heard a sniffling, snarling growl behind him. Phil turned abruptly to the sound. Again the snarl, arriving through a thicket of fog. He stepped towards the noise as the fog grew dense around him; his sonar capability revealed a tall and monstrous steel fence not more than a few feet from where he stood. He stepped closer and gripped the thick bars as the fog thinned within reach inside the fence. He could see monsters crawling on all fours. Lycan, thought Phil. Tons of Lycan growled as they inched closer to him.

He clenched his fist, staring at the werewolves that approached him when a clear vision of a wolf humanoid gripped his thought. And as quickly as the image arrived, it faded into the subconscious. He placed his palms on the steel bars when those growls and snarls turned to whines and whimpers. Phil's heart sank looking over the Lycan, the horde of werewolves. He scanned across the clearing. There had to be a thousand inside the fence.

Torture. Conditioning. Words and revelations gripped his thoughts. He knew then the species had been subjugated, forced to abide by the will of Drac. And the Lycan all bowed like an abused pet, confused by its orders. He bowed in return when another Lycan barreled through the horde, a monster of a werewolf, panting, its tongue lapping as its claws sank into the belly of the Lycan it had barreled over. Tore its talons up the torso, shredding the wolf in its grasp. The others cowered before this abusing Lycan, moving back and into the shadows. The abusing wolf eyed Phil, its red eyes beaming hate, as it jumped and tore towards him. Phil stepped back as the Lycan rammed into the fence, barking and yipping when it hit the ground, having bounced off the fence.

Phil's heart sank watching the wolf jump and claw at the fence continuously. He could see madness in its eyes. Its rage for blood as it reached its claws through the fence. Its jaws chomping on the thick steel bars like a diseased rabid dog. The Lycan then dropped to all fours, started pacing back and forth, all the while glaring at Phil with those deep red eyes. Phil backed up, backed all the way up until his back touched Drac Tower.

"Sorry buddy," said Phil. "But that's a fight I don't have time for."

He looked up at Drac Tower; the pinnacle reached so high he craned his head all the way back and still couldn't see the top. There had to be a few hundred floors.

He tracked his trajectory to the thirty-third floor docking bay before igniting his jet back. Floor after floor raced by with glints of silver as he thrust out of the misty gallows to the thirty-third floor, ceased the jet pack's anti gravity mechanism and dropped feet first on the docking bay.

Where Calla was waiting for him.

16

SANDY followed Diagon through the gallows. They were heading towards the main docking bay; from there they would commandeer a starship and be gone from Drac City within moments. According to Diagon, Moth had no recourse but to kill Sandy, recent events being the straw that broke the camel's back. Not that he would have allowed her to live despite current circumstance, as Sandy had suspected he was a devious and manipulative vampire and he was going to rip out Sandy's heart no matter what had happened.

Once he received answers, that was. Apparently, according to Diagon, Moth suspected the greys were responsible for Sandy's change. Also, according to Diagon, he refused to acknowledge that Sandy could have been spawned naturally from the universe, as was the point of view possessed by the red robes.

But the genuine concern for Sandy was the fact that she required Moth's intelligence on the whereabouts of Adam. And as she continued to follow Diagon, she could feel the ability to secure his location slipping into the void. She will need to confront Moth to find her answers, not run and hide.

"Live to fight another day," Diagon had told her. "You will need all your strength and wits to confront him. You're not prepared for such a conflict. Not yet." She stopped at the end of the hall, her back to the wall as she closed her eyes. A moment later she opened her eyes, said, "All clear," and rounded the corner. Sandy following close behind.

Diagon's footsteps were soft and seemed to glide across the floor. At the end of the hall was a glass door; beyond was the docking bay. Sandy could see the multitude of starships on the dock. Diagon went to the door, hid by the wall, peering out, assessing. She turned to Sandy. "Good to go," she said, a small smile across her lips as Sandy's eyes lifted to the vampire, now standing beyond the door. He craned his head, and the door exploded. Diagon was thrown into the hall from the sheer force of the explosion. Glass shards tore through the air as the ground shook beneath Sandy's feet and she felt herself reeling back, landing with a thud as she slid across the ground. Her head rocked against the wall, shooting pain to the back of her skull as she scampered to her feet, watching the vampire stomp down the hall.

On Sandy's left, three more vampires approached. Diagon was down, unmoving, and the vampire raced towards Sandy.

"This will be easier for you should you choose to come with us," said the vampire barreling towards her.

"Moth requires your attendance." He held what looked like a halo between his hands. "This won't hurt you; it'll simply incapacitate your telepathic ability."

The three vampires on Sandy's left moved with caution towards her, stealth and seething, guns drawn as the head vampire stopped cold not a few feet from Sandy. Behind him she could see Diagon, a small pool of blood beneath her skull, but she stirred, the movement proof she was alive. Sandy could see her body flop over to the side as Sandy gritted her teeth, snarling at the vampire in front of her. She looked left, assessing, looked back to the vampire in front of her, craning her head, glaring, her eyes wide. She turned from head vampire to the left then back to the head vampire. Watched as Diagon struggled to her feet.

"Are we going to do this the easy way or the hard way?" asked the lead vampire.

In that moment, the click kicked in. *Move like a snake.*

The lead vampire stepped closer as Sandy kicked her right foot over her head. Her torso bent forward as her foot burst into the vampire's nose. She swung the same foot back around and connected with the halo, now tossed from the vampire's hands into the air. Sandy lifted into the air, her left foot connecting with his jaw that flung the vampire back into Diagon's arms as Sandy flipped over onto her feet. All Sandy heard was the snap of his neck from Diagon's grip. She caught the halo as the three vampires rushed at her, snatched it to the head of the first vampire, then forced him into the wall with a furious telepathic thrust that crushed the back of his skull with a burst of blood that smeared across the wall as his dead body slumped to the floor. Sandy moved fast, she caught the rifle held by the second Drac and side stepped the particle blast that tore a hole through the wall behind Sandy as she chopped the gun in half with a quick thrust, then caught the vampire's throat and tore his windpipe from his neck.

The final vampire received a fist that tore through his torso and through his back, his spine clenched in Sandy's fist. Strange thing happened then. The vampire's emerald eyes pleaded with Sandy as if he wished to offer an apology, receiving sympathy before slipping into the unknown. She thrust her first from his torso, spine still in hand as he dropped with a thud to his knees, collapsing backward, dead on the floor.

Snarling, Sandy dropped the spine on top of the body, said with a hiss, "The eassssssssy way," as she wiped the blood from her hands. Her red robe now stained with dark crimson Drac blood.

When she turned to Diagon, the stare in Diagon's eyes was wide and wondrous, despite the fact that another Drac soldier had fit a halo over her head, holding a gun to her temple, her throat caught in the crook of his arm. She attempted to speak, but the halo must have cut off her ability to do so. Sandy eyed the gun at Diagon's temple.

"Don't try it," said the vampire. "You're fast, my lady, but no one is that fast."

Now a new slew of vampire soldiers arrived on Sandy's left and outside the shattered door. A horde of vampires in all directions.

The same vampire said, "Even with all your strength you won't be able to fight off such an attack and your friend here will be dead." He shook his head as he clucked his tongue and squeezed Diagon's throat. "I can crush her larynx with just one more squeeze." Diagon gasping, eyes bulging, the vampire sniffing her skin as he raised her off her feet, standing tall, erecting his shoulders. "Moth requires your presence. There is no need for further loss of life."

The vampires on her left approached with caution, surrounding Sandy, stepping over the dead, halos held in their hands. Sandy turned to Diagon, choking, her eyes rolling up.

Sandy raised her hands in surrender, her nose curled, grinding her teeth.

"Allow them to slip on the halo," said the vampire.

Sandy's lips trembled, clenching her jaw as they attached the halo to her forehead with an immediate sinking sensation that raced from Sandy's head to her feet. She dropped to her knees, weary, her eyes rolled to the back of her skull, then lazily fell forward.

"Good girl," said the vampire. "Cuff her too," he

ordered, and two Dracs pulled her forward, securing her wrists.

Sandy could feel her strength dissipating. The rose ability tapped from her veins as she fell back on her ass against the wall. Her eyes, bleary and narrow, saw Moth behind the vampire with Diagon. He put his hand on the vampire's shoulder.

"Excellent work Zon. You'll be honored for your bravery." He may have been referencing the vampire next to him, but his eyes never moved from Sandy.

Zon said, "What do you wish to be Diagon's fate?"

Moth stepped away from Zon and Diagon, stepped over the dead vampire, and moved forward, glaring at Sandy. He gestured quickly to Zon and Diagon, brief, then turned that sinister scowl back to Sandy when he said, "I have a special brand of torture waiting for the dear prophetic Diagon." He craned his head; his lips pursed a cold dark purple. "She'll make no more trouble for Drac ever again."

Sandy's right hand shook as she cursed herself for allowing the halo. The thought of tearing him limb from limb, to claw through his mind to find Adam until Moth was nothing more than a feeble and pathetic mental weakling tore through every vein in her body.

Moth, walking towards her, snarling. As he approached, his ether preceded him, barreling down on Sandy with the weight of a planet. Hard to breathe. Air caught in her swelling throat as her head bobbed back and forth as she fought to bring air into her lungs. Hands trembling now, pressure in her skull to the point she was sure her eyes were going to pop. Felt blood seep from her ears as her heart swelled in her chest, ballooning and struggling to draw a beat. Felt blood stream from her eyes when her vision turned red. Moth, crouched in front of her, gripped Sandy's temples. Pain now like a knife in her skull, stabbing, twisting, churning in her brain.

Lock the room, she thought as her tongue fell limp across her lips. *Go dark.*

She forced her eyes to cease rolling, staring directly into Moth and the rage revealed in his eyes.

"Useless," he seethed, slamming the back of her head against the wall as he sprang to his feet and Sandy flopped across the floor.

Her eyes found Diagon; a terror filled stare gripped her countenance. And the last Sandy heard was Moth's instruction.

"Bring her to the pod," he said. "Allow this phantom to find her there."

17

CALLA thrust his boot into Phil's chest. Pain shot
through every part of Phil's body as if the heavy foot
snapped his bones. Reeling back off the ledge into free
air, he thought his chest had cracked as he flipped over,
ignited his jet pack and rushed at the anticipatory Calla
who gripped Phil by his neck and leg and tossed him,
whirling into the docking bay door with such a force
Phil crushed through the door and into a wide open
empty floor with fifty foot high ceilings. Phil slid across
the floor, spiraling, flipping, turning, tumbling. His
eyes snapped shut as the pain writhed up inside his
skull and he slid to a stop, clutching his chest as he
gasped to bring air into his lungs.

He heard feet stomping towards him. Calla,
thought Phil as he forced himself to his knees,
retracting his visor as Calla's heavy fist crushed across
Phil's jaw. Saw the lights go out, darkness awakened as
he felt himself being thrown backward, landing with a
heavy thud to the floor, legs over his head as he
stumbled back onto his knees. Blood in Phil's mouth,
he spit a tooth and blood filled dribble to the floor, his

eyes bleary, wet with tears, and he felt blood across his lips, seeping into his mouth, across his tongue.

Calla stomped towards him. "I'll use your bones to pick human flesh from my teeth," Calla snarled as he snatched Phil's shoulders in his talons, lifted him like a child into his arms and squeezed like a bear when an immediate blood-curdling scream erupted from Phil's throat; felt like his spine was on fire. Calla grinned with a chuckle. Phil slammed his hands across Calla's arms, attempting to wiggle himself free from Calla's grasp.

"Human," Calla taunted him, grinding his teeth. "No phantom no more."

He thrust his forehead into Calla's face and immediately saw stars and darkness. Phil shook his head; Calla's skull was like iron. Phil's back cracked and popped, the pain excruciating as Calla laughed before heaving Phil over his head, then thrust him across Calla's knee and his back just about snapped in half. A painful groan escaped Phil's throat. He dropped to the ground on his hands and knees and Calla thrust his boot into Phil's side. Pain seared through his ribs, racing across his chest, wrenched with burning, furious heat in the back of his skull. The kick so powerful Phil lifted across the air, tumbling head over feet yards away from Calla.

Phil on his hands and knees, hard to breathe and he thought his lungs were on the verge of collapse. Calla took Phil's head between his hands and lifted him off the ground, felt his skull on the verge of cracking and splintering, his eyes about to pop from his skull as Phil ignited his jet pack propelling him from Calla's grip towards the ceiling, but Calla gripped his ankle.

"Where are you going, little one?" taunted Calla as he whirled Phil across the air and slammed him against the floor. Another kick to Phil's stomach. Again, he felt himself reeling back, slammed against the ground and crashing into the wall. Phil's eyes wide, a heavy breath, his mouth wide open, needing air, needing oxygen in his restricted lungs, watching as Calla thumped towards him and Phil forced himself to his feet just as Calla thrust his blade towards Phil's head.

He caught the blade with his own, sidestepping away from the wall and Phil advanced, blade against blade, Calla's heavy arms barreling down across Phil's blades. Heavy swooping arms brought Phil to one knee, his arms heavy and hurting as he ignited his claws and stabbed Calla's right leg. A grunt escaped Calla's throat. Phil swiped his free blade across Calla's stomach; Calla's face pinched in pain as he gripped Phil's neck and tossed him backward where Phil slid across the floor on his back, tumbled over, and onto his knees. Calla, nursing his wounds, snapped his head towards Phil, his breathing heavy, as he stood tall, revealing his massive height and advantage.

Calla stepped forward. "Is that all you got, phantom?" goaded Calla, his voice thick, sinister, seething. Blood seeping from his leg, his stomach, pain pinched across his face as he advanced. "There's no way you can defeat me."

Phil ignited his jet pack, raced towards Calla, close to the ground, and swiped Calla's leg from under him. He fell face first against the floor as Phil stood. Calla groaned when he raised himself to his hands and knees and Phil propelled up and over to Calla, thrusting his knees down into Calla's spine, then took hold of Calla's skull, yanking the oversized Drac stretching the throat. But Calla thrust his massive frame over, releasing Phil's hold as he tumbled across the floor and Calla clambered to his feet, his mouth dripping with blood. Phil, his legs beneath him, looked up at the massive Drac. His eyes darted up above Calla.

There's only one way, thought Phil, as he snapped his visor over his eyes.

"Think that'll help you?" seethed Calla, head shaking.

Phil used his visor to bring about the sticky bombs in his armor. Aiming his arm at Calla, he brought it up, and aimed at the ceiling.

"What's that you have there, human?"

Phil shot two bombs from the gun that projected from his armor into his hand that whistled past Calla's head into the ceiling above. Calla watched as the bombs attached to the ceiling.

Calla snapped his head towards Phil. "You missed," he snarled.

Phil, head shaking, watching the massive Drac,

counting down the seconds in his head, said, "Some things were meant to happen."

Calla's face pinched, confused as Phil manipulated the surrounding ether, stepped forward and clapped his hands together. His ether barreled towards Calla, wrapping around him and squeezed. Calla grunted in its embrace and Phil stepped forward, clenching, tightening his arms to squeeze the ether stronger over Calla. Squeezing his bones and holding him in place.

"Sorry Calla," said Phil. "But I haven't got the time to continue this game."

The bombs exploded and quickly Calla's head snapped to the ceiling where a thick blanket of marble and silver barreled down towards him and Phil released his ether, allowing Calla to be covered in debris. An oversized piece of ceiling crashed across Calla's skull before he plummeted to the ground and a plume of debris and smoke rifled off Calla's body. The Drac lay unmoving on the floor, his skull cracked, a deep gash flowing blood across his forehead.

Phil dropped to his knees, catching his breath.

18

SANOS waited for Moth in Moth's personal quarter, raking his nails across his arm. The itch was intense, skin crawling and all he could do was scratch like a wolf suffering flees. He sat across from Moth's desk, windows beyond the desk, beyond Moth's throne. Moth's living space was vast and open, tables and chairs strewn across the room. Perhaps to entertain or hold those so very important COR meetings, Sanos scoffed. His thoughts on Plagesous and the sound vibration that tore the Drac into a pool of ghastly blood and bile; an effect Sanos hadn't fully expected, albeit an effect he savored in the vast spell of his consciousness. There was only a matter of time before he used the same on Moth. No wings will allow Moth to fly away from that threat.

Moth sent for him, for obvious reasons. The phantom was alive and he, Sanos the great, had ushered him into Drac City. He was sure Moth was not pleased, not that Sanos cared much for appeasing the COR leader. The phantom's actions brought shame to Moth, cracking the esteemed image his vampires held for him, but this shame was in Sanos' favor. One more step, thought Sanos, towards total dissension for Master Moth.

This was a game; a cosmic game of chess, and he, Sanos, was the knight that would take over all. And like all games, strategy was paramount to victory. First, make Moth appear incompetent, gather favor against Moth from within, then create deception among his own soldiers. Now that Plagesous and Dalious were dead, only Calla stood in Sanos' way. Not even Zon would confront Sanos in this effort; that vampire's loyalty was as hypocritical as a human politician to his own people, absent from day-to-day business.

After he destroyed Plagesous, Sanos went hunting in the human fields, where he feasted on three humans. Their blood fed his veins, but the taste was different, more metallic than normal and the effect-the sensation brought on by required nutrients-lacked the heightened awareness and primal high he'd received from new blood. His stomach churned thinking about feasting on new blood. The thought drove insanity through his mind as he breathed shallow, his lips stuttering, raking those nails across his bloodied cracked skin with a snarl.

Where is this wretched fiend? thought Sanos. He despised waiting, his plan placed on hold. He had to think through to the next step, the next move on the chessboard; a play that required an understanding of Moth's strategy in the wake of present catastrophe.

(Knowing his mind is the key to COR.)

Sanos snapped his head around when the door opened. Moth stomped into the room as Sanos stood and bowed with a slight hesitation. Moth's stare had blood in it, rage and ferocity as he walked past the attentive Sanos who couldn't help the small smile that curled across his lips, seeing Moth so unnerved was a victory in itself.

Moth went to the far side of the desk, across from Sanos, and stood beside his chair. The two vampires staring, sizing the other up; Sanos could feel Moth's distaste for his presence. Moth craned his head, glaring, then closed his eyes with a sigh before addressing his subordinate.

"The phantom is alive, Sanos. How do you account for this?"

"How do you account for it? You saw he was dead the same as I."

"Humans don't come back from the dead, Sanos, there are systems in place to prevent such occurrences."

"Perhaps," retorted Sanos, "he's figured out the mystery of life and death." His sarcastic grin was ear to ear. "Or perhaps he really is a phantom, a ghost in our machine." Sanos craned his head to the right. "What will you do now, Master Moth, to rein in the ghost once and for all? Quite obvious you yourself didn't believe he was dead, considering how you ordered Plagesous and Calla to stand guard in case of an insurrection."

"Of course," retorted Moth. "Never trust a

human. They are sneaky little vile manipulators."
Sanos caught Moth's eyes staring at his clawed flesh.
Sanos stood tall and proud as Moth's eyes returned
Sanos' stare. Now that conniving smile graced Moth's
lips. "Perhaps we have gotten off on the wrong foot."

"What do you mean?"

"The two of us," Moth said, gesturing to Sanos
and himself. "We should work together, Sanos. A
human is loose in our city, murdering Dracs, and we
are both to blame." He raised his finger. "But we must
see the good in our predicament."

Sanos' eyes narrowed. "What good Moth?"

"In my calculation, Sanos, it would be best if we
can question him. Break his mind to gather intel on the
human rebellion. Don't you agree? My opinion is for
the phantom to never leave Drac City. Every vampire
here can feed on him. Every drink a victory to our
cause."

Sanos thought through Moth's declaration. "He
believes the human female is alive," said Sanos. "He
will undoubtedly look for her. Perhaps a trap can be
set?"

Moth said with a slight bow, "Indeed. I have
already set the trap. He's being led to the pod on this
very floor. I presume he is headed this way now."

"Have you requested the necessary protocol to
capture him?" Sanos was sure Moth ordered Zon to
capture the phantom.

"I have not," said Moth. "I want *you* to capture

him."

"Me?"

"Of course," said Moth, stepping away from his desk, his hands clenched behind his back, staring at Sanos. "Who better than you, Sanos? You've already faced this human, you've seen him in action and you've won the battle. Why risk further Drac life when you are clearly capable? Plus, this is a chance for redemption... it was you who brought him here. I'd say that comes with a bit of responsibility to handle this most dire circumstance appropriately."

Sanos clenched his fists, grinding his jaw. He smelled a rat.

Moth stepped closer. "Will you?" he asked. "Will you redeem yourself, Sanos, and bring this phantom to his knees? Do you have the strength to dismantle him?" Moth regarded Sanos' bloodied arms. "Or has your battle with the phantom made you weary and weak?" Moth's smile curled in the corner of his mouth, his eyes mad with rage. "Perhaps I've overestimated your use?"

Sanos craned his head to meet Moth's eyes.

"The great and powerful Sanos," Moth continued. "Please tell me you still have some strength left. A member of COR knows no bounds of strength or determination. Can you handle this most dire assignment?"

Sanos breathed deeply, his stare stoic. "With pleasure," he snarled.

"Good," muttered Moth. "Go then," he said. "We will lead him to the pod, Sanos. Go, and have your day in the limelight."

Moth went to leave, but stopped when Sanos asked, "And where will you be?"

Moth waited in the doorway. "I have another situation that requires my attention," he said. "I need to put a traitor in their appropriate place." His eyes narrowed before walking out the door that closed behind him.

Sanos looked through the window to his beloved city, his thoughts cycling through Moth's strategy. Why the order? Why him when an appropriately placed military team would take down the phantom easier than one lone warrior could? Moth could care less about the loss of his Drac soldiers. There was another reason.

His skin crawled, that itch burning up his arms. Sanos mindlessly raked those long talons across his skin. Blood streamed from his open wounds as his lips curled in a snarl.

What he knew, without a doubt, was that he was being set up.

He would need to counter Moth's move.

19

CAM and Grimes watched from the cockpit as Cameron walked through the door at the far end of the docking bay. The door shut tight after he entered; even Perseus wasn't able to catch the door before it closed.

It all happened in a flash. One moment the door was closed with no Cameron in sight, the next the door opened and Cameron moved through it quickly. All too fast for Cam and Grimes to even move. Cam and Grimes burst out of the cruiser.

"Why would he do that?" asked Grimes.

"How am I supposed to know?"

They ran to the door and past Cat. Perseus was in front of the door, observing it, seeing how he could open it. There was no knob, no hand or eye scanner, nothing to open the door.

"What happened?" asked Cam to Perseus. He pushed on the door with his palms, hoping to slide the door open manually. "Why did he do that?"

Perseus turned to Cam with a growl.

"I don't speak grunts Perseus. What happened? Where's Annie?"

Perseus gestured to the cruiser.

Cam said to Grimes, "Go check on her," as he pushed with all his strength on the door. Perseus doing the same.

"Roger that," said Grimes before darting back to the cruiser.

"Problem, gentlemen?" said Cat. He came out of nowhere. His finger to his temple, his eyes scanning the door with that blue electrical spark raging in his pupils.

"Cameron went through this door not more than a minute ago."

Cat looked at him like he was insane. "How did he open the door?"

Cam continued to push on the door. "I have no idea. It just opened, and he went through. Looked like he was gliding across the floor. It happened so fast." He stepped away from the door in frustration. "Damn it." Perseus kept pushing the door. Cam looked at Cat. "Can you open it? Use that mind… whatever the hell it is." His voice shaky, felt his face turn blotchy and flush. His heart racing, pounding in his chest.

"I don't have telepathic abilities outside of devices specifically equipped for that purpose."

"Wonderful." Cam tried the door again, gaining a good hold with his palms pressed tight against it, and said to Cat, "Get Annie." Perseus growled, using all his strength to force the door open.

"Here," called Grimes, he had Annie with him. Her face was flushed white and red, her hair matted;

apparently she'd been sweating. But all of that took a back seat to the fear that gripped her eyes.

"Why are we here?" asked Annison. "Cameron said we were going back to Robyn Winter?"

"We took a detour," said Cam. He backed away from the door, then turned to Annison. "Cameron went in there. We need to find him. Can you open the door?"

She looked like she was mulling over the situation. Her eyes moving in rapid motion as those two nubs erected from the back of her head, her face scrunched as if she were in pain.

"This may not be in our best interest," said Cat.

"What?" Cam, shaking his head. "We don't leave anyone, Cat. That may not be part of your robotic calculations, but we don't leave anyone behind."

"That's not exactly what I was referring to."

"What do you mean?" asked Grimes.

Cat looked at Grimes as his eyes returned to a blue shade. "It is likely that Cameron did not just wander through this door of his own accord."

"Meaning?"

"Meaning," Cat went to the door, smoothing his hand over it. "Someone on the inside opened the door and brought him through."

"Wonderful," said Cam. "Annie?" Her eyes were moving in such a rapid motion, Cam was sure the girl was on the verge of passing out.

"Got it," she said, and the door opened. There wasn't more than a three-foot opening before blue and purple electrical sparks raged across the door, and with it an energetic hum as if that hum were gathering the electrical current into its embrace.

"What the…" Cam's eyes were wide, watching the current, when it burst like lightning towards Annie with an impact that drove Annie back, slamming the young one to the ground as her body slid across the floor.

"Jesus," said Grimes as they raced to Annison. Perseus continued to pry the door open. "What the hell was that?"

Smoke slithered off of Annison's body. Cat was the first to her and placed his hand over her heart.

"She's alive," he said. "In shock but alive." Annison's eyes clamped shut. Cat looked at Cam. "We need to bring her to the cruiser." He scooped Annie into his arms as Cam rose to his feet, nodding. "The regeneration chamber will help her heal."

"Get her to it," said Cam. He eyed the door and Perseus continuing to force the door all the way open. He'd only managed at most another foot. Cat was heading towards the cruiser. "Cat," called Cam, and Cat turned to him. "Once she's stable, get the cruiser fixed. We may need to leave in a hurry."

"Understood," said Cat before trudging off to the cruiser.

Cam regarded Grimes. "Stay with Annie; help Cat get this cruiser fixed."

"No way," Grimes said. "There's not much I can

do for her after she's in the chamber." He shook his head. "I'm coming with."

Cam stepped closer, gestured to Grimes' shoulder. "You can hardly hold a weapon. If something happens to us, Annison will be alone with only a robot by her side. I trust no one at this moment, even that robot. Stay with her, corporal. Perseus and I got this."

"I don't like it."

"I know," Cam said, walking towards the door. He turned to Grimes. "But we need to make sure at least one of us makes it out of here." He raced to the door, Perseus still struggling, got it five feet. "That's good Perseus," he said. "We can get in."

He slipped through the door, and immediately the stench invaded his nostrils. The room was barren, vast and wide. Cam was sure this room had been a conference room or training room in its heyday. Two sets of doors, one on the left, the other on the right. Perseus grunted behind him.

"Stinks to high heaven," said Cam. "Like something died."

20

ANOTHER strike across Diagon's jaw, courtesy of Zon. They had her chained to a chair, her face swollen, bloodied, and bruised. She spit a wad of blood to the floor, then eyed Moth with a scowl as he sat, enjoying the beating she was taking. It's not as though they were needing answers or information. The beating was simple blood lust, punishment for what Moth deemed was a traitorous act.

Zon paused, holding his fist high. Diagon stared at him, her right eye swollen shut, blood in her left eye as she snarled at him.

"Go ahead," she scolded. "Do what you must, but know the end of everything in Drac history is coming to an end."

Zon turned to Moth, his lips trembling, his body shaking with adrenaline and fury.

Moth ran his tongue inside his mouth. Looked at Zon, said, "I'm rather enjoying myself Zon, please continue."

Zon asked, "Is she to perish? Is that our purpose

here?"

Moth shook his head. "Of course not, we're not animals." He turned to Diagon. "But since we can't have this little bee buzzing around our hive causing an insurrection among our most weary Dracs, filling their heads with lies and myths long proved nonexistent, I have a special plan for our dear Diagon here. My Drac warriors are gathering the required consequence to these actions as we speak. They should be here shortly."

"And the beating?" asked Zon.

Moth eased back in his chair. "Fun," he said with a grin. "A little aggression to relieve the stress from Diagon's actions." He looked at Diagon. "Your behavior has a direct consequence. Here it is. Punishment by the hand of Drac for your betrayal against Drac." He eyed Zon. "Continue."

Moth enjoyed watching Zon deliver the punishment, a stout reminder that Moth was in control. Never turn your back on Moth, the consequence will be dire.

Zon drove his fist across Diagon's cheek. Another across her already bloodied lips, rocking her head back as she slumped in the chair, all disfigured and disoriented.

Moth looked at Zon as if he were a child, unsure of himself. "Continue," he ordered. "We need to teach them all a lesson. All the red robes, that the time for their delusion stops now. We cannot evolve under such duress, waiting for mythos to come and deliver us from evil."

Zon hesitated, Diagon unmoving.

"Now Zon!"

Zon steadied himself. Started whaling one fist after another into the already bloodied Diagon. Her skull splintered, her bones cracked, beaten to an all bloodied pulp until she, with the chair, fell backward. Moth rose from his seat, a sinister smile across his lips.

"Is she alive?" asked Moth.

Zon stepped over Diagon, crouched down, his hand over her solar plexus. "Yes," he said.

"Good," said Moth, when he received a telepathic message.

Master Moth, we have located Calla.

Stellar, answered Moth. *Bring him to me.*

Hesitation, followed by *He's unconscious. The ceiling fell on him. We think it was the phantom.*

Moth closed his eyes, grinding his jaw. The last of his three most trusted warriors, his massive Calla, defeated by the phantom. Seemed like the walls were closing in on him. Who could he trust to provide undying loyalty? Certainly not Sanos; his rebellious and traitorous acts were on the way to a private hell. Sanos secures the phantom, or the phantom kills him. Either way was fine with Moth, and if he does best the phantom, Sanos will meet with an untimely accident of sorts. No way does Sanos receive his seat with COR; that would be a catastrophe for all Drac. He looked at

Zon, but Zon's teaching was far too evolved for Moth to take him under his wing. Like Dalious, Calla, and Plagesous, Moth selected his warriors at their earliest age. In order to educate them in his ways, it was vital for their minds to be unadulterated from opinions and programming from others; he wanted them schooled and loyal to his philosophy and his philosophy alone. This revelation over his warriors' demise gathered a new conundrum for Moth to contemplate. Those walls were closing in, closing in and suffocating the life breath from his Drac lungs.

Master Moth?

Yes, complete your assignment and gather with the rest of the soldiers outside the pod.

Orders received.

"What is it?" asked Zon. "What's happened?"

Moth looked at the ceiling, breathing deeply.

"Master Moth?"

Moth turned to Zon, eyes blinking when he said, "They have found Calla. The phantom has done a number on the poor Drac." He shook his head.

The stare on Zon's face registered disbelief. "Calla," he said, more to himself than to Moth. "But he's one of our most feared warriors. How…"

"The phantom," Moth interjected. "Plagesous and Dalius have fallen under his blade as well. Seems the devil has come to Drac City."

Diagon broke into a fit of coughs and groans. She must have heard their conversation. "Gone because the prophecy is true. The phoenix has come. She will right all wrongs and set us free."

Moth rolled his eyes, seething he said, "It is that exact blasphemy that is required to be snuffed out." He gestured for Zon to return Diagon to her seat.

Zon lifted her up, slammed her down, seat and all. Blood rushed from every pore and every contusion across Diagon's head. The door slid open.

"Ahh," said Moth. "The time has come." He turned to Diagon as three Drac warriors entered the room, wheeling in a cart with a large glass tube on top of it, each one holding a tall staff in their free hand. Inside the cube was a black and slimy slug, a foot long. The slug slithered in the cube, tentacles sputtered into the glass as if attacking. Moth smoothed the cube over as if he were admiring a pet. "Marvelous," he said. "Seems your narrative, Diagon, will be no more."

Moth watched while Diagon's one eye grew wide with fear.

"Told you I had a special surprise for you."

Diagon's head shaking, "You can't do this. There's no justification. No Drac has ever been under the control of a symbiote." She looked at every Drac in the room. "You can't allow this to happen." No response. They did nothing but stand quiet, jaws hung open. "This is against the rule of law." A slight whine in the back of her throat.

Moth was handed a thick wool bag, which he used to gather the symbiote, never touching the slimy slug. He wrapped the bag around the cube, opened the end where the bag was and wiggled the slug into the bag, which he quickly held tight, keeping the bag closed as the symbiote within thrashed and slithered inside.

He stepped towards Diagon, said, "Diagon of Drakulon, I have charged you with high treason. Since we do not put our own to death, your charge dictates a life of servitude. This symbiote will allow you to live, but to live under supreme Drac control, and never will you be a threat to Drac again."

Diagon said simply, "Please, don't do this. Send me back to Drakulon. Banish me to the netherworld, but this... I'll do whatever is necessary. You don't have to do this."

The room tensed around Moth. He could hear heavy breathing from his Drac soldiers. *But they must know, they must know who is in control of Drac City.* Diagon gave him no other choice. He thrust the bag over her head and immediately Diagon started thrashing, screaming through the bag.

"So be it, Diagon."

Blood stained the bag, starting small and growing as Diagon's feet shuddered before her body fell limp, her head lolled back. Two quick jerks from her torso as Moth watched the symbiote slither beneath her skin, taking control of those vital organs. Moth craned his head to the left, watching, then pulled the bag from her head. The symbiote was wrapped around her throat, her skull, and slithered into pores in the back of her head as it squeezed Diagon's throat. Her eye bulged when a breath was forced from her throat, the breath stained red over her lips and the symbiote tentacle morphed into a mouth, inhaling the breath.

Moth gestured to his soldiers. "Take her to the gallows with the rest of the symbiotes." He turned to Diagon. She may have a symbiote wrapped around her, but she could still see with her one good eye. Pain. Fear. Rage was in her eye. "Your day in slavery has begun." One of those tentacles reached towards Moth and he quickly stepped away, cringing at the sight of it.

The three warriors who'd brought the cube in used their staffs to release Diagon from the chains used to tie her to the chair. Electrical sparks raged from the top of each staff, snapping the chains. They used the same sparks, forcing them into Diagon's body to get her to move, continuing the same as they took her away.

Moth hollered to them. "And let it be known. Drac City has not only been breeched by the phantom, but he also comes with traitorous Dracs by his side. And those Dracs must be dealt with in the harshest manner." His voice rose to meet their ears. "Behold the first traitorous Drac. Diagon the prophet has conspired with humans to destroy the ways of Drac." His smile grew ear to ear. "See her consequence as a warning to all… Never betray your own."

21

THE hall was barren. All was quiet, and Phil's gut instinct told him he was walking into a trap. Moth was here, on the thirty-third floor. Phil's seed guided him, projected on the screen over his eyes; a beacon to Moth. Blinking beacon revealing that Moth was inside a room with some pod sitting center stage. Phil closed his eyes, wanting to see the seed, to see through the seed. Moth was a powerful Drac, more than likely the most powerful of all Dracs, and Phil understood the possibility that Moth had recognized the seed Phil had disguised in Moth's ether, setting up this most dire trap for Phil to walk into. All he could see through the seed was the pod, a silver crypt lying on a pedestal in the center of the room. Inside the pod he could see closed eyes, Drac skin over those eyes.

Moth?!

He came to the end of the hall, leaned against the wall. He knew no one was on the other side of the wall. Sonar revealed that much, but he required further intel. Phil closed his eyes, going within, scanning his internal system.

See through it all. See through this time. Where are they? What is waiting?

In his mind's eye, images raced across his internal screen, his ethereal seed projecting further into the room with the pod, through the walls where a horde of Drac warriors waited, his seed like a fly on the wall. Dracs conversed, but the sound was muffled, like listening under water. They did not look pleased. On the wall in front of them was a window they could see through, although on the other end this window was disguised, apparently to allow undisclosed observation. Phil counted the Dracs. Six warriors waited, more than likely waiting for Phil to arrive, protecting Moth as he lay in the crypt. But he wanted to know more. He followed the seed obeying his command, scanning the room the Drac warriors occupied. Seems the only entrance in or out of that room was the one they waited behind. Phil could locate no other way in or out.

Except?

The seed rose to the hundred-foot high ceiling. Access portals existed in the roof and there was an obvious entry to the Drac warriors below. He followed the seed through the ceiling, inside the roof, mapping the ceiling towards his current location.

Works like a charm, he thought, looking up as he lifted into the air, his jetpack quiet as he hummed to the ceiling, removed the marble tile, sliding it over and then projected up and through the open tile. Steel beams held the tiles in place. Phil landed softly on those beams. His sonar clicked over to account for the lack of light, the crawl space bathed in darkness. The crawl space wasn't a crawl space, he could walk with no issue. The ceiling here was ten feet high. Phil crouched down, replacing the tile.

He swerved towards the location of the pod room, sonar mapping his destination. He made his way to it, walking across those steel beams.

Supreme focus, he thought.

And once Moth is within my grasp…

Total obliteration.

22

SANOS perched outside Drac Tower, outside the window of the room where the pod was located. The lip that jutted from beneath the window allowed Sanos to watch all that happened inside the room.

Who's in the pod? he wondered. Apparently the pod held a Drac, but which Drac he couldn't be sure. Something was rotten in Drac City, and it stunk like a putrid, decayed and rotting animal. Sanos snarled while observing the room. All was quiet, but he was sure there were Drac warriors beyond the wall, in the observation room, although he couldn't tell how many. Obviously, the trap had been set. He was supposed to be in that room and he was sure the Drac warriors waited for him. Him, and the phantom.

Perhaps this was Moth's plan; do away with his most dire threats, the phantom being the first, Sanos himself the second. Or first? Moth was indeed devious, and Sanos had no trust in the COR leader. He was sure Moth would destroy Sanos when given the chance. Maybe this was his chance?

Sanos was supposed to be waiting in the room, waiting for the phantom as if there was a reason for the phantom to arrive in this very room. He'd thought the dead human female's body was going to be on display. How wrong he was.

His skin swarmed with an itch that couldn't be satisfied. His arms clawed and bloody, even when his arms would heal, he'd reopen the gashes with the next rake over his skin.

He thought about confronting the warriors but decided to leave them to the phantom, and if they were victorious, he would then have a pleasant surprise waiting for them. Deliver the phantom myself and deem Moth a murderer of his own. Sanos snickered, thinking about his rise to glory in the eyes of Drac. Moth's incompetence, his lust for power, would be his downfall. He'd even murdered Dracs to advance his cause, is what Sanos would proclaim. Sanos breathed hoarsely through his nose, noticed how his nose drew in snot, his nose wet and running.

He waited. Waited for the phantom to arrive. Waited for the trap to spring, all the while raking his arms as dribble snot raged from his nostrils when the door to the pod room opened and Sanos stepped beside the window, behind a slab of silver wall that cut through the windows. He craned his head around, looking through the window to see who entered the room.

His eyes grew wide, staring.

It wasn't the phantom who entered.

It was that insipid Kaal.

23

Caammmmmeeerrroonnnnn!

Cameron followed the trajectory of the voice that had taken him through the double doors on his right when he first entered from the docking bay. He felt like he was being led by the hand through each door. The first door he'd gone through opened to a large lobby, completely barren except for some wires that hung through missing tiles in the ceiling. The only light was from emergency alarms on the walls, dim and soft. In the lobby center, a staircase led to the floors below, the top of which was on the floor where he stood. The staircase descended, but Cameron couldn't see exactly where they led other than down. A waist-high wall surrounded the opening where the stairs descended; Cameron went to it, looked down. All he could see were ocean waves four floors below. Nothing else, no signs of life, but the voice called again, driving him down the hall past the stairs. He followed it, sensing urgency brought on by the voice, hurriedly down the hall, noticing how his feet were sloshing across the carpet when he halted. He looked down; the carpet was saturated in the hall, but that made sense considering there was water everywhere. Except around the staircase, which he found odd.

Caammmmmeeerrroonnnnn!

His head snapped to the voice that raged from down the hall. He raced towards it, passing closed door after closed door to the end of the hall, where he paused. The hall went left and right. Across from him, another closed door. He went to it, but the moment his hand touched the doorknob, the voice raged again. On his left, he snapped to it, ran down the hall, his feet sloshing through the saturated carpet. Racing towards the door at the end of the hall, a sign above, tattered and worn, hung loosely above the door. **Emergency Exit.** He was racing to a staircase.

As he neared the door, a sense of dread seemed to thicken in the air. He could see the atoms that made up the surrounding particles, thickening as if blocking him from the door. He ran through it, felt a wash across his skin, a cool mist on his skin like parachuting through a storm cloud as he barreled through the door that slapped against the back wall.

Caammmmmeeerrroonnnnn!

Up above. Cameron eyed the concrete stairs leading to the next floor. He stood there, looking up, calculating his exact location, remembering how the docking bay was below the roof, not by many floors, maybe one or two, which meant he was going to the last floor before the roof or the second to last. And as he took the stairs up, he tried to remember, tried to remember how he got here. That, and wanting to know where the electrical current raging from the floor above was coming from.

24

AT first, Cam had second-guessed himself for allowing Perseus to come with him. Someone could easily notice the giant, and there weren't many places the big guy could hide, either.

But when Cam was weighing his options over which door to go through, which door could Cameron have possibly taken, Perseus led the way. He could smell Cameron, and the giant seemed mad as hell, stomping through the door on Cam's right. He followed the giant into a lobby, Perseus continued into a hall on Cam's right. Cam was confident the giant knew exactly where he was going. Cam followed. Door after door passed by them in a blur.

Déjà vu, Cam thought. The strangest sensation gripped his heart. All was familiar. When he looked up, Perseus was at the end of the hall, stopped, assessing, sniffing. He seemed lost. Cam went to him. Perseus' grimace revealing he'd lost the scent.

Cam looked down both halls, first on his right, which led to a windowed wall. Turned left, another door, leading to a staircase. He gestured to Perseus to follow him; the giant's mouth gaped open and closed as if to tell Cam he agreed and Cam led the way down the hall, all the while knowing. Knowing he'd been here before.

25

PHIL moved the tile from the ceiling, where the six Drac warriors were waiting over a hundred feet below. Two stood at attention, as if watching some events unfold in the room beyond. The others stood idle. They looked frustrated until something drew their attention.

"That's him," the lead Drac said. "That's the traitor?" They all looked through the wall. "Kaal?"

"Master Moth said we would not believe it," another said.

Phil lowered himself down, his jet pack quietly humming, descending on the Dracs. They gathered their weapons, particle beam rifles hung from their shoulders.

"Moth said no survivors. Destroy them both," said the leader.

"I can't see Moth wanting Kaal to die."

The leader snapped, "He said the traitor and Kaal is the only Drac who has entered the pod. There's no other to account for."

Phil watched as his feet drew closer to the Dracs. Any second now and they'll be able to notice him, about fifty feet above.

"What about this phantom?" asked a warrior.

Phil could see how they were watching the opposite room through a mirror, saw the crypt in the room, the pod containing Moth.

"He'll be here shortly," said the leader. "Let us prepare."

Phil turned up the full force of his jetpack and barreled down on top of one of the Dracs, crushing his head into the floor. The two Dracs closest to him turned on a dime. Phil drove his blade claws into their torsos, ripped through their armor and into their stomachs. A Drac stood between them. Phil used the Drac stomachs as leverage to flip over, sending his boot into the Drac's rifle and jaw as his blades twisted in the Drac's stomachs. He landed on his feet and spurred his claws out. Skin, blood, and intestines whipped across the room. A Drac rushed at him and Phil drove his claw into his throat, then used the momentum to lift off the ground, spin and kick the two remaining Dracs. Their rifles flung across the room, his claws tearing at the vampire's neck and throat, severing the head that lopped off the shoulders and dropped to the ground with a slight roll. Blood sprang from the severed neck as the body slumped to its knees and fell forward. Phil landed with a slight bend and swiped his blade across a Drac throat when the remaining Drac warrior wrapped his arms around Phil's neck. Phil sunk his claws into the vampire's thighs; thrust his head against the Drac's face as he yanked his claws from the vampire's leg bones.

The vampire, blood spewing from his nose, his legs seeping blood into a pool beneath him, snarled and rushed at Phil as he ejected the blades across his arms. He swiped across with his right arm. Phil side stepped to his left and drove his claw into the Drac's ribs. A painful hiss tore from the vampire's throat. Phil curled his lips then swiped his free claw across the warrior's face and throat, the force so powerful the vampire fell back ten feet with a thud, his throat torn open, thick gashes across the vampire's face and neck.

Phil breathed deeply, looking over the carnage in the room. Blood slithered from each body and Phil made sure not to touch any part of the slippery dark crimson as he went to the window, his breath heavy, his heart pounding. He expected to see Moth. But there was no Moth in the room. A Drac hovered over the open pod, he seemed feeble and Phil felt a nervous vibration surrounding his ether. Another Drac was lying in the pod, staring up at him; she was thin and looked tiny below the vampire above her. Apparently, the room he was in was soundproof, because neither vampire appeared startled or alerted to his presence. Phil craned his head to get a better look at who was in the pod. The standing vampire was saying something, gesturing to the door. He moved slightly and Phil earned a clear view of the vampire in the crypt.

And Phil thought, Is that? Not possible.

It can't be...

26

SANDY tried to breathe. Kept forcing her throat to draw air into her lungs as she watched Kaal open the crypt, realizing she was at the mercy of Moth's most trusted confidant.

He seemed nervous, his hands shaking. His entire body was shaking, trembling. He kept looking around the room, nervous and afraid. As the crypt opened, Sandy's first thought was to jump and protect herself, but the halo restricted movement. The electrical impulses refused to connect her thoughts to her muscles. Her heart raced, pounding, beating against her chest with a thick hammering that drove that heartbeat into a pounding echo between her ears.

Kaal's eyes snapped to the window. He craned his head, nervously searching when Sandy saw dried blood across the back of his skull. A moment later, he looked at Sandy. His mouth opened, but no words came. Kaal closed his eyes, shook his head, and breathed deeply before addressing Sandy.

First he said, "Will you promise not to hurt me?" His voice cracked with the word hurt. He swallowed hard, and a gasp released across his lips. Sandy felt her eyes narrow, her brow furrowed. Kaal looked over the room again, then back at Sandy. A painful wince across his face. "If I release you, do you promise you won't hurt me?" Sandy tilted her head, staring, confused.

He's going to release me?

Kaal continued, "I know that if you promise you will keep it." He looked over the room again, his beady eyes scanning, and Sandy could feel his heart thumping like a rabbit in his chest. He looked back down at Sandy. "And another promise," he said. He seemed like he was in pain, with the way his face scrunched as if he'd just bit into something bitter and nasty. He whispered, "The human is here. We call him the phantom, but I believe you refer to him as… Phil." Kaal's eyes lit up. "Such a strange name," he said, as if to himself. He turned back to Sandy and gritted his teeth. "I wish for no more loss of Drac life. This Phil has already murdered many Drac. Please take him and go. Go far away. Moth will stop at nothing to destroy this phantom and when he does, he will come for you." He looked up and over the room before returning to Sandy. "Moth has planned to execute you in the morning. Execute you as a traitor to all vampires." His head moving back and forth. "He's already incapacitated your powers. If I don't release you now, you will certainly be dead by morning. You will never see your son then. He will be raised by Moth, here in Drac City."

Sandy went to speak, but no words connected from her mind to her lips. She felt her lips moving, but no words were spoken.

Kaal said, "You can't speak. The halo prevents it. Just blink, blinking is fine. I will have to trust you. Do you promise to leave Drac City with this phantom?"

Sandy hesitated. Moth was her only way back to Adam, this she knew, but if she were dead, there would be no Adam. There would be no future and the thought of Moth raising Adam was the equivalent of driving a stake through her heart. But alive, still alive, she could find the resources to fight Moth and discover her son's whereabouts.

Sandy closed her eyes, opened them a second after. A small smile graced Kaal's lips. He took a key from his pocket and unlocked her handcuffs; her arms fell limp by her side. Kaal craned his head, looking over the halo, pinched the halo on both sides and unlatched the back, pulling with all his strength to remove the halo from Sandy's forehead. His arms and hands tense, grunting in his throat until...

Snap!

Sandy's eyes went wide as a rush ran through her body, head to toe, reviving sensation to her bones, muscles, and joints, like a breath of fresh air. Felt her pounding heart calm to a soft rhythm. Kaal stepped back, halo still in hand, as Sandy scurried her legs out of the crypt and stood.

"Where is Diagon?" she asked.

Kaal's eyes seemed to widen and sink into his skull at the same time as he backed away from Sandy. "Moth gave her to the symbiote," he said. "The first ever Drac to be under their wretched spell."

"What's a symbiote? Is she alive?"

"The life of a symbiote is not any life to live for the host. There is no helping her. Even if the symbiote could be detached, it leaves a chemical in the host that ultimately causes death." He locked eyes with Sandy, head shaking. "She is best left discarded."

"We have to try," said Sandy.

But Kaal kept shaking his head. "I've risked my life to help you. Make good on your promise and find this phantom and leave Drac City. My life, all I hold dear, I have risked by setting you free. I beg of you to keep your promise." He seemed like he could cry; instead, he swallowed those tears.

Sandy craned her head, staring at Kaal. "Why would you do such a thing?"

"Because this must all end. I value Drac life; I value our ways and our heritage. There's no reason for further loss of life. Enough Drac have already perished. What I do today is for the best of all Dracs; whether they are aware of my sacrifice or not does not matter. Death has come to Drac City, my lady. And that death is by your hand should you not leave. There is a star cruiser in the docking bay, number CCF11. I've had the ship prepared for takeoff. Use it and go." He pursed his lips, swallowed hard. "Go Sandy. Take the phantom and be gone... please."

Sandy looked over the room, then at Kaal. "How do I find him?"

To this, Kaal's face scrunched with surprise. "You are a powerful Drac, my lady." His head moving side to side. "Search your feelings, Sandy. Search your mind and you will find him."

27

SANOS listened from the perch outside the pod chamber, watched as the female Drac walked cautiously from the room, Kaal still standing, halo in hand. Sanos grinned as he craned his head looking up and ejected the claws from his blades, then started scaling Drac Tower.

He needed to get to the docking bay. Needed to get there before the phantom and this female Drac took off.

Kaal's actions were a surprise, and Sanos was sure he acted alone. The why behind it mattered not, and Sanos was sure Kaal would have to answer for his actions, answer for them in front of Moth. Sanos grinned, thinking about it, wished he'd be able to see the look on Moth's face when he discovers his beloved is the very vampire who betrayed his order.

Yet another spoke on the turning wheel towards Sanos' rise. A pawn on Sanos' chessboard.

Sanos scaled three floors up, then scaled across the floor to the docking bay where he entered Drac Tower. From this floor, he could sneak down to the docking bay in the gallows. He gnashed his teeth while moving through Drac Tower, ready to dismantle any Drac that came his way.

28

NOW Rodek stirred with a groan on the floor. His neck hurt something awful, the same for his head. He could feel blood seeping from his skull as his eyes drifted open, immediately alerted to the carnage around him as he gathered himself to his hands and knees. His Drac warriors were all dead, lying in pools of their own blood. He lifted to his unsteady feet, caught himself from falling backward as he surveyed his fellow warriors while holding his head. He looked up, watching as the tile above slipped into place.

The phantom!

His head snapped to the window, looked through. Empty, and the crypt was open, the female Drac gone. Rodek shook his head.

The phantom was still loose in Drac City. Rodek's head was fuzzy; using telepathic communication would prove difficult. He tore a communication device from his belt, used his thumb to locate Moth. He was waiting for their intel.

Moth appeared on the com, a hologram on the small device.

"Master Moth," Rodek said. "We have failed. The phantom attacked from above." He placed his hand beside the window and the wall opened. Rodek stepped through. "My team is dead. The female prisoner has escaped."

"Escaped?" said Moth. "How is that possible?"

"The traitor Master Moth. He… he released her."

"Sanos?" said Moth.

Rodek was taken aback. "No," he said, shaking his head. "Kaal. The traitor you spoke of was Kaal. It was Kaal who released her."

Rodek looked down at his master, the stare across his face likened to someone who had just received a punch to the gut.

"Kaal?" said Moth. "Are you sure?"

"Without doubt. It was Kaal."

Moth paused, his head bent, thinking.

"What are your orders, Master Moth?"

But he received no answer; Moth's stare turned from concern to rage. "I want all warriors searching for the female and the phantom. They are not allowed to leave Drac City. Do you understand me?"

"Yes, my master. Orders confirmed," he said as he stomped to the door that slid open as he approached. "What about Kaal?"

Moth considered the question before he said, "Have him secured, I'll meet with him soon."

29

CAM and Perseus climbed the staircase to the floor above, Cam in the lead, Perseus behind him. The door's window painted over in black, impossible to see through. With his hand on the doorknob, he turned to Perseus.

"You smell something?"

Perseus grunted, gesturing beyond the door.

Cam put his ear to the door, listening. Silence greeted him. His breath heavy as he twisted the knob, slowly, and the door opened a crack, held in place by Cam as he looked through to another hall, a replica of the floor below. Cam slipped through the door, stepping cautiously into the hall. A mirror image of the same below, with one exception, there was no window at the end of the hall, instead a second staircase, this one all concrete, narrow, and dark. Cam moved towards the stairs. He counted five steps as he approached where the hall divvied off on his right. He leaned against the wall before the opening, craned his head to look through. No one was there. He was staring at a replica of the floor below, although the hall held no stairs leading down to the next floor, instead the area was wide open and barren.

Where is everyone? Cam thought. All those ships belong to someone.

His thoughts ceased from the sounds coming from above, from the concrete stairs at the end of the hall.

Electrical. Sounded like electricity accompanied with a hum, chatter beneath the hum and electrical sparks. Cam looked back at Perseus, whose mouth gaped open and closed, his eyes tracing across the ceiling. Perseus, his body shivered.

"What is it?" asked Cam. He couldn't help the notion that Perseus was frightened to all bloody hell. His head snapped towards Cam, gritting his teeth and snarling. "Not good," breathed Cam when he turned to the stairs. Took another look down the hall on his right then stepped towards the stairs. The never-ending rainstorm outside the once famed hotel raged outside as a roll of thunder rattled the building. The stairs led to a dark room, a hint of red light in the room. Cam turned to Perseus and put his fingers to his lips; the giant's grunts were loud enough to be heard over the thunder as Perseus rolled his lips inward.

Cam cautiously stepped up, and the air thickened with humidity. Beads of sweat gathered on Cam's brow, his breath heavy. At the top of the stairs, another short staircase emerged on his left. The red glow strengthened as he took the steps up, searching, scanning. The top of the steps looked over the adjacent room. A third staircase led up to another room.

Cam stepped up cautiously as blue and purple electrical beams cascaded across the ceiling from the room below. Those electrical sparks gathered strength, the hum they emitted growing loud as if converging with each other. Cam turned to Perseus, gestured to keep quiet as he stepped up to the landing, crouching low to view the room below.

"Shit," he muttered.

Deep below, Cam assumed must be two floors down, was a large round table surrounding a bronze pod in the shape of a bell. Computer screens were inserted inside the table. Displayed on the screens was an image of the bell shaped pod in what Cam assumed was an x-ray type of vision. He could see on the screen that there was a body in the pod, covered in electrical waves that moved back and forth inside the pod. The hum heightened and Cam put his hands over his ears to muffle the noise. Surrounding the table in front of the screens was a host of aliens and a few humans, eleven in total. Four were alien greys, three were humanoids, they looked absolutely human if it weren't for their short stature–they were tiny, maybe just over four feet tall and super thin–two were the vampires Cam knew all too well, clad in black armor with black cloaks, and two were undoubtedly human. One wore a white scientist coat, while the other wore a general's uniform.

"Friggin' alien council meeting." Cam shook his head as the hum continued to strengthen; apparently whatever was in the bell pod was receiving the brunt of the electrical current. Lining the walls, six feet apart from each other, guards stood at attention. Cam likened them to Egyptian pharaohs with their helmets of gold in the shape of horses, dragons, and reptiles. All holding golden spears.

The electrical current reached high overhead, then spiraled down into the pod, enveloping the pod in an indigo light of electricity. Cam watched as the monitors flickered and the landscape surrounding the pod traveler dipped into the far reaches of the universe, as if the pod raced across the dark recesses of space. He could see how the hand and arm in that pod shuddered. Could see how the pod traveled as if spiraling into a vortex, a wormhole.

The human scientist hollered over the humming electrical current, "One minute to us will seem like an eternity to Alexa."

A grey answered in a language Cam didn't recognize as the sparks and currents rippled towards the pod and vanished, except for the continuous tiny sparks on the pod itself, which moved from its position, raising six feet above the ground. Cam watched the audience waiting in anticipation as the pod opened, the cover sliding from the top to the bottom of the pod. A white mist spewed into the room from the open pod.

From out of the mist a screech followed by a full-blown scream filled with pain as a vampire fell from the pod, its legs caught in some thick block of concrete and the vampire's skull conjoined with what Cam thought was a plastic sheet driven into the vampire's skull.

"Damn it," hollered the scientist. He was standing now, staring at the vampire. And the general beside him did not look pleased.

The vampire kept screeching, crawling across the floor, its new appendages obviously heavy; the vampire struggled to move even an inch. Now the general stood with a disgusted stare.

"Destroy the thing," he said, gesturing to the guards. "Its cries are irritating."

Cam watched as two guards gathered the whining vampire, escorting their captive to the far end of the room, where a door opened. Cam stood up, watching the greys and humans.

"I need more time," said the scientist. "There's got to be a reason behind all of this."

Cam closed his eyes and shook his head, then looked for Perseus, who was no longer behind him. He stepped up into the room bathed in red light. On his right, a wall of concrete blocks lined with what looked like a workstation, although the tools were foreign to Cam. On his left a waist-high wall. Beyond the wall a large open room that led down, onto the next floor. Cam could hear movement and chatter coming from below. The room he stood in was long and narrow, fifty feet deep and twenty feet wide. In the middle of the workstation, a bronze square sat in the middle of two iron rods, held in place by bolts of electricity that reached from the four corners of the two rods. The square had the shape of an old movie clip, but this square was thick, at least an inch thick. Symbols graced the outer edges.

That sense of déjà vu gripped Cam's thoughts.

On the far side from where Cam stood, he observed what looked like a massive hive covered in dark black slime reaching from the bottom to the top of the wall, six feet wide. Cam craned his head, looking into it, and thought he heard a snarl coming from that hive. Directly in front of the hive, a crypt sat horizontally four feet above the ground on top of a thick silver pedestal.

Cameron was in front of the crypt, standing. He looked like a child who'd been scorned by his teacher and forced to stand in a corner, his back to Cam and Perseus. Cam stepped towards him when Cameron opened the crypt, revealing the vampire inside.

30

PHIL was watching Sandy, following her every turn, using his sonar to look through the ceiling.

The vampire he was following was indeed Sandy. Even though her skin had turned Drac, her facial features held the same stare he knew as Sandy. The revelation turned his gut nauseous.

How? That was his only question. *How is it even possible?*

Genetic experimentation was the answer his thoughts provided, remembering Robyn Winter's instruction: You will come upon things that seem unnatural and impossible. But there're many things in the universe for which you have not had experience, things that will test your resolve, and your heart.

Was he referring to Sandy's current predicament? There was only one way to be sure. He still had his mission, and Robyn would know what to do with Sandy. One thing was certain; Phil knew he could not bring Sandy to meet the eyes of every human in Robyn Winter's hidden base. He'd have to meet with Robyn and Sandy in an undisclosed location until

Winter could figure out what to do with her. This was an unprecedented situation; only Winter would know what was best.

Phil stopped moving, allowing Sandy to continue. As he removed the tile to lower himself and meet Sandy eye to eye, he thought, I really hope she doesn't bite.

31

SANDY could feel Phil's presence; his ether carried a distinctly human vibration, and she could smell him. The scent of his human flesh, mouthwatering, and seemed to come from every wall and door she passed, up above and below. Was he waiting, she thought, assessing what she was, what they had turned her into? She couldn't blame him; she didn't know herself.

Maybe, she thought, Robyn Winter would know. Possibly, if there was anyone who would know it would be him. According to Phil, it was his mission to deliver Sandy to Robyn Winter, and he'd gone through great strife to make good on that mission.

Now Sandy could sense how the air behind her turned with a thick spiraling contortion as a breath of air rushed across her skin, and the smell of human sweat gripped her nostrils. And blood! Sandy turned on a dime, seeing Phil in the hall, or what looked like Phil, with his new armor stained blood red, a visor over his eyes beaming white with electrical currents raging across the screen. He pressed the side of his helmet and the screen and helmet retracted. His eyes were narrow and mistrusting. He drew the blades down his arms as he stepped forward. Sandy looked down, a foolish attempt at hiding her vampire features as Phil stomped towards her and Sandy lifted her eyes to him, his face tense and his jaw tight.

"How?" he asked, head shaking, his voice curt and angry. He lifted her chin, scanning her skin, every pore, every scale, and stopped when his eyes locked with Sandy's. She could feel how his ether slackened then. "There you are. I can't... can't believe it."

"They did this to me," she said. "It was not my choice." Her lips trembled as she stared into his eyes. She moved his hand away, stood tall. "They took Adam too. I don't know where. I can't lock in on him."

"Who took him? Drac or grey?"

Sandy considered this, said, "Moth sent him away with the greys, those witches from the compound, and another vampire." Head shaking. "They must be doing something to block me from his location."

Phil grunted beneath his breath. Sandy could see the cogs churning over in his mind, thinking. "Highly possible," said Phil. "Dracs have a psychic link to their children." He shook his head. "They obviously don't want you to find him." He looked around the hall. "Come on. We need to go. Robyn will know what to do." He stepped back, then stopped and looked at Sandy. "This time, don't leave. Stay put if I tell you."

Sandy's brow furrowed. "You've got nothing to

worry about."

Now Phil's brow furrowed. He led the way down the hall to the ceiling tile still open when Sandy said, "We've got to get to the docking bay." Phil turned to her and Sandy sensed his skeptical nature. "Do you have a ship to get us out?"

"I do not, but that was my plan."

"Good," said Sandy when she stopped cold. There was a vampire at the end of the hall.

"Not good," said Phil when Sandy turned to him, his gaze fixed on the opposite direction. Sandy followed his gaze to the horde of vampire soldiers at the end of the hall. Sandy and Phil locked eyes. "It's never easy, is it?"

A small smile graced Sandy's lips. "No, it never is and honestly," she said, turning to face the horde behind them. "I've grown weary of these assholes." Sandy stepped forward as the horde of vampires lined against the wall, slithering across the floor towards them. She looked over her shoulder; the vampire there was closing the gap between them. Phil's helmet was back on, scanning the hall, up, down, right, and left.

"I've got a plan," he whispered, but Sandy had stepped closer to the Dracs coming down the hall. "Sandy?"

"Don't be so concerned, Phil," she said when she stopped cold, raising her arms, palms up, the air around her hands spiraling into a thick cloud where lightning pumped from within. Sandy raised her hands above her head. "I come with many new surprises." She slapped her palms together as she threw the ether across the hall with a powerful explosion that ripped through the vampires. The hall enveloped in a thick cloud of smoke. She looked over her shoulder as the Drac advanced towards Phil when she heard the screech and turned to face the vampire barreling towards her.

32

NOT that feeble and naïve anymore, thought Phil, as he watched Sandy confront the horde. The air around her palms pumping with lightning. He turned to the advancing vampire and his eyes narrowed, head cocked to the right. He'd seen this vampire before.

"Next time you drop down on a Drac," snarled the vampire. "Make sure they're dead."

Now Phil understood; this was the vampire he barreled down on top of from the ceiling. "No worries," he retorted with a slight shake of his head. "I'll finish the job this time."

The vampire attacked, blade against blade. He gripped Phil's throat, slammed him into the wall, lifting him off the ground. Phil's knee found the Drac's ribs, another to his chin releasing Phil's throat as the vampire reeled back. Phil dropped to his feet. The vampire weakened as Phil raced at him, jumping; two kicks to his chest and the vampire dropped on his back, flopped over and got back to his feet.

Phil advanced as Sandy fought off the Dracs down the hall. She held a Drac by the throat, crushed his windpipe and dropped the dead body with a thud as a second vampire attacked from the smoke-filled hall. Phil advanced with a boot to the vampire's chest; again he dropped to the ground then scampered to his feet in a rush. Sandy spun around, catching the next vampire's neck in the crook of her knee, brought his head down, rattled against the floor and twisted her body, snapping the neck as the weakened vampire advanced towards Phil with heavy, labored breath. Blade against blade, and Phil could sense how weak the vampire was. His thrusts carried no strength. Phil caught the vampire's wrist, twisted the Drac's arm, and the vampire grunted a painful groan before Phil sliced his arm in half and the vampire hollered something awful, blood spewing from the severed limb. Phil thrust his claws into the vampire's face, crushing his skull against the wall. He retracted those claws, and the vampire dropped dead to the floor. He looked up to find Sandy had dismantled the entire legion of Drac warriors.

"Took you long enough," she said.

Phil ignored her retort, stepped into the center hall and raised his arm towards the windows at the end of Drac Tower, igniting a glove over his hand, fingers formed a gun and from the sleeve on his armor he shot a small bomb that barreled towards the window, and stuck to the thick glass.

"What're you doing?" asked Sandy when the sound of rushing footsteps descended on the opposite side of the hall.

Phil turned to Sandy. "Getting us out of here," he said when down the hall, in the mist of smoke and carnage, a new vampire stood in the mist.

Sandy stepped forward, said, "Zon," while glaring at the vampire. Another horde of vampires joined him. "What did you do to Diagon?" Sandy seethed.

"That pathetic traitor got what she deserved," said Zon. "And soon the two of you can join her."

Phil took Sandy by the wrist and she spun around with a hiss. Phil's head shaking. "We can't take on all of Drac City and expect to survive." He eyed Zon and the vampires approaching, slithering around him. Some carried particle rifles. Phil looked at Sandy, said, "Live to fight another day."

"Take them," ordered Zon. "Now!"

Phil gripped Sandy's waist and wrapped his arms around her. "Hold on," he hollered over the screeching, wretched, advancing vampires, igniting his jetpack and barreling towards the window that exploded a second before they reached, racing out of the window into Dac City as Phil turned on a dime, moving at lightning speed into the gallows, disappearing into the thick mist below.

33

THE vampire in the crypt wore a red robe. Her wrists bound with thick chains attached to the floorboard. Her face disfigured, lacerations across her skin seeping blood and puss. Her legs completely encased in the same concrete block Cam had just witnessed on the floor below. She coughed blood and groaned. She looked as if she were dying, left in the crypt to hasten death.

Little Cameron never stirred. He stood over the vampire without moving a single limb. Cam wanted nothing to do with the vampire; he approached Cameron cautiously, gripped his shoulder, and the young boy turned with a startled stare.

The boy's eyes blinking rapidly. "Cameron," Cam whispered. "What're you doing?" The boy seemed to be in the throes of a trance. He stood there, saying nothing, mesmerized. More chatter from below followed by electrical sparks as a blue, white light reached towards their floor. And a snarl lifted from the slimy hole in the wall opposite the crypt.

And the vampire hissed at Cam. "Release me,"

she said as she tugged at her restraints.

Her eyes fixed on Cam.

"Please," she said. "Don't let them eat me."

Cam could see the pain in her eyes, the fear, as he backed away from the crypt, forcing young Cameron with him. She had blood in her eyes-*or are those tears*. She pulled and yanked at the chains in a frenzied panic.

"Please, Cameron, please," her voice groveled and pleading.

"You did this?" said Cam. "You brought him here?"

The vampire stopped moving. She looked from Cam to Cameron. "He's my only hope."

"Hope for what?"

"Please Cam," said the boy. "Let her go… before…" His voice trailed off as he swallowed the lump in his throat. "There's so many of them here. It's not fair what they're doing to them."

Cam ignored the boy; obviously he's under some vampire spell as the blue and white electrical storm below raged high on their level.

The vampire said, her eyes on the light, "They're sending another through." She looked at Cam. "Are you a part of it, too?" Her head shaking. "It won't work, it doesn't work." She looked away. "Can't work." She turned back to Cam. "Traveling through time has come to an end."

The snarl from the slimy pod.

"Please," pleaded the vampire, holding her wrists and chains. "It's coming."

"Please Cam, release her."

Cam snapped. "I'm not releasing a bloodthirsty vampire. She'll kill us all."

The vampire shook her head. "I promise not to hurt you. Please." Her voice hurried, urgent. Her breathing heavy as she looked to the far wall. Looked at Cam, then back to the wall. "Take the chip," she said. "If I attack you, use it and leave me here."

"What?" Cam looked at the wall and the chip held in place by electrical currents.

She coughed more blood over her lips and chin. Another growl. "The chip is a teleporter. Take it, just hurry, please."

Cameron tugged Cam's sleeve. "Please Cam." Cam snapped towards the boy. "She's going to die."

Cam eyed the chip.

This is insane!

"Please," pleaded Cameron. "I know she won't hurt you. Please trust *me*."

Cam looked at the boy tugging on his sleeve. Eyed Perseus when the snarl grew loud from the slimy pod.

The vampire's eyes widened, struggling to break free. "Hurry!"

Cameron said in a soft voice, "Please trust me."

Cam went to move, but his feet refused to follow his train of thought. Again the growl, but closer, louder.

"I can't believe I'm doing this," said Cam, as he went to the chip and pulled it from its electrical bondage. Electric shock ran up his arm, but the chip was in his hand. Cam gripped it in his fist, turned to the vampire and hesitated.

"Please," she muttered. "Before…"

But she never had time to finish her sentence. What erupted from the slimy pod had teeth.

34

"WHERE are they?" hollered Moth to Zon.

"They've gone into the gallows."

"Why didn't you follow them?"

"We're on the thirty-third floor. None of us have wings."

"How is it possible that they have wings, Zon?"

"From what I saw, Master Moth, the phantom is capable of flight."

Moth closed his eyes, thinking.

Zon continued. "We're searching for them in the gallows. We suspect they may have escaped. Considering their ability to fly, I wouldn't be surprised if they went into the tunnels."

"No Zon, they are here in Drac City. Can you not sense their presence?" Head shaking, gritting his teeth. "I want all available soldiers looking for them. Station warriors in every corner of Drac City until we weed them out. No Drac is allowed to leave their home until that time."

"Understood Master Moth. We will do our best."

"Do better, Zon; it's quite obvious that your best

hasn't been good enough."

"Yes, sir."

Moth could sense Zon's shame; he was in over his head. Sandy posed a threat unlike he'd ever seen, and this phantom continued to plague his people and his leadership. And if they escape? That possibility tore at his heart; having to explain to his people that not only had the phantom survived, he'd wreaked havoc in Drac City and escaped without a scratch. How infantile and incompetent would he appear to his people?

"Zon," said Moth, "Where is Kaal?"

"He was escorted to the gathering room; he waits for you there. I've placed three soldiers with him."

"Let them know I am on my way. I need to speak with Kaal immediately. Continue your search, Zon. I want them found."

"As you wish, Master Moth. As you wish."

35

PHIL had flown into the gallows, then steered towards the docking bay, landing behind a cruiser to conceal their position. Standing eye to eye with Sandy, he put his finger to his lips as his helmet retracted.

"How did you do that?" he asked, knowing they had little time, but what he just witnessed rattled him to his core. "Where did you learn that kind of power?"

"It… it's hard to explain. I don't know how I do it. I just know that I can. It comes easy, this power. It's like it's always been there." Her eyes downtrodden. "Hidden away." She looked at him, those human eyes with a vampire face. "The only thing that makes sense is that whatever they did to me either created it…. or let it loose."

Phil took her hands, studied the skin and fingers. All vampire. "Is there any part of you that hasn't changed?"

Sandy shook her head. "Only the eyes. I don't know why they haven't. Everything else has, but why not the eyes I don't know."

Phil considered the enigma. He'd never come

upon such a happening. He'd always heard about the genetic experiments, knew they were trying to make a Drac Human Hybrid, but to his knowledge they had always failed, until the boy Cameron appeared, and Adam, and now this change in Sandy. Somehow, they decoded the necessary science to make it happen. Robyn had been cryptic about his explanation. Robyn was always cryptic as there were situations and circumstances he cannot reveal. Nonetheless, Phil knew the reasons behind the experimentation. Understanding the why behind it had to do with the indigos and the Draconian's desire to destroy the trait, and with it, the hope for humanity.

His chief concern, if they succeeded once, they will no doubt repeat the procedure. Sandy now represented what Phil had been attempting to derail most of his life: a significant threat to the indigo children and the future. He required Robyn Winter's wisdom now more than ever. Footsteps caught his attention. Phil moved Sandy closer to the cruiser as he crouched down, securing his helmet across his eyes. As he scanned the dock with sonar vision, he counted ten soldiers standing guard, hiding, all carrying particle rifles, the closest Drac not more than a few feet from where they were now. He continued scanning, finding the three ships he'd come across earlier. Scanned their mechanical structure, all three were at the ready. All three with guards waiting and he was sure more were on the way. He craned his head, assessing the distance between the furthest ship and the portal into hollow earth.

Fifty meters, thought Phil. His concern was with the particle beams. Did he have enough strength within his ethereal manipulation to stop a particle beam in his ether? Phil knew that his ability with the rose had increased substantially since his battle with Sanos, but a particle beam erupted at lightning speed; it would be difficult to capture the beam in his rose manipulation.

Keep your wits about you, he thought. Stay in the moment. See through to the future.

He turned to address Sandy, but she was nowhere to be found.

"Sandy?" he whispered. He heard a muffled grunt behind him, and his head snapped around to see how Sandy had choked out the soldier closest to them. He heard the snap from the vampire's neck in the crook of her arm before she dropped him dead to the floor. Watched her as she walked further onto the dock.

Get the ship, Phil, said Sandy telepathically, a voice in Phil's head. *CCF11,* she said. *I'll be done in a minute.*

Glad she's on our side, he thought, and turned his sonar to the floor above and the commotion that now erupted in Drac Plaza. There were vampires up there.

A ton of them.

36

SANDY strolled to the dock's center, her attention taken by the commotion up above. She could sense the vampires a few floors above, could sense the multitude of warriors scattered across the city, all for her, all for Phil, all to stop them from leaving.

They picked the wrong woman to screw with.

She started skipping when the warriors in hiding moved from their positions into the bay, rifles drawn. She put her hands up.

"Don't shoot," she said when she stopped walking, sensing the vampires circling around her.

"Don't move," said the vampire behind her. "Where's the human?" he asked.

Sandy heard the crackling from the vampire's communication device. "We've secured the Drac traitor. Waiting on the human's location."

"Oh, he's here, that's for sure," said Sandy, staring at the ground with her hands up. She could feel their steady approach.

"Halo her," ordered the vampire behind her, obviously the leader of this small faction.

She couldn't help the grin that crossed her lips, her eyes staring, scanning the surrounding warriors. A fear vibration writhed off their skin, and she absorbed the emotion; it helped to clear the mind. Their fear transformed into Sandy's ambition, cause, and strength. She eyed the one in front of her as he removed the halo from his back belt. His eyes twitching as he approached.

"My dear boy," said Sandy, "Whatever do you mean to do with that thing you hold?"

The young vampire warrior stopped cold, holding the halo in his shaking hands. He looked at the leader behind Sandy.

"No worries, Adonis," said the leader, "we've got her point blank. If she tries to resist, she'll be talking to Hades."

Sandy stepped back. Not by much, just a slight step.

"I said," the leader hollered, "don't MOVE!"

When Sandy felt the rifle inch into her back, she made her move, twisted around just as the particle beam raced by her, tearing a hole through the Drac's torso in front of her as the halo dropped with a rattle to the floor. She bent down with a fist to the leader's sternum. He bent over and Sandy twisted his neck with a crunch and snap.

Three down.

She swiped the legs of the two vampires closest to her then stomped on their skulls as another particle beam raced towards her, Sandy caught the beam in her ether and turned the beam into lightning bolts that raced back towards their origin, exploding the rifles and vampires with it.

Eight down.

She readied herself, knees bent, arms outstretched, hands drawn into claws at the ready. She waved at the remaining vampires to advance. They looked up, listening to the rumbling commotion above.

Sandy shook her head. "No time, gentlemen. Either you advance or leave," she said. She could hear the hum of the starship behind her. The vampires looked at each other, then at Sandy. "I'm getting used to all the fighting, so do me a favor... attack," she said in a hiss.

They dropped their rifles, obviously useless, extended the blades, and started circling. Sandy dropped her arms, stood tall. "Now you're just boring me, biding time till the cavalry arrives." Head shaking, she caught Moth's ether in Drac Tower, his anger so strong it raced towards her. The first vampire attacked, but Sandy stepped back, sidestepped, and gripped the vampire's wrist, then tore his arm from its socket and dropped the limb, the vampire screaming with agonizing pain as blood spewed from the shoulder. She put her fist through the last vampire's skull and dropped him dead to the ground. She felt Moth's disappointment, his anger over losing more vampires.

She turned to the ship hovering behind her. Phil

was in the cockpit, the ramp open. Sandy stepped on, looking high above, knowing Moth was watching.

Get in, said Phil.

Drac warriors were propelling from Drac Plaza down towards the docking bay.

She wanted Moth's throat in her palm, wanted to squeeze Adam's location from his choking windpipe. She glared up at Drac Tower.

In time, she thought. "In time," she hissed, "We will meet again."

She climbed on board, and the ramp retracted. She caught herself on the wall when the ship moved, and she raced to the cockpit. Phil in his seat, pushing buttons, one of those halos over his head.

"Buckle in," he said.

She could see the ropes around the ship as she strapped in.

"This is gonna be fast."

She looked at Phil and then to the portal as the ship spiraled through faster than she could ever possibly imagine.

37

MOTH watched as the starship raced out of the docking bay; his heart went with it. He was on his way to meet with Kaal when he received word that his soldiers had surrounded Sandy. He stopped at the window in Drac Tower and with his ether used his mind's eye to watch the outcome.

He should have listened to Kaal, should have torn Sandy's throat and burned her body. Now, she escaped, and the phantom with her. A dire loss in his string of victories. His soldiers failed him. Kaal failed him. The bastard traitor will get his. And *he* had failed. He thought he had the plan in place, the perfect plan that would have revealed Sanos as the traitor, giving Moth reason to dispatch him as a symbol to all Dracs not to betray their own. His only victories: one was now under the control of a symbiote. The other, Adam, and there was no way he would allow Sandy to find him. Not a chance, no matter how powerful she was becoming. No matter how strong her telepathic ability was to her child, he'd do all that was necessary to keep her from him, knowing such a task was close to impossible. Drac mothers always find their spawn; there was no question about it.

Should have killed her when I had the chance, he thought. Why Kaal, why? Why did you release her? It was the perfect plan. Perfect! Now, all has been compromised.

Moth stomped towards where Kaal was being held. He wanted answers and that right soon. Wanted to stare into Kaal's eyes when he explained himself. Moth's blood curled, thinking about the betrayal that stung more than any battle he could ever lose.

And for the sake of his leadership, where was Sanos?

38

CAM wasn't sure, but what raged out of the slimy pod was covered in a black shell, its long head bared teeth with a growl when the thin arms punctured the vampire, its hands the shape of thick massive pinchers. The creature's tail whipped from behind the creature's body, wrapped around the vampire, cutting the chains, then disappeared into the pod.

Mesmerized, it took Cam a few moments to realize the vampire was screaming. A whining echoing wail filled with blood and terror quickly cut off when the creature's tail wrapped around the throat and choked that scream from her lungs. The last Cam witnessed before the vampire disappeared into the slimy pod was the blood pouring from the vampire's throat. The remaining blood-curdling scream was coming from the boy. Blue and purple electrical bolts raged from below, quickly vanished.

Cam gripped Cameron's shoulder. The boy's screams never ending as Cam put his finger to his lips and Cameron's scream dissipated.

Cameron said, "Why did you wait so long?"

Perseus grunted, gesturing to the slimy pod when Cam heard the trampling.

Is that thing coming back?

Commotion on the floor below, Cam went to the waist-high wall. Those greys were looking in his direction; the pharaoh-like soldiers were circling, getting ready to advance on their position. And the humans were escaping, back towards the door behind them. Cam turned and scanned the room, knowing there was no place to hide. Cameron's face still scrunched in disappointment and fear. Perseus put his hand on the boy's shoulder, a desperate act of consolation. Cam eyed the staircase when the waist-high wall was blasted with an explosion that tore through the wall as Cam hunched down to ward off the shrapnel barreling towards him, clenching his fists around his head. His heart pounded in his ears. Three more blasts ripped through the room, more debris falling on top of him and when he looked up, he could see that Perseus had grabbed Cameron, shielding him from harm.

More blasts, more growls from the slimy pod and now he could hear footsteps, hurried commotion coming from the hall, down the steps.

Trapped, he thought. We've got to get to the cruiser.

His thought wasn't completed before he found himself in the docking bay, staring at the cruiser. Cat looked at him from the cockpit with a confused stare as

Cam caught his breath, his chest heaving, his shoulders rose, then fell. Looked around…

Where are Cameron and Perseus?

Felt sweat bead off his upper lip as he tried to wrap his head around how in blazes he'd gotten from the room to the docking bay when he opened his palm, as if the chip within his palm wanted to be revealed.

Teleportation, he thought when he squeezed his palm and thought of…

Back in the room with Cameron and Perseus, more blasts erupted, and he could see that slimy carnivorous alien's head spout from the pod, its teeth chattering. Saw one of the pharaohs on the steps, his staff in his hands, aimed at Cam when the soldier spoke an order that Cam didn't recognize.

Cam stepped quickly, wrapped his arms around Perseus and Cameron, and thought of the docking bay as he closed his eyes and opened them safely on the dock. Looked at the confused stares of Cameron and Perseus.

He looked at Cameron, said, "Never do that again. Next time you want to leave, you need to tell one of us." His head shaking. "You could have been killed."

The boy was in tears, holding onto Perseus. "You could have saved her."

"Trust a vampire? Cameron, that's insane. She could have killed all of us."

To this, Cameron stood tall. "That's what I am. Do you not trust me?"

Not that he didn't trust the boy, but this was insane. Cameron was human, not a vampire, but Cam had no idea how to respond. He put his hand on the boy's shoulder. "We'll talk about this later. Right now, we need to go before..." his voice trailed off when thick gates, one by one, sealed off all exits out of the bay.

His attention caught by Cat, now standing outside the cruiser. "I suggest we depart immediately."

"Agreed," said Cam as he took a few steps, turned to Cameron and Perseus, walking backward. "Let's go." he demanded.

Perseus grunted, gesturing towards the door, then gathered the boy and raced to the cruiser. Cat was on first, Perseus and Cameron next, followed by Cam. Cat made a beeline for the cockpit, while Perseus brought Cameron to the back of the cruiser. Grimes sat beside the sleeping Annison, said, "What the hell happened?"

"No time," Cam blurted. "We'll talk later." He stomped towards the cockpit.

"After what?" Grimes hollered, although Cam never answered; he took his seat in the cockpit as Cat placed the halo over his head.

Cam looked at the steel door. "Will we be able to get through the blockage?"

"Yes," said Cat, as he gripped the steering knob in his right hand. "While you were gone, I made some adjustments to our weapons system."

Two blasts, one a white circle that spiraled

towards the enclosure, followed by a green laser blast, tore through the steel, creating an opening wide enough for the cruiser when an explosion erupted across the cruiser from behind. Cam and Cat jutted forward from the blast.

"They're shooting at us," Cam hollered.

Cat said, "I know," and the cruiser leapt out of the docking bay into the raging storm outside, banked a hard left and raced into the night sky.

Cam breathed a sigh of relief when a raging, buzzing emergency signal erupted in the cockpit. On the computer board in front of him, several ships were advancing from the roof of the hotel.

And Cat said, "It appears we are not out of the woods yet."

39

MOTH trampled into the room to confront Kaal, found him sitting, and Kaal immediately turned away from Moth's stare as he stopped and stood a few feet from Kaal.

"Leave us," Moth addressed the three soldiers standing guard, his heart thumping, his blood hot in his veins, waiting to be alone with Kaal.

"I know what you're going to say," said Kaal when the door slid closed. The stare in his eyes burrowed into Moth's ether. He stepped towards Kaal, not allowing him to complete his sentence. Moth slashed Kaal across the cheek, first the left then the right. Two slits that seeped blood that dripped across Kaal's chin. And the stare in Kaal's eyes, pain and betrayal.

Moth muttered, "I've experienced my share of betrayal, Kaal, but this event burns me like no other." His head shaking. "Why Kaal? I want to know why?" He saw himself with Kaal's throat in his grip, wanted to tear him apart, cause pain and suffering to the extent he was feeling now. Even more.

Kaal wiped his face, but the blood kept coming, his eyes glassy, his lips trembling. He turned away, said, "I did it for you."

"You betrayed my order in some deranged show of loyalty? No Kaal, what you did was allow two sworn enemies to get away and with it..."

Kaal jumped up, eye to eye with Moth. "You think Sanos was falling for your trap? You think that vile female has no powers. Look at what she did." His head shaking. "You allowed yourself to be deceived. I told you to kill her when you had the chance." His voice trailed off. He turned from Moth's stare, wiped his cheeks again, and stepped away.

Moth cringed at the sight of his loyal subject. "You haven't answered my question."

Kaal stopped cold, turned to Moth. Went to speak, but no words came. Kaal shook his head, breathed deep and gritted his teeth.

"Speak!" Moth raged. "Before I attach a symbiote to you, Kaal."

To this, Kaal stood tall. Raising his chin, he spoke in a stern voice. "Sanos is gunning for your seat in COR."

Moth craned his head, glaring at Kaal. "How do you know this?"

"Insignificant how I know, only know that it is true."

Moth breathed deep, turned from Kaal, then looked back. "Continue," he breathed, staring down at his subordinate.

Kaal stepped closer. "Sanos was waiting for your trap," he said. "He wants you discredited, wants to make you look like a fool."

Moth interjected, "And you wished to help him achieve this task?"

Kaal clenched his jaw, his lips trembling. "She is who you refuse to acknowledge, Master Moth. What I saw in Drac Plaza proves it. She is…"

"And now you wish for her to lead." He raised his hands as if in prayer. "In honor of the SST Queen," he mocked. "Spare me the righteous blasphemy. She is nothing more than a diseased and disfigured freak schooled in our ways by our human enemies."

"Whatever you wish to believe is on you."

"And that's the why behind the betrayal, Kaal. So you can have your cherished coming of the phoenix?"

Kaal shook his head as he closed his eyes. He unclipped a small device from his belt, pressed a button, and the screen lit up, a small red dot blinking on the screen.

"What is this?" asked Moth.

Kaal eyed Moth. "Her location. When she was in the throes of the halo, I clipped the chip to her robe. Wherever she goes, you can find her." Moth's eyes narrowed, Kaal's hand shaking. "And the phantom. And the rest of the rebellion. And… Sanos."

"What do you mean, Sanos?"

"Sanos has followed them. I provided the exact ship they would use so Sanos could track them. He's certainly ambitious, that Drac. But now you have him, in the employ of the human rebellion. You can destroy all of them. All of our threats with one swipe of your hand and implicate Sanos in the betrayal."

Moth raised his brow, took the transponder from Kaal's hand, studying the device.

"Are you satisfied?" asked Kaal.

Moth stared at his subordinate. "Just one more question. Should she be who you say she is, then why destroy her? Isn't this what you've been waiting for?"

Kaal responded, "Such an event will cause insurrection among our people. It is best if she is dead."

Now a smile spread across Moth's lips. "Now Kaal, be careful. You're beginning to think like a genuine leader."

Kaal raised his chin. "What is our next move, Master Moth?"

To which Moth responded, "All out war."

40

SANOS had placed a transponder onto the hull of CCF11, then climbed aboard his own ship, watching in dire amazement as the battle raged in the docking bay. He'd never seen such a powerful Drac before, other than Moth, and even his power may have difficulty advancing against the female. Obviously she is schooled in the old ways, her power like perfected magic played with genius and mastery.

She could be a powerful ally. Or a dreadful enemy.

After Phil's ship had flown into hollow earth, Sanos waited for the Drac warriors to leave before taking off to follow them, his transponder blinking with the phantom's location. His skin crawled with that insipid itch, gritting his teeth and snarling. His blood like fire in his veins, his bones aching, his stomach twisted, skin moist and drawn.

Side effects.

New blood.

He ran his tongue over his lips as a shudder ripped across his body, head to toe, and cold, like ice within his organs. Hot and cold. Cold and hot. His lips trembled with a throaty gasp as his throat swelled with a painful, suffocating sting. His hands shook as he steered his ship through hollow earth and the dendrites raging electric blue and white.

The blinking red light on his transponder ceased moving. The phantom has arrived at his destination, thought Sanos, communicating with his ship to map the location and his ship jumped ahead, propelling out into the vast void of planet Earth.

His plan was complex, requiring apt focus and stealth acumen. Like the phantom, Sanos will be the proverbial fly on the wall and gather intel on the rebellion's secret base. Then use his knowledge to gain trust with the Drac Army, bringing the cavalry to decimate the rebels while revealing Moth's plot against him, and, in turn, against all Dracs. Moth's incompetence led to the phantom's escape from Drac City. His foolish antics and desire to hold power over his people have placed Drac lives in danger. He must pay for his ineptitude. Him and Kaal.

The foolish Kaal, Sanos thought. The feeble Drac, who handed Sanos his victory on a silver platter. He would serve useful to further Sanos' cause. After Moth meets his death by Sanos' hands–in the name of Drac– he would have no choice other than pledging his undying loyalty to Sanos; it was a matter of survival. If not, Sanos would take great pleasure sending Kaal to the grave.

Traitors deserve a treacherous death.

He flew over Atlanta, towards the north where the phantom had landed, across rocks and trees, landing his ship a mile from the location. From here he would trek through the forest, unseen by human eyes, under the cover of night. Once he was inside, he'd send for the Drac warriors, Zon being his best chance of conformity. Sanos knew Zon had grown weary of Moth's treatment towards Dracs, as was the talk among fellow warriors. He may prove useful to advance Sanos' cause.

Exiting the ship, Sanos took the transponder and extended his blades.

One never knows what's lurking in the woods.

He could smell the human scent from where he stood under the stars. His blood curled, mouth watered.

Save your hunger, he thought.

Save the ravaging thirst for the phantom.

41

THEY were in a halo driven rat race, traveling across the earth. One moment they were over Russia, the next India, then Ireland. Alaska. Mexico. Puerto Rico. China. Japan. Every jump to another location happening within seconds. Cam gripped his seat's arms, his stomach jumping with every turn of the cruiser.

"How do they know where we're going?" hollered Cam, the noise as the cruiser jumped through the vortex deafening. "I thought this thing ran on thoughts. How are they reading your thoughts?" His voice panicked as his heart raced inside his chest. He could feel the thick beat in his throat, his ears.

Cat said, "Now that they have eyes on the ship, they can map the location to follow."

Cam's head shaking, his knuckles turning white. He gripped those arms tight as the cruiser banked right, disappearing into the vortex. Cam's face pinched, the force from the propulsion nerve racking, tensing every muscle and bone in his body.

Canada now, over Niagara Falls. The cruiser jumped forward and on the screen, Cam could see how the ships followed close behind. Inside of a five second count, Cam watched as they jutted out of each vortex after Cam's cruiser. Four ships in total on their heels as laser blasts ripped past the cruiser. Cat dipped the controls, the ship twisting and turning, then banked up into the vortex, coming out over Panama.

"This is useless," Cam hollered. "If they can track us, we'll never get them off our tail."

"No worries," said Cat. "I have a plan."

The vortex erupted in front of the ship; Cam held on tight. Over the North Pole, barreling towards an iceberg as Cat shifted quickly as if he'd expected the berg in front of them, skimming the top as they passed, lifting high into the air, twisting, turning upside down and over and back down, racing towards the iceberg.

Explosions below, Cam's eyes opened wide as the ship headed down towards the iceberg and the smoke and flames that lifted towards his ship. Cam saw on the screen that two assailants had crashed into the iceberg, obliterated on impact. The cruiser pulled up just before crashing into the iceberg, another dip down closer to the frozen ocean, and the cruiser raced forward.

"Have you done this before?" Cam hollered.

Cat turned to him, brief as the cruiser gunned forward into another vortex. "I have," he said. "UFO movement has been a hotbed of activity for a long time. I have flown many missions in my time."

Shanghai now. Barreling towards Shanghai

Tower as a horde of particle beams raced from the cruiser to the tower like a monstrous demonic hand. Explosions ripped through the skyscraper, billowing into a ball of fire. Cam's eyes wide as the tower gave a steel crunching belch, and started falling, collapsing on top of them. The cruiser moving at a breakneck pace towards the devastated floors where fire and smoke raged and Cam held tight to those arms, thought his heart stopped as they propelled forward into the fire, into the building as the tower fell behind them crushing the two remaining ships now gone from the cruiser's screen.

The vortex opened, seemed to draw them into it, gripping the cruiser and propelling it forward like a metaphysical slingshot. Cam's eyes wide and tense coming through the vortex over the ocean and kept moving, moving fast.

"No more ships on the screen," Cam hollered. "I think we lost them."

But Cat kept going, another vortex.

"Holy shit," hollered Cam as the ship raced through it and the speed settled to a humming slow ride outside the vortex and into a calm, starry night.

Cat said, "I apologize, but I needed to make sure they did not return."

Cam could finally exhale, his chest and shoulders calming with each breath. His eyes blinking, he shook his head when he looked at Cat. "You dropped a building on them. I think that was a sure bet that they wouldn't follow."

"Perhaps," said Cat. "Even so, I needed to be sure. Jumping through twice guaranteed the necessary outcome."

"Can't argue with that," Cam whispered, looking through the cockpit. "Where are we?"

"I've brought us to Coba, Mexico."

"What's in Coba, Mexico?"

"Nothing anymore. We should be safe here."

"You said the same about Miami."

"Well," Cat said, landing the cruiser in the forest. "Let us hope I am not wrong this time. I would like to assess the girl Annison for complications, although I do not expect there to be any. The regeneration chamber has never failed before."

Cam remembered the teleporter device he'd placed in his breast pocket. He took it out, said to Cat, "Have you seen one of these before?"

Cat observed the tiny chip in Cam's hand. "Yes, it is a teleportation device. I have not seen one in a while." He looked at Cam, those eyes raging with electrical currents. "Where did you get it?"

Cam gripped the device, put it back in his pocket. "In Miami."

"Seems there was a lot happening in Miami."

"You don't know the half of it."

"Then why don't you tell me?"

Part III

Something Wicked Has Come!

1

"WAIT here," Phil said to Sandy. "Robyn will be in soon." He gestured to the cave, bathed in darkness except for a soft white glow from the floor, where small square grates lined across the bottom of the rock walls. A soft cool breeze against his skin. The air was moist and thick. He paused before he said, "I apologize for the accommodations, but until Robyn can figure out what we need to do to help you, my people may have a difficult time with your current... change."

Sandy looked over the cave, twenty feet in diameter; the floor was dirt and rocks. In the center, a flat rock formation made up of three tiers reached three feet above the ground. They'd come in through the forest, into the cave, through a narrow hallway they accessed after Phil's eyes were scanned for entry. They walked forty feet through the hall to the cave they were standing in. Beyond the cave, they could hear rushing water.

Sandy forced a small smile. "It's fine," she said when she locked eyes with Phil. "Believe me, if I saw what I looked like I'd be afraid too."

Now Phil forced his smile. "Understood," he said, then gestured to the flat rocks. "Have a seat while you wait. He won't be long; that I can assure you."

"You're not staying?" she muttered and Phil could see how her body tensed.

Phil shook his head. "No," he said, his voice soft and caring. "What happens between you and Robyn is not my business. We all have our own evolution... what happens here is for you. Remember that, Sandy. Life happens for us, not to us. There's reason and meaning behind every change. Some are more difficult to accept is all." He paused, watched as Sandy turned from his stare.

Sandy tensed her jaw, said with desperation in her voice, "Are you sure he can help me?" Her stare cold and stiff. "I'm just not sure what he can do."

A thin smile graced Phil's lips. "If there is anyone who can, it's Robyn. He... He's one of the very few who can transform living tissue." He cocked his eyebrows and his eyes lit up. "The rose," he continued. "Robyn is its master. He can help you clear your mind to find your child." Phil could see from the look in Sandy's eyes she did not believe him. "Look at your own power with the rose, it's..." He shook his head. "Rather inspirational. How you harnessed that power so quickly... is amazing. Think of where that power will take you as time progresses. You'll be able to move mountains should you choose to do so."

Sandy seemed to consider the possibility, her

eyes downcast, head bent when she raised her eyes to Phil, her head shaking. "Why do we have this power? I... I don't understand why only a few are capable?"

Phil stepped closer. "All have the power. Every human being and every species in existence has it. It... is our birthright. The few do not claim the rose; the power comes from within. Most are just unaware of its existence. Think about what would happen if every human being knew the power that lives within themselves. It would level the playing field and those with power stand to lose all they hold dear with the discovery that we are all equal. Unfortunately, human beings are taught to be dependent, always looking away from the heart, away from the self for power and strength. Looking to the stars, to government, to gods and myths for hope when we carry that hope within our hearts already. We are born with the power. It exists within us from our very first breath. We can self heal, with an ability to go deep within ourselves to open a path to our dreams. Look into your heart, Sandy, you will find all you need, including a clear path to divinity."

Sandy nodded, and Phil could see the cogs turning over in her brain. He pursed his lips before asking, "Are you... hungry?" catching Sandy's attention. "I mean, is that part of you still human? We do have synthetic blood I can get you." Sandy's stare was skeptical. "We keep it in case we capture a Drac. Seems like the right thing to do if a vampire surrenders."

"That's… odd," she said.

Phil laughed, "I think we're way beyond odd at the moment."

Sandy laughed too. "I definitely agree," she said when the laughing ceased and an awkward silence fell over the cave.

"Would you though… I mean, are you hungry? I can get you whatever you need."

She shook her head. "I'm fine, really," she said, looking over the cave again. "Where will you be?" she asked. "You're the only one I know here. I'm comfortable with you around."

Phil nodded. "Understood. I'd like to go see my family first. My wife and… daughter. Haven't seen them in a few days."

Sandy tensed once again. Phil understood how Sandy was feeling. Yes, she was turned into a vampire, but that circumstance took a back seat to a caring parent. She wanted her son, and Phil knew she would stop at nothing to find him. He would do the same if the situation were reversed.

Sandy answered with a slight bow, "Go to them, then. I will be fine." She forced another smile.

"Thank you," Phil said. He stepped to the rock wall, placed his hand over a rock, and a door opened on his right. Outside, the sound of rushing water turned thunderous. He stepped through the door, then turned back to Sandy; she sat on the flat rock formation. He could feel her eyes on him. Phil said, head bent and eyes downcast, "For what's its worth, I am sorry. Sorry for all you've been through. Sorry... that I failed you."

She didn't need to respond, and Phil did not expect a response. Some apologies don't require one; they simply just need to be said. He put his hand to the outside wall, said, "He will be along soon," as the door closed, leaving Sandy alone. Phil took a deep breath before he walked down the rock hallway towards the light and the thundering water. He continued to sense Sandy's strife, her pain, her heartache, and confusion. Those sensations stabbed at his heart, turned his blood hot and furious.

The water raged with thunderous fury, growing stronger and louder as Phil stepped to the end of the hall. Outside the rock hall, his home was in view, a garden within an underground copse of trees. Bright-colored flowers, plants, and shrubs flourished, scattered around a winding lake fed by a waterfall that gathered water through a vestibule beyond the cave. Beneath the rushing waterfall, crickets called to one another. Insects, snakes, birds were all welcomed, a graceful invitation to bring harmony to the garden. Phil stood at the end of the hall, standing over the garden. On his right, stone steps led down into the thicket.

The garden had been brought to life by harnessing the lifeblood of mother Earth. A symbiotic relationship between earth, air, water, and fire—once nature ran its life course, they would burn the foliage to honor its life, giving back to the earth what it created. Sunlight reflected into the cave through the many vestibules scattered across the cave, a hundred feet above. During the day, the garden was lit up with the rays of the sun, as if the foliage were above ground. The energy was immaculate and unadulterated, clean and pristine, although it did little in this moment to calm the fears that balled into a thicket within Phil's gut.

His heart sank thinking about Sandy. All she'd been through, all she'd lost, and all she'd become. I failed her, he thought. I failed, and she lost her child...

"There is no such thing as failure. In every situation there is information that leads to the correct solution."

Phil turned on his heels to see Robyn standing on the steps below, his eyes blazing with white electrical currents.

"Stop thinking about failure. Such beliefs lead to internal chaos, the same as deriving conclusions. Both place limits on our ability to understand the complexities of life."

Robyn stepped up towards Phil. Phil's lips trembled as Robyn met him eye to eye. Phil looked away.

"Do you have information for me?" asked Robyn.

Phil turned to meet his stare. He swallowed

before answering. "Yes, Sandy waits for you." He gestured down the hall, then turned his gaze to Robyn, trying to stifle his tears.

Robyn pursed his lips, staring at the dried blood, gashes, and swollen bruises across Phil's skin. Looked down, briefly, as if he were looking for the right words to fit the moment before he raised his eyes to meet Phil. "You are indeed a valiant soul, Phil." Robyn's head shaking, slow and empathetic. "The best of all of us. It has been a privilege watching your evolution." And he bowed.

Robyn had never bowed to Phil before.

Robyn returned his gaze to Phil. "Go now," he said. "Find your family and embrace them. Hold them tight. Wish the best for them and rejoice in their glory."

Now Phil bowed. "I will," he breathed, choking back the lump in his throat when Robyn placed his hands on Phil's shoulders, put his hand on the back of Phil's head and dipped Phil's forehead to his. Eyes closed, silence like the void in space, distant stars spiraling across the universe in silent accord and joy.

Phil's neck, shoulders, and head shuddered as his face scrunched; he felt a rush, a rushing ball of electricity plume from the center of his brain to Robyn's forehead. Phil raised his head with a gasp, his mouth agape, eyes wide. And the stare across Robyn's face carried the weight of disappointment.

Phil craned his head, said, "What is it? Why do you appear so distraught?"

Robyn placed his hands on Phil's shoulder. "One day, you will understand. For now, go Phil. Be with your wife and child." Phil nodded, his eyes and skin wet with tears. "It is my turn now. Let me be all that Sandy requires."

"Yes, master Robyn," Phil said, with a bow and closed eyes. A single tear fell from his chin.

When he looked up, Robyn was gone. Phil turned around, saw Robyn by the door, and watched as he entered.

2

SANOS followed his nose; the mouth-watering scent of human flesh grew stronger as he approached a rock formation that raised a hundred feet above the earth with a flat surface that stretched for what Sanos could surmise was more than a hundred yards across. A vampire in the woods, the situation reminded him of times long gone, when unsuspecting humans lived by meager means, before industry, before technology had changed the world. His breath heavy, his hunger burning rage in his mind, he could hear crickets in the forest and the sound of rushing water coming from within the rock formation.

His nose crinkled with the scent of vampire and human, staring, observing and analyzing the rock in front of him. The scent grew knowing they were inside the rock and how convenient was it that humans had taken refuge beneath the earth, hiding in plain sight from the scavengers sent to secure their location. Thought it ironic how surface dwellers had taken to live beneath the earth. He came upon an out-of-place rock, discolored and perfectly shaped into a rectangle as a grin erupted across his lips. Sanos touched the stone, not stone though, just a box made to look like stone. He felt over the rock, flipped it up. The screen embedded in the rock had a single star floating across the screen that quickly turned to a camera with the words blinking on the screen that read: Eye Scan Enabled. Look Into The Camera.

He flipped the box back and covered the screen.

"They are here," he snarled as he looked up. Sanos gripped the rock, propelled himself up, grunting and seething, blood dripped from his arms with a subtle sting he'd grown comfortable with, the itch now beneath the skin, bone deep, climbing, one rock hold to another, scampering to the top where he crawled across to the center and stood tall, head raised to the full moon. Sanos raised his arms, drawing power from the moon's energy, drenching himself in moonlight. Eyes closed, mouth agape, swallowing energy into his system, devouring strength into his veins and bones. Shallow breath. Fluttering heart. His hands and arms raised, palms up, the moon framed inside his arms. Fingers curled, he felt the energy in his palms, brought it to his chest and breathed deeply, tongue pressed to the roof of his mouth, sensing the energy, oxygen in his spine as his back, shoulders, and neck drew in energy and breath into the back of his head, to the crown. His lips opened, jaw tight, when he let the breath out with a hiss, clearing his ether with pure energetic calm and focus.

He will need to be clear. Will need to be on point, focused and conscience, wielding the rose within his commands.

Sanos opened his eyes with a slow flutter. The moon's brilliance was a light in his eyes. He looked around, took three objects from his armor. The first, a beacon locater that he secured to the rock formation. The second an explosive capable of tearing a hole through the cave for surprise access below. And the third, a military communiqué, specifically designed for Drac warriors. Part of his plan was to provide intel to Zon, who Sanos considered his ace in the hole. Sanos concluded the Kaal insurrection was a farce, designed for Sanos to take the bait and be deemed a traitor once they found him in the rebellion's employ. Zon's lingering resentment towards Moth would serve Sanos well. Communication was a must, planting the seed in Zon's mind, a sliver of doubt Sanos could exploit for his purpose. Moth betrayed Drac, set up a Drac warrior for the fall on his own incompetence and if he will do this to one, he would do it to all.

He sent a private message to Zon with the rebellion's location, along with a warning.

Something is rotten in Drac City. Trust no one, weed out the deception; for whoever wishes to destroy Drac has no loyalty to all Dracs. The traitor will be revealed for those who practice deception have no recourse but to destroy all in their path. We must keep Kaal under a watchful eye.

447

He laughed over his inclusion of Kaal in his message, which he sent along with the recording he'd taken on the ledge on Drac Tower, proof of Kaal's traitorous antics against Dracs. All Dracs were aware of Kaal's supreme loyalty to Moth. And if Kaal had indeed betrayed Dracs, Moth wasn't far behind the betrayal.

The last his message reported was that he would wait for further instruction; ready to battle when the brigade arrived. Sanos marveled over his devious manipulation as he walked across the rock, analyzing any possibility of escape for the humans when he came upon a vestibule where the sound of rushing water turned thunderous. He looked inside, and the grin that tore across his lips was never ending.

His phantom was beneath the rock.

3

SANDY stood when Robyn entered the cave. His first remark when he saw Sandy's transformation was, "Your eyes have yet to change."

There was no fear in his eyes, none that Sandy could see or feel. As if the very sight of Sandy's change, the vampire in front of him, brought no recourse to separation of identity or isolation. No cringe or startled response. Sandy felt, for lack of a better word, comfortable, at ease in Winter's presence. Acceptance and empathy were in his heart, not fear or judgment. His words were subtle, calm, and understanding.

And she had to admit, while she sat in the dark cave waiting his arrival, the thoughts rolling over in her mind were cataclysmic and anger filled with a conclusion that she was all alone, and no one could offer solace or resolution to her situation. All that changed the moment Robyn stepped through the door, as if hope had arrived with a resolution she wished to embrace. And, as if the tables were turned, it was Sandy who cringed when Robyn had entered, with his white eyes, and his scarred skin that slithered from the top of his smooth round skull across his eyes and down his face and neck beneath the tightly wrapped white short-sleeve shirt revealing those same scars across his arms to his wrists. He wore rust colored cargo pants. He was not at all what she expected. At first sight Robyn Winter didn't look like much, but the ether that followed him, his demeanor screamed knowledge with an ultimately wise nature.

He asked, in a gentle although commanding tone, "What is it you wish for, Sandy? What do you want?"

Sandy paused before she answered; her first thought was for the change to reverse. She wanted to be human again, but she squelched this response for what she searched her heart for. "I want my child."

"And then?" he asked as he stepped from her, his back to her, looking up. "Where in the universe will you go?"

She looked around the cave. "Away," she muttered. "Away from all of this. To raise him peacefully."

Robyn craned his head. "And then?" he asked.

No answer as Sandy thought through her line of thought. Robyn turned to her, staring. He stepped closer.

"Every parent wishes to give their child the world. Every parent discovers the moment when that child goes out into the world as they think about all the moments that have led to the commencement. Seems that moment has already arrived for you."

Sandy's eyes narrowed. "Parents get to raise their children. I was never even able to spend more than a few hours with him. He's all I think about. I... I can't locate him. I did and then, some way, somehow I lost the ability. I lost him before I even had a moment to show him how much I love him, to carry him and care for him." Her head shaking. "I never had time to be with him."

Robyn's smile was tight across his lips as he looked around the cave as if he were staring at the stars above. "He's always been with you. Soul energy is attracted from one life to the next." Sandy watched as he paced across the cave. "What if I told you he was safe? What if I told you that should he be with you now, that should your wish come true, that if you turn back from this duty bestowed upon you, the furies will be your attendants?"

"I don't understand. You speak in riddles." Her heart racing, blood hot in her veins.

Robyn stepped eye to eye with her. "There is only one way this all ends for the betterment of all in the universe. Only one way for your wish to manifest... to usher forth the basking glory of eternal joy with your child." He craned his head and Sandy could feel his stare as electrical currents raged across his eyes. "And it requires pain."

Sandy's body shuddered, then tensed, felt her chest constrict as she forced her eyes to turn from his dire stare. Robyn gestured to the flat rocks. "Please, sit," he said.

"Why?" Sandy scoffed. "For what purpose?"

Robyn eyed Sandy, his eyes beaming with electricity that Sandy believed was calling to her. "Let me show you, Sandy. Show you how to reach your child. And then, and only then, will you be able to choose the fate of the universe."

4

MOTH had ordered his army assembled and ready for battle. His official story to his warriors was that Kaal had gained intel on the traitor Sanos and the female Drac's conspirator nature with the human rebellion. A revelation that flew in the face of Sanos himself. Zon had known Sanos for a long time; they'd waged many battles together, and although his nature was primal, Zon always knew he held Dracs in the highest regard. But Zon knew also that Sanos, like himself, had grown weary of COR. And now Sanos had sent a communiqué warning Zon of Kaal's insurrection against him.

Sanos was right, there was something rotten in Drac City. Rotten to its core and the fate of Drac hung in the balance between Moth and Sanos. Lies and deception were a tricky business to engage in. He would need to be on guard, stealth, and conscious during battle. Moth had reported that he informed the greys of the rebellion's location. The same location Sanos had provided. All were on their way to battle, all were on their way to put an end to their concerns for the future, where Dracs will rule over the earth at the behest of their Draconian overlords.

But there was more, from what Moth had
alluded to. The traitors must be destroyed, but proof
was necessary. Moth wanted the dead bodies to burn in
front of Drac City; a warning to never betray the orders
given by COR. Such an outcome would require Drac
warriors to infiltrate the rebel base, find the traitors,
and walk out with their dead bodies. Moth also
ordered for the phantom to be captured and prepared
for sacrifice in front of Drac City.

The fear was with the fabled Robyn Winter. His
power will prove difficult to counter. Zon secretly
wished Moth would call upon the great and powerful,
the one known as Sephtis, to aid in their battle with
Robyn Winter. Zon wished for no further loss of Drac
life that he was certain would come by the hand of
Robyn Winter during the battle. Of course, there was
more. Zon received intel that the Miami experiments
were infiltrated, the assailants lost in battle. The project
was being brought to Drac City, a desperate attempt to
continue what some believed would ultimately secure
their victory here on earth. The ability to time travel
offered many ways to assure victory. He could feel the
energies combining, planets and stars, solar systems
and galaxies aligning over what has taken millenniums
to accomplish. Along the timeline, once the stars
aligned across the universe, the Arcturians will arrive
at the precise moment of the Earth's inevitable
cataclysm. All must be in place before then for his

people to be victorious. And that time was spiraling towards them, the proverbial timeline inching towards finality.

As Zon looked over his army of a hundred Drac warriors, he understood the importance of this moment. And as his eyes stared from one Drac to the next, his heart dropped, knowing, knowing so many of them would not be returning; their sacrifice given freely in the name of Drac, for the future...

For Moth!?

5

PHIL stood over his daughter Cathryn as she lay sleeping. He brushed her hair from her eyes and she laughed in her sleep as if whatever dream engaged her thoughts brought comfort and joy. Phil couldn't help the adoring smile that graced his lips as he leaned forward, planting his lips against her forehead.

"Sleep, my baby," he whispered. "Daddy loves you. Loves you always." He closed his eyes when he touched his forehead to hers and she laughed out loud once again, widening Phil's smile as he brought his lips to her ear, whispered, "Be bold. Be brilliant. Be beautiful. Be... extraordinary," then kissed her temple before standing tall, staring adoringly at his daughter.

"Welcome home," his wife whispered, now standing in the doorway.

"Esta," Phil breathed, turning to her when Esta's jaw dropped, her eyes wide, staring at the carnage that had become her husband. "Did I wake you?" His voice gentle.

His question never registered as her eyes narrowed, head shaking, looked like she was on the verge of tears. They'd had the same conversation before, Phil's incessant need to fight, to win the battle no matter what the cost. "When will the fighting stop?" she'd asked a hundred times over.

"Looks worse than it feels," Phil muttered, needing something to say. He had little time before he had to meet with Silas and debrief, didn't want his limited time to be an argument. Her eyes cast down now and Phil could sense her ether, her unacknowledged fury. "I… I've missed you," he said, casting his eyes down. "Missed you both," he said, turning to Cathryn, brushed his fingers across her forehead, tucked a strand of hair behind her ear before returning his gaze to Esta.

Tired eyes, dark hair tussled with sleep, and the baby bump showing beneath her dark gown, she gestured for him to follow her. "Let her sleep," she whispered when Cathryn laughed as if in her dream she was being tickled. Esta walked towards the bed, staring at her daughter. "It's the first pleasant dream she's had in a week." Esta pulled the blanket over Cathryn. "Are you hungry?" she asked, her tone soft. "You must be. Come," she said, "We picked some fresh fruit yesterday." She took Phil's hand.

"Okay," he said, allowing Esta to lead him to the door, but Phil stopped in the doorway, and, turning to his daughter, said, "Love you, my baby. Always and forever. Sleep tight. Dream beautiful things."

Cathryn rolled over on her side. Phil took a step

back, his hand on the doorframe as he looked over the room.

So quiet. Quiet is the night, Phil thought. For dreams with laughter hold no bounds.

He could hear the waterfall in the distance, could hear the crickets and gently slithering snakes in the grass as he looked at his daughter once again before he took the doorknob in his hand, went to close the door when he heard Cathryn giggle and say, "Love you too nana," and Phil stopped cold, face pinched in confusion.

"Phil," Esta hushed. He looked back at his wife. "Let her sleep."

Phil nodded, closing the door, then joined Esta in the kitchen. The hut they lived in was carved into the rock, much like the multitudes of living quarters scattered across the miles of cave beneath the earth. All were sleeping, all dreaming, hopefully good dreams.

Phil said, "I've got to debrief with Silas."

Esta looked at him. "Have you not already?"

Phil shook his head. "I just returned. Wanted to come here first."

Esta offered a small smile. "Did everything go okay? I heard about the safety camp." She shook her head. "So sorry about the team. I heard they fought gallantly."

"As always," he said, thinking about the team he lost when they first arrived to rescue Sandy.

"Is she here?" asked Esta.

Phil nodded. "That she is," he said.

"What a relief," Esta breathed. "Aries will be more than ecstatic. Does she know yet? Did you tell her he is alive?"

Phil paused, his bottom lip pursed, as he moved his head back and forth. "I did not," he said. "Robyn wanted to tell her."

Esta moved her head back and forth as if she were considering Robyn's decision. "If I thought one of my children were..." she swallowed hard. "Not with us any longer, but he was, I'd want to know immediately."

Phil craned his head. "I know," he blurted. "But, there are... other matters to consider." His eyes narrowed, downtrodden, thinking about Sandy's change. Thinking about Adam. "Plus," he raised his eyes to see his wife. "Aries is not her blood-born child. Robyn wanted an appropriate assessment of the situation before reuniting them."

Esta smiled. "He works in mysterious ways, Mr. Winter."

"That he does," agreed Phil when Esta handed him a cup of water and a ripe pomegranate. He drank the water, gulping it down to empty. She took the cup from him. He turned towards Cathryn's room.

"You okay?" Esta asked.

"Yeah," he said when he met his wife's eyes. "Just glad to be home."

Esta was analyzing him, he could tell. She knew

his ways better than he did. Knew him better than he knew himself. "That's not it," she said, her eyes narrow, staring. "Something's on that mind of yours."

Phil didn't answer; he bit into the pomegranate, the taste sweet and bitter on his tongue. He said, "Perfectly ripened," his mouth full.

Esta laughed at his antics. "Nice try. Changing the subject."

Phil nodded. Put the fruit on the counter between him and Esta. There was so much he wanted to tell her, so much he wanted her to know. His eyes downtrodden.

"It's okay," she said. "Whatever it is, you can tell me."

"I know," he muttered, nodding. "I do."

"But... some things are just too difficult to say, aren't they?"

Truth be told, Phil wasn't sure what was eating away at him other than the usual battles and blood; carnage and evil he'd been confronting since birth. Now that he'd arrived home, processing and decompression slammed into conscious thought, but there was more, something he couldn't put his finger on. Something about when he was under, after he'd taken the pills provided by Silas. Something in his subconscious nagging at him, and every time he was sure he'd be able to remember, the thought ran from conscious thought like a thief in the night. He didn't know what to say to his wife, nodding instead.

"Come here," she told him, walking around the counter, and offering her embrace, which Phil took immediately. He felt safe in his wife's arms. Always had. Ever since the island. Ever since they shared a cell, waiting for death together. Esta kissed the back of his head as he rested on her shoulder. "My precious angel. So much fighting. Always in the battle. I hope one day we can be in peace, away from all of this." Phil shivering in her arms, trembling, an empty pit in his churning stomach, hollow and wrought with pain. He wanted nothing more than to stay with her, take her and Cathryn and go, but go where? To do what? All his life, he's been in this fight for humanity. When will the fighting stop? "Go," said Esta. "See Silas," she told him. "Maybe after, Cathryn will be awake, and we can all be together."

Phil tightened his grip with shuddering arms. Cold air rippled goosebumps across his skin, a certain chill down his spine. He closed his eyes, wishing for the day all the fighting would stop.

6

THE cruiser remained in the woods. Cam had built a fire where Grimes and the giant warmed their hands, Grimes joining the misfit crew after he'd gone into the regeneration chamber. His shoulder now completely healed. Cat was gathering more wood from the forest. Contact to outside sources, to Robyn Winter, was still down. Cat was monitoring all communication from the greys, assessing their position on the happenings in Miami and whether they found Robyn Winter's secret base. So far, they had not.

Cam sat outside the cruiser, his back to it, away from the fire, looking over the teleporter in his hand. There was something strangely familiar with the device, like meeting a stranger who seems as if you've known them forever. And that sinking feeling returned, the disconnection to everyone, to himself, gathered inside his heart, made prominent by the surrounding quiet. He was still fuming over Cameron's disappearance into the hotel.

He could have been killed.

They all could have met their fate; if it weren't

for the teleporter, he'd be fodder for an alien monster. He could still hear the screams, the vampire's blood curdling wails when that monster claimed her.

What was he thinking? Cam thought about Cameron. Maybe he had no choice, some vampire hypnosis he can't control. Not yet anyway. Robyn had said the vampires could find him telepathically. Perhaps the ailing vampire, in her most desperate moment, latched on to Cameron and brought him to her. Maybe he couldn't control himself; or he had to go because of some sense of loyalty to his own.

That's ridiculous. Cameron's a human. A human turned vampire through genetic manipulation.

"There they are," hollered Grimes when Cam turned to the cruiser. Annison and Cameron stepped off, Cameron helping her, escorting the young lady to the fire, where they took a seat close together.

Cam could see that Cameron held her in high regard, and he understand why. She didn't judge him and saw through the fangs to the heart within. Saw him as the child he was and not some monster come to sneak into her room at night with a deadly kiss. Grimes waved his hands through the fire as the flames licked his palms, pretending to grab the flame. He thrust his arms up and sparks raged into the night sky, thumped, then disappeared.

"Oooh," called Grimes as if his antics would bring some mystical pleasure to mystical children, although they did laugh and Cam laughed under his breath, knowing they were laughing at Grimes and not his little fire sparks. A laugh to cut the tension.

Cameron turned to Cam and Cam noticed how Annison nudged the boy's leg. A second later, he gathered himself to his feet and walked towards Cam. He's so small, Cam thought. Just a kid, a baby. How could I be angry with him? He wanted nothing more than to reach out and wrap his arms around the boy. Wanted to tell him it was all going to be okay, but he couldn't. Couldn't, because he didn't know if that was true or not. Cam wasn't sure about anything anymore. With all that's going on in the universe, he wasn't sure if humanity could even survive. His people were being wiped out, that was for sure. Eradicated and turned into slaves. Cam wished in that moment he could hide, hide so the boy wouldn't see the lost stare in his eyes because then he'd know. The boy would know that Cam had lost his faith.

Cameron stood in front of him, the boy searching for the right words. His hands shook, and Cam shook his head.

"It's okay," said Cam with a shrug, an attempt to shrug off the lump wrenching in his throat. "We just have to stay together, is all. That's what is most important. Right?" Cam's brows pinched with narrow eyes as if he was asking himself the question.

"I just couldn't help myself," said the boy. "It was like she took control of my thoughts; my feet moved on their own."

Cam noticed how Annison was staring at them, Grimes and the giant, too.

"It's okay," said Cam. "There's a lot we all don't know about." He lifted his chin. "But we'll find them out together."

Without warning, Cameron jumped into his arms, holding tight around Cam's neck to Cam's startled surprise. His first thought was that Cameron would bite into his vein and his heart jumped, cursing himself for the thought as he held the boy tight.

"It's gonna be okay," said Cam. "We'll figure this out. All of us."

The boy pulled from Cam's embrace, put his hand on Cam's shoulder, said, "Together?"

Cam stared into the boy's eyes, gave a slight nod. "Yes," he breathed. "Together."

A smile across the boy's lips, he turned to Annison. "See," he hollered. "I told you he's staying."

Cam's brow furrowed as the boy turned to him when the sound of hurried footsteps approached. Cam shot up, grabbing the rifle he had leaned against the cruiser as Cat emerged from the woods, hurried and tense, as if a robot could ever be tense. His eyes flashing electrical sparks.

"Gentlemen," Cat said in a raised voice. "They have found Robyn Winter."

7

SANDY'S scream echoed through the cave. Her hand on her temple, pain between her temples like a knife twisting in her skull.

"The eyes," she hollered. "Those eyes."

Every time she found Adam, her thoughts slammed into grey eyes like some mystical blockade that turned fire into her skull. She felt sweat on her lip, her forehead, the heat on her skin burning.

"Why can't I break through?" she whined as Robyn placed his hand on her shoulder, standing behind her.

"The greys are powerful," said Robyn. "They know what you've become. Of course they would place a block within your ether, or his." He paused as Sandy caught her breath, her hands trembling, her skin fluttering. "May I ask something?"

Now Sandy's stomach wrenched and twisted, her lips trembling as she nodded approval.

"From what you have seen of Adam, is he safe?"

Sandy's hand drifted from her temple to her stomach as she leaned back against the rock. Robyn stepped to the side, crouched in front of her, his head craned to the right, eyes white with electrical flutters.

"What sense do you receive of his condition?"

Sandy gasped, having difficulty breathing, her chest rising in quick successions with every breath. She pursed her lips, catching her breath. Her eyes moved across the cave, catching visions and scenes from her mind. "Safe. Being cared for. Somewhere beautiful. Lots of grass and trees, butterflies, water. Like a garden or something, on the top of a hill or mountain. But the sky is different."

"How so?" asked Robyn.

Sandy closed her eyes, seeing, remembering the thought, the scene. "Two moons in the sky. White sun blazing hot."

Robyn seemed to consider her vision as she watched his downcast eyes.

"So many systems to consider. Two moons, white sun, there's got to be at least a thousand systems with the same." He looked at her, reached his hand to her forehead. His eyes, adoring, empathetic, twitched with an electrical current, but Sandy couldn't shake the sensation that Robyn was hiding something, some unknown cause or trifle. "Perhaps," he said, "We should take a moment before reconvening. You have blood coming from your nose. I'm afraid continuing may cause cerebral damage." He took a cloth from his pocket, wiped her nose with it.

Sandy stayed his hand. "No," she said, turning

from his stare. "I have to find him."

Robyn stood. "You will," he said, as if to give her hope when Sandy snapped her eyes to him.

"How do you know?" she asked.

"It is inevitable," was Robyn's response. "You will find your son. I have no doubts that you will."

Sandy watched as he stepped away. The pain in her skull thumped into her lungs, her breath heavy as she raised herself back to a sitting position. "There's something you're not telling me," she said. "I can feel it. I know it's true." Her head shaking. "What is it?"

Robyn stood tall, craned his head, staring, as if he were pondering his thoughts. "There is something I'd like to show you."

Sandy nodded as Robyn went to the wall, pressed his hand to it and the wall moved with the shape of a rectangle, a foot across and equally high. Beneath was a screen that quickly gleamed with life. On the screen, Sandy could see were children playing and running. The screen closed in on one child, a boy who appeared no older than fourteen. Confusion, face pinched, staring. She recognized the boy on the screen. Although his face had matured, she knew all too well the boyish stare and the uncanny reflection of Ben. She stood up, ambled to the screen.

It was unmistakable; the boy she was staring at was Aries, Ben's son. Her son.

Her head shaking. "How is this possible?" Her voice stern, disbelieving. "We were told he was… lost in the war." She turned to Winter. "How is he here?"

Robyn said, "The bus you and Ben put Aries on was not going to the safety camp. All the children on that bus were indigo children, very capable indigo children. Children who demonstrated the evolved unadulterated indigo trait."

"What does that mean? Indigo?"

"The indigo gene is the Draconian's greatest threat and the only chance for humanity. All human beings carry the indigo gene, but the gene has been suppressed for centuries in the larger populace. At one point in history, human beings were a highly evolved species, but also a dire threat to the established order. Many years ago, our enemies devised a plan to halt its power and suppress the gene. As a result, the devolution of the human species was initiated in an attempt to disarm the indigo gene." He stared at Sandy. "Did you not notice this yourself? Did you not notice any strange or gifted traits in Aries? Within yourself? Is it really a coincidence that you met his father, Sandy?" He pointed to the screen. "There's reason behind everything. Your paths were meant to cross, and that bus was never meant to arrive at the safety camp. For millenniums have they attempted to eradicate the indigo gene." He shook his head. "They have failed, and we were able to secure the bus. Aries has been here with us since then. He told us about you and his father. It took us some time to discover your whereabouts but when we did, I dispatched Phil and his team to rescue you from them."

Sandy whispered, thinking of Phil, "Why didn't you tell me?"

Robyn answered. "Because I told him not to."

Sandy spun around, head shaking. "Why?"

Robyn said, "Would it had made a difference? All that happened in the medical compound happened as it was meant to. We've been waiting for you, Sandy. All in the universe is now aligned in the stars. This is a time for action, a time for change, and a time for the future course of humanity to be set on the right path. As is this time, the safety camp rescue, the genetic manipulation. And the here and now. Every once in a while, the universe opens a window. It is through this window that we can set the future on the right path. That window is now open, Sandy, and the actions we take will determine the fate of our species. You are a part of that. You and your children will play a role in the future, whether that future will be greeted with peace or destruction is up to you, Phil, and the indigo children."

Sandy clenched her fists, anger swelling in her hot veins.

"My purpose is to ensure the future of our species. I have witnessed our destruction. I've gone through portals filled with pain and suffering, held star systems in the palm of my hand, and yet, still, our destruction seemed inevitable. The Draconians have done their work with care and caution, but like all who hold power, their arrogance allowed a sliver, a window to open, capable of allowing survival. As I said before, Sandy, there's only one way this all ends, only one way for the human species to survive. And it requires pain for all who are involved. Including yourself and your children."

8

PHIL had gone to see Silas. The cave was quiet; few were working at such an early morning hour. He gave nods to those he saw. His body ached, his neck where Sanos had bitten him was swollen and stiff. He'd need to gather himself in the regeneration chamber, heal his wounds, and gather strength.

After Silas, he thought. After my questions are answered.

He was hoping Robyn had made progress with Sandy. If anyone could help her, it would be him. Perhaps he had answers? Answers to Sandy's questions; namely, how she turned? Why she reflected a vampire's skin with vampire abilities far greater than his own?

Was Robyn aware of the change? Did he know she would change, or is this all a part of the master plan? Phil was not sure. Thoughts rolling over in his mind when he entered the communications department, finding Silas sitting in front of a computer monitor, his lips close to a microphone.

"Base one to NM9. Come in. Do you read me?"

Static, white noise from the speaker.

"Having trouble?" Phil said when Silas turned in his seat and Phil could sense his admiration, as if, perhaps, a wish was fulfilled with Phil's return.

Silas pushed his seat from the desk. "Yes, we've lost contact with NM9. No signals coming in or out." Silas rolled his tongue inside his cheek, staring at the monitor.

"NM9?" said Phil. "Isn't that where Cam was going?"

Silas nodded. "We've lost contact with them, too. With the cruiser."

Phil's eyes wide. "Have you tried the other bases?" He craned his head, staring at Silas. "Maybe they've heard from them?"

"Not yet," said Silas when he turned to Phil, his eyes wide as he took in Phil's wounds. "I thought I told you to play nice with the vampires."

Phil laughed. "Yeah well, they're a rowdy bunch."

Silas chewed the inside of his cheek, seemed to consider Phil's statement. Phil stood looking at Silas' monitor, where darkness swept across the screen. On the bottom of the screen in white letters within the thicket of black blinked NM9. "They should have been there hours ago." He stepped closer, put his hand on the back of Silas' chair.

Silas talked into the microphone, "Base one to NM9, come in." Static returned from NM9, nothing more.

Phil craned his head, his chest tight, felt his jaw tense.

Something is most definitely wrong.

"Check in with the other bases," he said. "See if you can get someone online."

Typically, all bases checked in at the same time; an effort to maintain anonymity and to ward off the possibility of communications being retrieved by outside sources. Even though the code was scrambled, a seasoned IT veteran could lock on to the signal and break through. The less communication, the better other than in an emergency.

"Of course," said Silas, dutifully progressing with Phil's request.

Phil felt a tug on his elbow. He turned to see the boy who had been waiting for his arrival. Green eyes gazed upon Phil with an innocent stare, his dark hair disheveled as if he'd just awakened, and his skin carried the complexion youth so often brings, soft and unfettered. Thin, although cut and tone, he stood just under Phil's chin like a beanstalk on the rise. Robyn and Phil had trained him since the rescue; however, his rose training was about to begin. According to Robyn, he would evolve into a great warrior. A powerful indigo, his evolution was unadulterated as a side effect of the war; if he had been raised in the wider population, he would have received the same devolution process as the other captive humans.

"Aries," Phil sighed. "Why are you up at such an early hour? You should be sleeping."

The boy's green eyes gleamed. "Are they here?" he asked. "Did you find them? I heard things took a turn for the worse." His eyes drifted. "Heard the team... didn't make it."

Phil put his hands on Aries' shoulders. "They fought gallantly," he said. "Their sacrifice is just; your mother is here. She is being debriefed by Robyn as we speak." Phil was careful in his choice of words.

Aries caught on. "She?" he asked. "What about my father?"

Tightness in his chest again. Over the years Phil had gotten used to giving bad news, but telling Aries his father had perished in the night, a victim to a vampire, was not news he wished to provide. He didn't have to. Looking at Aries, his mouth open, jaw slackened, staring into Phil's eyes with a disappointed and painful stare. "He didn't make it, did he?"

Phil's head moved back and forth. "I'm so sorry."

Aries said nothing in response. Phil watched as his eyes filled with tears.

"It's okay to cry, Aries. I know the pain you feel."

Aries lips trembled as a single tear fell from both eyes.

"Stay with me here," said Phil. "Stay close. I'll bring you to your mother soon." He turned to Silas.

"Just as soon as we get someone on the line."

Commotion now coming from the cave dwelling, the entrance to their base. Muffled words, a roar, and moving feet. Silas looked at Phil, his eyes revealed fear drenched in pity and shame.

"What is it?" said Phil as he went to the far wall, put his hand to the palm reader, and the door opened to the cave.

And Phil said, "Cam?"

9

THEY arrived within seconds from Coba after Cat's informed information about Robyn Winter's whereabouts. According to Cat, the vampires tracked the location after the rebel's flight from Drac Tower. But that wasn't all the information they received. Apparently, after Cam and Cameron's exploits, the greys moved their project to Drac City, believing they had compromised the Miami location. And the last communication revealed that not only were the Dracs headed towards Winter's base, so were the greys. An elite show of power capable of destroying the rebellion, wiping out all threats to their established order. All other bases were destroyed, just as Cam had witnessed the New Mexico obliteration.

It took some time for Cam and his crew to gain entrance into the cave, and now they were standing in the cave dwelling, with Cam shouting bloody hell to every human he could see, requesting Phil's, Winter's, and the nine's presence when he saw Phil.

Cam called to him, "We need to evacuate immediately."

"What?" Phil shook his head. "What's going on? What happened in New Mexico?"

"Gone," Cam said. "Total annihilation. They were dead before we even got there."

Cam watched as Annison tore past them and wrapped her arms around a young man with green eyes.

"How?" Phil said.

"Doesn't matter how," said Cam. He paused before saying, "They're on their way here now. They know your location. They're coming."

"Who?"

Cam's eyes widened. "Everyone! Greys. Vampires. Everyone they have. All your bases have been destroyed." He shook his head. "You're all that's left."

Phil seemed to consider this. He looked over at the giant, Grimes, Cameron, and his eyes narrowed when he saw Cat.

Cam said, "We need to evacuate."

Phil shot Cam a stare. Looked around the cave, noticed Silas beside him. Phil took him by the elbow. "Get on the communiqué, gather all remaining soldiers…"

Silas interjected, "There aren't many left," said Silas.

"Doesn't matter," said Phil. "Sound the alarm; we need to get everyone into the tunnels."

"And go where?" said Silas. "You don't even

know this is real."

Phil looked at Cam, who nodded twice. Phil said, "I believe him." He looked at Silas. "And you haven't been able to contact any of our bases. Can't you feel it, Silas?" His eyes searched over the cave, as if he could see beyond the cave to the stars above. "There's something wrong with the air tonight."

Cam stepped up. "Is there an entrance to hollow earth?"

"What?" said Phil.

"A… hole, a pit that leads to hollow earth? That's how they came in from the other bases. A sneak attack from within and…" he looked up. "Above."

Phil's eyes widened, his body tensed. He turned to Silas. "Close the pit," he called. "Sound the alarm now, Silas. Order all remaining soldiers to the pit." Phil pointed to a few human adults. "Seal the cave," he ordered. "NOW!" He looked at Cam. "Come on," he said, and Cam followed with his crew. Followed Phil back into the room as Phil called to Silas. "Start the evacuation procedure." Silas took a seat by the microphone. Pushed a button and an alarm wretched through the cave.

City Evacuation Procedure In Effect.
Proceed to Cave Dwelling AR77

Red flowing lights erupted in the cave. Phil looked at the young man with green eyes, said, "Aries, gather the children with you. Take them to AR77 immediately."

Aries nodded, looked at Annison and Cameron. "Come with me," he said. "All children need to come with us."

Phil said to Silas, "And find Robyn," he told him. "He's in the decompression room with Sandy. Channel 219." He was walking with a hurried step towards another wall where he placed his hand on the palm reader and the door opened, weapons behind the wall. Rifles, handguns, bombs and devices Cam had never laid eyes on. Phil took a rifle when the lights went out with a dying hum. Cam looked around. All computer monitors that had been on now revealed dark screens. A second later, the red lights went on, bathing the cave in a red glow.

"My god," said Cam, locking eyes with Phil. "They're here."

10

ROBYN, his arm stretched, palm up, curled his hand into a fist, and said, "One life is not worth the extinction of an entire species."

Sandy said, "But if we're all indigos, why not just tell everyone that aliens exist. If what you say is true, they'll have to leave and the Arcturians will bring order when they arrive."

"Because of the blanket," he said.

Sandy looked at him, puzzled. "What blanket?"

"The electronic blanket… a frequency signal wrapped around the earth. It provides cover, like camouflage, for aliens; the frequency, the wavelength, disturbs their features. Humans think they're looking at a human when it's an alien in front of them. But the frequency also dumbs down brain activity, turning the human mind easily. It holds all frequencies within the planet. Nothing can get in or out, no thought, no message, no clarity from above. No ships can enter or leave unless specifically allowed. Whoever controls the blanket controls the planet. Not even our ether can pass. All exceptions are when one is aware, conscious that the frequency exists; only then can a supremely trained soul tear through its boundary. The earth…. was once a place of marvel, an oasis, a grand utopia filled with magic and wonder. Now…." He gripped a handful of dirt in his palm; let it slip through his fingers. "Nothing but dirt and rock with boundaries that begin in the mind. It used to not be this way. Before the frequency, communication with outside worlds was immediate."

Sandy remembered the glow above Drac Tower. "Where is it located? Surely we must have seen it in all this time?"

Robyn turned, took a few steps to the rock formation. "The location is a secret. They move the towers frequently. From what I know, there are seven transmission towers scattered across the planet. Towers like electrical beacons used for electricity and phones. Every time we get close to finding one, they move the location. We have been searching, of course. Access to the blanket would provide an opportunity of dire importance. The signal can't be stopped but it can be neutralized, sped up. Understand, the Draconians set the blanket to thrive until well after the coming of the Arcturians and the Earth's cataclysm, an arrival beset by the stars and the alignment of the universe over the planet. Should we be able to find it, we could advance the signals output to dissipate prior to their coming. Such an occurrence would offer an opportunity to take back the planet once the Arcturians arrive."

Sandy said, "Purple and blue electrical currents, reaching high above."

Robyn stared, perplexed. "Yes," he breathed.

Sandy turned her chin up, locked eyes with Winter. "I've seen one," she said.

Robyn craned his head, his eyes beaming with wonder, said, "Where?"

Sandy saw a white and yellow glow before she heard the boom, saw how the rock above rained down on Winter before she was thrown backward. The back of her head rattled against the rock wall. Rock shrapnel ripped through the cave, billowing dust that choked the throat.

An alarm, an intermittent beeping, rang through the cave, now bathed in a red blaze.

System Breach.

Evacuation procedure in effect.

Go to the nearest exit point.

Cold vapor erupted in the cave as Sandy looked up; saw the thick rock ceiling falling.

And then, darkness.

11

MOTH'S ship, one of four Drac vessels, spiraled towards the rebellion's pit into hollow earth. The greys were attacking from above, deploying their robotic army with a direct attack, and strict orders that Moth's Dracs would enter the rebel base from below. Force them into a bottleneck where Moth and his soldiers will be waiting.

He addressed his soldiers before the armada arrived.

"Take prisoners," he told them. He wanted a show, a grand display to parade through Drac Plaza. A display of power and fear his people would never forget. He also provided intel on Sanos and Sandy, who he deemed traitors in the eyes of Dracs-take them dead or alive. It didn't matter to Moth.

No one would ever think to question Moth's leadership after tonight. His only concern came with Robyn Winter. A battle he was all too eager to engage in, Sephtis being his ace in the hole. A call to him would take mere seconds should it be required. An entanglement he wished to avoid. He already had the message with Winter's location set to send to Sephtis if needed. Should Winter cause more concern for Moth, he would send the message and all his Dracs would need to be ready to leave at that moment. Sephtis didn't take kindly to distractions; he just destroyed all who were in his path.

"Master Moth?" Moth received communication from his pilot as they neared the rebel's pit. Moth himself watched the advancing ship from his private hull. The pilot on the screen in front of him, Moth provided acknowledgement. The pilot returned, saying, "The entrance has been sealed. Our scanners reveal human rebels inside the pit."

Moth sat forward. "Then blast the entrance and advance." The pilot acknowledged the order as Moth communicated with Zon. "Have all Drac warriors ready to depart. Human rebels will advance upon our arrival. Be ready and capable."

Moth knew his order meant death for many Dracs, but soldiers were expendable and he had many. Breach the hull, he thought when Zon hesitatingly acknowledged the order.

"Don't think, Zon," ordered Moth. "Simply do as I say."

Zon bowed to Moth. "As you wish," he said when Moth's screen transferred to the sealed pit. His pilot hovering beneath the circular entrance and shot bombs that clung to the door, four bombs north, south, east, and west and a fifth in the center when the ship moved away from the entrance. On his screen, Moth could see the countdown on each bomb, counting down from 5…

Moth grinned when he thought about the human's destruction.

4…

Fantastic day, he thought.

3…

He sat forward, his lips curled in a snarl.

2…

Here we come, Sandy, mistress of the night.

1…

Sanos, come and find me.

The pit was torn apart in a raging ball of fire as the enclosure fell down into hollow earth. The first ship raced into the opening.

I beseech you. Come… find… me!

12

"HERE they come," hollered Phil, looking through his sonar visor, two small screens on each corner in his visor, revealing the Gatling weapons his soldiers were using against the grey army from the two corners of the cave, ripping green lasers across the robot horde. Cam and Grimes and this new guy Cat acknowledged him, all at the ready. Silas had sent the soldiers to the pit to ward off the attack from the Dracs. Aries, Silas, and Perseus were gathering the children into AR77, following the evacuation protocol, along with the council members. Should the rest not survive the attack, Silas and the council will continue with the indigo children; their only hope for a future. For freedom. His thoughts went to Esta and Cathryn. He'd gone over the evacuation procedure with her a million times. Esta, being one of the most capable people he'd ever known, would make it to the tunnels, he was sure.

The children had to survive; he would risk his life for them to escape. The future always remained with them, with the children; the indigo trait had advanced under Robyn's command, strengthening from one unadulterated generation to the next. What he needed in this moment was time, time to give Aries and Silas an opportunity to reach the water and the hidden base they had there. The future depended on their escape. Nothing else mattered.

Phil's attention caught by the immense door leading into the cave with a sound likened to bending steel; the door seemed to buckle, as if being pulled inward and away from their location. Sonar revealed multiple soldiers behind the door, lined in single file to the left and right of the door, rifles in their hands. The grey's robot army. He'd come across a few in his lifetime, easily dismantled by particle technology, but what waited outside was an onslaught. Yes, they could disseminate the multitudes of soldiers about to arrive, but their advanced numbers would ultimately lead to evacuation on the rebel's part. Time was of the essence and when the door caved inward in a vast heap of smoke and steel, as he ordered his people to fire, particle blasts disappearing into the smoke and beyond as green lasers returned fire, watching as the robot army began marching through the smoke filled door, Phil could only think of the one they needed…

Where is Robyn Winter?

13

ESTA'S eyes opened with a hurried snap of emergency. Raging alarm, the cave drenched in red light and a mechanical voice calling for evacuation as smoke and cold vapor–the vapor extinguishing the many fires raging in the garden–gripped her attention.

She'd been knocked unconscious the moment the bomb detonated. Beneath the raging alarm, she could hear people evacuating into the tunnels, towards AR77. Esta was well aware of the evacuation procedure; she was sure the others scattered across the cave and garden were heading there now. She could hear screams and hollers, blood-curdling screams filled with terror coming from the garden. Esta clambered to her hands and knees, her throat arid, her eyes burning from the thick smoke billowing inside the cave as she coughed violently sitting on her legs as her vision blurred, her head weary when she felt tiny hands and arms wrap around her chest.

Cathryn!

Her daughter was behind her, her tiny frame attempting to help her to her feet. Esta wrapped her arm around Cathryn's shoulders, forced herself to her feet as she coughed and gagged, her stomach heavy. Her hand went to it, feeling for the baby when the kick within her stomach told her all she needed to know. She looked at her daughter, said, "We've got to get to..."

"AR77," said Cathryn, those big sea-blue eyes panic-stricken yet calm. Cathryn had always been an advanced child; she was Phil's daughter, this was true.

Esta looked over at their home. The far wall had caved in, furniture overturned, scattered across the floor. Vapor and smoke outside in the garden. She needed to get through the garden to the entrance into the tunnels. She gripped Cathryn's hand in hers.

"Stay close," she said, and Cathryn responded with a nod and cough before Esta led them outside into the garden as a thick rock fell from the ceiling into the lake fed by the waterfall. She led her daughter through the thicket of smoke, alarm blaring, her throat burning. Difficult to see more than a few feet ahead, but Esta knew the path; she'd walked it with Phil so many times she could find it blindfolded.

She looked back at Cathryn, the child's eyes burning red, and Esta scooped the child into her arms. "Keep your eyes and nose in my shoulder." Cathryn did as instructed, clinging to her mother for dear life. Esta's hand rested on the back of Cathryn's head as she stepped forward, climbing over rocks and dirt, her feet padding through the burning, smoke filled garden.

Following the path as smoke filled her vision, now thinning as she hurried to the tunnels when she saw the first body, torn open, lying dead on the ground. She recognized the woman immediately. Laura had always been a loyal friend; she taught the children history and mathematics. Her throat torn open, and that was when Esta knew; Laura's death wasn't a result of the explosion.

Her eyes widened as the smoke slithered into a thin mist, revealing a line of dead bodies scattered across the ground, leading to the tunnel's entrance as if they had clawed for the door to open. The door that was closed.

"Don't look," she told Cathryn as she scampered towards the door, her heart on fire with a thick successive pounding in her chest, stepping over dead bodies, men, women, and children. Her friends, her confidants, children she'd helped raise within their sacred community. All dead, their eyes black to the core as she came upon the door, pressed her hand to the palm reader then gripped the back of Cathryn's head as she turned to see if anyone had followed, if anyone was coming to issue the same fate as her neighbors, listening as the door hummed open. Her breath heavy, another explosion and she snapped to it, watched as a thick cut of rock fell from the ceiling into the lake as she gripped her daughter tight and turned to the open door.

And the vampire who greeted them.

14

ROBYN Winter's eyes snapped open in a hurried frenzy, realizing he was trapped beneath rock and rubble. Felt warm liquid cascade across the back of his head.

Blood, he thought as he inhaled hoarsely, recognizing then that the alarm was raging inside the cave.

They are here!

Tried to steady himself with his palm, to force himself up, but his unsteady arm gave out. Pain in the back of his head, Robyn gritted his teeth, clenched his jaw.

Settle down, he told himself, widening his eyes. The cave was thick with smoke and vapor, bathed in red light; it felt like a mountain had fallen on top of him, the weight like an elephant with pressure that choked the lungs and wrenched the back.

Buried.

Sandy is here… somewhere.

I am not my body.

I am not crude matter.

I am luminous and made of stardust.

Robyn closed his eyes. The pain in his skull deterred his concentration, but briefly, only a moment of hesitation when the pain cringed the neck and pinched the face before he felt himself break free. The cave now a ball of light. Rock dissipated into light as Robyn stood while sealing his wound, feeling the gash in the back of his head heal instantaneously. Through his eyes, he could see where Sandy was, beneath a thick heap of rock and debris. He could see her ether and body heat under the rock. Robyn waved his hand, and the rock rose from over Sandy. He dropped it to the ground a few feet away.

He could see she was breathing, albeit shallow. Her heart thumped with a thick wallop in her chest and then lay still. A thick gash across her forehead, blood down her face and neck. She was dying; he knew. The weight of that rock just about did her in. If she were human, she would be dead from its weight. If he didn't act now, she'd be dead by morning. Robyn looked over the room, looked to the wall behind them, unscathed.

Good, he thought when he gathered Sandy in his arms and, with a thought, ejected the regeneration chamber embedded inside the rock wall. Vapor, healing oxygen, poured from the bed into the cave. Robyn placed Sandy inside.

"They'll be searching for you," he whispered. "You must survive this night."

Robyn stood tall. The alarm blaring. A hole in

the roof where the bomb had exploded. He could see clearly to the night sky and the pending twilight that bathed the sky in a dull but dark bluish glow. He turned to Sandy, and the bed hummed into the wall.

Moth has come for her, thought Robyn as he looked over the cave. Sealed shut with debris. Robyn craned his head; the rock seal was the perfect protection for Sandy. He manipulated his ether, his matter, and slithered through the rock like rays of sunlight through the crevices, and materialized outside the enclosure.

Now, he thought, where is Moth?

15

ARIES led the children with Annison and Cameron on his heels, and the giant holding the back of the line with Silas, through the tunnel towards AR77. He walked with a hurried, although cautious, pace. No alarm in the tunnel, but he could hear the continuous buzzing raging in the cave. No red lights here either, the only light a soft white glow from the floor to lead the way. Not that Aries needed the light, his helmet was equipped with sonar.

His comrades, fellow soldiers he'd trained with for years, had taken up arms in the pit. Phil led the rest of their tight community in the entrance. Aries understood this moment was about survival; how the vampires found their base was insignificant. What was true was the fight and their ability to save as many as possible, to live to fight another day. His heart sank when not one of his people made it from the garden.

Keep moving, he told himself. That was protocol, to keep moving to AR77, an access point where underwater vessels waited for their arrival to take them down into the ocean.

An explosion on his right, far up ahead; he saw the blasts wallop into a raging ball of dust and debris. Aries stopped short, held up his hand, a signal for everyone to cease moving. Aries craned his head, staring, assessing. Waved his hand for everyone to sit against the wall, hidden behind the thick rock protrusion he was hiding behind now. He scanned the wall, looking for an access point, a hidden door in the rock where another tunnel would bring them to AR77, a longer and tightly narrow access point but if the tunnel they were in was compromised the secondary tunnels would have to do. The closest access point he found was well beyond where the cave had exploded. He looked back, scanned the wall there. Since access points were strategically placed every thirty feet, he found one close to the giant and Silas. He locked eyes with Silas, then gestured to the access point. Silas nodded his understanding.

They'd be taking the long way to AR77. Aries watched as Silas opened the door through a retinal scan.

"Are they coming?" whispered Annison, the boy next to her hugging her shoulders.

Aries put his finger to his lips, gestured to the door where Silas was ushering in one child after another when Annison screamed and Aries turned on his heels to the vampire barreling towards him. Behind him another vampire, a third behind him.

"Come out, come out, little ones," said the first

vampire. "I can smell your blood."

Aires stepped into the center, revealing himself, and rushed at the first vampire, who fired a particle beam from his rifle. The beam raced towards Aries as he jumped to the wall, running across rock and dirt and jumped with a spin towards the vampire, hooked the neck and throat into the crook of his knee and brought the vampire's skull down against the ground. He could hear how the particle beam tore through the wall at the end of the cave with an explosion that billowed dirt and rock into the cave. Aries twisted his leg with a quick thrust, snapping the vampire's neck.

The second vampire advanced. Aries sprang up, took two quick steps forward, jumped and flipped over, his heel crashing against the top of the vampire's skull, when he continued to roll behind the vampire, extended his blades and sliced up the vampire's back, from the base of the spine to the nape of the vampire's neck with a roll across the vampire's back. He dropped to his feet and extended his claws and thrust the steel talons into the throat of the third. His claws wedged in the vampire's throat. Aries tugged his claws, blood flowing across his hand and arm. He tugged again, no use, then retracted the claws, and the vampire fell to the ground.

He turned back to Silas, all were through the door except Annie, the boy, Silas, and the giant. The giant who had no chance of getting through the narrow tunnel. He stepped forward, assessed the giant, the boy, and Annie.

"Go," he ordered Silas and after a brief hesitation, Silas entered the door.

Annie screamed bloody hell.

And Aries felt hands on his shoulders, felt himself flying back, crashing against the ground. His head and neck rattled against rock and cold dirt.

And then darkness.

16

PHIL was in a firefight like he'd never seen. Watching, as his people were dying, one by one, life gone in a hail of lasers, disintegrated upon impact. The coming AI were relentless. How many were still to come he could not be sure. He lost communication with his soldiers secured in the base's corners, and the Gatling weaponry was no longer being used. On his visor screens he could see nothing but darkness, knowing they had all met their demise.

It was a losing battle. A losing battle that he'd need to end in catastrophe if necessary. Phil had the pulse bomb, the bomb that would tear through the cave and destroy all within its vicinity, his ace in the hole. His last attempt to give Aries enough time to AR77. Certain death had come to Phil; it was the only way the rebellion would continue.

The only hope for humanity.

A laser tore into the blockade he hid behind, and he felt himself propel back, crashing and sliding across the floor, slamming into the wall to a stop. Smoke filled the cave, covering debris and the dead scattered across the cave. Pain welled from his back to his neck as Phil attempted to get up when the pain rushed across his spine, his face pinched in pain and agony. Through the smoke filled cave, he saw Cam rushing towards him as Phil forced himself into a sitting position.

"I think we're going about this all wrong," said Cam, crouched down in front of him. Grimes and Cat continued blasting. That Cat was on point. Every blast found its target, but the AI were vast in numbers. They kept coming.

"What does that mean?" said Phil when Cam revealed a tiny device, looked like an old film reel. Phil looked at him with a narrow, confused stare.

"It's a teleporter," said Cam. "You know this cave and the outside better than anyone. Get us outside and we can fight from behind them." Cam smiled. "Sneak attack. They won't see us coming."

Phil took the teleporter as Cam helped him to his feet. Phil took the pulse bomb from the back of his belt. Showed it to Cam.

"I've got a better idea," said Phil when he locked eyes with Cam. "Get everyone into the tunnels. Sound the retreat. The blast will destroy all in this entrance once it goes off."

Cam followed Phil's gesture to the tunnel, and Cam's eyes widened.

"Now," Phil hollered, seeing in his mind's eye outside the cave. Three massive UFOs overhead, their ramps down, hordes of AI marched down the ramps.

AI in the entrance, single file, smoke filled the cave, green blasts raged in multitudes into the smoke. Looked to the starships again, their location and height perfect for the pulse to destroy when he was noticed by an AI. He couldn't hear what was said over the lasers, didn't have to, when a horde of AI turned their weapons on him.

"See you on the other side," hollered Phil to the starship as he tossed the bomb into the air.

Back in the cave, behind Cam, Phil screamed, "Get down," when the pulse bomb erupted with a massive wallop of fire and heat that tore into the cave as the earth rumbled and rattled, knocking Phil to his feet in a cloud of dust and debris.

17

ANNISON'S scream was never ending. Screaming in fear, fear that Aries was dead, and fear of the vampire coming towards them.

Cameron stood up when the vampire had come behind Aries and tossed the young warrior backwards, stepping in front of Annie to shield her from the vampire.

"You want her? You've got to get through me first," said the young naïve Cameron, cringing when the vampire turned to him. But the vampire stopped cold just before Perseus slammed into him. The vampire thrust back but Perseus reacted quick, catching the vampire's head with lightning speed and tearing the vampire's skull from his neck.

Another vampire, and Perseus grabbed his shoulders, tossing him through the exploded hole in the tunnel. Cameron craned his head, watching as Perseus leapt through the hole confronting all who would come to claim Cameron. He wasn't sure when Annie stopped screaming. Cameron crouched in front of her. "We've got to go," he said. "Perseus won't be able to hold them off for long."

Annie shook her head. "Not without Aries," she said. "We've got to see if he's alive."

Cameron turned to see Aries unmoving far down into the tunnel. Looked for Perseus battling a handful of vampires when he turned to Annie.

"Okay," he said, offering his hand.

They raced down the tunnel to Aries' aid. They could see he was still breathing. Perseus growling, vampires groaning, breathing heavy, a dog fight if there ever was one. Cameron's head snapped to Aries when he groaned beneath his breath.

"Help him up," said Annie, draping an arm across her shoulders and Cameron did the same, lifting the young warrior to his feet. "We need to get him to AR77."

Aries moaned, clutching his head, leaning against Cameron as they stepped towards the tunnel. Perseus was thrown back into the tunnel, landed on the ground with a thud onto his knees, and then a laser beam slammed him back into the wall.

Cameron could hear breathing, heavy breath from Annison and Aries; from himself. Frozen in the tunnel, Perseus unconscious as the vampires stepped in front of them.

18

ZON, with four Drac warriors, raced through the cave. Hurried steps, weapons at the ready. They'd come in through the pit and were met with immediate gunfire. They lost many warriors in the battle; nevertheless, in the end, they were triumphant, able to break through the rebellion barrage. His warriors were the best with seek and destroy missions. On his ear com, he'd learned a few prisoners were captured. Moth wanted a show, and it was a show drenched in blood.

Moth had taken a faction of Drac warriors with him, his nose seeking the female Drac Diagon had attempted to free. He could have the woman, Zon thought, his own nose picking up the scent of vampire. Sanos was on Zon's radar, knowing Moth would squeeze the life from Sanos' throat once he was in his clutches. That was not how Dracs operated, Zon knew. There were protocols to follow when it came to Drac soldiers and part of him wanted Sanos to tell his story. Something was foul within COR; he could feel it like poison in his veins.

They were travelling through a dark tunnel, but

he could see light at the end. A drop off into a round room filled with stone seats. His nose crinkled. The scent of Drac was in that room. He arrived at the tunnel's end, gestured for his warriors to halt as he looked in and down.

Sanos was sitting, drenched in blood, his talon scraping his arm as he stared at the dead humans in front of him.

Zon dropped down with a thud. Sanos never stirred. It wasn't until Zon walked closer, rifle at the ready, aimed at Sanos, that Sanos noticed his arrival. Zon's warriors dropped into the room and Sanos grinned, watching them circle around him. Zon approached closer.

"Did you receive my message?" said Sanos, not looking at Zon, staring at the dead eyes in front of him.

"I did," said Zon.

Sanos snickered, a guffaw in his throat. "And now you're arresting me for revealing the rebels' base." He turned to Zon. "How noble," he growled.

"Master Moth," said one of Zon's warriors, "wants him dead."

Zon shook his head as Sanos answered, "Of course he does. Those who deal in manipulation always want those who can point fingers to be destroyed." Sanos shot up to his feet; the warriors flinched and tensed. Sanos' eyes wide with rage as he stared into Zon's soul. "What will you do here, Zon?" He raised his hands in surrender. "Here I am, unarmed.

You can kill me now or…"

Zon answered, "You're under arrest, Sanos."

One warrior retorted, "That's not what Moth wants."

Zon looked at his warrior. "Then he can kill him himself. Sanos will stand trial in front of Drac City. Let him tell his story. He will be judged by all Dracs should his report be foul."

Sanos grinned, hands still up as he slowly bent to his knees. "There you go Zon. Such a righteous Drac you are. But do tell me, where has our little treacherous Moth gone?"

19

MOTH followed Sandy's scent with ten Drac warriors at his command. He'd lost communication with the greys after the cave rattled and hummed around him. He wondered if Robyn Winter had handed the greys their demise. Or was it the phantom? He could not be sure. The rebels' base was in chaos and mayhem; he and his warriors had torn through the rebel fighters who advanced on their ship in the pit, and he'd dispatched his warriors to secure prisoners–just a few, enough to parade in front of Drac City as a display of power and unfettered resolve–and leave the rebel base in ashes.

His enhanced sense of smell brought him towards a garden where Sandy's blood grew ever the more prominent. A unique scent it was, vampire for sure, was in her veins but also human. The faintest stank of human beneath the fragrance of a vampire. They arrived at a tunnel, round and ten feet high, fifty yards long. Sandy's scent strengthened in the tunnel and he could see beyond, bathed in red, an alarm raging, faint and mixed with rushing water. His warriors assessed the tunnel, guns at the ready; a cold, quiet wind greeted them.

Eerily quiet and Moth could feel how the air turned thick in that tunnel, gnashing his fangs, his jaw tense. His soldiers waited for his instruction.

"Advance," he said when the closest soldier turned to him with wide, fearful eyes. "NOW!" Moth hollered, and his soldiers, five on the right and left, stepped into the tunnel. Moth could hear their panting breath, felt the rapid beat of their hearts thundering in their chests. Perhaps, Moth thought, they are aware of their pending sacrifice. He grinned as he stepped into the tunnel behind them. He didn't get more than two steps in when his warriors stopped cold.

Up ahead, just outside the tunnel, flakes of light, seven of them, converged into a bright, striking white light. Momentarily blinding, Moth's warriors shielded their eyes, turning away from the light. Moth's eyes wide.

"I can't believe it," he whispered, earning stares from a few warriors when the light dissipated. The human behind the light now revealed. "Robyn Winter lives." Moth craned his head, staring at the human with a confused stare. "Where did you get the body, Robyn? You look so young for someone thousands of years old."

"It's called dying," said Robyn when he stepped into the tunnel, his white eyes narrow, glaring at Moth. "You should try it."

Moth wasn't sure if he froze because his heart skipped a beat or if the mere presence of a sworn enemy centuries old stopped him cold in his tracks, but when he looked down, he knew why.

The rock had wrapped around his feet and ankles, the same for his warriors.

"Neat trick," said Moth to Winter, when the rock around his ankles broke apart and he stepped away. "But you'll have to do better than that." His warriors gasped, their eyes wide and fearful as Moth broke their rocky restraints, one by one, with a pop and crack. They looked at Moth. He wasn't sure if their stares meant a plea for their lives from Robyn Winter, or pride that their master had released them. Didn't matter, Moth ordered, "Attack," in a restrained, matter-of-fact voice.

Robyn stepped closer as the warriors aimed their rifles.

"Particle beams," said Robyn. And he grinned, staring at Moth, when he said, "My favorite."

The first two warriors fired upon Winter, who raised his hand, absorbing the beams into his palm. The beams raced into his arm as if engrossed by the sun. His arm then turned into steel and shot the beams towards them, through them, each gripped by the beam that dropped them to the ground, unmoving, although alive. Winter looked at the ailing unmoving vampires as electrical sparks raged across his pupils and the ground, the earth, rock and dirt wrapped around them and pulled them into the ground, embedding them inside the rock. Winter then turned to Moth.

"Perhaps I'll keep them," he said. "Like pets."

Moth, head shaking in disgust and disappointment, snarled at Robyn Winter, when behind him a second horde of his warriors rushed into the cave and gathered arms. Moth's breath shallow, regarding his multitude of warriors, before he turned to Winter.

"Trust me, Robyn, I wouldn't want this to be too easy for you."

Robyn craned his head, assessing the warriors with their rifles, when he grinned at Moth, stepped forward, grinding his foot into the cave and slapped his hands together.

Moth's wings covered him in a protective shield as Winter's etherical thrust barreled towards him and his warriors. The air rippled, thrust towards them, turning the rifles into dust and dropping the horde to the ground where the rock floor wrapped around them, entombing them inside the rock.

Robyn Winter stepped back, arms at his sides, said, "No worries, Moth…" The warriors groaning with fearful panic, their screams stifled under rock formed arms. "But I appreciate the sentiment."

Moth retracted his wings, looked around him before his eyes settled on Winter. Sandy's scent carried on the breeze. She was beyond Winter, his stance a clear sign Moth was not getting through this tunnel without a fight. His agitation reached a fevered pitch as he raised his arms, palms up manipulating the surrounding air into a thick ball of energy which he barreled towards Winter who, seeing the coming ether, raised his hands and braced himself as his protective light circled around him and Moth's ether slammed into Winter's shield. Moth held the ether, an onslaught against Winter's protection, and flew through the tunnel.

Barreling towards Winter to hand him his fate.

20

CAM rushed to Phil's aid. Phil was buried beneath rock and debris. Cat pulled one boulder after another, and Cam feared the worse as he tore at the rock. Their little ruse had worked. No longer was the AI army advancing. After Phil called for everyone to take guard against the coming blast, Cam had turned to see Phil fall when the ground quaked beneath them. Watched as the rock fell over him.

And then darkness bathed the cave, briefly before he fell himself. Cat removed the last boulder. No Phil, the ground was empty.

I saw him here, thought Cam. Saw it rain down on him. Cam slapped his hand against the empty floor.

"Cam," said Phil, and Cam turned to see Phil behind them. His sonar visor blaring in the darkness. Cam looked from Phil to the floor beneath him, then back to Phil as he raised his hand, revealing the teleporter in his palm. "Works like a charm."

Cam shook his head as he rose to his feet. Looked at Phil as he stomped towards him. "I thought you were dead," he said.

"Guess it wasn't my time."

"Guess not." Cam looked around the tunnel. "Where to from here?"

"Simple," said Phil. "We meet the others in AR77. Aries should have gotten everyone down there by now."

"Hopefully," said Grimes, earning stares from Cam, Phil, and Cat. "Remember the sneak attack," he said when he looked down the tunnel, swallowing hard. "There're vampires down here." He looked Phil dead in the eye. "They won't stop until we're all dead. That's... what this is. Annihilation."

Phil seemed to consider the statement when Cam said, "What happened to the optimism?"

Grimes glared at Cam. "They've destroyed every rebel base capable of challenging their agenda." He shook his head. "We... everyone in this base... we're all that's left. No matter what, they have to eradicate us from the planet. Doing so would hand them certain victory."

"What are you saying?" said Cam.

"I'm saying," answered Grimes. "That no matter what, we have to be sure some have survived."

Cam, nodding, said, "Go down in a blaze of glory?"

"Whatever needs to happen needs to happen. What I saw during our travels, what that girl Annie could do. They are the future and I'd be proud to hand it to them." He pursed his lips. "Even if it means my life."

Phil turned from them, walked into the tunnel a few feet from where they stood, looking around the tunnel.

"To the pit?" Cam said. "Seek them out while they're looking for us."

"Go forth to be free," said Grimes. "And we'll take out as many as we can."

Cam looked at Cat. "What are your thoughts?"

Cat's red eyes locked with Cam. "Depending on how many are still here, we may have a slight chance of driving them back. Communications with the greys have diminished. Your plan worked, the ships and army were destroyed in the blast, but the greys will not remain solitary for long. They seek retribution and have dispatched a mother ship to this location with Nero at the helm."

"Nero?" asked Cam.

"Yes," said Cat. "Nero is the leader of the greys. The mother ship will eradicate the base in one immense blast."

"Why not just send that ship to begin with?" asked Grimes.

"According to my intel, the vampires are looking for one of their own, a traitor whose location was tracked here. They are also looking for Robyn Winter, which is why they have not sent the mother ship to prior bases. They want to see his dead body."

"What vampire?" muttered Cam.

"Sandy," said Phil, appearing behind them.

"That lady with the baby?"

"Yes," said Phil. "That exact person."

Cam shook his head. "Isn't she one of us?"

Phil said, "It's complicated."

"You're telling me."

"Where is she?" asked Grimes.

Phil said, "With Robyn."

Cam stepped towards Phil. "We should help him. Obviously that's where they're going."

"Robyn would not want that," said Phil. "He'd want us to survive." He looked at each one of them. "Our best bet is to join the others in AR77. If what your... robot here says is true, we can use the mother ship to the best of our ability."

"What do you mean?" Cam, his eyes narrow, brow furrowed.

"I have a plan. Follow me," he said and turned into the tunnel.

Cam said, "You don't want to help Winter?"

"No," retorted Phil. "That is one person I never have to worry about."

21

WINTER sidestepped Moth's thrust of his arm, and countered with a breakneck fist to Moth's jaw and a straight punch into Moth's solar plexus, the force so powerful, Moth was tossed back, crashing into rock with a heavy thud. His wings fluttered as pain shot to his head. Internal bleeding. Moth could feel his blood curl into his throat.

Winter was relentless, never giving Moth a moment to breathe. Robyn moved like water, his movement fluid with speed like hurricane wind. Winter was on top of him before Moth could collect himself. Robyn Winter curled his fingers around Moth's throat, raised him overhead as Moth's feet dangled, kicking air before Winter tossed him across the garden, crashing into rock and debris. His right wing sore, blood from his nose pooled across his lip as Moth shook his head, touched his nose, saw blood, his blood, on his fingers. Winter standing, waiting for Moth to attack.

Why doesn't he attack? thought Moth. He had me. Had me at his mercy? Why did he not deliver death? He's like ether. Smoke. A ghost. A raging ghoul.

Moth had yet to land one hand on Robyn Winter, a first in his lifetime. It was as if Winter was the wind. Moth rose to his feet with a wince when his wing shuddered, pain in his ribs tore to his skull. He could see his warriors beyond the tunnel, muffled screams and wails, wrapped in rock.

"Perhaps you should surrender," said Winter.

Moth's face pinched in a scowl.

Winter turned to regard Moth's warriors before turning back to Moth. "Seems your trusted warriors have lost their ability to offer assistance." And he smiled, a goading, conniving grin. "What's wrong, Moth? You seem so feeble."

Moth stepped forward, tripped, and fell to his knees.

"Has old age taken its toll? I remember you so much stronger." He shook his head. "Haven't you been keeping up with your training? Let me guess, too much grandstanding? Too many political speeches to write?"

Nothing from Moth, as he forced himself to stand. "Whatever you are," said Moth, "You are not Robyn Winter. Just his ghost. A shell of the former man."

Robyn grinned once again, his white eyes gleaming. "You have no idea," he said in a hush.

Robyn stepped to his right, turned to face him, a direct line of sight to Moth as he stretched his arms, palms down, in front of him. Moth watched as Winter turned his arms into steel and extended the blades down his arms. "What do you say, Moth? For old times' sake? Let us battle in the ancient ways." He twisted his arms back and forth, his blades glimmering with red light. "I promise," he said, staring at Moth. "I'll be gentle."

Moth could smell Sandy. She was everywhere in the garden. His mouth salivated just thinking about tearing her heart out. But he was truly outmatched. How Robyn Winter had grown so powerful was a conundrum, a freak of nature that shouldn't exist. As if he were a hologram, but a hologram with bite. Nothing he was witnessing seemed even remotely possible. And yet Winter hadn't delivered a deathblow. And his Drac warriors were alive; trapped in rock, but alive. With this type of strength, Winter could end the Draconian and human alliance himself; why did he not?

Even more, he wondered, was this a power he, Moth himself, could conjure? To be all-powerful was to be a GOD!

"But you have to die first," said Winter when Moth snapped to him. "You see, Moth, where you're standing…" he looked around the cave. "This is my doing, my dimension. When you realize what has been happening, when the future is set, the only way to change the outcome is to become… something more than the physical. To go beyond the reach of life and sacrifice your undying soul to the cause. Are you willing to do that, Moth? Death is not the end; it is only a beginning."

"Of course it's always about you, isn't it, Robyn?" Moth seethed, blood dripping from his mouth over his lip. "And it always has been. I remember you Robyn. I remember who you were. Nasty little tyrant hell bent on revenge with an appetite for death that could never be satisfied. I saw you, Robyn. I saw the things you did. All in the name of a revenge filled with hate. Who are you to receive this power you now have?" His head shaking, gnashing his fangs. "I saw you destroy all you held dear all because you couldn't admit when you were wrong. You said you came in peace and then unleashed holy hell."

"Against the manipulation, nothing more. It's the wise and the just who seek change when the error of their ways is revealed. When you're responsible for the extinction of an entire species, we all seek a second chance. Perhaps you should try it." He raised his hands palms up, then stretched his arms, hands tensed into fists, and arched his back. "Whatever you do now, Moth, you will not take Sandy from me."

Moth glared at Winter's blades, followed them to the white gleaming eyes. The white eyes, he thought. The white eyes. White eyes. Moth craned his head, staring into Winter's eyes. And in his mind's eye he could see the young and tempered Robyn Winter, lying down, an Arcturian over him, a blinding white light as the thick greyish brown Arcturian swiped its talon over and above Winter's body. Moth's eyes narrowed when in his mind's eye he could see how the young Winter's eyes beamed with a hologram into this world.

Cosmic creation under cosmic law, a voice in Moth's head said. The voice was Draconian, sinister and groveling.

Bound by cosmic law, thought Moth as he raised his chin to stare at Winter; a grin spread across his lips. "You can't kill me, can you?"

"There are worse things than death, Moth. And truthfully..." He craned his head, his lips curled. "I'd like to show them to you." Robyn Winter then stepped towards him.

Moth's smile erased when he saw the Drac behind Winter, in the tunnel. The size of his warrior was unmistakable, but even Calla would not win this battle with Winter. There was only one who could remove Winter from the planet. Only one who would offer escape from the rebel base with enough time for Moth to survive and return to Drac City triumphant. And if Sephtis fails, it would be no matter. Robyn Winter, bound by cosmic law, could not take life, only influence it, a partiality to the prime directive. This, at least, had now become apparent to Moth. Plus, he'd received Nero's message. The rebel base would be in ashes soon, and Sandy with it. The only person capable of surviving such an attack would be Winter, but his use in the rebellion then would be for naught. Moth would make sure of it with the help of his human counterparts. The only war surviving humans were now under control. Winter's ability to awaken them to the truth would take decades. Well past the time necessary for Draconian rule and the Arcturian arrival.

These rebels Winter has amassed are his last hope for redemption, thought Moth. Sometimes, the battle is won not with the fist but with the mind. Calla posed the possibility for Moth to advance his position and escape. And then, bring in Sephtis. Calla would be his sacrificial lamb to ensure Moth's survival.

Moth arched his back and his right wing flapped; his face pinched in pain. Calla advanced, stepped from the tunnel, his fists tight, lips and nose curled as he approached Winter. "May I introduce you, Robyn," said Moth, goading him, "to Calla."

Calla wrapped his massive arm around Winter's throat and squeezed when Robyn's ether, his body, turned to atoms, seeped through Calla's gigantic frame like a ghost, materializing behind Calla and wrapped his arms around his throat. Moth launched into the air, flying above his beloved Calla and Winter, swooped through the tunnel, landing on his feet in a crouch. His eyes found one of his warriors by his feet, embedded in rock, whose eyes revealed panic and relief, relief his master was here to help him. Moth rose to his feet and turned as he took a thumbnail sized communiqué from his belt, his ticket to Sephtis. Winter, ahead through the tunnel, Moth could see, brought Calla to his knees.

"Help me," said the Drac by his feet.

Moth turned to him, said, "We all die my noble

warrior, have the dignity to die with pride." His voice swam in blood.

When he looked up towards the tunnel, his eyes widened, watching as a boulder was barreling towards him, courtesy of Robyn Winter. But Moth rose into the air, face pinched in an onslaught of anguish as he erected his injured wing with a quick thrust up. The boulder spiraled across the room, crashing into the far rock wall with a rock filled explosion. Moth looked down to his thumbnail, pressed the side button that initiated his message to Sephtis as he floated down to his feet.

When he looked up, Robyn Winter was in the tunnel, coming towards him, when Moth felt a talon around his ankle. He looked down; his warrior pleaded for help and Moth thrust the warrior's hand off him. Looked around the cave and then to Winter, now halfway through the tunnel.

Robyn Winter called, "Never seen you so afraid, Moth. Could it be you're not as powerful or heroic as you say you are?"

Winter at the end of the tunnel, not fifty feet from Moth as his wings flapped by his sides.

"Master," his warrior pleaded. "Are you not going to help us?"

And Moth said, "Not at all," before he raced from the room, his wings flapping through the tunnel away from the threat of Robyn Winter.

22

ZON stopped outside his starship, Sanos in tow, held at gunpoint by Zon's warriors.

"Such a nice ship," said Sanos. "Will Moth be joining us?" Sanos looked around the ship and the pit. His eyes found Zon then, a grin plastered across Sanos' lips.

Zon shook his head; ordered his vampires, "Secure him on board."

"Always the professional, Zon. I knew I could count on you."

Zon looked at his warriors, gestured for them to go on board.

"Move, Sanos," said Illam, the head warrior under Zon.

Sanos looked around once again before boarding, and Zon breathed a sigh of relief. Drac warriors stood on guard in the pit, dead humans at their feet, as additional soldiers ushered in human prisoners, the captives being placed on board additional starships.

Where is Moth? he thought. The time to

evacuate had arrived. Nero was on his way to destroy all that was here, leaving a hole in the earth, soon to serve as a graveyard for the human rebellion. How many humans made it to safety was the question on his mind. Have they attained a safe distance, free from Nero's coming attack?

Zon didn't like loose ends. He wanted assurance to know they were all dead. Moth should have allowed Nero to destroy the base from the onset. So many Drac lives were now lost. The humans proved capable in their resolve to fight off the attack. The war would continue if any had survived. A seek and destroy mission would need to be established if necessary. He and his Dracs would come back to comb through the destruction, assessing any possibility the humans may use for escape.

Never stop fighting until the fight is won, Zon told himself. One could never be sure until the enemy was vaporized.

But his Dracs were still gathering prisoners for Moth's parade.

Why hadn't Moth given the evacuation order? What was holding him up?

The order was required and required immediately. If not from Moth, the responsibility passed to Zon, and he couldn't wait any longer. Zon pressed the communiqué on his wrist, was about to speak when he caught Moth stomping into the pit, alone.

Moth ordered, "Begin the evacuation procedure," as he continued through the pit to his starship.

Zon went to him. "Where are your Drac guards?"

Moth passed him without notice. "Gone," he said. "By the hand of Robyn Winter."

"You left them?" Zon's face pinched in a scowl of confusion when Moth stopped cold, turned slowly to meet Zon's eye.

"They are expendable, Zon. As are you. Start the evacuation order. We leave now."

Moth turned from Zon, who watched him as he entered his starship. Zon's jaw hung loose before he gnashed his teeth, clenched his fists.

So many Drac lives gone in an instant. He looked at the ship that held Sanos and his stomach twisted.

Between Sanos and Moth, the future seemed uncertain.

Zon gave the evacuation order.

It was all he could do to save Drac lives.

23

PHIL moved with swift indignation. Cam, Grimes, and Cat followed close behind through a dark tunnel.

Cam said, "Where are we going?"

Phil stopped by the wall, said, "Weapons room," as he retracted his visor, pressed his thumb to the rock and the wall moved–a small compartment one foot by one foot revealing an eye scanner. Phil looked into the scanner and the rock moved opening to a large room with metal walls, concrete floors, a long counter in the room's center, and guns, weapons, armor, and bombs behind steel cages. "Follow me," said Phil as he stepped into the room.

"What're you thinking?" asked Cam as he stepped in. Grimes and Cat behind him.

Phil opened the steel cage, surveyed the rows and shelves filled with weaponry. Found what he was looking for, a small device, another pulse bomb, and brought it to the counter.

"You're gonna blow it all up?" said Grimes.

"Not at all," said Phil, showing the teleporter.

Cam said, "You're gonna send it up to the

mother ship?"

"Exactly."

Cam cocked his head. "But you have to know where you're going to use it. If you don't know what the ship looks like from the inside, you may end up on the wrong ship." Cam locked eyes with Phil. "Have you been on a mother ship before?" He wouldn't be surprised if Phil had.

"No," said Phil, pointing to Cat. "But he has."

Cam's heart jumped when he looked at Cat, his red eyes unwavering.

Phil stepped to Cat. "Are you okay with this mission?" he asked. "Once you teleport to the ship, drop the bomb. We'll give it five seconds so you can return."

"How will he know where to find us?" asked Grimes.

Phil looked at Grimes. "AR77," he said. "We're going there now." He turned to Cat. "How long until the mother ship arrives?"

Cat's red eyes gleamed. "ETA is twenty minutes."

"Perfect," said Phil, "Plenty of time to get to a safe distance."

"But the mother ship will crash down on us," said Cam. "Why not just send him now?"

Phil shook his head. "Because I want the mother ship to fire first."

"You want them to do what?" Grimes hollered.

"I want them to fire their primary weapon at the same time that Cat goes up there." Phil went to the steel cage.

"Why?" huffed Cam.

Phil surveyed the weaponry, looked back at Cam. "We'll be gone by then, but with the blast, they'll think we all perished. Computer intel will reveal an intruder on the ship before the blast." He looked back at the weaponry. "They'll conclude we attacked first, and that's why the mother ship went down. Logical conclusion then is that we were still here on the base when the ship fired."

Cam bobbed his head. "That's one hell of a risk."

"It's friggin' insane," said Grimes.

Phil laughed under his breath. "My experience fellas... those are the plans that work best."

Phil reached his arm across the shelves of weaponry, to the wall behind the shelves, and the wall moved, revealing a compartment six inches across and six inches wide. Vapor slithered from the compartment as Phil reached his hand through, took hold of a tiny glowing white orb, and secured the orb within a compartment in his armor.

"What is that?" said Grimes.

Phil turned to him. "I don't have time to explain," he said, tapping his armor where he placed the orb.

"This is crazy, but I like it," said Cam. "How do we get to AR77?"

Phil regarded all three of his comrades. "Gather around, gentlemen." He gripped the pulse bomb and teleporter. "We're going for a ride."

24

WINTER ejected the regeneration chamber where he placed Sandy. Cold vapor rushed against his legs as he pressed his hand to her abdomen, checking her vital signs.

Sandy's heart thumped with a thick struggling beat, her breath labored and shallow, still unconscious, brain functioning was at a minimum. But Winter knew what was coming, and Sandy was required to secure future victory. He had to get her to Silas somehow, down to AR77.

Sandy's head was healing, the thick gash now a thin cut over her forehead. Winter scanned her robe after his vision caught sight of the tracking device the size of a pin. He pinched the device, pulled it from her robe and dropped it to the ground. Winter gathered Sandy in his arms, then turned the rock enclosure into dust, stepping out and towards the garden.

He needed to bring Sandy to AR77, knowing that Sephtis would arrive soon. Winter was certain Moth had sent the transmission, giving him little time before the arrival.

The universe works in a cryptic geometric gathering, with codes across the universe. Someone who understands these codes can manipulate future outcomes. But those codes only reveal the surface, the outcome, to the individual seeking them, excluding fine details and the effect on others. The future is always in motion, he thought, always transforming with every choice taken and not taken. Tracing steps back and forth across time, ironically, took time. Crucial points on the timeline, if manipulated, added to or changed completely–like when a certain someone is inserted into a situation where previously on one existing timeline they had not been, you can change the coming thread in time–the geometry on that timeline then bends into a new direction. The Draconians had been manipulating time. Winter was a master with time. So why not fight fire with fire. But time was never an exact science, as time exists within its own dimension. It took millenniums of trial and error to find the exact points and manipulations necessary to secure the desired outcome. Only concern is that the changing geometry opened new possibilities because of the cause-and-effect law of the universe. In turn, nothing could be counted on with absolute certainty. There still remained the unknown. And now that Robyn had manipulated time in his favor, knowing Sandy's presence was required for ultimate victory, he hoped he could secure Sandy before Sephtis arrived. The future depends on her involvement.

And Phil.

Winter stomped across the garden. The alarm had ceased but the red light bathed the garden as if caught in a surreal sunrise, as vapor, smoke, and sparks raged across the roof, drowning the cave in a red smoky film. The bodies lying dead on the ground stopped him cold after he passed through the garden, rushing towards the huts and cave dwellings towards the door that led to the infirmary and further towards AR77. Humans, his people, children, adults, torn apart by Drac hands. People whose lives he had taken into his cause, people whose safety he was responsible for, their black eyes staring at him like a last plea for help. His arms trembled holding Sandy, his heart stabbed with a thick wave of emotional hell.

My babies! I am so sorry, my angels.

Please forgive me.

Winter could hear their screams, their terror, inside the cave, inside his head. And the children, their cries and wails going unheard, their pleas for life cut short by fangs around their throat. Winter had seen enough of death to last eternity, and yet, still his heart ached, dying an eternal death by a million cuts with every loss of life. Winter had given up on embodying any notion of peace a long time ago.

He looked over the bodies to the door that led to AR77, opening the door with a thought when he heard the coming sonic boom overhead. The sound like a stealth bomber tearing through the sky. Winter tightened his grip on Sandy, the diving whistle growing loud and deafening as he raced across the dead, through the door and stopped. The coming boom was inching closer. He looked down the hall, assessing how long it would take him to bring Sandy to AR77 and come back to meet Sephtis eye to eye. What he knew couldn't happen was allowing Sephtis the opportunity to destroy Sandy. Sephtis enjoyed the hunt, and nothing satisfied his desire for blood more than the destruction of the innocent. A sleeping Sandy would prove a grand prize for him. There was no way he could make it back without giving away AR77 to Sephtis. Winter assessed the tunnel, looking for an alternative path for Sandy's descent into AR77. He found his means inside the walls, where thick roots bulged within the rock and dirt. Winter billowed his ether towards the roots, communicating with the natural order within the rock and the trees standing tall in the forest above. The roots rippled from the wall, forming a surface large enough for Winter to place Sandy on. She groaned, a growl beneath her breath, followed by a hiss. Winter placed his hand above her abdomen, the other across her forehead, as the sonic whistle grew louder.

Vital signs dwindling, she needs to be kept in regeneration.

Winter looked up. Sephtis was entering the earth's atmosphere between the moon and the earth. Wouldn't be long now, he thought, looking back at

Sandy.

"This is not your fight," he whispered when he placed his thumbs across her forehead, his fingers over Sandy's temples, and bowed. "See," he said. "Know, in your mind's eye. Think of me and know I will arrive."

Robyn stood tall, craned his head, his eyes staring at the roots and dirt as those roots wrapped tightly around Sandy, rolling her body into the rock. Winter watched as the roots brought Sandy below, towards AR77. The thick wiry roots bulging and rolling within the rock.

Silas will find you, he thought, thinking of Sandy. He knows what to do.

Robyn looked up; listening to the sonic whistle, then stepped out and closed the door, locking it in place. The sonic thread growing. He stepped from the door into the garden.

He looked up, waiting for Sephtis to come and claim his bounty.

25

IN a flash, they were in AR77, courtesy of Phil and the teleporter. AR77 was a vast under earth cave dwelling with a large fresh-water lake that dove more than a hundred yards down. Towards the bottom, a cavern led to the ocean where the rebels had been building an underwater base. It was there where they could hide and reconvene. When they arrived, Silas was helping a child onto one of the multiple underwater vessels. Phil watched as another vessel dipped into the water.

"Silas," Phil called.

Silas gently graced the young girl's chin and offered a smile. The girl's lips trembling, tears in her eyes, when Silas stood tall and the vessel's hatch closed over the small pod. Phil looked over the number of vessels not being used. His heart sank when he counted them; the meaning behind them idly floating was that there was no one to use them. There had to be hundreds that remained of the four person vessels.

Silas looked at Phil, the stare in his eyes lost, shaken, and heartbroken. He tapped the top of the vessel before it dipped into the water before he regarded Phil. His head shaking with disappointment.

"We've lost over three quarters of our people," he said. "This is an annihilation."

Phil couldn't take his eyes off the remaining vessels and their vast numbers. His heart pounding in his chest, listening to Silas.

"Aries is not accounted for," said Silas. He regarded Cam. "Same for Annison, Cameron, and Perseus."

Cam stepped up. "I thought they were with you?"

Silas shook his head. "We were separated in the tunnels after the Dracs found their way in." He looked at Phil. "Aries fought gallantly to save us, but I fear the worst for them. And our own nine have been eradicated," he said. "Torn apart by Dracs. Our army defeated. We're being wiped off the face of the earth."

Phil thought of the young Aries. How could it be so? Aries gone? Such an occurrence flew in the face of Robyn's prediction. He had to be alive.

"Robyn has yet to arrive. Sandy too."

Phil looked at Silas, his jaw hung loose, confused.

"You said they were in the cave beside the garden," continued Silas, his head moving right and left. "We've lost communication with that sector."

Phil watched as Silas swallowed the lump in his throat, his lips trembling. There was something he hadn't said yet, so Phil said it for him.

"Where is my family?"

But Silas didn't have to answer. The look in his eyes told Phil all he needed to know. They had not made it. How? The huts and dwellings offered almost immediate access to AR77. He looked up at the door that led to them. A set of rock stairs led to the door above. He turned to Cat, pointed at the vessels waddling in the water.

"After you plant the bomb and come back, take one of the vessels under water. There's a homing beacon on the control panel that'll take you to the underwater base."

"Where are you going?" asked Cam.

Phil shot him a stare, eyes wide with rage.

"Not alone," said Cam. "I'm coming with."

"Me too," said Grimes when Phil regarded him, Grimes replacing the clip in his 9MM. "We don't leave anyone behind."

Phil gave an appreciative nod before he turned to Silas. "If we're not back in ten minutes, get yourself to a safe distance. There's a mother ship headed this way." He shook his head. "You need to be gone before it arrives."

Silas put his hand on Phil's shoulder. "I understand," he said when the wall leading to the garden rippled. Popping cracks like a bulldozer crushing stones and rocks raced down the wall.

Phil's eyes wide as he watched embedded roots tear down the wall and stop five feet above the ground.

Watched as tree roots rippled from the wall in a makeshift bed, and Sandy rolled out from the wall, lying unconscious on those roots.

"My god," breathed Silas. "But that means..."

Phil shot Silas a wild-eyed stare. Silas' eyes, bloodshot, red and teary, turned to Phil. It looked like Silas' heart dropped to the floor.

"Sephtis is coming."

26

SANOS looked up to the ceiling as the starship docked in the bay, back in Drac City. A wide smile stretched across his lips, a curl in his nose. The itch had ambled up his arm, his skin crawling with maddening bone deep penetrating desire. He would claw out his skin if he weren't bound. Instead, all he could do was grin at the warriors standing guard around him.

"Ahh," he said, "We've come home." He looked at each Drac, one by one, scanning across their eyes; contempt stared back. Sanos cocked his brow. "There's no place like home."

The ship settled in the bay with a clank and slight rock. Sanos shuddered to his left, then right.

"Such an eager pilot we have," said Sanos, grinning. "I guess he too is happy to be home."

"You're mad, Sanos," declared Illam when he stepped closer to Sanos, head shaking. "Look at your arms, they look like rotten human. You've got the fever of madness. Zon should have killed you, as Moth said to."

Sanos puffed out his chest. "Would you be all

too willing to take up that task?" He raised his chin, staring. "Is that so Illam?"

"Do I hear a throat, Sanos... begging to be cut?"

Sanos grinned once again. "Are you so eager to drink from the fountain of my blood?" He craned his head, glaring at Illam. "Go ahead," he raised his arms. "Try some. I'm more than sure you'll find it exquisite."

Illam thrust the back of his hand across Sanos' face, his skull rattled against the wall. His face pinched in pain.

"Watch your vile tongue," seethed Illam when the door opened and Zon walked in.

He assessed the immediate situation. Sanos lapped his tongue over his chin, licking his blood. Zon looked at Illam. "What has happened here?"

"Oh," answered Sanos. "Just vampires having an existential conversation that seemed to have gotten a bit out of hand. Isn't that right, Illam? Dracs will be Dracs after all."

Illam, panting, said, "You're disgusting, Sanos. A true disappointment to all Dracs."

The grin wiped clean from Sanos' lips. His beady sunken eyes glaring at Illam. "That may be true, but before this is over, I'll enjoy tearing out your entrails with my claws. Perhaps, only then will you bow to me."

Illam raised his hand to deliver another strike.

"NO," called Zon. He stepped further into the room. "We do not treat prisoners in such a manner."

"Prisoner?" said Illam. His hand stayed as he turned to Zon. "Moth wants this Drac dead. He has betrayed all of us and yet you insist on this inquiry." His lips trembled, his eyes narrow, mad with rage. "If you wish to betray Lord Moth you shall do it without me."

Illam went to rush from the room, but Zon stepped in front of him, grinding his jaw and gritting his teeth. "Do not question my judgment, I am still your superior officer."

"Not for long," seethed Illam. "Once Master Moth discovers your treachery, he will have *you* attached to a symbiote."

Zon snatched Illam's throat and squeezed. "And yet I am still your superior. You will not question me."

"Oh boys... boys," said Sanos. "Surely there must be some peace between us. Let go of him Zon, embrace him as your brother." He looked around the room to the other warriors, standing, watching the tiff play out. "As we all should. All together. One Drac for all." Sanos laughed in his throat, enjoying the insurrection.

Zon snarled at Illam before releasing him. Illam's talon went to his throat when he stepped up to Zon, and Zon did the same. Eye to eye, heavy breath.

Illam said, "You want this disgrace detained... do it yourself."

Sanos grinned as Illam trampled through the door. Zon watched as he went.

"He's just a bit too high-strung," said Sanos, garnering a stare from Zon and the others. "It's never good when one acts like that. He should be given leave, let him rest his loins in more suitable arrangements."

Nothing from the others, no response.

"Or not," said Sanos with a shrug.

Zon regarded the warriors. "Help him up," he said. "Follow me to containment." He looked at Sanos. "At dusk you will have your time in front of Drac City. And then, you will be judged and your fate sealed."

Sanos, his eyes narrow, said, "I only wish to tell the truth. To… inform all Dracs of the blasphemy existing within COR."

Two warriors took Sanos by the shoulder and arms as he stood eye to eye with Zon.

"You'll have your chance," said Zon. "As all Dracs should be given the opportunity to speak." He craned his head. "But if what you say proves to be false." He shook his head. "I'll kill you myself."

Sanos shot his head back, gnawing on the inside of his cheek and beneath his bottom lip, took a deep breath. "I expect nothing less," he replied, when that grin once again graced his lips.

Zon stepped away. "Go," he said, gesturing to his warriors.

Sanos followed the warriors through the ship, listening, his eyes wandering from ceiling to wall, door to room, as they reached the ramp descending into the docking bay and Sanos stopped cold.

So quiet, he thought, a subtle stillness drenched in coming chaos. He looked over the docking bay, head moving slow, scanning the bay as his eyes turned up, his head and chin followed, regarding the roof and above the roof the many levels of Drac City, all the way up, thinking of Drac Plaza.

"What is it?" said Zon, now to the right of Sanos.

Sanos trained his eyes on him. "You hear that?" asked Sanos as he raised his head once again. "It's so quiet. If you listen carefully enough," he whispered, closing his eyes. "You can hear all of Drac City breathing while they sleep."

"Dawn has come," said Zon. "Of course it's quiet."

Sanos looked out into the bay. "But there's something more to this silence," said Sanos when he turned to Zon.

"It's the quiet…" he said, "before the storm."

27

THE sonic boom grew ear piercing, deafening. Robyn stood in the garden as the whistle barreled down on him. He closed his eyes when that same whistle suddenly ceased. No boom, no tear or ripple through the air, no thunderous quake in the earth, nothing more than quiet beneath the soft waterfall.

He could feel the ether expand in the garden, turning thick and hot around him. Pressure drawing down from above, like a thick heavy air pressurized and weighted across his shoulders. Beneath the quiet, a rickety, deep-throated growl quickly cut off, raced to his ears. And Winter felt the heated, burning rueful waves thicken.

And Robyn Winter opened his eyes to see Sephtis had come.

Sephtis was eight feet tall, and thin, although the dark armor he wore concealed this except for his thin neck and hands. His skin was like burnt charcoal, long bony massive hands gave way to sharpened nails stained with blood. His mouth–likened to a wolf's snout-opened, snarling, revealing rows of jagged razor-sharp teeth that dripped mucus and bile over his darkened thin lips. Nose almost non-existent, coiled and huffed thick heated breath. His eyes, the size of chestnuts, all black, like staring into death. The forehead towered above his eyes, revealing the brain as an imprint in the skull beneath. The cranium smooth, dark, and elongated as if stretched to a finely pointed tip that jutted from his skull a foot away from his back.

His voice a permanent garble as if he were gnawing on bones, a thick baritone born from the depths of despair. When he stepped forward, the surrounding air moved with him as if the atoms feared death for not paying homage should they refuse, revealed in a permanent skew like chemtrails that refused to waver, thick around his ether.

"There you are," said Sephtis. "I have waited eons for this moment." He craned his head, his black eyes wide, staring at Robyn Winter. "Nice body," he said. "What poor human did you take it from?"

Winter gritted his teeth. "You're not welcome here, Sephtis. This isn't your fight; engaging me is against cosmic law. Trifling in business that doesn't concern your species can only bring doom to your people."

Sephtis snapped his head back. "Oh, please, Robyn. Spare me your speeches. I grew bored with them years ago. As I see it, this is no longer your planet. Your human leaders have made sure of it; handed their kin over to Draconian rule without a second thought. If any species deserves extinction, Robyn…" He curled his claws in front of him, snapping his fingers into fists. "It would be yours." He scanned around the cave. "Where are those vile humans hiding? Those pets of yours make excellent fodder for the insatiable appetites in Xibalba. I shall take a throng of them back with me."

"None are here, Sephtis. The base has been evacuated. I am all who remain."

Sephtis then caught sight of Calla, embedded and restrained inside the rock floor, his throat choked by a rock arm.

"Still waging war against these revolting hybrids, Robyn?" He stepped towards Calla, stood over him as Calla's voice was stifled. Sephtis crouched down over him, his head then moved to the vampires scattered behind him. He sniffed; his nose curled as if the foul stank of vampire insulted him and turned his eyes back to Calla. Saliva dripped off his lip as his jaw opened and closed, glaring at Calla. Robyn could see how Calla, the great gigantic vampire, shivered under Sephtis' sinister gaze. "Be not concerned, vampire. You will still serve a purpose. Like the humans you eat, you too will know what it is like to be eaten alive." And he laughed, thick and sinister, bellowed in his chest as Calla attempted to scream. "No concern," he said as he stood. "No concern at all. There's enough meat on this one to feed the horde." From his hand, lightning bolts raged as a staff was erected from the lightning. The bottom slammed into the ground with a heavy crack, as the top erected into a trident, the three tips just above his jaw. Flashes of lightning surrounded the trident, wind swirling around the staff. "I'll take them all with me, and those humans you have lied about, Robyn. I can smell them, hiding beneath the earth."

"Your cause is for me, Sephtis. Come and get your prize."

Sephtis, head shaking, glared at Winter, and said, "I know what you've become, Robyn. I've always known, biding my time until I received the call. I know you, Robyn. I know you can't kill me; doing so will undermine your agreement with the Arcturians. You are bound by cosmic law, a fitting price to pay for immortality. And it comes with a certain irony, doesn't it? Considering your reputation is one of death and destruction. Remember, Robyn, I'm not the only one in the universe who's been waiting to get their hands on you."

Robyn scoffed, "The Verieseans have cause." He reached a finger towards Sephtis. "You do not."

"Please, Robyn, one cannot insult the dark lord and not pay retribution."

"Even so," said Robyn, "There is no just cause for the dark lord. Your presence here is irritating and does not suit the law."

"Take it up with the Arcturians then. Either way, you're coming with me."

"No," called Robyn, "I don't think so."

Sephtis grinned. "There you are; there's that

anger I know. Some things never die do they? You'll need all of it to defeat me."

Robyn closed his eyes, briefly, as he stepped forward. Sephtis gripping his trident tight.

"I won't make this easy, Sephtis, that I can assure you."

"I never planned for this to be easy. An all powerful Robyn Winter with the incapacity to take life; there's only one way I can capture you. All the resources in the universe have been delivered to me for this purpose. I know how this works, and it requires pain, your pain. For every cut I offer you, every slice of my blade across your skin captures your consciousness into the body you hold." He clenched his fist. "Death by a thousand cuts, Robyn, and yet all you will become is human." He shook his head, disgusted, disenchanted. "Pain will manifest your physical presence and then, then Robyn, will you be open for a proper killing. The fools you've been battling with since this newfound presence you've manipulated are too quick to assume your physical presence. They lose because of your advantage." His head shaking. "I will not make the same mistake. I know how to capture you to drive the pain from your mind and manifest your physicality. I know how to stop you Robyn, it just takes a greater being. Someone who knows what you are. Someone whose speed is quicker than lightning and capable of causing pain, continuous pain with a thousand thrusts across your flesh, too many for your

ether to heal. An onslaught of pain, Robyn, and then…
and then I hold the necessary substance to imprison
your mind for eternity. Allow the dark lord to feast on
your ether or toss your bones to his minions. The choice
will be his."

"And all wait with bated breath. They will be
disappointed once again."

"No, Robyn, it is you who will be disappointed."
He slammed his staff with a powerful thrust against the
ground; pulsing waves erupted towards Robyn like
ripples in the water, rushing towards Winter.

Robyn ground his feet into the earth, clenched
tensed hands, curled fingers. Winter stretched his
hands apart as the wave poured over him, around his
ether, the force pounding against the encapsulated
mass of energy sprouting from his hands. His feet
moved back under the weight and force from Sephtis'
waves of thunder and still Robyn held tight inside his
protective ethereal shield. Sephtis' ether blast
dissipated and Robyn Winter drew his ether into his
hands, standing tall.

"This won't be easy, Sephtis. You should not
have come."

Sephtis clawed his hand around his trident
when Calla grunted beneath his feet. With a snarl, he
yanked his trident from the earth and slammed it
between Calla's eyes. Waves rippled across his body,
smoke filled the cave, burning flesh and bones,
smoldering in a thick cloud that concealed the body. "I

haven't time for whining vampires." He twisted the trident left than right and pulled it from Calla's skull. Beneath the thinning smoke, Winter could see how Calla's massive body was reduced to a skeletal mass.

"Are you done?" said Robyn and Sephtis snapped his head to him. "Or are you just afraid?"

Sephtis raised his chin. "Why do you care for Dracs, Winter? They've been a scourge on humanity for centuries."

"All life has its place, Sephtis. You should learn yours."

"I have," declared Sephtis as he extended his blades down his arms.

And Robyn turned his forearms into blades of steel.

"How ironic," said Sephtis, staring at Winter's blades. "Your gift from the dark lord after learning our ways. I'm sure he'll be eager to have them returned."

Winter clenched his fists, a fighting stance. "Come on," he hollered.

Sephtis rushed at Winter, trident in hand, and Robyn did the same, flipped over, his boot connecting with the mouth of Sephtis, thrown back, crashing against the wall, crushing rocks and wall. But Sephtis reacted upon impact, propelled himself from the wall towards Winter, dropped down in front of him and jabbed the trident at Winter. Robyn sidestepped the attack, gripped the trident and sliced across it with his free blade, the trident cut in half as Winter stabbed

Sephtis in his armored chest. A grunt in Sephtis' throat. His boot slammed into Robyn, sending him crashing across the garden, tumbling forcefully into a boulder. His back arched as pain shot up his spine. He dropped to his knees. Sephtis stood in the middle of the garden, looking down at the trident in his chest. With a snarl, he pulled the trident from his armor, looked at it, then tossed it to the ground with a steel clang.

"That," he said, "was my favorite weapon."

Winter shook his head as he rose to his feet, arching his back as he manipulated his ether, sealing the wound on the back of his head from when he'd hit the rock. He stretched his neck, bones and tendons popping and cracking. "It won't be the last," said Winter, tensing his arms to his sides.

Sephtis stepped forward, arms outstretched, those black eyes roaming over Winter as he stepped closer to Sephtis. The two circling each other, waiting, anticipating, assessing threat and exposure, drawing closer; Sephtis' hands stretched into claws as he snarled that rickety growl from the depths of his throat, his jaw tense, mouth open wide, revealing rows of jagged teeth. He attacked first, thrusting his blade towards Winter, his arm swiping open air, finding nothing more than atoms, ether, as Winter materialized behind him. Sephtis twisted. His elbow rocked against Winter's jaw. Sephtis was on top of him, had his throat in his hand. Sent his fist into Winter's gut, lifting him off the ground, Winter's throat still in hand. Another fist to the sternum, followed by another to the chest that propelled Winter back, slamming into the rocky ground.

Winter groaned, his face pinched in pain, holding his ribs. He rose to his feet.

"C'mon," he goaded.

And Sephtis obliged, meeting Winter's blade with his own.

28

CAM was following Phil as closely as he could. Phil was like the wind, rounding corners through the tunnel towards what he dubbed was the garden and huts. Cam understood Phil's need to know where his family was. Were they now prisoners of war or had they been destroyed in the battle?

Cam hoped for the former.

Grimes was close behind Cam; Cat was waiting in AR77 until the very last second before teleporting to the mother ship, aiding Silas by transferring Sandy, on the brink of death, onto one of the water vessels. Time was running out, closing in on them.

And then there was the Robyn Winter situation. Whoever this Sephtis was, he brought fear to Phil and Silas. Robyn had instructed Phil to never engage in battle should Sephtis come for him. The result could be catastrophic; a possible end to the rebellion and the decimation of humanity. Robyn always said how Phil and the other refuges were the future; he himself, a simple cog in the wheel of that freedom.

Cam could hear what Phil said in AR77,

repeating Winter's words verbatim, *The survival of the species far outweighs any one life.*

As he inched closer, Cam was overcome with a sense of loyalty to Robyn Winter. A kinship that boiled his gut knowing that Winter may become no more by the hand of the one known as Sephtis.

Phil flashed up ahead, rounding a corner and out of sight. Cam sprang into the tunnel, hurried steps, rifle in his hand leading the way. Rounded another corner and Phil disappeared down the hall. Cam's breath heavy, he paused briefly to see Grimes behind him who gestured to keep moving and Cam did, springing into the tunnel, a long tunnel. A door up ahead, thick and grey. He could hear crushing booms and swiping steel raging from behind it.

No Phil. The tunnel held an eerie quiet, as if death had filtered inside the cave. On the right an opening, bathed dark red.

He ran to the opening when he heard Phil screaming. Grimes on his heels. His jaw and rifle dropped when he saw Phil cradling his child in his arms. A dead body beside him cut open naval to throat. Cam clenched his fist, looking over death and carnage, acid in the back of his throat from the stank of open bodies when he saw the writing on the wall, written in blood with streams that poured down from each letter.

Phil's wails reached a fevered pitch, clutching his daughter's limp body against his chest as if his pain could raise her from the dead. But Cam couldn't take his eyes off the writing.

WHO'S THE PHANTOM NOW?

Cam's eyelids fluttered while staring at those words. He swallowed hard when he heard a boom rage from beyond the grey door.

29

WINTER spun around, swiping Sephtis' leg from under him. Sephtis dropped to the ground with a thud. His head sprang forward and Winter slammed his boot against his nose, rattling Sephtis' head against the ground.

Sephtis swiped Winter's legs from under him, pulled his leg around and thrust his heel into Winter's nose, returning the favor. Blood splattered from the force as Robyn turned over. Sephtis was up, gripped Winter by the back of the neck, and tossed him across the garden. Rocks crumbled under his weight.

Winter wrangled himself to his feet just as Sephtis' mighty fist rapped across his jaw. Robyn flew back, crashed into ground tumbling over, head over feet into the wall.

Sephtis relentlessly barreled towards Winter, seething and snarling. He gripped Winter's shirt in his massive talons, but Winter brought his arms down across Sephtis' hands, releasing the hold, then brought those knotted hands up across Sephtis' chin, snapping his head back. Sephtis returned with a snarl and gripped Winter's skull with both hands and squeezed, pulling him off the ground, his feet dangling. Winter thought his skull was going to crack. Winter used the leverage, gripped Sephtis by the hands and sent kicks to his sternum, chest and jaw. Sephtis released his hold, and Winter flipped over to his feet, crouched down, and swiped his blade across Sephtis' leg above the knee, then forced the wincing, grunting Sephtis across the garden with his ether. He hit the wall and slid down as more boulders and rock fell on top of him.

Winter limped a few steps and stopped when the rock moved off of Sephtis, holding the boulder in midair as he forced himself to his feet.

"Block this," said Sephtis as he thrust his hands and the boulder spiraled towards Robyn.

A single thought, thought Robyn as the boulder turned to dust before reaching him. His eyes closed briefly as dust billowed over him. Winter snapped his eyelids open, watching as Sephtis raced towards him. Winter ran to meet him, jumping and flipping, his foot met Sephtis with such a force Winter's leg just about snapped below the knee. Sephtis slammed against the ground as pain shot up Winter's leg, and Sephtis bounced off the ground. Winter seized Sephtis' armor in his ether, turning the dark matter into steel bars that wrapped and squeezed around Sephtis, whose anger fueled his insurrection, returning his armor to the stealth black it was before. Robyn grunted before he raised Sephtis within his ether, jerked his hands and

Sephtis was tossed across the garden, scuttling and tumbling across the earth. Winter used the moment to turn his leg into steel as he stepped forward, watching as Sephtis rose to his feet.

"There's no way to win this battle, Sephtis. You may injure me but the injury is temporary."

Robyn watched as Sephtis snarled at him. Stretched his arms and cracked his neck. Stepped forward, pain pinched across his curled face. Winter could see blood seeping from his leg.

"Give it up Sephtis. Go home."

"You're so foolish Robyn. You think because you are not of this earth, you can't be captured. While your real body may be in Arcturian isolation, your mind is still here. Among us mortals. All it takes is speed and pain, Robyn. And time, and I've got all the time in the universe to play out this little game of ours."

He stepped forward, baring his teeth.

Winter stepped back, head shaking. "Don't try it," hollered Winter. "Don't."

Sephtis laughed beneath his breath, a guttural laugh that transformed into that rickety hiss and snarl. "You can't kill me, Robyn, but even if you do, it will mean the end of your rebellion. Tell me, are your people able to survive and withstand without you?" Another step towards Winter. "I'll be content in the afterlife knowing they eradicated your precious species from the earth. And all because you simply refused to die."

He barreled towards Winter with such quick and relentless force Robyn hadn't time to react. The force crushed against his chest. He spiraled back and scuttled across the ground, flipping over to ward off the oncoming attack gripping Sephtis in his ether and tossed him against the wall, manipulating the rock to hold Sephtis in place, those rock arms tightened around the large frame, across his mouth, his black eyes, stifling his wails as the rock brought him within.

Robyn watched as Sephtis became consumed within the rock and vanished beneath its trapped embrace. He huffed and breathed deeply. Hunched over, his hands on his knees, when the rock exploded.

The last Winter saw, before he was catapulted across the garden, was Sephtis re-emerging from the rock.

30

PHIL knew time was running out. He didn't care. He wanted to hold his baby in his arms and join her in the afterlife.

His worst fears had come true. His mind racing with the how. How did the vampires know his wife and child? Clearly, the message had been written for him.

Sanos!

The Drac's face etched in Phil's mind. He could see him sinking his teeth into Cathryn's neck, tearing his talons through Esta's stomach. And the baby, his unborn child. He refused to allow the thought to manifest. He held it at bay, his body shuddering, tense, swallowing pain and anguish. Phil hadn't recognized he was screaming, wailing cries so profound the gods wept for him. Didn't recognize how his heart had shattered, leaving in its place an eternal void wrought with agony. Not until he felt Cam's hand on his shoulder.

Cam's words arrived as if under water, shallow and garbled.

They're gone.

So sorry Phil.

I'm so sorry.

Phil could feel his anger rising in his throat, burning rage into his mind. Gnashing his teeth to the point where his jaw was on the verge of splintering. His head jutting in quick successions as tears raced down his skin. And then Grimes, his voice the same as Cam's, shallow and garbled.

What do you want to do?

Mother ship is coming.

ETA five minutes.

Phil could hear Grimes swallow his breath.

Phil's hands shaking, trembling, as he laid Cathryn next to Esta.

Esta!

How many times had she comforted him? How many times had she been his strength, his courage, his conviction to move forward? To keep battling. Keep fighting until the fight was done?

Always. Ever since the island. Ever since they shared a morbid cell waiting for death where he rested in her arms and discovered enough comfort to take him to the afterlife. Now she lay dead before him, cut open. He couldn't look at her other than her eyes. Those black dead eyes staring at him as if pleading for him to join her, to follow her to the unknown depths of death. He could feel her touch on his skin and his body cringed and tensed. Cold over his skin, he could feel it in his bones. The cold burning in his heart.

He'd rose to his feet, when and how he didn't know. Standing over his family, lying dead at his feet. For a moment, the briefest of moments, he thought they were sleeping, just sleeping. But that dream dissipated quickly as if the thought was thrown at him; meant to add insult to pain. His head shaking as he inhaled with a shudder from head to toe, his fists clenched by his sides as he raised his eyes to see Grimes.

Heard Cam say behind him, "What do you want to do?"

Phil turned to him, his eyes wide, tense.

"Do you want to stay here with them?" said Cam. "I… I don't know what to say."

Inside, the thought kept coming, the voice, his voice, in his head: Get control. Get control.

A loud boom erupted behind Grimes. They could feel the impact in the cave. Grimes went into the hall.

Phil noticed his hand was shaking, his fist so tense and tight, rattling against his hip.

Get control. Now, get control.

But the thought of leaving them to a shallow unmarked grave brought a second wave of hurt that slammed into his heart and mangled the organ.

Get control.

His lips pursed, his throat thick with tears and anguish. Every bone and muscle tense, trembling. Waves of sorrow swirled around his head. He couldn't think beyond the moment. All he could see were Esta and Cathryn, as they were, happy and content.

Grimes back in the cave. "It's Winter; he's in trouble." he said, although his voice was still shallow. "And an enormous demon looking alien."

He heard Cam jump to his feet.

Phil felt his lips move, heard his voice like a whisper. "Sephtis," he said as he breathed deeply, nodding, sucking down the pain.

"If Sephtis is some demon looking evil alien than yes," said Grimes.

Cam behind him, Phil could hear how he loaded and cocked his rifle. "I'll go," he said, his hand on Phil's shoulder. "Get to AR77 with Grimes. We..." he paused as Phil turned slowly to him. "We've got mere minutes before the mother ship arrives."

Phil closed his eyes, an attempt to find some sort of clarity in the moment. Cathryn. Esta. Winter. Sephtis.

Grimes behind him. "Are you ready to go?"

Another boom outside the cave. And Phil raised his eyes to the ceiling.

Where are you?

Give me strength.

Phil opened the compartment on his armor. He took the orb from the compartment. Offered it to Cam. "Be sure Silas gets this," he said.

"What is it?"

"Silas will know." He handed Cam the orb. "Now, GO!" Cam looked into Phil's eyes.

Cam nodded, pursing his lips. Hesitation.

"NOW!"

"Are you sure?"

Phil turned when he said, "Yes." His jaw tense, gnashing his teeth. "It's about to get bloody."

31

SEPHTIS pressed his arm against Winter's throat, his blade inching into Robyn's jaw. He had Winter off his feet, raised to meet Sephtis' eyes, his left hand adding pressure, forcing Winter's skull against the rock. Sephtis' attack was never ending and unwavering and Robyn understood that Sephtis was accurate in his assessment; speed and pain drove the protective thoughts from Winter's mind, manifesting in a physical existence and stealing time from Robyn, scattering his healing thoughts into oblivion as his body reacted to the oncoming threat, giving no time for Robyn to close his wounds and heal with enough time to counter Sephtis' next strike. But was this a never ending battle to last for eternity or did Sephtis have an ace in the hole he had yet to reveal? Robyn was certain Sephtis had brought a means to bring this ruse to an end.

"You can't kill me Robyn but I... I can send your soul into the dark void."

Robyn felt pressure on his windpipe. Air strangled from his throat, knowing his death was soon approaching.

"Dead or alive," growled Sephtis, "your bounty is the same."

Robyn thrust his knee against Sephtis' ribs. One strike, two, three. His thoughts wavering along with his breath, his consciousness wavering. Seeing death. Seeing himself lying down projecting the moment, attempting to fight, to break free from Sephtis, too weak in mind to keep fighting, his physical body withering, dissipating, fading like the evening light, solidifying his holographic form in this world. His will to live, to continue, to breathe and lead the rebellion to victory willed in these dying moments.

"You're growing weak," seethed Sephtis. "What's wrong, Robyn?" Robyn's feet kicked at the air. "Am I squeezing those thoughts from your brain?"

Robyn knew what killing Sephtis would do. Breaking cosmic law meant an eternity in the void, incapable of even the slightest influence. Absence would be his consequence. But death, should Sephtis kill him now, would render his ether incapacitated. Robyn would gain knowledge but have no use in it; he would be a passive observer to all events with no ability to provide aid or counsel. He could feel it slipping from his grasp and there was only one conclusion, one option to put a stop to Sephtis, but killing Sephtis also came with a dire consequence. For Robyn, yes, but even more for the rebellion. The dark lord would not have it and would rain down hell and damnation upon the planet. An effect Robyn knew he could never allow to happen.

Sephtis tossed him to the ground and Winter cracked his skull against the earth as Sephtis stepped from him, two steps, and turned around as Winter pushed himself to his feet, blood dripping from the gash across his forehead. That rickety growl in the back of Sephtis' throat.

"I'm not here to kill you, Robyn," said Sephtis as he approached, his fingers pinched, holding a vial. "That would be an injustice to Xibalba and all who you've wronged."

Pain tore across Winter's chest, radiating down his body, felt like a third-degree burn extending across his torso from his throat as he sought to see Sephtis, gritting his teeth. The burn born from Sephtis' hand on his throat. That's what happened when hell offered its touch.

"There's only one way to isolate a ghost," continued the goading Sephtis. "It takes lightning."

Winter eyed the glass vial; saw how lightning raged within it. Winter knew what that vial contained. He'd seen it in the record. Conjured from the depths of Xibalba, in the forest of pain, the lightning within seized upon atoms, rendering them incapacitated. A hell in itself; the lightning strangled the atoms, consuming their energy, crushing them down with a weighted force. The process could take millenniums before certain death.

Robyn winced as he stood. His arm shaking by

his side.

"Don't do this Sephtis," Robyn hollered. "I won't allow it." Robyn eyed the vial, his eyes rising to see Sephtis.

"Afraid, Robyn?" said Sephtis. "You should be."

Sephtis went to open the vial when the garden, cave, and all in it rattled and quaked. A sound like crunching steel, like a crack in the atmosphere the moment before an avalanche, ripped across the garden as a blinding dark red light beamed into the cave from the cracks in the door to AR77. Winter looked at the door as Sephtis followed his gaze.

Winter swallowed the pain in his throat. "My God," he breathed.

Sephtis whispered, "What in damnation could that be?"

Winter looked over the quaking, shaking, trembling cave, then to the light growing ever stronger beyond the door. He looked at Sephtis and his heart sank.

Winter whispered to Sephtis just before the boom.

"Rage," he said. Sephtis' eyes narrow.

Winter repeated, "Rage!"

32

HE had no thought other than pain. No emotion other than hate. When Phil stomped into the tunnel, hate came with him.

Sephtis was beyond the door. Robyn required help; something he'd never thought would happen. Phil understood Robyn could not kill Sephtis, understood where that would lead, and the thought of knowing Winter was in the throes of absence turned his gut.

But to defeat Sephtis, he would need to become more.

Light filled his eyes, beaming and gleaning, his ether expanding to the door, and he could feel the weight of the cave as his ether slammed against it. Phil breathed deeply, his nose curled, his arms and hands tense, seeing how the ether encapsulated the door, sending blinding dark red light beams through every crevice. Watched as the door melted, disintegrating with bubbling boils raging with heat as if that light carried white piercing heat. The door exploded into the garden, accompanied by rock, dirt, and debris that Phil manipulated into daggers driving towards the waiting Sephtis. The force from those daggers thrust Sephtis back with a grunt and groan as his back arched over the boulder he landed on.

Phil ran through the tunnel, lifting off the ground once he entered the garden, propelled across the cave and brought his fists down across Sephtis' skull. Pain pinched across his visage as the back of his head rattled against the boulder. Another fist across Sephtis' chin. Another and yet another as Phil could hear the crack of Sephtis' bones beneath his fist. Blood spewed from his face, his mouth, nose, and eyes.

All his strength. All his power. A lifetime of rage manifested in pounding this alien demon into oblivion.

The words "Who's The Phantom Now" etched into his thoughts, driving his hands, his fists. Blood on Cathryn's neck. Esta's torn body. His mother. Vampires eating away at him, at his family.

Esta.

Cathryn.

Mother.

Robyn.

Phil gripped Sephtis by the armor, raised him to meet his eyes and screamed bloody hell into his face before slamming his skull against Sephtis' bloodied, mangled head. Phil stepped back as Sephtis lay unmoving. His ether floated above him, dark and grey.

"Phil," said Winter, struggling to move across the garden. Bloodied, battered, and bruised.The stare in his eyes, nervous and frightened as Robyn shook his head. "Stop," he said.

Confused, Phil eyed Robyn Winter from his feet to his eyes. Those white eyes grew faded and sunken. "Why?" Phil asked, his hands clenched in front of him, shaking with rage when the laugh bellowed through the cave and Sephtis rose to his feet.

Phil stepped back as Sephtis rose over him, laughing a cackling rickety growl.

"Foolish boy," declared Sephtis and he stomped his foot into the ground, stepping forward. "Don't you know me?" His voice echoed across the garden, thick and sinister, as he sucked in air through his deformed, bloodied nose.

Phil stepped back, beholding Sephtis in his field of vision.

Sephtis curled his fingers into fists. "You can't kill me with rage, boy."

His fist moved with such fierce ferocity, indignation, and speed Phil hadn't seen it. All he felt was pain when Sephtis' fist crashed against his jaw, and catapulted him across the garden, landing in the lake with a heavy suctioned thud. Pain raced across his jaw as he gulped water. Suffocating, choking on water, Phil sprang for air with a gasp. His knees in the water, his eyes burning, but he forced them open. Sephtis was approaching, stomping towards him. Robyn hurriedly moving to receive him.

Sephtis standing over him. "I live off of fear,

boy. I devour hate to feed my heart. Rage brings me strength."

His massive fist hurled across Phil's skull. He felt the crack across his head as he dropped into the water. Saw blood in the water, his blood, rise to the surface.

And over him, Sephtis stood.

33

"GET in," hollered Grimes to Cam. He was in the underwater vessel, Cat beside him. "You can't help them." His voice weakened with defeat. Cam standing beside the water.

He looked at Cat. "ETA for the mother ship?"

Grimes shook his head. "This is insane."

"Two minutes," said Cat. "With an additional two for them to advance their primary weapon."

Cam bit his lips. *Four minutes.*

"Cam, get the hell on this ship right now," ordered Grimes.

Cam looked to the steps and the door that led back to the garden, assessing time and purpose.

"Now," hollered Grimes, and Cam turned to him. "They're gone," he said. "There's no way they can make it back in time. It's over."

Cam looked over at Grimes and Cat, both of them staring with weighted, hurried anticipation. He looked over the vessel, every inch, every crevice.

"Cam?" Grimes hollered.

Cam shot him a stare, said, "No. I've got a plan."

34

ROBYN trudged across the garden. He had little strength left; Sephtis had done his job well, weakening his ether, his body, and even more, his mind, which, Robyn had become aware, was the strategy all along. Weaken him enough to unleash the lightning across his ethereal cells. He could see his body, his real physical body, entombed as he had requested, on the other side of the universe, cast into his own dimension, hidden away from the real and the physical, groan with a shudder he felt in his chest as it writhed down his bones to his toes.

Sephtis had bludgeoned Phil with the force of an anvil. Robyn feared he may be dead beneath the water when a wave rippled across the cave, glimmering and shimmering like dominoes, the air thick as if it had taken on physical form.

The record, Robyn thought. It's changing in real time.

He looked at Sephtis standing over Phil as Winter's body tensed, climbing and standing on the boulder where Sephtis had been draped across not a minute ago.

Shimmering to reflect an alternative course stained with the blood from this moment.

What will it reveal?

What will it show?

A driving wind ripped through the cave. Winter felt its effervescence tear through his bones. Sephtis raised a scepter over his head, a long black scepter with the heart of a purple glowing orb.

Heard Sephtis speak, "I'll kill you now, boy, and swallow that rage to feed on for centuries."

Robyn gathered his strength, all his power, all his love. One last thought as he slapped his hands together and his ether barreled towards Sephtis; the force catapulted the massive evil lord across the lake into the waterfall where he dropped into the water. And Robyn huffed to catch his breath, dropped to his knees, depleted and raw, holding his ribs that wrenched in anguish as he looked to where Phil had sunk, watching, nervous, when a single air bubble rose to the surface.

Alive!

He gathered himself to his feet, his chest heaving, tasting blood in the back of his throat, gasping for air. He climbed down the boulder, and limped over to Phil, sank down to his knees, and pulled Phil from the depths of despair. Held him in his arms, Phil's breathing shallow as Robyn gasped before pulling Phil to the surface, trudging his heavy body from the water.

Phil's head bleeding, the cut over his forehead thick. Robyn placed his arm over the wound, closed his eyes and felt how his skin fluttered, white light beaming from his hand sealing Phil's wound, sensing how his heart beat, once slow and wavering, raced within Phil's chest as his breathing caught with the heart and he gasped awake, his eyes wide.

The first words off his tongue were, "Go, Robyn. The future waits for you."

Followed by a thick hum over the cave. Robyn knew that sound all too well; the greys had sent a mother ship. There was no way to escape the blast. And Sephtis then rose from the lake.

Winter gritted his teeth. All was lost.

"If you like that pitiful human so much," said Sephtis, raising the scepter over his head. "Than we'll just have to take him with us."

Sephtis tossed the scepter, but not before he was blasted with a particle beam that disintegrated part of his torso. He stood there, wavering, unblinking, confused. The scepter spiraled into the lake.

Winter whispered, "Love saves the universe," when he looked over to see Cam standing in the doorway leading to AR77.

"No way," said Cam, "will I allow you to hurt my friends."

Sephtis steadied himself. Pain trifled across his visage. "You can't kill me with fear," growled Sephtis.

And Cam stepped forward, aiming his rifle at

Sephtis. "Go to hell asshole." Another shot, another particle beam raced towards Sephtis as the hum above the cave grew ear piercing. Robyn helped Phil to his feet. The beam took Sephtis' arm. And Cam fired again, the blast disintegrating Sephtis' right leg as he dropped into the lake. The bleeding seething, decimated Sephtis, refused to relent as he forced himself to rise above the lake, manipulating his ether to draw a new leg and repair his torn torso.

Robyn draped Phil's arm over his shoulder, walked with him hurriedly towards Cam, who raged another blast at Sephtis and the force bowled him over into the lake. Cam dropped the rifle and met Winter and Phil in the garden. Phil's breathing labored in between waking and dreaming consciousness.

The hum overhead ear piercing.

"They're firing their primary weapon," said Robyn. "You should not have come back."

Sephtis rose again from the water, as the hum ceased.

"I told you, human," said Sephtis. "The only way to kill me is to scatter my atoms." Sephtis stopped cold and looked at the roof, then snapped his head to look at them.

"You were saying," said Cam when he wrapped his arms around Winter and Phil, teleporting to the waiting underwater vessel when Grimes raced down into the water and Cam handed Cat the teleporter.

35

SEPHTIS watched as his prize vanished before his eyes. Winter was gone, his chance at redemption with him. In their place, a blue light beamed down and filled the cave.

His jaw tense, snarling when he breathed his last word, "Humans."

The blast tore through the cave, decimating all in its path. Sephtis watched it, watched as it ripped towards him, mercilessly unforgiving. Above him he could hear a great explosion and he knew, he knew, the mother ship had been destroyed. Mere seconds after he felt his body shatter and tear into pieces as the explosion ripped through him, scattering him into atoms across the devastated rebellion base.

36

MOTH received notice from Kaal that the mother ship had annihilated the rebellion base. Information received from the ship revealed an intruder had boarded, seconds before the mother ship met its demise.

The greys, he knew, would demand blood. But blood from who? Nero was gone, and another grey will rise from his ashes. Now that they have wiped the rebellion off the planet, whom will the greys seek to offer redemption?

The humans? Moth scoffed at the notion. When had they ever taken responsibility for their deeds, let alone the actions of the few who opposed them? Never was Moth's answer as he gazed over his city from his living quarters, hands clamped behind him, thinking, assessing, contemplating what had taken place in the rebellion base.

The greys were a finicky species; Moth would need to call on the Draconians to settle the matter or hand over his prisoners to settle the score. Either way, didn't matter, not to Moth and not in the least. Moth had other more dire concerns to deal with, namely Sanos. Moth could eat Zon for not killing Sanos, a direct disobedience to Moth's order. And a leader of Moth's stature could not allow those directly under his command to provide insurrection. Such actions made him look weak in front of COR. Zon would need to meet a dire fate, but how and when was the matter. When you're skating a thin line between betrayal and loyalty, Moth knew, it was best to strike at the precise moment with a calculated, well planned, formidable foray. The game was chess, not checkers, and he would need to be cerebral and diabolical in his treatment of Zon.

Allow Sanos to speak? He gnashed his fangs just thinking about it. Sanos would belittle Moth in front of his people, would raise red flags and cause insurrection. His people were already on edge, had been on edge since the war began, those insipid red robes leading the charge with their myths and calls for peace. No, Sanos provided with a forum to spread his infection into the minds of Dracs could never be allowed.

He would find a way, somehow put an end to all of it, dismantle all possibility of a Drac insurrection despite what little time remained before Sanos would be allowed his podium to speak rage into Drac ears. Time was of the essence, and Moth would never have thought he'd be celebrating the end of the human rebellion by planning the demise of fellow Dracs. But his seat at the head of COR could not be given to any other than him; his future was waiting to join him, his rise to power over the planet, handed to him freely by the Draconians.

He raised his chin, thoughts rolling over in his head.

Sandy.

The rebellion.

Sandy's death was required; she had indeed proven to be a powerful vampire, how, he could still not decipher. Take away the mythos and vehement bedtime stories and you had a simple explanation: genetic manipulation by the hand of Mono alone because surely Jayda would have provided intel that the witches caring for the child were compromised by now if they were. Jayda's instincts on these situations were the reason Moth sent him to begin with. He would need to contact Jayda soon with another report on current happenings, assess his demeanor and ethereal vibration for any possibility he, too, had become compromised.

At least Sandy no longer posed a threat. He could bring the baby back to Drac City after Sanos and the Drac City Council had adjourned. His people would raise the Drac Human hybrid to loathe humans; all it took was an attachment and appropriate programming. If history taught anything, it was that programming a mind took time, care, and persistence. In time, Moth will destroy all attachment Adam has to his human species. *The scourge of humanity from humanity,* Moth grinned, thinking about it. Under his tutelage, Adam would destroy the indigo children. Now that they abolished the rebellion, identifying the indigo threat among the current human populace would prove easy and, one by one, they will meet their demise between Adam's jaws.

Winter failed. Moth could see Robyn's eyes, those white holographic projectors from the unknown. Moth's wing curled around him, his face pinched with pain, remembering the power Robyn manifested, treating Moth like a feeble child. None in history had ever held such power over him; apparently, death had served Robyn with promise.

You have to die first. Moth could hear Winter's declaration from the garden.

No, thought Moth. I don't believe it.

But where did he receive his power?

Even the Draconians had never revealed such a power before. He wondered how Sephtis had fared against Winter. Better than himself, he thought. And with the call to Sephtis, he may have opened Pandora's box. Should the armies of Xibalba be sent by the dark lord, the entire planet, himself and his Dracs included, would suffer by their hand. Those Xibalban's were a unique class of torturous beings. Power and control were foreign to them. They lived for one thing and one thing only, fear, and they had no care what species provided it to them. But they'd never get through the barrier; the electronic blanket barred all from entering the planet without strict consent. Plus, the Draconian colony on Titan would be the first alerted to any coming from Xibalba, and any others, for that matter. He assumed Sephtis had been triumphant in his endeavor to secure Robyn Winter, or he'd perished when the mother ship unleashed holy hell scattering his atoms across the globe.

He had to put Sephtis out of his thoughts. He would need to answer to the Draconians on why he had called Sephtis.

Robyn Winter being his sole reason.

Robyn Winter!

But how? How did he get his power?

I must know how.

I must know.

I must.

37

ARIES was escorted down a thick concrete hall. The stench was god awful, a mix of feces, urine, and sweat. He wondered how long it had been since the facility he was in had been used. Considering the thick film of dirt and grime on the windows, he concluded it had been ages since anyone stepped foot in this prison. Four Drac warriors stood around him, walking down the corridor, a set of double doors on his right; he could hear murmurs behind the walls.

He'd been stripped of his armor, cut down to his t-shirt and cargo pants, then beaten within an inch of his life. He could feel the wounds from Drac claws across his face, bleeding with a sting he knew wouldn't relent. His right eye swollen, a gash across his forehead.

Not once had he been asked a question. They made no inquires of the young Aries. They simply beat him into submission, clamping steel cuffs around his wrists with a pinch and wince. He wondered who had escaped from the rebel base. Wondered how many had made it to AR77. Phil? Robyn? Silas? His mother? He never had a moment to embrace her, and now his chance may never arrive.

Aries sucked his cracked and bloodied bottom lip into his mouth, an attempt to stifle his tears as the lead Drac opened the double doors with a metal scrape. Inside, he could see the captive children from the rebel base. His eyes jumping from one to the other, counting ten including himself. His eyes stopped when he found Annie and that boy sitting across from the door. Annie rose to her feet when she saw Aries. The boy continued to sit.

A Drac unchained his wrists, grinning before he smacked Aries across the face with the back of his hand, the force so great, Aries fell into the arms of the Drac behind him.

Laughter. Snickers from vampire throats.

"I'd bet my rations on this one," said the Drac who hit him. Aries' eyes narrowed, staring at the Drac vehemently. "Once the hunger drives the mind into a frenzy, he'll eat his mother to relinquish the craving."

The Drac behind him said, "No matter, it'll be a sight to see no matter who wins." He gripped Aries' dark hair in his claw and tossed him inside the cell, where he fumbled to his knees and Annie raced over to him.

"Are you okay?" she asked, her hand on his arm.

"Take good care," said the Drac before closing the door. Aries could hear the key twisting, locking them in.

"C'mon I'll help you up," said Annie, but Aries waved her off, got up on his own and scampered to the wall, where he turned to sit, holding his knees against his chest, his back to the wall. He had to catch his breath. His ribs hurt something awful. Pain jutted to the back of his head when he breathed deeply, exhaling with a sigh as he looked over the others in the cell, all standing, standing over him, waiting with bated breath. Aries scanned their eyes, all young, some only four. He was the oldest in the cell. He took a minute to catch his breath.

"Do you know what happened?" Annie said in a whisper, as if she sought to conceal the answer from the others.

Aries pulled his hand away from his ribs with a wince and shudder. Shook his head. "No," he answered. "I lost consciousness in the tunnel." He touched his lips; saw blood on his fingertips when he locked eyes with Annie. "Are you able to call to them? Communicate with base operations. Maybe someone is listening."

Annie shook her head before looking around the cell. "We're blocked off," she said. "All of us." She gestured to the rest of the children. "It's like this place was made to suppress frequency communication."

"I'm not surprised," Aries grunted. "They've been planning our demise for centuries." He coughed into his hand as pain shot up his ribs to his chest when he noticed the boy standing over him crouch beside him, his hand on Aries' shoulder.

"Thank you for trying," the boy said, and the other children followed suit, offering gratitude.

"Don't thank me yet," he said. "Considering we're all trapped in some vampire prison, I'd say that was an epic fail."

Annie shook her head. "Remember what Robyn always says: failure doesn't exist; what does exist is feedback."

The boy asked, "Did you see Perseus by any chance?"

"That giant guy?" The boy nodded, his eyes wide with anticipation as Aries shook his head. "They took him somewhere. I don't know where, though. Cameron, right?" he said. "Your name is Cameron?"

The boy nodded, sucking back his lips. Seemed on the verge of tears when Aries noticed his eyes; something was off about the eyes.

"Do you know where we are?" asked one child, an older female, no more than eleven.

Aries looked around the cell. "I don't," he said. "Beneath the earth, for sure. Somewhere in hollow earth."

"Did they say what they're going to do with us?" asked another, her voice cut off with a swallow of fear.

A question Aries refused to answer. He looked at the children, and his eyes must have provided the answer, for they all looked away.

"I don't want to stay here," cried a little one. He had to be no more than seven.

"Won't master Robyn or master Phil save us?" asked another.

"We don't know if they're even alive," hollered another with a shaky voice, clearly irritated.

"Cam will come," said Cameron. "I know he will. He'll always come for me."

Aries looked at Annie.

"It's a long story," she said.

Aries looked at Cameron, his fists clenched, pacing. The stranger among them. *Something's off with him*, thought Aries.

"What're we going to do?" cried the eleven-year-old.

"We stay together," said Aries. "There's strength in numbers. We need to be observant. Only our wits will get us out of here."

"We're doomed," cried another as the eleven-year-old attempted to console her. "They're going to kill all of us. We're the biggest threat." She moved her head back and forth, tears rolling down her cheeks. "They're going to kill every one of us."

"We can't think that way," said Aries. "We..."

His hands went to his body, feeling over his torso. *Can't believe I forgot.*

"What?" asked Annie. "What is it?"

Did they find it?

He searched his back, remembering on his belt

Robyn had placed a homing beacon. Relief washed over him when he found it, holding it in his palm as the children gathered around him.

"What is it?" asked Cameron.

Aries couldn't help the smile that crossed his lips. "A homing beacon," he said as he pressed the button on the side of the tiny device, no bigger than his thumbnail. "Robyn will be able to track our location."

"If he's even alive," said Cameron. "If… any of them are alive."

Aries responded, stern and poised, "Never give up hope," he said. "Never."

38

ROBYN, crouched in front of a fire pit, inside an underwater pod bathed in blue, the hue reflective of the ocean water outside the windowed enclosure, stoked the fire. Four couches, one on each side of the raised floor, were gathered around the sunken fire pit. Silas sat on one of those couches. He looked like he'd seen better days.

"They're alive," said Robyn, referring to the prisoners. "I can feel it."

"But we don't know for sure," said Silas. "We should assume the worst."

Robyn closed his eyes, not wanting to hear it. What happened in the garden was not supposed to end the way it did. The shimmer, he thought, referring to the shimmer in the record he'd seen in the cave. Now he understood Nin's message, the one she'd provided to Phil when he was under the influence of the red pill. Nin was referring to what the shimmer had revealed, and the effect to the rebellion. Nin's army would not be offering the assistance Robyn expected.

Nin's words, *"The armada cannot fly,"* was a

reference to Nin's army being incapable of following through with the plan Robyn had set in place. But what was even more peculiar was the added message from Nin, *"Proceed as such,"* indicating for Robyn to continue to push forward despite the current shimmer in the record. Or, in more coherent terms, protect the indigo children no matter what the cost.

But who had changed the record? The Dracs? The Greys? Humans? Robyn had dismantled the time machine himself. How were they able to break through? His calculations had been precise; only he could unlock it. Robyn knew all too well that traveling through time was not in anyone's best interest. Time was its own dimension, with natural intelligence that did not care to be altered. The consequence to the one who fought to change time was dire. His own heart couldn't break through it. He knew there was only one who could.

Hearing his own words repeat in his mind: *The one who masters the rose master's time.*

This was true, from a certain point of view. But not time travel; linear time being what he had been referring to. Phil was supposed to become something greater than himself in that garden, but he barely escaped after the shimmer. And his family? Esta was an important part in the rebellion's success, Phil's children too. Robyn snapped a branch, tossing it into the fire. Someone changed the scene, for what purpose he did not know, wouldn't know until he could gain access to the record, a trip he would need to take soon to discover the ins and outs the future held. He wondered if the mother ship had done its job, or had Sephtis escaped? Tricky Xibalba soldier he was. Now his whereabouts could only be speculated. Robyn knew he would need to be conscious of any Sephtis resurrection.

"Sandy is recovering," said Silas as if he couldn't stand Robyn's silence. "She should be at full strength soon." Robyn looked at him when Silas cleared his throat. "No more than a few hours."

Good, Robyn thought. We will need her now more than ever.

"And Phil?"

Silas paused before answering, as if looking for the appropriate words to describe Phil's current mental state. He didn't have to answer.

"What happened in the garden, Robyn? This was all…" He clenched his fists. "This part was supposed to be over."

Robyn stood, holding his hands over the fire, listening to the crackle and pop. "I know, Silas. Someone's changed the record. We're riding on unfamiliar ground."

"But who?" asked Silas. "Did we evacuate for no reason?"

Robyn stepped back and turned, stepped up to the raised floor in between the couches, looking over the potions lined on a shelf in front of him. "Not at all," said Robyn. "We did what was necessary."

"Considering a certain time line that by your own account has now changed."

Robyn shrugged him off, taking a bottle of amethyst from the shelf. "Not all was changed before that," said Robyn. "We proceeded with what we knew on that timeline during the timeline; it was only in the garden that things changed. All we did before then was on the correct timeline. It is the here and now that we must adjust to." He uncorked the amethyst bottle, breathing in the effervescent scent, and his body shuddered. He tossed some into the fire and the flames raged above him, licking at the air.

"What does this mean for the future? What are the vibrations telling you?" asked Silas.

"Strange," said Robyn, his eyes fixated on the fire. "I feel it was us who changed the record."

"Why?" Silas scoffed.

"At this time, I do not know," he said, staring at the flames, his thoughts lost in the fire. "But I intend to find out."

"Will you go to the record, Robyn? Will you seek the answers?"

Robyn said, "Of course, but I have a good idea who proffered the change. And it wasn't Draconian..."

Cam walked into the room now with Cat behind him. They stopped behind one of the couches, in front of a wall with a small desk and computer monitors, three of them hanging from the wall. The decimated rebellion base on one monitor, the second the underwater refuge, and the third was the waterline revealing the risen sun over the horizon. Silas jumped to his feet, his nerves on high alert. Robyn was the first to speak, inquiring about Phil's status.

"He's…" started Cam. "Not good. I can't imagine what he's going through."

"Go to him, Robyn. He needs your counsel," said Silas.

"Phil is my top priority. I will meet with him after our hero here has said his peace." He offered Cam a seat, which he declined.

"What is the plan?" asked Cam. "From what I've learned, they took prisoners. Cameron, Annie, and Perseus are among them."

"And Aries," added Silas.

"Yes, Aries too," repeated Cam.

Robyn tilted his head, staring at Cam, noticing how unfazed the soldier was. "What do you recommend?" asked Robyn, receiving peculiar stares from Silas and Cam.

"I say we send a search and rescue mission to find them. They've got to be somewhere with the vampires. Can't be too difficult to find where they're hiding."

Silas scoffed. "There's multiple alien cities scattered across the planet. You might as well be searching for a needle in a haystack. They could be anywhere."

"But we've got to try," pressed Cam, his head

shaking. "We can't just sit here and wait. We need action and action soon."

Robyn bowed to Cam. "I am in complete agreement," he said. He turned to Silas. "How many are accounted for?"

Silas eyed Robyn. "Fifty," he said, "And twenty who were already here on the underwater base."

"Then we go, all of us, fight to the death," said Cam.

"And if we all die, then the future will be lost. They'll eradicate the indigo children and the planet will be handed to them. No." Silas shook his head. "We must survive for the future."

Cam looked at Robyn. "Then a minor operation," he said. "I can't leave Cameron alone," he said. "He…"

The monitor behind Cam started blinking, a red beeping blinking dot on the bottom of the screen. All turned to it, but Silas hurried to the screen, clicked on the red dot that then took up the whole of the screen. Silas scanned over the information received.

"My god," he said.

"What is it?" asked Cam.

Robyn watched the reaction, sensing how time was catching up.

"It's Aries," said Silas.

"How do you know? Can you communicate with him?" Cam said, his voice relieved and hurried.

"It's his homing beacon." Silas punched a few

keys on the keyboard, then pointed at the screen. "We have his exact location."

"Where?" asked Robyn.

Silas read over the monitor, then froze. Robyn could cut the tension with a knife. "Silas?" His eyes roaming from Silas to Cam and Cat, then back to Silas as he turned to face them.

"Where?"

"The island," said Silas. "They've taken him... to the island."

Robyn then understood why the record had changed, or at least one reason why. It had to do with Phil. Perhaps, he thought, becoming something more took a bit more of a push.

"Well," said Robyn, looking at Cam. "It appears you will have your mission soon."

39

PHIL could hear the screams, the terror his family endured; their voices were everywhere; he couldn't shut them off. Couldn't stop seeing their torn bodies. It drove him mad, pacing and clenching his fists, tears in his bloodshot eyes.

Their death was not part of the plan. He fought his whole life to keep them safe, an endeavor now filled with failure.

My fault. All my fault.

He was foolish to not go back; foolish to think they would be safe. Was anyone ever safe from a vampire? No, and he knew this better than anyone.

Cuts, slices across the torso. He could hear cries from his unborn every time he closed his eyes.

Help us. Esta's voice.

Heard Cathryn scream over and over, calling for him, for Phil to rescue her.

Saw Sanos tear into her throat to stifle those pleas.

Help me daddy. Help us.

Saw the words written just for him: **Who's The**

Phantom Now!

Written in their blood.

Phil pursed his lips, fighting off an all out bellowing scream.

He couldn't think, not any clear thought manifested other than images wrought with carnage.

Help us.

Daddy, please.

"I know, baby," he whispered, as if Cathryn could hear him. He tried to feel, to see where they'd gone. Kept seeing a light on the top of stairs, Esta and Cathryn wandering in the darkness, confused. Not knowing what had happened or where to go. Wandering confused for eternity.

The thought stabbed at his heart. His hands shaking in front of him when the monitor beside the bedroom door blinked with a red dot. Phil craned his head while looking at it. He understood what it was, a homing beacon sent by someone who had survived. Phil jumped to the monitor, pushed the blinking red light, and the screen shifted, revealing the intel attached to the beacon.

"Aries," Phil breathed, scanning over the location. His jaw dropped with the revelation.

Phil, it now appeared, would be going back to his dreaded island.

He hoped he would find Sanos, too.

40

SANOS was tossed into his holding cell, courtesy of Illam. His fellow Dracs had beaten and tortured him. Zon was nowhere to be found. The torture was expected; Sanos knew Illam wouldn't allow the opportunity to pass. Moth's lackey seemed to enjoy himself thoroughly as he beat Sanos to a bloody pulp. But Sanos refused to relent from his traitorous story regarding Moth.

And after they locked him in, after the beating and berating, Sanos grinned welcoming more, hollering down the hall where the Drac warriors disappeared. "The future is set," he screamed. "And it is I, Sanos, who will rule over all on this planet. There is nothing that can stop me." He gripped the bars in his chained hands, the same chains Saiph had used on him. He would not be using the rose to release himself from his cell. And he wondered then who Moth would send, calculating the many ways the COR leader would attempt to stifle his voice.

No way would Moth allow Sanos to speak in front of the Drac City Council. There was too much at risk. Sanos looked up, assessing his cell before he yanked on the unmoving bars.

"It's useless," said a voice behind him, garbled and rickety like a hushed baritone.

Sanos turned to the voice but saw only darkness. Darkness and a thin stream of smoke, like a cloud that refused to dissipate.

"There's only one way to escape this cell." The voice again and Sanos clenched his fists, waiting for a fight to fly from the darkness.

"No need for those," said the voice when Sanos felt pressure on his hands and his fists opened. "I mean you no harm."

Sanos snickered, his nose curled, craning his head, attempting to see.

"Who are you?" asked Sanos.

"I… am the reason you have come here, Sanos. My redemption began with death. I'm the reason you fight so vehemently. I've given you purpose, Sanos."

Sanos repeated, "Purpose."

"The formula," said the voice. "My gift to you."

Sanos shook his head. "No," he declared. "I took the formula myself. I had no help."

The voice laughed at this notion, a deep bellow that rocked the cell.

"Please, Sanos, I've been following you for a long time." Sanos wasn't sure, but he thought he heard a change, as if whatever body the voice was attached to had shifted. "No Drac has ever presented themselves with such ferocity. You should be proud, if not satisfied with your endeavors."

"Of course," said Sanos gleefully.

"And you want to leave here, don't you? Leave before they come to kill you?"

Sanos turned away, said, "I'll make my own way out."

"You want Dracs to bow before you," continued the voice. "You want all on this planet to bow to your will."

Sanos snapped his head around to the darkness.

"You want them to drink from new blood and be your slaves."

His head turned slowly, looking over the cell, lips curled in a snarl.

How could the voice know? Know his private thoughts.

"Of course I know," said the voice, and Sanos turned on his heels. "I'm the one who gave you the idea."

"I'm done with the inquiry," raged Sanos as he stepped into the dark, swiping at nothing more than clouds and air as the laugh raged in the cell. On his left, his right, in front, behind. Everywhere.

"You can't take hold of me, Sanos. I exist inside the ether."

Sanos clenched his fists, his irritation boiling with frustration. Snarling, he trounced across the cell. "Where are you?"

"Everywhere!"

Sanos stood tall, looking from corner to corner.

"Do you want to take your rightful place in COR? Do you want to squash the rebellion and that insipid Robyn Winter for good?"

"Of course," breathed Sanos. "It is my destiny."

"Star systems will bow to your leadership. I can offer you all you want, Sanos. All I need is for you to do one thing for me. Just one."

Sanos looked over the cell. "Doesn't seem like I can do anything at the moment. Not until…"

"I require a promise, Sanos, before I allow you to leave this cell."

"I can get out myself," said Sanos. "I need help from no one."

"No?" said the voice. "I can give you new blood right now, Sanos." The laugh raged in the cell. "I know you want it. And you'll be able to spring from this cell and trample all over Moth's dead bones."

"The pills?" said Sanos as his mouth salivated, uncontrollable, dripping off his lips. "How do you have new blood? No one is even aware…"

"I know all you've done, Sanos. I know about the change new blood brings to you."

Sanos licked his lips, his mouth arid, thinking about the change, the power it held. His ability to strike genuine fear in his Dracs came with the change, and the change was an effect born from new blood.

"Will you promise or no?"

"What is it you want me to do?"

The voice laughed, rattling the bars and walls. "That will be revealed when the time is right, Sanos. I assure you it is something you will enjoy."

Sanos swallowed his breath, head down, thinking of new blood.

"Yes or no, Sanos?"

Sanos raised his chin, his hands shaking, body trembling, and offered a resounding, "Yes."

Sanos felt a brush across his palm, looked down at his fist, and opened his hand. Two blue pills, new blood pills, were in his palm. He cradled them, brought them to his chest as if they were precious stones. His body aching to swallow them. His hand shaking as he closed his fist around them, looking over the cell; the still quiet was maddening.

"Who are you?" said Sanos. "Another phantom? Some horrific Draconian ghost?"

The voice let out a single chuckle before answering as the clouds, the thin grey smoke, billowed towards him, revealing the face that proffered the pills.

"I am the one known as Sephtis," said the demonic face.

Sanos' eyes wide, staring at the demon head.

"Sephtis," Sanos repeated.

"The dark lord has given me refuge," said Sephtis. "To bring hell to Robyn Winter."

Sanos grinned at the complexion born from the fires of Xibalba. He looked down at his hand and the tiny blue pills sitting inside his palm. Closed his eyes to feel the wheels turning. Turning in his favor when he swallowed one pill down his gullet and his body shivered from his head down his spine, tensing his legs, feeling change coming, his body already pumping with the effects, heard a rumbling in the cell, his skin fluttering.

And Sanos snapped his eyes open; wide, maddening, breathing,

"Something wicked has come."

Coming Soon From PD Alleva

Horror

Jigglyspot and the Zero Intellect

Sci-Fi/Fantasy

The Rose Vol 3

Urban Paranormal Fantasy

Girl on a Mission: The Dead Do Speak

Also by PD Alleva

Sci-Fi/Fantasy

The Rose Vol 1: A masterful, dystopian science fiction thriller of telepathic evil greys, mysterious rebellion, martial arts, and Alien Vampires.

Dark Fantasy

Presenting the Marriage of Kelli Anne & Gerri Denemer: One known terrorist. A protest about to erupt. A family on the brink of collapse. Is the bond between husband and wife strong enough to defeat evil?

Twisted Tales of Deceit: Three supernatural tales of horror (*The Calculated Desolation of Hope, Somnium, & Knickerbocker*) chronicling evil's influence on innocent hearts and our uncontrollable desire to give in to their calculated transgression. Features Knickerbocker, a novelette and reimagining of Washington Irving's classic tale, *The Legend of Sleepy Hollow*, with a modern day twist; all characters are recovering addicts employed as teachers at the prestigious Sleepy Hollow Private School. And yes, heads do roll.

Literary

A Billion Tiny Moments in Time...

Indifference

Horror

Golem: A haunting tale of suspense, loss, isolation, contempt, and fear.
The Devil is in the details!